The
FRENCH
BOOKSHOP
Murder

GREG MOSSE is a 'writer and encourager of writers', husband of internationally bestselling author Kate Mosse. He has lived and worked in Paris, New York, Los Angeles and Madrid, mostly as an interpreter and translator, but grew up in rural south-west Sussex.

In 2014, he founded the Criterion New Writing playwriting programme in the heart of the West End and, since then, has produced more than 25 of his own plays and musicals. His creative writing workshops are highly sought after at festivals at home and abroad.

His first novel, *The Coming Darkness*, was published by Moonflower in 2022, followed in 2024 and 2025 by The *Coming Storm* and *The Coming Fire*.

Following his successful 1970s cosy crime series, the Maisie Cooper Mysteries, his new collection of Provençal village whodunnits begins with *The French Bookshop Murder*.

Also by Greg Mosse

The Maisie Cooper Mystery Series:
Murder at Church Lodge
Murder at Bunting Manor
Murder at the Theatre
Murder at the Fair
Murder at Sunny View
Murder at the Wedding

The Alex Lamarque Trilogy (Moonflower):
The Coming Darkness
The Coming Storm
The Coming Fire

Secrets of the Labyrinth

The FRENCH BOOKSHOP Murder

GREG MOSSE

HODDER &
STOUGHTON

First published in Great Britain in 2025 by Hodder & Stoughton Limited
An Hachette UK company

The authorised representative in the EEA is Hachette Ireland, 8 Castlecourt
Centre, Dublin 15, D15 XTP3, Ireland (email: info@hbgi.ie)

3

A CIP catalogue record for this title is available from the British Library

Paperback ISBN 9781399746885
ebook ISBN 9781399746892

Typeset in Monotype Plantin by Manipal Technologies Limited

Printed and bound in Great Britain by Clays Ltd, Elcograf S.p.A.

Hodder & Stoughton policy is to use papers that are natural, renewable and
recyclable products and made from wood grown in sustainable forests. The
logging and manufacturing processes are expected to conform
to the environmental regulations of the country of origin.

Hodder & Stoughton Limited
Carmelite House
50 Victoria Embankment
London EC4Y 0DZ

www.hodder.co.uk

For Carrie

Zoe's drawing of Sainte-Catherine

Cast of Characters

Zoe Pascal
Thierry Maurice, car hire assistant
Barbara Ercollani, elderly tourist
Brigadier Antoine Grenelle of the Sainte-Catherine police
Antoinette Grenelle, haberdasher, his sister
Napoléon Etienne, second-hand bookseller
Marcel Maurice, winemaker
Caroline Robin, solicitor
A team of removal men
Patrick Lagrasse, waiter at the Auberge Sainte-Catherine
A team of cleaning women
Elise Guillaume, horticulturist
Robert Petit, butcher
Russell, a Jack Russell terrier
Clare, Toby and three-year-old Benjy Day, English 'van nomads'
Firmin Séchan, an elderly large-animal vet
Gato Merino and his son Lali, builders
Denis Allard, guest-house proprietor at Chez Denis & Davide
Davide Quillan, his partner at Chez Denis & Davide
Father Julien Calmet, Catholic priest
Maisie Cooper, Zoe's elderly half-sister
Oskar Weiss, German tourist
Inspector Thibaud Sicarie of the Aix-en-Provence police
Simouno Simone, waitress and proprietor of Le Gourmand
Cécilie Guillaume, garage cashier, Elise's daughter
Frank Séchan, garage mechanic, Firmin's grandson
Ambroise Caille, estate agent – and, in passing, his family
Odile Charpentier, Marcel Maurice's wine farm manager
Bernard Dupin, minibus driver and tour leader

Prologue

The city of Aix in the gorgeous landscape of southern France has, for many years, been known as 'the place of a thousand fountains', each with its own dedication or meaning. There is not one in all those thousand, however, that commemorates a burglar.

The people of Aix are known as 'Aixois', a word whose spelling might have been deliberately contrived to confuse non-French speakers. That summer, there were a hundred and forty-five thousand Aixois, easily sufficient for someone with malign intent to blend in with the crowds, pursuing their evil goals in devious anonymity.

Or, on this particular occasion, to operate in the dead of night, just before the onset of morning, a time when the human engine is at its weakest and wakefulness is rare.

The plan was fourfold.

First was a break-in, effected via a courtyard, inadequately protected by a wooden gate whose broken-down boards were rotten with age and extremes of weather – from a record minus twenty degrees centigrade in winter to a scorching maximum of forty-two in high summer. Once in the court-yard, it was easy to find a window left ajar and climb inside, taking care to leave no trace of DNA, neither blood drawn by a splinter nor a hair trapped in an iron hinge.

The second phase of the plan was the location of a set of keys. The burglar knew that the one to the front door would be made of iron, heavy and old. The other, on the same ring, would be more modern, suitable for a replacement rear door.

They would both be found easily enough in the key safe on the wall.

The burglar paused to consider this security flaw.

If you put your keys in a safe, that probably means they're easier to find than tossed randomly in a drawer.

The door of the key safe wasn't robust. The lock held, but the hinges on the other side were easy to force with a strong screwdriver and the application of Archimedes' ideas about levers and fulcrums. The keys in question were on the top-left hook. A second or two later, they were secure in the burglar's pocket.

It was now time to embark on phase three of the plan, the controlled and oh-so-quiet vandalism of the whole office, a strategy designed to disguise what had been taken.

Because of the need to proceed with this vandalism in near silence – broken towards its end by a pre-dawn chorus of Provençal songbirds – the destruction took some time. Then came the wary exit, carefully astride the windowsill, with the eastern sky beginning to glow a fiery orange.

For the burglar – slipping away into the anonymity of the maze of irregular, crooked streets of Aix old town – only phase four, the final step of the plan remained.

I must get into that bookshop before it changes hands. It might already be too late.

It was too late – and the consequence would be murder.

I

A New Life

One

DEPARTURE AND ARRIVAL

Zoe Pascal – a handsome woman in late middle age with short grey hair that she refused to dye an unnatural colour – felt a strange and unexpected energy fizzing through her. She looked at her fellow passengers and wondered if they felt the same.

I know this feeling. I've been searching for it these last few years, not knowing where to find it – freedom.

They were flying at twenty-five thousand feet, above a ceiling of cloud. Zoe had taken the precaution of bringing two books with her, in case of delays, so she had a choice between the new Kate Mosse novel and a substantial non-fiction volume, purchased by post from an independent bookseller in the beautiful southern French city of Aix-en-Provence, a glossy guide to *Le Parc Naturel du Verdon* – the beautiful 'Verdon nature park'.

The vista on the cover of her guidebook was magnificent – green rolling hills, some of the slopes divided up into vineyards, others hedged for pasture, dotted with sheep and cows, and snow-capped mountains beyond. In the sky were wheeling birds of prey with enormous wingspans. The book's subtitle was a sort of slogan with an internal rhyme.

'*Une autre vie s'invente ici.*'

Zoe smiled.

That's exactly what I'm doing. I'm about to invent another life for myself in this beautiful place.

In business class for a treat, Zoe plumped for the novel and politely declined the offers of in-flight food and drinks, duty-free spirits, perfumes, watches and inexplicable model planes. Around page one hundred, Kate Mosse's heroine experienced a dramatic loss and was left uncertain what to do. Somehow, the skilfully described emotion aroused in Zoe a painful slide-show of memories from her own childhood: growing up in foster care, unloved and uncared for, finally abandoned and homeless as she turned sixteen. A feeling of desperation – which she knew well – rose from her solar plexus into her throat, tightening her breathing in a vice of anxiety.

This isn't good.

She focused on drawing in steady calming breaths, trying to return her mind and her emotions to the present. Then, all at once, the spell was broken as the pilot announced the locking of the toilets so that the plane could begin its descent into Marseille.

Zoe relaxed and her breathing returned to normal. She was even able to smile, watching passengers – who, only now, were discovering an overwhelming desire to relieve their bladders and bowels – being politely ushered back to their seats. The plane banked and, with a thrill of recognition, Zoe spotted the impressive and influential River Rhône, sinuous and grand in the gorgeous landscape.

They touched down with the slightest of bumps and, from the rear of the plane, came a round of applause. With the midday sun bright on the windows, they taxied to a stand close to the airport buildings and, agreeably, a mobile set of stairs instantly appeared alongside. Just a few minutes later, Zoe was on her way down, into the sweltering air, beneath a startlingly bright sky, wishing she could remember which of the numerous pockets in her rucksack concealed her sun-glasses. She could smell kerosene, of course, but also hot grass and that indefinable mixture of lavender, rosemary, pine resin and joy that characterised the south of France.

First off and, therefore, first through Marseille airport's passport control, Zoe's passage was very much eased by the fact that she was the proud possessor of a set of French identity papers as well as British. By a quirk of the internal workings of the baggage machinery, her bright-blue suitcase was third out on the carousel. Dragging it behind her through the smooth-tiled halls, she hurried through customs and headed straight for the counter of the car hire company recommended by her French *notaire* – the conveyancing solicitor, Caroline Robin, who had diligently helped her through every step of the purchase of her new business and home.

The boy behind the counter – according to his name badge, Thierry – looked too young to drive, let alone run a car hire business. Their conversation began on the wrong foot because, without looking up, he assumed that Zoe was a monolingual tourist and addressed her casually, routinely, in poor English with an execrable accent. Not wanting to show off with her excellent French – taught to her by her half-sister Maisie Cooper – Zoe replied in the same language and Thierry, thankfully, proved efficient and well informed. The transaction was soon complete, though – to Zoe – unsatisfactory.

'You're sure you have nothing but this enormous vehicle?'

'The SUV is a good car, *madame*. I upgrade you. You will like. Do not be frightened.'

'I'm not frightened. It's just that, where I'm going, the streets are very narrow and I fear it won't fit.'

'Where are you going?'

'Sainte-Catherine-en-Verdon.'

'*Oh-la-la*,' replied Thierry, bursting into French in his eagerness. '*Que c'est joli.*'

Zoe switched to French, too, agreeing that Sainte-Catherine was, indeed, 'very pretty'. She spent a pleasant few minutes, pumping Thierry for knowledge of a region that he clearly knew well. In the end, she was sad to leave him, but an impatient queue was building up behind.

'Thank you very much,' she said, adding kindly, though unjustifiably: 'You speak very good English.'

'*A bientôt,*' he told her.

Wondering why it was that he thought he would see her again '*bientôt*', meaning soon, Zoe exited the building, dodging a man with a rotary floor polisher, back out into the sweltering Provençal air. Dragging her wheelie suitcase along a smooth pavement, she found the car park, the vehicles all sheltered beneath a roof of photovoltaic panels so, once she had located her ridiculously bulky Peugeot SUV, she could at least take pleasure in the fact that the cabin was not roasting from the lunchtime sun.

Leaving Marseille airport took no time at all, the access roads being well marked and the direction clear. She headed out of the city, into gorgeous pasture and – quite soon – through a narrow gorge cut by a tributary of the Rhône.

★

After watching the attractive Englishwoman – in personality and appearance – walk away, Thierry Maurice dealt with his remaining customers. Several of them found their allocated vehicle unsuitable, even though it was, in each case, the one that they had chosen online.

Finally, he was alone at his counter, gazing across the shiny marble of the arrivals hall floor at the accoutrements of modern travel: the plate-glass dividers and soft, low seating; the payment machines for the car park; the money changers and cashpoints; the unstaffed help desks; the swiftly emptied waste bins.

Odd she should be on her way to Sainte-Catherine.

Thierry was torn. Yes, of course, there was plenty to love in the gorgeous Verdon nature park in which he had been brought up by his uncle, Marcel. But there were also huge swathes of empty time where he felt purposeless and lost.

It isn't Uncle Marcel's fault.

Was there anything more fulfilling than working the fertile land and producing high-quality wine at fair prices for an appreciative public?

But it's not the pace and energy of Marseille.

Thierry sighed.

After all Uncle Marcel's done for me, I can't just leave him in the lurch, can I? If I could find the Vulture, though, that would change everything.

★

Zoe spent a good deal of her journey singing to herself in the privacy of her cab. Then, just as she was beginning to lose confidence in her sense of direction, on the point of admitting defeat and trying to connect the satnav, she saw the sign she was looking for, one of the brown ones that indicated sites of historic or cultural interest.

Sainte-Catherine – village du livre.

The same feeling of fizzing excitement – of freedom and new beginnings – took over once more. Two minutes later, her destination appeared, profiled against the distant mountains, a lovely ancient hill town built of biscuit-coloured stone.

This is it, my new home: 'Sainte-Catherine – the book village.' I'm going to be very happy here.

She decelerated as she approached the slip road, then frowned, wondering if that was a kind of metaphor for the decision she had taken.

Am I retreating into a side road from life?

The tarmac veered sharply right so she touched the brakes more firmly.

No, I don't think so. It's more like turning the page of a novel and finding, in the new chapter, that time has moved on, the action is somewhere new and different people are becoming important.

She had taken off her sweatshirt, discarding it untidily on the passenger seat, and was driving with her windows down for the cooling rush of air. The friendly analogue clock on the dashboard had ticked round beyond teatime, but slowing down made her aware of quite how hot the day had become. Winding through a field of sunflowers at just thirty kilometres per hour, the air felt superheated and parched.

But also cleansing.

Emerging from the sunflowers, the road followed a straight stretch of canal, the water dark green and placid, almost like a mirror. Then she came to a magical place where the canal met a natural river, marked by a roadside panel indicating its name, the Rigolet. Canal and river were separated by a low, dry weir. In the rainy season, six months before, Zoe had seen the canal replenished by fresh river water running over the top. Today, there were ten or twelve children jumping in and out, enjoying the autumn weather – or, rather, the end of summer in the south of France. They were laughing as they dived from the rounded concrete rim, hurling themselves onto their lilos and inflatable rubber rings, then splashing out again.

Zoe was now very close to her destination. She navigated a small suburb of identikit villas, built on the flat land of the periphery of Sainte-Catherine, each with its own garden and wiry hedges, set in quarter-acre plots. She slowed further, obliged to take care to avoid a somnolent dog, lying fully in the middle of the road.

As if it owns the place.

Two municipal tennis courts in tall cages gave Zoe an urge to put on her whites.

I'll need some proper exercise after a day's travelling, but that may have to wait. I fear I'll have too much to do for a week, at least, getting things shipshape. At least my racket will soon arrive with my sports kit and the rest of it.

The road curved round beneath the slopes of Sainte-Catherine. Zoe passed a Total petrol station and a Hyper U supermarket, plus an example of what she believed to be one of France's greatest innovations, more important than the metric system, the Napoleonic legal code or the network of impeccable motorways.

A drive-through bakery.

She almost pulled in, dreaming of a *pain au chocolat* or maybe a leek tart, either one doubtless extravagantly rich with butter. Right there, however, was another sign indicating the entrance to the narrow, cobbled streets of historic 'Sainte-Catherine – *village du livre*', so she resisted the temptation.

It calls itself 'the book village', but it's really a town.

As Zoe expected, there was no way the enormous Peugeot SUV hire car would fit into the narrow streets. Fortunately, the residents had anticipated this problem, providing a spacious car park at the foot of the incline, in front of the *mairie*, the town hall, an impressive civic building adorned with geraniums in window boxes and a proud *tricolore* French flag, hanging limp in the breezeless heat.

Zoe parked, taking care to fit her car between the white lines painted on the scorching tarmac, among a dozen other vehicles, including a couple of motorbikes and a lightweight moped – a *mobylette*. She opened the door and got out into what felt like a sauna. A frail-looking elderly woman in a purple tracksuit was tottering past a row of four garages, built into the hillside, with an open book in her hands.

'*Puis-je vous aider?*' Zoe asked, meaning 'can I help you?'.

The woman tottered on, utterly absorbed in reading and walking.

I wonder what she's up to?

★

The elderly woman's name was Barbara Ercollani. She had been in Sainte-Catherine for a few days but intended to stay on until she had achieved her goal – one that she had shared with no one and had taken pains to obscure.

Anyone might be spying on me.

Passing out of sight of the new arrival in her enormous SUV, Barbara found a bench that faced the sun, giving her a view of flat lands either side of the wandering Rigolet. There, too, in plain view, perhaps two hundred metres away on the far bank, was a large tree, its leaves just tinged with yellow autumn colour.

That tree is important. Why can't I remember why it's important?

Barbara frowned.

Is it because of the Vulture?

*

Standing in the bright sun beneath the dome of the rich, blue sky, Zoe took a few deep, joyful breaths, smiling and counting her blessings. At first, she thought she might now be alone, most people sensibly indoors, sheltering from the heat. Then she noticed a man with his back to her, in a blue shirt, sitting on a bench at the edge of the car park, looking out across another glorious field of sunflowers. Beside him was his picnic, set out tidily on a red-and-white-checked cloth: French bread, a gooey camembert and a bottle of red wine from which he was pouring a measure into delicate crystal glass.

Becoming aware that he was being observed, he turned his head, revealing his lush moustache, and greeted her in French, his voice rich with the twang of the local accent.

'Good afternoon. Lovely day.'

'It is. What a wonderful place to sit.'

He turned more fully to face her and she recognised the insignia of the French police.

'Join me,' he invited her, raising his glass. 'Do you have a receptacle somewhere in that magnificent vehicle?'

'How very kind, but I can't. I'm expected.'

12

Belatedly, he stood up, brushed crumbs from his uniform shirt, and came to meet her – slightly unsteadily, she thought.

'Brigadier Antoine Grenelle of the Sainte-Catherine police,' he told her. 'I am, in fact, *the* Sainte-Catherine police. And you must be Madame Pascal.'

She admitted as much, wondering to what extent she was already a subject of gossip: '*Enchantée*.'

He surprised her with an expression of sympathy in his rheumy eyes: 'And you speak French with no accent. Was it the *coup de foudre*?'

'I beg your pardon?'

'Did you see Sainte-Catherine, profiled against distant snowy peaks, and fall in love with the place?'

'I suppose I did.'

'I hope,' he told her, his tone very serious, 'you won't fall very quickly out of love again.'

'I don't think that's likely,' she told him, unnerved. 'I'm not a changeable person.'

'Though this is a new life for you, as I understand it, leaving everything behind and beginning again.' He went back to the bench and drank from his delicate crystal glass. The wine dampened his lush moustache. To her surprise, he gave her a wink. 'In Sainte-Catherine, there are no secrets. Everything is known.'

'I see,' said Zoe. 'I hope I don't disappoint.'

'Oh, that would be impossible,' he told her with tipsy gallantry – he was definitely tipsy, she thought. His eyes travelled up and down her body. '*Vous êtes une très belle femme*.'

He sat back down, using the crusty bread to scoop up a portion of his runny cheese. For a moment or two, Zoe didn't move, thinking about how, in London, a stranger telling her that she was 'a very beautiful woman' would almost certainly have seemed creepy and intrusive.

Not here, however.

She wondered why that was.

Is it because he's older than I am, or is it because it's sort of normalised as a mode of conversation, fitting an everyday pattern and somehow, therefore, unthreatening? Had I been a handsome gentleman with greying hair at the temples, tall and distinguished, would he have called me 'a fine figure of a man' or something like that? Perhaps not necessarily.

'You are sure you have no cup to share my wine?' he asked.

'You are very kind but no, I must get on.'

Zoe returned to the SUV and fetched her suitcase and rucksack out of the boot, lifting the latter onto her shoulders. She headed for a tight, cobbled lane that sloped up the hill beside the *mairie*. Her wheelie suitcase – that had run so smoothly through the arrivals hall and on the tarmac of the car park – began to bounce and swerve, but she had no choice.

Climbing between largish houses, she found the air much cooler in the delicious shade. She came to a junction with a small well in the centre, a galvanised bucket swinging damply on a metal chain, indicating that it had recently been used, perhaps for watering the ubiquitous geraniums in their heavy clay pots.

From the well, the lanes branched left or right. She took the latter, curving uphill between houses that became more compact, most of their shutters closed. Whether that was because they were unoccupied or because they were shut up against the heat of the middle of the day, she couldn't tell.

She doubled back, round a hairpin, past a *coiffeuse* or ladies' hairdresser and a *mercerie*, a haberdashery, selling cloth and wool and thread and so on. The owner, a generously proportioned woman in a floral apron, was sitting outside, subsided on a wooden kitchen chair, smoking a fragrant cheroot.

'That looks like hard work,' the woman remarked, her eye on the disobedient suitcase.

'It is,' said Zoe, pausing to adjust the straps of her rucksack on her shoulders. It contained her laptop and her iPad, as well as all of their associated bits and pieces of baffling but useful technology. She hadn't wanted to entrust them to the baggage handlers. 'Nearly there, though.'

'Madame Pascal, is it?'

'Yes,' said Zoe, warily. 'It is.'

'Welcome to Sainte-Catherine.' The woman drew on her dark-brown cheroot, then dropped it on the cobbles alongside several other butts, crushing it under the heel of her black, masculine, lace-up shoe. She offered a hand to shake. 'My name is Grenelle, but you can call me Antoinette.'

'My first name is Zoe. Are you related to the brigadier?'

'My brother,' said Antoinette Grenelle. 'But we do not speak.'

'Good heavens. Why not?' asked Zoe, before she could stop herself.

'Do not ask. You will be friends with him or you will be friends with me. Not both.' Antoinette Grenelle flopped back down on her hard kitchen chair. It gave a groan and a creak. Then she winked and added: 'In Sainte-Catherine, it is normal to take sides.'

'Oh, I see,' said Zoe, though she had no idea what the woman meant. 'Well, pleased to meet you, in any case.'

With a smile for the *mercière* – the haberdasher – Zoe pressed on.

I don't want to get involved in any feuds and it feels strange that, already, two strangers know my name and, no doubt, my business.

Two

Getting In

Zoe next found herself in a lovely square called Place Saint-Bertrand, just big enough to accommodate two restaurant terraces. The outdoor tables of Le Gourmand were sheltered by a gorgeous vine, dripping with bunches of ripe grapes. The other establishment, Auberge Sainte-Catherine, was more utilitarian, shaded by branded umbrellas advertising pastis, the popular aniseed liqueur, drunk with lots of ice, diluted with fresh water.

The idea of sitting down for a quarter of an hour with a cooling drink felt so delicious that Zoe had to exercise all of her willpower to force herself to press on, climbing Rue des Templiers towards the summit of the town. On the right, she found a short cul-de-sac of cobbles that led only to a *chambre d'hôtes* – a guest house – with a sign by the door, hand-painted on a piece of rustic timber: *Chez Denis et Davide*. Beneath the sign was a tarred wooden barrel in which a magnificent oleander grew, with clusters of pink flowers at the ends of long fronds with many narrow, dark-green leaves.

I hope that accommodation works out for my removal men.

Further on, the lane levelled out at the impressive front door of Sainte-Catherine's octagonal Templar church, with half a dozen tourists on their way in and out. From there, it was a short step to Place Sainte-Catherine where Zoe found herself weaving through a crowd of locals and visitors, busy with a street market that occupied the whole of the square, a lovely open space at the summit of the hill, shaded by centennial lime trees. Swerving and apologising, she and her cumbersome bags navigated stalls selling olives, garlic, onions, cheese, fresh meat, local wine and – of course – all kinds of delicious-smelling bread. There were also two tables of second-hand books, managed by a small man in a blue painter's smock.

Zoe paused because she was interested to see what he had on sale, but the look he gave her was so unpleasant and angry that she changed her mind.

What on earth is that about?

She glimpsed her destination through the crowds and the awnings of the market stalls, in the far corner of the square, shuttered and sad. She weaved between a butcher's rotisserie full of delicious-looking chickens and a wine merchant. When, at last, she reached the door, she became suddenly aware of the huge step she was taking.

What, precisely, have I done?

There was a vast cobweb stretching from the iron door handle, through the ornate bars on the glazed portion and across onto the jamb. In two concrete boxes either side, a handful of parched weeds had taken over from what looked like deceased geraniums. The sign above all this was rotten and peeling, but could just still be made out.

La Librairie de Mes Rêves.

Reading it, Zoe's brief trepidation dissipated and, for a third time, she felt a fizz of expectation and excitement, not in the slightest discouraged by the dust and grime, nor by the dark interior behind the filthy window glass, nor by the untidy crush of advertising leaflets crammed into and overflowing from the letterbox, nor by the filthy frayed doormat. Her face creased into a broad smile. She eased her rucksack from her shoulders, popped it on top of a square granite bollard, then took a step back, beaming with pleasure.

The name is one thing I won't change. This genuinely is 'The Bookshop of My Dreams'. My new life starts here – one I've been dreaming of for years and years.

★

The second-hand bookseller, Napoléon Etienne, watched the newcomer from a distance, through the crowds and the stalls. There was a nasty look in his eye, composed of suspicion and jealousy. No one noticed because he had no customers just then. The other stallholders – his neighbours but not his friends – would have expected nothing else, because he was not well liked.

How dare she?

The 'nasty look' became a sullen frown.

We don't need outsiders in Sainte-Catherine.

★

Weary from her climb through the winding, bumpy lanes, Zoe moved her bag off the bollard, sat down and took stock. The market was in full swing. She wondered how many of the people browsing were active customers and how many were simply enjoying the sights and sounds, intending to do their real shopping at the Hyper U supermarket. It was a good sign for commerce in Sainte-Catherine that the market was open well into the afternoon. She knew that in lots of Provençal villages the traders packed up at midday.

It would be useful to find out what proportion is local and how many are tourists, simply passing through.

Close to where she was perched, a jolly-looking man of her own age was beckoning passers-by towards his stall, inviting them to sample his wares: three different wines – two red, one white – from bottles without labels, served in tasting measures in lovely tulip-shaped glasses that sparkled in the bright sun. On a blue-and-white awning above his counter she read his name: *Marcel Maurice, viticulteur.*

What a lovely name that is for a profession – 'one who cultivates vines'.

Amused by his spiel, she watched three couples try Monsieur Maurice's vintages, one after the other, each ending up purchasing two or three bottles, the transactions accompanied by his steady flow of entertaining patter. Feeling refreshed by her sit-down, she got up in order to go and speak to him, but was interrupted by a tap on the shoulder.

'Madame Pascal, Zoe, I'm so sorry I'm late.'

Recognising the voice of her charming and intimidatingly glamorous *notaire*, Caroline Robin, Zoe turned to greet her, then her face fell. Caroline was dressed, as usual, impeccably, having chosen today a white linen suit that looked as if she had only just put it on, implausibly clean and pressed, paired with pristine white trainers and a white silk scarf knotted at her throat. Her left arm, though, was held in a black neoprene sling.

'What on earth has happened?' Zoe asked.

'It's a long story. How was your journey?'

'Draining, as travel always is, but efficient, as you see.'

'I ought to have got someone to meet you in the car park to help bring up your bags.'

'Don't give it another thought. The exercise did me good.'

'You seem already to be *en pleine forme*,' said Caroline, meaning 'on top form'.

Zoe reflected that it was a wonderful bonus that she had become fast friends with the solicitor who had helped her through six months of tiresome paperwork for the purchase of 'The Bookshop of My Dreams'. With a thrill of impatience, she demanded: 'Do you have the keys?'

Caroline's face fell. 'That's just it. I'm so sorry. I don't. There was a break-in at my office and everything got turned upside down.'

'You mean someone stole the keys to my bookshop?'

'It's possible, or more likely they simply haven't turned up yet in the mess.'

'Are there any special reasons why someone would want to steal from you? Did they take your computers?'

'I'm not sure computers are worth stealing these days. I remember when someone I know was devastated because their CD collection was taken while they were away on holiday – more devastated about that than their jewellery and their television. But times change.'

'What about your arm, though? Are you badly hurt? Did you confront them?'

Caroline didn't answer. Her haughty features expressed uncertainty. She pursed her lips and Zoe saw, in her eyes, that she was weighing up whether to share something possibly slightly shameful. She never got the chance, however, because Marcel Maurice, the winemaker, came to kiss Caroline on both cheeks and ask the same question with which Zoe had started.

'What's happened, my dear Caro?'

Like Antoine, the tipsy police officer, Marcel spoke with the distinctive accent of the '*terroir*', the local soil. He seemed charming and open, but Caroline clammed up.

'I can't tell you, either of you. It's too embarrassing. You will both think me a fool.'

'I'm sure I won't,' said Zoe, then introduced herself to Marcel.

'Ah, the book lady,' he replied.

Zoe concealed a sigh.

Is there no one within five kilometres who doesn't know who I am?

'You were very clever and entertaining with your customers,' Zoe told him. 'Business looks like it's going well?'

'Oh, the market is little more than a hobby. The important thing is a big chain taking thirty thousand bottles, not whether I sell a few dozen on a Saturday.'

'Thirty thousand? That's a very substantial business.'

'Perhaps I exaggerate a little,' he told her, modestly.

'But selling at a higher margin must be handy, without the costs of distribution or a powerful bulk buyer forcing down your prices?'

'Those are good points,' he said, looking as though he was adjusting his idea of who she was and whether she was worth speaking to as an equal in commerce. He asked: 'This bookshop venture is not a folly of retirement? Though, of course, you are too young for retirement. Perhaps you have a husband who has made a lot of money and likes to see you enjoy yourself by spending it?'

Marcel Maurice asked this so simply, so openly, that Zoe almost found herself answering in the same frank tone, but Caroline interrupted on her behalf.

'On two minutes' acquaintance, Marcel, these are not suitable questions.'

'I don't mind sharing,' said Zoe. 'I've had a lifetime working in theatre as an actor and then, for the greater part of my professional life, in management. But a bookshop has always been my dream.'

'A lovely one,' confirmed Marcel.

'Now,' said Caroline, 'I've had an idea. You are packing up, yes?'

'I will, shortly,' said Marcel.

Zoe glanced round the square. It was true, some of the stallholders were in the process of dismantling their awnings and counters. Two tiny elderly Renault vans had actually managed to climb up through the steep lanes, ready to transport away goods, tabletops, trestles and frames.

'My boy is not yet here,' said Marcel. He gestured with his right hand and, for the first time, Zoe realised that his left sleeve was empty, folded back on itself and pinned. Then Marcel added in a voice full of disappointment – or perhaps resentment: 'I cannot manage on my own.'

Caroline didn't respond to his appeal for sympathy. Instead, rather brutally, Zoe thought, she replied: 'For the time being, I am in the same boat. We are both damaged goods, but Madame Pascal is very athletic, very strong.'

'Is that so?' asked Marcel with a wolfish smile that suggested that he had already reached the same conclusion. 'What is your idea, that the book lady should help carry my unsold wares down through the town?'

'No, Marcel, pay attention. I don't have the keys to open up the bookshop. Look, there's a window half open on the first floor. We could use the frame of your stall as a ladder and Madame Pascal will scamper up and climb in.'

All this was news to Zoe.

'But if the door is locked—' she began.

'Yes, the front door is locked, but it can be opened from within,' said Caroline. 'The button can be turned on the inside. You know the style? The keys are not needed. And I have called a locksmith. He will be here first thing on Monday morning.'

'But that means I'll be trapped inside all weekend?'

Caroline shrugged in a way that suggested Zoe ought to recognise that some things can't be altered and there was no point complaining about problems that already have a solution. She said: 'It was the best I could do.'

'What about overnight?' Zoe insisted.

'Perhaps there is also a manual bolt. But what do you have to fear?'

That's true. I'm bringing my London consciousness of ever-present crime to somewhere it perhaps doesn't exist.

She told them: 'Okay, I'm willing to try.'

Because Marcel's 'boy' hadn't yet turned up, the three of them took apart Marcel's stall together, Zoe using her two hands and Caroline and Marcel – for their different reasons – using one each. Brigadier Antoine Grenelle arrived, just as they were leaning the ladder-like framework against the façade of the bookshop, and he wondered aloud what was going on, making Zoe think about old-fashioned police dramas on TV in which the stolid uniformed sergeants always wanted to know: 'What's going on here, then?'

Caroline explained as Zoe, in her trainers and loose cotton trousers for travel, began to climb with Marcel grasping the steel frame, looking up at her.

'Nice view,' he remarked, admiringly.

'I agree,' said Antoine.

'Be quiet, both of you,' said Caroline.

Zoe paid no attention. She had arrived at the first-floor window. It was open wide enough for her to put an arm inside and lift the window stay off its spigot, allowing her to swing it open, outwards, casement style.

Before climbing through, she took a moment to inspect the room. It was dingy, of course, but seemed reasonably clean. There was an open fireplace full of sticks, meaning some determined bird had attempted – and presumably failed – to build a nest at the top of the chimney. There was no furniture of any kind, but there was a built-in hanging space beside the chimney flue. The floor was covered with a square of linoleum that didn't quite reach the walls, meaning she could see some of the boards beneath.

I do hope they're in good condition.

Zoe put a leg over the sill and climbed in, eliciting a cheer from the stallholders left in the square. Glancing back outside, she saw that at least two-dozen people were watching her progress, including – to her surprise – the boy, Thierry, from the car hire company at the airport in Marseille. She called down to Caroline.

'Is the electricity on?'

'You will discover, I suppose.'

Zoe crossed the room and flicked an old-fashioned Bakelite switch on the wall.

Not on.

23

The bedroom door was closed and a little sticky in its frame, as if there had been movement in the property. Zoe wasn't worried about that. The bookshop was firmly supported by the buildings on either side and had stood for at least five hundred years. No one knew precisely when it had been built, using heavy round stones from the local riverbed, set in lime mortar. She gave the door a wrench and it swung open.

The landing was darker still, though there was a skylight in the angled rafters of the roof, covered over with something. She found another light switch but that, too, flipped up and down to no purpose. She proceeded into the back bedroom, her hands out in front so as not to bang into anything, finding her way towards a few slivers of light that described the shape of the window shutters in the far wall. She located the mechanism by touch and flung them wide.

The light that entered from the northern sky almost made her wince. She turned away for a second to allow her eyes to adjust, then looked back through dirty panes of elderly glass – so old, in fact, that it had thickened at the bottom of each pane, drooping with age. Beyond the window, she counted four concentric rings of clay-topped houses.

Lots of new neighbours who probably all know who I am.

The roofs descended step by step, to the foot of the incline. Beyond them, the glorious countryside rolled away in soft folds. A heat haze in the distance meant she couldn't see whether or not the mountains were snow-capped, because they appeared like a range of ghost summits, merging with the sky.

It really is indescribably beautiful. I am so very lucky. It almost feels too good to be true.

Three

Making a House a Home

Zoe opened the window to let in the parched outside air, hoping to find it full of the fragrances of the countryside. Beneath her was a courtyard with a washing line strung across it and, to her disappointment, instead of rosemary and lavender, she smelt the unmistakable odour of a place used as a bathroom by cats.

'Oh dear,' she said aloud. 'That won't do.'

She returned to the landing. Now the rear shutters were open, she was able peer into a decent modern bathroom and well-appointed first-floor kitchen. Faintly, she heard a voice calling her and realised that Caroline must be wondering why she wasn't already downstairs, opening up.

She scampered down a solid wooden staircase, through the gloomy shelves of the bookshop proper and groped her way to the front door. Beside it was an old-fashioned coat stand and, at the top, an old-fashioned shop bell on a curved ribbon of springy steel. At the base was a manual bolt.

That's reassuring.

As Caroline had predicted, the lock had a knurled steel button, though it needed a key on the outside. Zoe turned the button, moving the deadbolt across, out of its retaining socket – a part of the mechanism that she knew, from some scrap of general knowledge, was called a 'keep'. Like in the bedroom upstairs, the door stuck momentarily in its frame and she had to tug it open, revealing herself to the assembled neighbours and passers-by with an unintended flourish and a loud jangle of the bell. This brought forth a second round of applause that made her feel silly and proud, both at once.

'I feel a fool,' Zoe told Caroline.

'No, you are a hero,' her friend replied, smiling.

Everyone soon went about their business. To Zoe's surprise, Thierry – the boy from the car hire company – set about removing the ladder-like frame of Marcel Maurice's stall. Zoe put two and two together and decided that Thierry must be Marcel's 'boy'. In an undertone, she asked Caroline if that was the case.

'Why, yes. It's very sad. Thierry is desperate to live in the big city and Marcel has no one else to whom he might want to pass on his business.'

'That's a shame,' said Zoe. 'Marcel obviously cares deeply about it, otherwise he wouldn't be here, hand-selling in the market. How did he lose his arm?'

'A farming accident. But he copes very well.'

'How will you manage with your own injury?'

'Oh, it's not so bad. I have an automatic car and, in France, we drive on the right and therefore steer with our left, which I have always thought dangerous, given that most people are more adept with—'

She was interrupted by Antoine Grenelle.

'I enjoyed your display, Madame Pascal,' he told them. 'But the bookshop, I've not been inside for two years. You will have your work cut out bringing it up to scratch?'

'I'm sure I will,' said Zoe. 'Would you like to see?'

'I dearly would,' he told her, giving a little hiccup behind his hand.

'Go ahead.'

As he brushed past, Zoe noticed Antoine's estranged sister, Antoinette Grenelle – the haberdasher – watching with a pinched expression on her fleshy features, standing alone in a huff, one elbow propped on the bare frame of Marcel Maurice's part-dismantled wine stall.

Oh dear, I hope I haven't made an enemy already.

*

Brigadier Antoine Grenelle of the Sainte-Catherine police had a good look round, then pottered home to a narrow village house halfway up the cobbled lanes, entering via an unlit corridor that led him to a kitchen last updated in the previous century. There was nothing on Antoine's square table but a bottle of wine, two-thirds drunk, and a cut-crystal glass. He picked up the former and poured the majority of its contents into the latter.

I never chose to become a lush. It crept up on me. But how is one to avoid it in a land of such excellent vintages at such reasonable prices?

It was perhaps due to this excessive consumption that, although a friendly, witty and – above all – employed gentleman, looking forward to comfortable retirement, he had no current relationships of a romantic nature or any prospect of developing one.

Sainte-Catherine is a lonely place when one is all alone.

As a lowly member of the rural police force, Antoine didn't earn a lot. Neither could his sister, Antoinette, put aside significant savings each month from the modest income of her haberdashery. They were 'comfortable', though. They had become orphans fifteen years before, each inheriting fifty per cent of the parental estate. As a consequence, neither had a mortgage to pay.

Is Antoinette happy?

He thought not.

If she were happy, she wouldn't be so desperately keen to find the Vulture.

His glass now empty, he replenished it by draining his bottle.

★

By bedtime, for Zoe, everything had changed – and entirely for the better.

Having located the fuse box, she had turned the electricity on and had had time to pop back down through the cobbled streets to the Hyper U supermarket to buy a few light bulbs, plus some bits and pieces for a picnic supper in her new home, while Thierry kept an eye. The next day, she intended to acquire cleaning products so that she could make her own contribution when the real work began, led by a team selected by Caroline.

Only a little later than planned, her removal van arrived, soon after her improvised supper, in the middle of the evening. The three men had taken turns at the wheel, driving down through France to meet her in a single day. They were just in time for Zoe to have her own double bed to sleep in, carried up through the cobbled lanes in their strong arms, like a kind of trophy. For simplicity, she had always intended to use a sleeping bag on the first night. One of them had that, too, together with her favourite pillow in a Waitrose bag for life.

Once the bed was ready in the back bedroom, she showed the removal men to the accommodation she had reserved for them, three small rooms in the guest house, hidden in the cul-de-sac off Rue des Templiers, run by two rotund men in their sixties with bottle-dark hair and lavish gestures: Denis Allard and Davide Quillan.

The back bedroom faced north and, with the window and the shutters open, Zoe was glad of the cool breeze that made its way down from the mountains to disperse the heat of the day, replacing it with a more bearable night. She was in bed by ten, comfortable in her White Company pyjamas, swiftly falling into dreamless sleep.

*

At about the same time, the burglar was cursing an unjust fate.

It is as I feared – I was too late.

The burglar gave some thought to the best method of approach.

Because it's a Saturday night and the weather so warm, there are lots of people eating and drinking and chatting out of doors. There's no way I can manage to approach the town square without being seen. Even very late, I might come across people staggering home under the influence and be recognised.

The burglar weighed up some competing options, none of which seemed completely secure.

I'll come back late tomorrow, Sunday, or very early Monday morning, before anyone is about – and we will see what we will see.

*

Zoe woke, the next morning, a little after seven, feeling refreshed and – simultaneously – intimidated by all she had to do.

For breakfast, she nibbled a little of the remains of her previous evening's picnic then went out into the quiet streets, seeking coffee. In Place Saint-Bertrand, the restaurant with the luscious vines – Le Gourmand – was still closed but the one opposite, with the pastis umbrellas – the Auberge Sainte-Catherine – was opening up. She spoke to a very lean and muscular waiter in his late twenties or early thirties, dressed in tight black trousers, a clinging white shirt and a traditional black apron. She explained that she was new to

29

the town and told him her name. He nodded and replied: 'Ah, the bookshop lady.'

Good heavens, he knows who I am as well.

Although the restaurant terrace was surrounded by low buildings, the sun soon climbed high enough to peep into the small square. Zoe drank her *café allongé* – an espresso 'stretched' by hot water – with her eyes closed and her face tilted up to it.

I'm like a lizard, kick-starting my day with renewed sunlight.

The church bells began to chime eight-thirty. She offered to pay. The waiter said his till wasn't yet working and asked her to come back. With a rewarding sense that this meant she was already a trusted local resident, Zoe hurried back to Place Sainte-Catherine.

The cleaning duo that Caroline had booked was just arriving, all their equipment in a four-wheeled cart with rubber tyres that, she supposed, they had dragged up through the cobbled lanes by hand. Two taciturn women with determined expressions wore matching company T-shirts printed with a slogan that translated as 'we love the jobs you hate'. They began by asking if Zoe had the wherewithal to make them coffee. Apologising that she hadn't, she turned round and went back to the Auberge to acquire more, asking the waiter for take-away cups, which he seemed to find baffling.

'What's wrong with the normal ones? You'll return them, won't you?'

While she waited, she caught two villagers she did not know clearly talking about her.

That doesn't look very friendly.

Soon, however, Zoe was on her way back up the hill with two large and frothy *café crèmes* and another middle-sized *café allongé* for herself. The cleaning ladies had already finished washing down the bare plaster of the front-bedroom walls with warm water in a bucket, provided by the copper

30

immersion tank, high up in the ceiling of the bathroom. Now, they were embarked on steam-cleaning the linoleum and the fringe of parquet.

With the casement windows open wide, by the time they reached the threshold on the landing, the floor was almost dry. One of them went back to swab the woodwork of the built-in hanging cupboard in the niche beside the chimney while the other moved on to the second bedroom, exasperated at the presence of Zoe's double bed.

She's only complaining because she thinks it's expected. She doesn't mean anything by it.

Sliding the bed from side to side slowed them down a little, then they attacked the window glass, remarking: 'It's very thin at the top of the panes. You should get Gato Merino to replace it before the winter.'

'Perhaps,' said Zoe, not wanting to get ahead of herself. She had an idea that she ought to live in the place for a while before she started thinking about making changes. 'We'll see. Who is Gato Merino?'

'The local builder and handyman.'

The cleaners moved on to attack the bathroom – which was only dusty, otherwise clean with a modern shower cubicle and two large mirrored cabinets on the walls. The kitchen, too, wouldn't detain them long.

Zoe went downstairs. Here, things were different. The entire ground floor was given over to the bookshop, a large space divided up by ancient timber posts and beechwood shelves, all of them bare because, two years before, when the bookshop had ceased trading, everything had been cleared out, except for two wooden kitchen chairs that stood, lonely and unloved, between the stacks.

Zoe ran a finger along the pale wood of one of the shelves, finding it dusty but not damp, which was a relief because spores of mould would have been a significant problem.

Of course, it may be different when the rains come.

Towards the rear of the open-plan shop was a vacant corner where she intended to install some armchairs, near a framed drawing of Sainte-Catherine on the wall – a bird's-eye view of the town inherited with the purchase of the premises – next to the back door, which had a slim key in a frail lock. She opened it onto the courtyard, assailed once more by the acrid smell of the cats' loo. The entire area was paved, except for a large stone planter the size of a big bath whose loose dirt had been used as a litter tray. The side of the planter was decorated with a bas-relief stone carving of a child reading from an open book.

I have to do something about this smell.

In a corner of the courtyard were some bits of neglected garden furniture in rusting, white-painted cast iron. She lifted the table upside down and put it on top of the planter, then she used the two chairs to make it even more difficult for the neighbourhood cats to get at it.

The cleaning ladies requested more coffee and Zoe obliged, remembering to return the crockery and coming back with fresh – only two this time, because the brew was strong and she thought she might get jittery if she had a third herself. By this time, the square was busy because the market traders had all erected their stalls for Sunday trading, though there was no sign yet of either Marcel Maurice or his son, Thierry.

Perhaps they are in church? Or is selling alcohol frowned upon on the Lord's Day?

When she got back, the cleaning ladies were busy on the stairs, applying a polish that smelt very wholesomely of beeswax. The removal men arrived, looking pleased with themselves, having lavishly breakfasted in their guest house, *Chez Denis et Davide*. Zoe told them that the upper rooms were ready for what she still thought of as her 'capsule' belongings.

Though I don't believe I've left behind or sold anything I'm ever going to miss.

She asked the cleaning ladies if the removal men might use their four-wheeled chariot and they readily agreed. Without a shared language, Zoe noticed, her two teams clearly found one another '*sympathiques*'.

The rest of the morning was spent equipping the upstairs rooms – the two bedrooms and the kitchen and bathroom. At one point, out of the casement window at the front, through which she had climbed the previous day, Zoe saw Antoinette Grenelle lurking in the square, watching the comings and goings, and she gave her a cheery wave, which was not returned.

After a moment, she realised that Antoinette was not looking her way. Instead, the haberdasher was fully focused on the elderly woman in the purple tracksuit Zoe had seen yesterday, who was once more exploring the town with an open book in her hands. In fact, Antoinette was clearly following the woman, keeping a little distance and attempting to remain unseen by her prey.

How extraordinary.

The removal men squeezed past and she saw that her new accommodation was beginning to take shape, her bits and pieces of furniture fitting very nicely into the ancient building because they were old themselves, picked up from auctions and charity warehouses, well made and thriftily unfashionable. She lined up her toiletries into one of the two mirrored bathroom cabinets and arranged a few personal things in the drawer of her bedside table. She told the men she would unpack the crates of kitchen things herself later, that they could simply leave them on the counters. Then she toured the upstairs rooms with a feeling of deep satisfaction.

Pausing on the landing, she looked up at the skylight. It was blocked by a sheet of cardboard. She was about to fetch a chair to climb up and remove it when the ladies called her from the shop floor. She hurried down, not wanting to undermine their goodwill and hard work, finding them in need of still more coffee.

This time, Zoe came back with pastries as well as caffeine, three *pains au chocolat* and three *croissants*, all golden and glistening with butter, to share with her two teams, male and female, exchanging a word with Marcel Maurice who, she learned, had simply arrived late because he'd overslept.

'Why was that?'

He looked shifty, then replied, vaguely: 'My farm manager Odile and I were studying a book.'

At an adjacent stall, Marcel introduced her to a woman in a green gardener's apron who sold flowers and shrubs, Elise Guillaume, who offered to replace the dead geraniums in the concrete boxes either side of the bookshop door.

'Could you put in oleanders, like that lovely one outside the guest house? Would they flourish there?'

'They would,' said Elise. 'I'll do it at the end of the day.'

She quoted a price that Zoe thought reasonable so they shook on it, then Zoe hurried away with the drinks and snacks. Once they had all been eaten and drunk, the cleaning ladies went through the building, polishing all the other windows, making everything look much brighter and nicer, while the removal men trundled up and down, bringing Zoe's initial supply of about three thousand books. It was a carefully curated list of literary and commercial fiction, plus popular non-fiction, mostly in French and English, but also including stock in the other major European languages: German, Italian and Spanish. She asked them to stack the boxes without opening them as she would take responsibility for sharing them out on the shelves herself.

By two o'clock, there was little left to do. The cleaning ladies had finished polishing the yards and yards of bookshelves, so the whole place now smelt deliciously of beeswax. Zoe paid them and they left, delighted both with the cash and her generous tip. Then Zoe offered to take the removal men to the Auberge Sainte-Catherine for a snack lunch at her expense. They accepted with alacrity.

The place was busy but, luckily, there was a table available, recently vacated by some Belgian tourists. Zoe paid for the morning's hot beverages and pastries, adding sufficient, in advance, for the men's three meals, accompanied by cold bottled lagers that the lithe waiter served with obvious contempt, remarking to Zoe: 'It's odd to order beer when one is dining in the heart of the finest vines.'

Without translating for the removal team, Zoe explained that wine was considered an evening drink in England. She discovered that the waiter's name was Patrick Lagrasse, and that he lived above the café-restaurant with his sister who worked in the kitchen. She asked him if he knew where Marcel Maurice's vineyards were and he gestured to the west, adding: 'Will you be going out searching?'

'I beg your pardon?'

Patrick was called away to serve another table before he could reply, rearranging some chairs to suit the large party, leaving Zoe confused. She thanked her removal men, handing each of them a fresh twenty-pound note 'for their kindness' and wishing them a safe journey home. They told her that they hoped to break their journey somewhere outside Paris that evening, but shouldn't delay getting back on the road.

'Rather you than me, though,' said the leader.

'What do you mean?'

'Living here. I mean, it's all right now, if you like that sort of thing. But winter will be something else again. It does get cold, you know.'

'Yes, I do.'

'And people are different, if you don't mind me saying.'

Oh dear. I hope he's not going to tell me: 'I'm not racist but . . .'

'Go on,' she told him.

'Me and my mum and dad went to live in Yorkshire from Hackney. Country people are funny. They don't like strangers. Or they like them up to a point, then they want rid.

We lasted eighteen months. What I mean is, it might be hard work breaking through, being accepted.'

Yes, thought Zoe. *It might. But I won't let that put me off.*

Four

DOG

Zoe left the removal men to their lunches and climbed back up through the lanes to the square. She was thinking about her first sight of Sainte-Marie when just a teenager, working as assistant to the celebrated French stage and screen actress Adélaïde Amour at the Avignon Festival, not far away in Provence. Adélaïde had been the star the previous spring when Zoe's half-sister Maisie Cooper had solved 'the murder at the theatre', as the *Chichester Observer* newspaper called it.

Driving along sun-baked summer roads, on a brief motoring holiday after the Avignon Festival, with Maisie's new baby sleeping soundly in a bassinet on the back seat, they had seen Sainte-Marie profiled against the gorgeous blue sky and the white-capped mountains and had fallen in love. Decades later, her teenage dream of living there had finally come true.

At the top of the town, Zoe found the market still humming. To her delight, the butcher was there again with his mobile rotisserie, slow-cooking chickens, their crisp and golden skin utterly mouth-watering. She introduced herself and explained that she had just moved into *La Librairie de Mes Rêves*.

He exclaimed: 'Oh, then you are Madame Pascal.' He wished her good luck, expressed his delight that the shop was reopening and gave his own name. *Je m'appelle Robert*

Petit.' Then he spoilt things by holding on to her hand for too long, a 'meaningful' look in his eye.

Zoe thanked him for his welcome and asked when the first chicken would be ready, only to discover that all of those on the rotating skewers had been pre-ordered. When she expressed her disappointment, he told her: 'No matter. The *notaire*, Caroline Robin, asked me to reserve one for you. Come back in fifteen minutes.'

Delighted and very hungry – she hadn't eaten any pastries herself – Zoe bought a baguette from one of two bakery stalls, wondering to herself if the competition between them was amicable, then exerted all her willpower not to start eating it. The second-hand bookseller was busy with a customer, a small boy who was looking through a pile of hardback *Tintin* comic books. Once again, he gave her an angry and unwelcoming look.

'*Bonjour, monsieur,*' she told him brightly, determined not to let his unpleasantness spoil her day.

He turned his back, his shoulders hunched defensively in his blue painter's smock.

Never mind. I'll get him onside soon.

Because the locksmith wouldn't come until the next morning, Monday, Zoe had left the door open, not without qualms. To her surprise, there on the welcome mat – brought from London to replace the filthy and fraying one left behind by the previous owner – was a white Jack Russell terrier with an endearing tan face, sitting upright and pert, like an ornament. It was the same dog she had seen the previous day, lying somnolent in the middle of the road, down in the little suburb of ticky-tacky villas.

'Hello,' she said. 'What's your name?'

The terrier cocked an ear, his lovely dark eyes seeming to understand.

Smiling to herself, Zoe repeated the question in French and the dog put its head on one side, taking an interest in her baguette. She crouched down, noticing that the dog had no proper collar, just a ragged bandana knotted around its neck. She tore what the French call the 'nose' from the end of her stick of bread and offered it to the Jack Russell who sniffed then looked her in the eye, as if to say: *'Is that all we've got? Isn't it dinner time yet?'*

Zoe stood up and told him: 'You can have a bit of chicken skin if you come back later.'

To her surprise, the dog – appearing to have understood precisely what she had said – jumped up and dashed away at top speed, slaloming through the stalls and past the ankles of the Sunday shoppers.

Weary from her busy morning, Zoe fetched one of the wooden chairs and put it outside to have a sit-down in the sun. Soon, she saw Caroline weaving through the square, a decorative carboard box tied with a bow of twine in her good hand. She was dressed in clothes identical to yesterday, except that the ensemble was powder blue instead of white, even down to her pristine trainers.

'I ordered you a chicken.'

'I know,' said Zoe. 'I discovered. That was very thoughtful.'

'I thought perhaps we could eat it down by the river, then follow on with this.' Caroline indicated the posh box, labelled *Patisserie Maguelonne*, a cake shop with an old-fashioned Provençal girl's name. 'It's a strawberry tart.'

'Lovely,' said Zoe, though she wasn't generally a fan of sweet things. 'But I don't like to leave the place unlocked.'

'It will be quite safe.'

'All my things are indoors. I went out earlier and it made me uneasy. And I don't want to have to climb through the window again. People will think I'm doing it because I'm odd. Your cleaners were wonderful, by the way.'

'Good, they are now putting some order in my office.'

'What do the police say?'

'I've had the visit of an inspector from Aix. The routine of investigation is under way,' Caroline added, giving Zoe the impression that she hadn't been impressed by the 'inspector from Aix'.

The roast-chicken man beckoned. Caroline went to fetch the bird while Zoe ran upstairs – once again enjoying the lovely scent of beeswax on the stairs – to find two trays in amongst the crates of kitchen paraphernalia. She brought them downstairs with knives and the butter from the previous evening's picnic, dashing back inside to fetch the second upright chair.

As it happened, they didn't need the butter. Zoe served and the meat was moist and delicious, eaten between fresh hunks of perfect French bread. While they ate, Zoe asked Caroline about the people she had met – Antoine and Antoinette Grenelle, Patrick Lagrasse, Marcel and Thierry Maurice, Elise Guillaume and so on. At first, her friend was too busy with her late lunch to give her questions much attention, then she began to pass humorous – though acid – commentaries on them all.

'Antoine and Antoinette are ridiculous. They keep their feud going out of habit.'

'On what basis?'

'And Robert Petit believes himself a man of the world and a catch, when he's never left Sainte-Catherine.'

'He seems to think a lot of you.'

'Have you seen Ambroise Caille, the estate agent, talking to tourists as if every one of them has millions to invest in a run-down chateau?'

'You're very critical. Weren't you born here? Don't you think you should celebrate his sense of enterprise?'

'Patrick Lagrasse is an odd one. You know he keeps himself under wraps, as it were, all summer long, then goes mad on his holidays when the season ends.'

'Goes mad in what way?'

'Women by the string, like sausages. Enough, now, let us eat in silence.'

Zoe decided Caroline was in a hurry to finish her rustic sandwich so that she could move on to attack the strawberry tart, which they soon did, Zoe finding it incredibly rich. Caroline savoured an enormous piece, licking her lips and the fingers of her one good hand, reminding Zoe of Nigella Lawson and her innocently suggestive TV cooking show. She noticed both Robert Petit and two gentlemen tourists looking over, mesmerised by Caroline's unconscious performance.

Lunch complete, Zoe took the trays inside and Caroline followed. They washed their hands at the kitchen sink then had a good look round. Caroline declared herself impressed with all that had been accomplished, though Zoe knew her solicitor's tastes were resolutely modern.

'You are making the most of its old-world charm, with the exposed beams and the crooked shapes,' Caroline told her, doubtfully.

'A bookshop should be a haven,' Zoe replied, 'a kind of nest for people to retreat into from the world and all its troubles.'

'You've said that before, but people order online these days, don't they?'

'They do,' said Zoe patiently, 'but they also like to touch and hold the works of their favourite authors. People buy cut flowers at the petrol station or the supermarket, but they also visit gardens and garden centres for a richer, deeper experience. That's what I'll be offering.'

'And have you thought about the competition?'

Zoe didn't answer straight away. She knew, of course, that there were other booksellers in Sainte-Catherine. One specialised in children's books and games, on the little ring road, near the supermarket. The second was essentially a newsagent beefed up with a good selection of non-fiction, plus the most popular crime and thrillers. Several market traders came on selected days with their own eclectic ranges, mostly local history, second-hand thrillers and French classics. Finally, there was the second-hand store where a pugnacious bibliophile sold dog-eared copies from a disorganised three-storey town house with piles of uncatalogued volumes scattered on every surface, including the treads of the stairs. It was he who had behaved so resentfully to Zoe on two occasions already, standing by his trestle tables in the square.

'For Sainte-Catherine to be "the book village", there have to be bookshops,' Zoe told her friend. 'We will all feed off one another's successes, I'm sure.'

'There was perhaps a reason why *La Librairie de Mes Rêves* closed two years ago, however. It wasn't making any money.'

'Thank you,' said Zoe, smiling.

'For what?' asked Caroline.

'I like a challenge.'

'You haven't taken offence?'

'Absolutely not. And I'm grateful for all your help – with the mystifying bureaucracy of the purchase, your wonderful cleaners, the magnificent roast chicken—'

'And the strawberry tart.'

'Yes, that too.'

Soon after, Caroline left, strolling away through the busy market, attracting admiring and – perhaps – envious glances as she went gliding over the cobbles. Elise Guillaume was busy turning over the dirt in the concrete boxes by the front door, picking out the dead geraniums and the moribund weeds and adding compost. Beside her were two substantial oleanders in two-litre pots, ready for planting.

'They will look an absolute picture,' said Elise. 'Due south. Would you bring me some water – lots of it?'

The only large receptacle Zoe could find was the saucepan she used for making stock. She had to fill it three times so Elise could give the shrubs 'a good soaking', after which the horticulturist stood up and rubbed her hands on her green apron. Zoe paid then, left alone, searched through the crates of kitchen equipment for a pair of heavy-duty scissors with which to cut the packaging tape on the book boxes. During the cleaning process that morning, she had begun to visualise how she would organise her stock.

The first box she opened contained a tightly packed selection of classical crime novels by Margery Allingham, Agatha Christie, Gladys Mitchell and others. She began placing them on some shelves deep inside the shop. Disappointingly, the light was not good. She promised herself she would make better illumination of her wares a priority.

The bottom layer in the box of books was made up of the thirty-odd novels of the New Zealand writer Ngaio Marsh, including a theatrical mystery entitled *Opening Night*, reminding Zoe of one of the adventures of her youth, when she was just sixteen years old and connected to a murder investigation in the provincial Sussex city of Chichester in the south of England, led by her half-sister, Maisie Cooper.

To Zoe's surprise, she felt suddenly homesick.

No, I'm not homesick. Nostalgic would be a better word.

The bookshop was not yet connected to the internet or to the French phone system. If all went well, that would happen the following week. She went and found her rucksack to dig out her mobile phone, wanting to call the now-elderly Maisie and find out how she was, whether she was recovering well from her worrying 'fall' which was, of course, one of the perils of old age. To her surprise, Zoe discovered that she had no signal, which was odd because, on her previous visit to Sainte-Catherine, she'd had plenty of 'bars'.

Never mind. I'll look into that later.

Zoe set to work. It took her until early evening to unpack the majority of the fiction boxes, the process delayed by the fact that she kept changing her mind about the layout. At seven o'clock, her mind weary and her back sore, she ventured out, finding the town very quiet and the restaurants on the little square closed up and shuttered. She returned to the bookshop and made herself another chicken sandwich, nowhere near as good as the first, now the bird was cold and the bread less fresh.

Reinvigorated, however, she carefully washed and dried her hands, determined to press on with her labours.

*

Caroline Robin belonged to that elusive segment of the consumer market so avidly sought after by advertisers. Of middle years and no longer 'a girl', she was still attentive to her appearance, an entrepreneur of independent means in a profession that would always be important. She lived alone but was not averse to what the French liked to call '*les aventures du cœur*' – adventures of the heart.

Caroline's two most recent affairs had taken place in her own professional milieu, in Aix-en-Provence, one with a doctor and one with an inspector of police. The first had begun a decade before and lasted several years, starting as a fling and then evolving into an undeclared devotion – on her part – which Caroline now regretted. The second, more recent, had been little more than a rebound, but it had lasted twenty-one roller-coaster months, leaving her with different reasons for regret.

Though it was Sunday evening, Caroline was in her notary's office, close to the centre of Aix, the 'city of a thousand fountains'. Her cleaners had done an excellent job, creating order. Like Zoe, she was tired and engaged in a routine task that was designed to help her start the new week with a desk as clear as her mind. She was moving active dossiers from her in-tray to the filing cabinet in which completed commissions were stored for six months, before being transferred to a secure facility where they would be looked after – apparently in perpetuity – by a dusty gentleman in a calico warehouse coat.

Closing the filing cabinet with relief, Caroline turned her attention to a communication from her accountant, addressing the issue of the rent rise that her landlord wished to impose – punitively, she thought.

The trouble is, I've made a success of these premises. The street was unfashionable when I took them on. He did offer me a ten-year lease when I moved in, but I was too wary to accept it. Now he has me over a barrel.

It was too late on an interminable Sunday to think about such fundamental issues of professional success and livelihood, about fairness and past mistakes. She reached into the bottom drawer of her desk and brought out an illustrated book – at one and the same time a hobby and an apparently unrealisable dream.

If I could find and sell the Vulture, pocketing the proceeds from the fund, I might even buy this place.

★

Zoe made some further progress but was soon yawning and dreaming of her bed. Finally, she ground to a halt with just four boxes left open, books scattered beside them on the clean floorboards.

I should stop. There's too much still left to do.

Abandoning the remainder for the following day, Zoe found she didn't even have the energy to look for proper bedclothes and resigned herself to using her sleeping bag once more. Before going upstairs, she remembered to shoot the bolt at the foot of the front door for a modicum of security.

The lock has not yet been changed. Somewhere out there, a burglar might be in possession of my front door key.

Ten minutes later, her teeth brushed and her face and hands newly washed, dressed demurely in her pyjamas, she stood at the window of the front bedroom, wondering if, perhaps, she might not like to swap her bed from the rear of the first floor, in order to be woken by the sun. It would mean reversing the arrangement of furniture but she thought that perhaps Patrick Lagrasse, the lithe and muscular waiter from the Auberge Sainte-Catherine, might be prevailed upon to give her a hand.

If he is the lothario Caroline suggests, I must be careful inviting him into my 'chamber' so he doesn't get the wrong idea.

The royal-blue sky was scattered with stars, just visible, despite the gentle glow of the orange street lamps. An elderly woman tottered past – the one Zoe had seen on arrival in the car park by the *mairie* – dressed once more in her purple tracksuit, again with a large-format book open in her hands that she seemed to be consulting on the move. Zoe saw a faint reflected gleam in the woman's spare hand, like from a watch glass.

No, not a watch, a compass. She's checking the orientation of the buildings.

The woman wandered away, towards the church at the far end of the square. Then Zoe saw that the elderly passer-by was not alone. Right in the centre of the cobbled space, standing out because of his clean white coat, sat the Jack Russell that she had met on her doormat. For a second or two, she had the odd sensation that the dog was looking her in the eye.

Surely that's not possible, given the distance and—

All at once, the dog barked, two sharp yaps, and Zoe felt utterly convinced that she was the one being addressed. Then a window opened over to her left and a dark projectile came flying through the air to land just a few centimetres from where the dog sat. Zoe thought it was a shoe.

The dog jumped up and skittered away across the cobbles on its little legs, disappearing down Rue des Templiers, following the elderly woman. Though Zoe waited several minutes, it didn't return. She took herself off to bed.

★

Several hours later, Zoe was briefly woken at some unknown hour of the night by a scratching sound and a very faint disturbance of the bell on its strap of steel.

Is that the terrier trying to get in? Or is someone knocking at the door?

Then the noise stopped, bone-weariness overtook her and, once more, she slept.

Five

DIGGING

The Jack Russell was a clever dog, experienced in its relations with humans. But his little canine brain wasn't equipped to wonder if, perhaps, had the woman in the window not already been in her pyjamas, she might have come downstairs and remonstrated with the neighbour who threw the unkind shoe. That would be a step too far in doggy conjecture. But he had formulated a vague idea that this new human was kind and that she might, given time, allow him to sleep in the warmth of her home, in relative comfort.

After the shoe had been thrown, the dog had made itself scarce, scampering past the church and through the square where the restaurants were still doing late business. He trotted round the well, sniffing the drainpipes that other dogs had marked with their scent, emerging onto the quiet car park.

Knowing the habits of the policeman, Antoine Grenelle, the dog went to forage beneath the bench that faced the field of sunflowers, finding nothing but a few stale crumbs.

Ever hopeful – as was characteristic of his terrier breed – the dog made a circuit of the tarmac but found nothing more substantial to eat. A family of tourists came merrily down to their campervan – a man, a woman and a small child. The dog didn't know it, but they were discussing the satisfying and reasonably priced meal they had just enjoyed in the Auberge Sainte-Catherine.

'When we come back, Toby, I want to go to that bookshop,' said the woman. 'The lovely one in the corner of the square.'

'Yes, Clare.'

A tiny blond boy approached, offering a hand to be sniffed and licked. The Jack Russell complied then raised its snout in enquiry: '*Nothing to eat, then?*'

'Come along, Benjy,' called the mother.

The little family got into their van and drove away, leaving the dog alone in the darkness of the night, the headlights and the engine sounds receding and a soft silence seeping back.

No, not silence. A night-time quiet, broken by the low noises of nocturnal creatures, exploring the nooks and crannies of the human world, taking advantage of the fact that the inhabitants of Sainte-Catherine were almost all in bed.

The dog became very still, tense as a hunter, aware that prey was near. After a minute or so, a rat came creeping along the edge of the car park, following its own ritual, along a very faint path through the grass that, on close inspection, could be seen as a 'run' for its tiny clawed feet, reminiscent of human hands.

Quick as a flash, the Jack Russell was on it, firm jaws clamped on the back of the rodent's neck. With a shake, the rat's bones snapped with a barely audible crack and the dog tossed the body away into the edge of the sunflower field, looking pleased with his swift despatch of the unhappy vermin. It was, after all, a terrier's role, even if the terrier in question had no home and no master or mistress, no farm or granary or pea store of his own to protect.

The Jack Russell trotted away, through the sunflowers, following the row until the tall stalks gave way to woody vines, heavy with grapes. In the mists of his doggy memory, he knew that grapes were edible, but only once their tasteless skins had been pierced, releasing the sweet juice.

Emerging from the vines, the dog stepped out carelessly and had to scamper to avoid the wheels of an oncoming vehicle, loud and bright. On the far side of the road, the land rose through more vines, onto soft hills where, he knew, there were rabbits.

Travelling on his little legs, the dog made slow progress in human terms – no quicker than an idle stroll – interrupted over and over by the need to investigate the compelling fragrances of other creatures, deliberately spread on the boles of trees, the feet of fence posts and the shanks of exposed rocks. Eventually, he came to a place of human activity, despite the fact that there were no houses or paved roads nearby.

The dog approached, warned by some sixth sense that he might not be welcome in this place where no voices sounded and no light shone, despite the grunts and heavy breathing he could hear. By scent, he found a shopping bag on the ground, containing a ham sandwich – baguette, rich butter, lean meat – which he delicately, silently removed, pulling it whole from its paper bag, with careful precision.

Before creeping away to eat his stolen meal in the privacy of the night, the Jack Russell stood for a moment with its head cocked on one side, dimly understanding what was happening in this lonely place.

Digging.

Because the dog's frame of reference was limited to his own experience, he came to a natural conclusion as to what the human must be digging for.

Rabbits.

The dog, of course, was wrong.

*

That was also the precise moment when, in the dark of the night, someone illegally in possession of the stolen keys tried the door of Zoe's bookshop, only to be denied by the bolt at the foot, but not before they had made the old-fashioned bell faintly ring, causing them to slip away, quietly cursing, in the shadows of the buildings, before they could be seen.

II

AN UNEXPECTED DEATH

Six

'She's Lonely'

Four weeks later, for reasons Zoe couldn't quite fathom, the
Jack Russell terrier had become her dog. He – for she had
quickly discovered that it was a boy – had formed the habit
of coming to see her at the same time each day, at more or
less the close of business, looking hungry and sad.

At first, Zoe was happy to give him scraps from her
kitchen, just to be friendly. She was aware that domesticated
animals are past masters at manipulating the humans they
live with. But she became more and more convinced that she
was the only person who paid the Jack Russell any attention.
She asked Marcel Maurice who told her he had no idea who
it belonged to.

'Unless it was those hippies that were hanging about the
town most of the summer. Did you meet them?'

Zoe hadn't, having arrived too late, but she thought the
idea made sense because of the faded and frayed bandana
that was the dog's only collar. Inevitably, she began referring
to the Jack Russell as 'Russell'.

It was now October and the weather had changed. The
night-time September breeze that Zoe had found such a
relief after the heat of a late-summer day, had abruptly
become a scouring, evil presence, forcing the inhabitants of
Sainte-Catherine to don winter jackets, scarves and gloves.
She asked Elise Guillaume if she ought to protect her oleanders from frost.

'No, they'll do, sheltered as they are from the worst of the weather.'

It was true. The frigid winds came from the north-east, plummeting down from the nearby mountains. Still, the change preyed on Zoe's mind.

Will the cold weather bring a sudden end to tourists and steady commerce? And what about Russell? He's unable to wrap up warm like me and my neighbours.

It was true. Russell's sleek white coat wasn't thick. Each evening, Zoe found herself more and more concerned about where the dog might be sleeping, cold and alone through each chilly night. Several times more she saw him sitting solitary in the darkened square, late at night, in mute appeal, as if asking, with his warm doggy eyes in his pointed tan face: '*Will no one take me in?*'

Then, one day, when she had to drive into Aix-en-Provence to visit the telecom shop, he fell into step beside her through the town, down the cobbled streets. In the car park, as she opened the door to her little Renault van – a vehicle that had come with the bookshop purchase, like the two lonely chairs and the coat stand and the dusty bird's-eye-view picture on the wall – he jumped in and sat alert and observant in the passenger seat. She picked him up to lift him out and he struggled against her grip. She felt his little bones standing out, sharp and angular beneath his fur.

'Oh dear.'

It wasn't easy to leave him behind. He looked so sad and lost on the cold tarmac, the hurt expression on his handsome little face haunting her all the way to her destination.

In the telecom store, she discovered that she had filled in the wrong forms, which explained why the bookshop was equipped with an internet connection but still no landline. She placed a new order to remedy the situation but was told it would take another two weeks before the absence was resolved.

'You were cut off, you see, Madame Pascal. It's no longer a reconnection. It's a new service altogether.'

On the way out of Aix, she passed a retail park with garish neon signs over the doors of several warehouse-style shops. She pulled in and parked in front of the sports shop, Decathlon, where she bought herself some new lightweight hiking boots, a quilted gilet and a modestly priced ski jacket. Next door was a pet superstore where she bought two bowls, one for food and one for water, plus a soft and comfortable dog bed that she determined would remain downstairs, among the bookshelves, not upstairs beside her own.

Just for the colder months. Assuming, that is, he wants the shelter and doesn't prefer to be out and about, smelling delicious smells and digging rabbits out of their burrows with his little paws.

With this determination fixed in her mind, Zoe drove home. Heartbreakingly, when she got back to Sainte-Catherine and parked in front of her garage, built into the base of the hill, not far from the town hall, Russell was still there, shivering but hopeful, sitting on the cold tarmac, precisely where she had left him more than two hours before.

'That settles it,' she told him. 'You're coming home with me – for good.'

*

Firmin Séchan was too old for his large-animal veterinary practice. Tipping a sheep to trim its hooves or wrestling an arm into the birth canal of a cow whose calf was breach demanded physical attributes that time seemed determined to erode. He persisted, however, because he wasn't ready to simply sit and think, twiddling the buttons of his cardigan, wondering how the years had flown so fast.

Firmin lived in the little suburb of modern houses on the approach to Sainte-Catherine, not far from the confluence of the Rigolet and the canal. His only concession to the expected hobbies of advanced age was the cultivation of a forest of large outdoor plants in enormous tubs, half-barrels and boxes. Just then, he was trimming summer growth from a bougainvillea that he had trained around the door of his reception, a converted car garage. The tender shoots fell around his feet and he persisted until the ache in his shoulders from reaching up above his grey and sparsely thatched head became too severe.

This is one more thing that will soon be beyond me.

He perched his bony backside on the rim of a huge clay tub containing a flourishing olive tree.

My life is practically over. People almost disregard me, if they notice me at all, because they know that soon I'll no longer be around. I miss Lucia.

He was thinking about the previous owner of *La Librairie de Mes Rêves*.

We used to have a good talk about books every now and then.

He took out his handkerchief and used it to clean the sharp edge of his vicious little secateurs.

Before I'm gone, I'd like people to look at me with respect – just one more time.

*

Because it was now the middle of October, the summer season was over. Zoe considered that her first month's trading had been a success. In the short term, she didn't need a vast turnover and she had anticipated that the autumn and winter would be much more difficult than the holiday months, but she hoped that Christmas and New Year – perhaps all the way through to Twelfth Night on the sixth of January – might give her figures another boost.

The business with the locksmith had been more expensive than she had anticipated. The entire mechanism had had to be changed in order to be brought up to the draconian modern standards that her insurance company would recognise as a viable deterrent. She now, however, had a single key that opened both back and front doors, with a fob she had bought at the Hyper U – a tacky Staybrite-brass vulture sold as 'a memento of the Verdon nature park'.

The insufficient lighting – wires stretched between the wooden beams of the ceiling with twinkly white LED bulbs strung along them – had been easily remedied. A local handyman recommended by Marcel Maurice, Gato Merino, came with his son and doubled the number and all was well. Gato, of course, had been the person mentioned by the cleaning women for replacing the elderly window glass in the back bedroom – something Zoe had so far refused to do.

She had solved the problem of the cats using her courtyard as their bathroom by adding to the dense, compacted soil a layer of compost from Elise Guillaume then a bed of large, egg-shaped stones collected from the banks of the Rigolet, planting the cracks with hardy alpine shrubs, leaving the feline invaders no loose dirt to exploit. It had done the trick.

The washing line was gone because, in the first place, Zoe found it ugly. Also, as she remarked to Caroline: 'At my time of life, I have better things to do than laundry. I will send it out. The dry cleaner at the supermarket offers a very reasonable service wash, giving it back bone-dry and nicely folded.'

'If you weren't French when you arrived,' Caroline told her with a smile, 'you are now.'

The problem with mobile phone reception remained. A mast or pylon designed to provide coverage to Sainte-Catherine was out of action. Patrick, the waiter, told her it had been vandalised. Antoine Grenelle, the brigadier of police, said that was nonsense, that the underground cables had been severed by mistake. Whatever the reason, it gave Zoe an uncomfortable feeling of isolation.

The sixteenth of October rolled around, a special date for the town, on which a saint of the Catholic Church, Bertrand of Comminges, was to be commemorated with a procession carrying an effigy of the eleventh-century churchman. Apparently, Bishop Bertrand had visited Sainte-Catherine in about 1080 AD and performed a miracle, causing a bedbound man to 'stand up and walk'.

Not being a person of faith, Zoe wasn't particularly interested in the religious connotations of the procession, but she was completely on board with the idea of bringing together the entire community with a shared goal of celebration and a delightful meal for which the two restaurants in the little square would combine their outside tables to accommodate the whole population, plus visitors.

And there was another reason. Zoe was a great admirer of the ghost stories of M. R. James, a Cambridge don who liked to share his creepy tales by reading them aloud at this very own Chitchat Society, around the end of the nineteenth century. One story in particular was pertinent and, as the sun dipped towards the roofs of the houses in the square and the sky became gloomy, she had the appropriate collection in her hand, angling the page to the improved lighting, opening it carefully so as not to crease its spine and prevent a future sale.

'Canon Alberic's Scrap-Book' was the story of an innocent English visitor to the decaying cathedral city of Saint-Bertrand-de-Comminges, in the foothills of the Pyrenees. Unwisely, the visitor is persuaded to buy a haunted book, inciting a demon from its pages to come to life and—

Just then, the front door opened, its old-fashioned bell jangling for her attention. She returned the M. R. James book to the shelf and went to attend to her customers – French tourists – showing them several different guidebooks to the region before they settled on the cheapest one. As they left, Russell the terrier slipped inside and came and sat at her feet, by the till, studiously ignoring the soft bed.

'You're not coming upstairs again tonight,' she told him. 'That's over and done with.'

He put his head on one side as if to ask: '*Are you sure? Do you really mean it?*'

'You're a manipulator, Russell,' she told him. 'And it's not yet dinner time.'

Another customer came in, the elderly woman in her late seventies or early eighties who wore the purple tracksuit, over which she had slipped a thick, fur-fringed gilet. Zoe saw a kind of mental slideshow of glimpsing her on arrival down in the car park, then followed by Antoinette Grenelle, then late at night in the square, always carrying an open book in her hands. She was staying in the same guest house that Zoe's removal men had used, on what seemed a solitary holiday.

A surprisingly long one, actually.

Zoe had also met the woman several times in the shop as a customer. An avid reader, the woman had bought a few books in English and French, including three different guidebooks and a very detailed local map, plus a volume from a popular romance series set in 1960s Milan, surprising Zoe because it came from a genre that publishers called 'spicy', meaning the sex scenes were unnervingly graphic. The novel was called *Infinite Desire* and the author's name was Erica Noll. There was an infinity symbol on the cover and the heroine was called Octavia.

The elderly woman wandered over to the bird's-eye view of Sainte-Catherine on the wall, then tried the door to the courtyard, which happened to be locked. Zoe asked: 'Do you need some fresh air?'

The woman came to stand wearily by the counter, making oddly disordered small talk. Then, painfully, she bent down in order to pet Russell, not seeming to need a new book at all. Zoe began to wonder if there was a second reason why the woman had dropped in and drew the obvious conclusion.

She's lonely.

Zoe felt sympathy. She was still a fish out of water in Sainte-Catherine herself. She had had another odd run-in with Antoinette Grenelle, with the older woman demanding to know if Zoe had 'any clues she would like to share', which seemed utterly baffling. Despite her constant efforts to exchange the time of day with people she recognised – in the square, at the dry cleaner, doing her 'big shops' at the supermarket – she often didn't feel much warmth in response. She almost felt like an object of suspicion. The only human contact she had really enjoyed was managing the work of her painters and decorators and odd-job men, Gato Merino and his enthusiastic son, Lali.

But I've developed no new intimate friendships, beyond that with Caroline Robin who I seldom see because her practice is away in the big city of Aix-en-Provence.

Zoe's elderly customer seemed to run out of steam, helping herself to her feet from the floor by using the back of one of the useful kitchen chairs that Zoe had kept between the stacks, then subsided onto it, her purple tracksuit legs rucked halfway up her blotchy calves.

'Have you been enjoying your stay in Sainte-Catherine?' Zoe asked.

'It's been hard work,' the woman said, with a frown, looking like someone trying to remember where they had left something important. 'Yes, yes . . .'

'I sometimes see you out and about, though the shop keeps me very busy. You've been here a month, I think?'

'That's true. Yes.'

Although it was only three little words, the answer sounded full of sadness.

'I wonder,' Zoe asked, 'were you intending to join the procession this evening?'

'I wasn't certain I would be welcome. There are the factions . . .'

'Factions?'

'And is it not a village affair? I did wonder if I could watch it from my bedroom window but, of course, we are in the cul-de-sac and there won't be much of a view.'

'Then you should come with me,' said Zoe decisively. 'We've never properly been introduced. My name is Zoe Pascal. I'm fairly new to the village, too, and would very much like you to sit with me for the dinner afterwards.'

'I enquired at the Auberge and the restaurant and was told that every table was booked, every seat taken.'

'Then I will ask Patrick to add a chair next to mine. It couldn't be simpler. If there aren't any more chairs, we will bring one – that one you are sitting on, for example.'

'Patrick?'

'He's the waiter at the Auberge, a friend of mine . . .' Zoe hesitated, struck by the depressing idea that Patrick wasn't her friend, he was just friendly because she was a regular customer. 'Would you like to tell me your name? I suppose I've seen it on your debit card each time you've bought a new book.'

'It's not like the old days with cheque books,' said her elderly visitor. 'Although people worry about their privacy, don't they? My name is very old-fashioned. It's Barbara.'

'Like a 1930s film star.'

'And, because I am old, people call me Madame Ercollani.'

'Which do you prefer that I should use?'

'If I can call you . . .'

Zoe reminded her: 'I'm Zoe.'

'You must call me Barbara.'

'In that case, Barbara, I will come by the guest house once I've closed up here. Shall we say at seven?'

Barbara Ercollani got painfully to her feet. 'This is very kind of you. What should I wear? Dressing and undressing are so tiring.'

'I don't believe there's a dress code. Sainte-Catherine is very much a "come as you are" sort of place.'

'Even though they are in competition with one another?'

Zoe frowned and asked: 'In what way?'

Barbara wasn't paying attention. She was struggling to her feet. 'Goodbye, er, Zoe. When did we say?'

'Seven.'

'Yes, seven. Goodbye.'

Zoe watched her go, feeling sympathy for her loneliness, wondering what she had meant by 'factions' and 'competition'.

In Sainte-Catherine? What a ridiculous idea.

Seven

TRAGEDY

As Barbara Ercollani left on weary feet, a hand on the door frame for balance, Russell the terrier slipped out with her into the cobbled square. Zoe felt a gust of very cold air, then the door was pulled closed by its spring-loaded mechanism with another clang of the bell.

Zoe made sure that her day's transactions had all been backed up to the cloud via her internet connection. She was glad that her experience in theatre management meant she was *au fait* with proper accounting practices.

That said, the numbers I'm dealing with here aren't exactly intimidating.

She spent a couple of minutes returning books that customers had left at the till or in other inappropriate locations to the shelves. Then she used a soft broom to sweep up, because the breeze kept blowing crisp, dry leaves indoors.

There's a chill at the beginning and the end of each day. I need to do something about that.

The bookshop wasn't a cash business but, now and then, someone would want to pay with notes and coins. For this reason, Zoe had acquired a safe, like those seen in hotel rooms. It opened and closed with a four-digit code and was bolted to the floor in a cupboard under her counter – a sort of island between the bookshelves, like a breakfast bar in a kitchen. She removed the cash tray from her till and put it away, using her own birth-date to lock it, 0511, Guy Fawkes' Night, the fifth of November.

Which is silly and eminently crackable, I expect, but the amount of money involved is so trivial that I can't be bothered to learn a different one.

Hungry from her long day, she made herself a quick snack in the kitchen and ate it standing up, with a small glass of white wine from an open bottle she kept in the fridge – a lovely crisp vintage from Marcel Maurice – and experienced once more a feeling of disconnectedness.

Marcel isn't a friend either. He's someone I see in the square. To him, I'm just another customer.

Back downstairs, she composed an email to send to Maisie Cooper, her half-sister by adoption, with whom she had shared several teenage adventures – including a number of murder mysteries and her first holiday trip to Provence. Once it had been sent, almost an hour had passed. From the old-fashioned coat stand by the front door, she put on her long winter coat, a very stylish camel-hair number that descended to mid-calf. Then she went outside, surprised not to find Russell lurking for his dinner.

Perhaps someone else has fed him. He is the master manipulator, after all.

To her dismay, contrary to the advice she had given Barbara Ercollani, Zoe saw that her neighbours – already out and about in preparation for the evening's festivities – were very dressed up. Even the smaller children wore smart dresses or little suits, the girls resembling bridesmaids and the boys tiny snooker referees. Underneath her own smart coat, she was wearing very everyday clothes but she didn't think that would matter because the evening was too cold for her to want to take it off.

There was a general flow of people down through the narrow streets. She joined them, past the front door of the octagonal Templar church where the procession was destined to end. In the cobbled cul-de-sac she found the guest house very quiet and dark, the front door closed. When she knocked, no reply came, which Zoe found odd because only sixty minutes before she had arranged to meet Barbara Ercollani at this very spot. Then, more peculiar still, from inside, she heard what she thought was Russell's voice, a plaintive whine followed by two sharp yaps.

Have Denis and Davide been feeding you, too?

Because of the cold night, the shutters of the windows either side of the front door were closed. She knocked again, without much hope. The building was completely dark. Checking her watch, she saw that it was now seven and she was at risk of being late. There were no more footsteps on the cobbles, except—

Zoe felt a sudden tension take hold of her because, in what had abruptly come to feel like a sinister quiet, someone was running up the lane towards her, their heavy tread and harsh panting reminiscent of the creepiest moments in the M. R. James story that, unwisely perhaps, she had been reading earlier on.

The figure came into view, beneath one of the gentle orange street lamps, its bracket bolted into the façade of one of the low houses. To her relief, she recognised him as either Denis or Davide – she wasn't sure which – looking short and round and flustered.

'Oh dear, Madame Pascal, I forgot my instrument. I'd forget my own head if it wasn't screwed on.'

He opened the front door – it hadn't even been locked – and there was Russell, seated on the doormat, as Zoe had first seen him, pert and attentive, like a little ornament.

'Will you excuse me?' said Denis or Davide, stepping over the dog and snatching up what Zoe thought was a piccolo from the hall table. 'I must run.'

'I came to fetch Madame Ercollani. Would you mind if I go up and find her?'

'I'm not sure she came back.'

'Really?'

'Never mind. Please, go and look.' From the bottom of the town, the sound of the local band tuning up drifted over the houses. 'I'm sorry, I really must dash. Pull the door to as you leave, won't you?'

Denis or Davide bustled away and Russell turned in the opposite direction, climbing the dark-timbered stairs on his stubby white legs. Zoe followed him to the landing and put on the light, seeing the doors to the bedrooms that her removal men had slept in and one which must belong to Barbara.

But which one?

She tried each door – they were charmingly labelled Rosemary, Lavender, Garlic and Thyme – finding the third one unlocked so in she went, putting on the big light. On the bedside table was a little pile of books that Zoe recognised as having been purchased in her own shop, plus a couple of others in a larger format that looked dog-eared and second-hand. The doors to the wardrobe were open, revealing a safe, very much like her own. In front of it was a suitcase, into which most of Barbara's clothes had been thrown in an untidy heap, as if a decision to leave had been taken very abruptly, then abandoned.

Not knowing what to do, Zoe went back downstairs and out into the street, pulling the door closed behind her but making sure that Russell was outside, too. He yapped and skittered a few paces away from her, towards the church rather than down the hill in the direction of the music.

'We can't go home now,' she told him. 'You'll have to wait for your dinner.'

Russell seemed more than usually determined, but Zoe paid him no attention, heading for Place Saint-Bertrand where the two restaurants were busy setting up for the community meal. She told Patrick about her spontaneous invitation to Barbara and he told her, kindly: 'We will do our best to make her welcome.'

Zoe continued downhill, past the little well, which formed a kind of crossroads in the steep streets. At the bottom of the town in the car park she met the procession, led by a village band that included both Antoine and Antoinette Grenelle carrying brass tubas, Marcel Maurice with a tambourine in his one good hand, his son Thierry with a side drum, and several other people that Zoe knew from the market and the shops. The instruments they carried were eclectic and, in other circumstances, might not have been thought harmonious, but the traditional song they were playing was folksy – by turns sad and jaunty – and wholly authentic. The bizarre make-up of the band didn't matter.

Zoe stepped back into a doorway to allow them to pass. At the rear of the procession were the children she had seen in the square, three on either side, the girls to the left and the boys to the right. They had been chosen so that they were all more or less the same height, carrying a small platform on which sat the effigy of the saint, half human size, the smooth features of its expressionless china face inscrutable and eerie.

Zoe followed, looking out for Barbara in case the elderly lady had misunderstood or had misread her watch. In amongst the crowd, she noticed the angry second-hand bookseller glancing back, looking daggers.

At the crossroads beside the well, the procession halted to play a song whose lyrics Zoe didn't entirely follow because they were in the Provençal language, a dialect different from modern French, as Catalan differs from Castilian Spanish. But, because the chorus was repeated several times, she managed to pick it up – something about how difficult it is to find fresh water in high summer and the importance of natural springs – and join in, encouraged by the roast chicken man, Robert Petit, beside whom she happened to be standing.

At the end of the song, he encouraged her forward with a hand in the small of her back – which she found annoying – and the procession moved on to the larger square, Place Saint-Bertrand, where Zoe, for the first time, made the connection with the evening's festivities.

Of course, the restaurant square is named after the saint.

Everyone paused while the villagers crammed in, edging between the tables and chairs, packed tightly against the surrounding houses. Three more traditional songs were played, including one that seemed to Zoe extremely risqué, about the voracious appetites of the 'beasts of the fields', for both food and sex. The boys in their little dark suits all joined in but the girls looked at one another and giggled.

Only at this point did Zoe notice the village priest, a gaunt but handsome middle-aged man with dark eyebrows and deep brown eyes. He was wearing a set of white satin vestments, heavily embroidered with bright-coloured thread, depicting flowers, farm animals and vines. The song came to an end and he raised his voice to declaim a sonorous grace for the meal that everyone would soon enjoy.

After the amen, Zoe was surprised to see all the villagers take their seats and the members of the band put down their instruments to join them, immediately filling glasses from the carafes of red and white wine, set every two or three places. Only the priest and the six children continued up Rue des Templiers, carrying the platform and the effigy of the saint towards the church.

'You look surprised, Madame Pascal,' said Robert Petit, standing unnecessarily close. 'I suppose it might seem odd, that we should all sit down to dinner without completing the pilgrimage.' He shrugged. 'But it is our tradition. Will you join me? I would be honoured.'

Zoe was wary of Robert Petit, remembering his hungry eye fixed on Caroline and his lingering handshake.

'Actually, I'm looking for an elderly lady, a guest of Denis and Davide. Do you know who I mean? She's been in Sainte-Catherine for a few weeks.'

'The purple tracksuit,' he said with a dismissive shake of the head. 'She is old. Perhaps she mistook the instructions and is already in the church?'

'Yes,' said Zoe, with a sense of relief. 'That makes complete sense.'

Russell rejoined her as she hurried away, catching up with the diminished procession at the church door. The priest pronounced a blessing then opened it onto a sombre, shadowy nave. To her dismay, Zoe saw Russell the terrier bolt inside, too late to stop him. The priest and the children laughed.

'I am sorry,' she said. 'He's not my dog – I mean, he sort of is, but only because he's nobody else's, if you see what I mean.'

'God's house welcomes all God's creatures,' said the priest, his gaunt face softened by a smile. 'Isn't that right, children? Don't we have a lovely service each year to which animals are welcome? Now, let us take Saint Bertrand inside.' As he turned, the heavy embroidered fabric of his vestments caught on the door handle and Zoe stepped forward to unhook it. 'Thank you. Madame Pascal, isn't it?'

'Yes, that's right.'

'Would you like to go ahead? The light switch is to the left of the door.'

Zoe did as she was asked, stepping in and finding the switch by touch. Before flipping it, thanks to his bright white coat, her eyes discerned Russell, sitting very still in the centre of the dark octagonal space. With a feeling of trepidation that she couldn't for the moment understand, she turned on the lights and had to screw up her eyes from the sudden illumination of many bright bulbs in a large brass chandelier.

Russell yapped twice as if to say: *Do you understand, now?*

Zoe looked through half-closed eyes, then gasped.

'Don't come in,' she said, urgently, not wanting the children to see.

On the stone-flagged floor of the octagonal church, sprawled like a broken puppet, clad in her unbecoming purple tracksuit and fur-fringed gilet, was the lonely form of Barbara Ercollani, her mouth agape, her eyes rolled back in her head, utterly still and lifeless.

69

Eight

SICK OR JUST OLD?

Zoe stepped aside from the church doorway, allowing the priest to look past her to the awful sight of poor Barbara Ercollani, lying dead on the cold stones. She felt shocked, of course, but also a sense of intrigue. Her mind instinctively began to wonder about what could have happened because it wasn't the first time she had looked upon death.

But I don't really want that widely known. People will think me strange if they discover that I was involved as a teenager in several separate murder investigations. I will keep it to myself unless I am asked directly.

'There is a little problem,' the priest told his junior pall-bearers. He instructed the three little girls and three little boys to put down the platform and the effigy and run off home. 'Or to dinner with the others, depending on your parents' instructions.'

The children skipped away.

'Will the community meal not be cancelled?' Zoe asked.

'What good could that possibly do?' asked the priest. He bowed his head and spoke a brief prayer in Latin. After the amen, he asked Zoe: 'Can I leave you here for a moment or two?'

'Yes, of course.'

'You will not be frightened or faint?'

'No, I will not.'

'Then I will go and fetch Antoine Grenelle.' He frowned. 'But, perhaps, it would be better if you joined the celebration dinner so as not to call attention to what has happened?'

'I wouldn't like to leave her alone.'

'True,' he said, thoughtfully. 'The idea does you credit. Perhaps, on reflection, you could go and ask Antoine to come, before he has drunk too much of Marcel Maurice's strong red wine. Be discreet, won't you?'

'I understand the need to avoid summoning a crowd,' said Zoe, irritated by the priest's patronising tone.

She slipped away down the cobbled street and found Antoine on his feet, glass in hand, about to launch into song. She went to draw him aside and he, surprisingly, put down his glass, took her in his arms and waltzed her a few turns, fortunately drawing her away from the tightly packed tables, giving her the chance to speak without being overheard.

'A tragedy has occurred. You must come with me to the church.'

To Zoe's surprise, despite appearing already the worse for alcohol, Antoine's eyes became sharp, his expression serious.

'My dear Madame Pascal,' he said loudly, to give an appearance of normality, 'I will come and help you, then we must return to the feast.'

'Yes, good,' she told him, hoping she wasn't overdoing the 'innocent' tone. 'Thank you.'

★

Two pairs of eyes watched Zoe and Antoine leave. One pair belonged to an outsider, visiting Sainte-Catherine for private reasons of their own, standing a little apart, not intending to join the feast.

The second pair belonged to the second-hand bookseller who, because he wasn't a very nice person, had a habit of nosiness and had noticed something odd about the tone of Antoine Grenelle's voice.

If Madame Pascal is in some kind of trouble, I wonder if there might be a way for me to make it worse.

★

Zoe and Antoine went back up the cobbled street, curving out of sight of the restaurant tables, and found the priest still at the door. Antoine took efficient charge, suggesting: 'It might be best if this sad event could be kept secret, between us, for the time being. You did not enter the church, Father?'

'No. Madame Pascal did so in order to turn on the light, but we went no further.'

'You did not take her pulse, for example?'

'I have seen enough death not to need any further confirmation,' he said, indicating the blank eyes and bleached-white complexion, the awkwardly posed limbs. 'She has gone over.'

'Of course, you would know,' said Antoine. Zoe wondered why the policeman took the priest's word so readily. He went on: 'Do either of you know how the lady came to be here?'

Zoe briefly told the story of her conversation in the shop, the appointment to meet at the guest house, then Barbara's absence.

'Her room was dishevelled, as if she hadn't been able to decide what to wear, or because someone else—'

'Did you touch anything?' Antoine asked, sharply.

'No, of course not.'

Did I though?

'Go on,' he prompted.

'I felt she was unhappy, lonely, perhaps. I don't know what she was doing in Sainte-Catherine.'

Antoine's eyes became very bright, as if she had told him something important.

'Everyone else did, however,' he surprised her by saying. 'She was old so death may have come innocently, but it's important to gather all the facts.' He turned to the priest. 'Will you ask Denis and Davide to come and find us, discreetly, of course. You can say it is to do with Madame Pascal who has a problem that needs their assistance.'

'Good idea,' said the priest.

He left and Zoe wondered what it was about her that lent itself so swiftly to the idea that she needed help.

Perhaps it was climbing in through the window on the day I arrived. I established, early on, a reputation for bizarre escapades.

Antoine asked Zoe to describe the precise order of events once more. She did so, feeling uncomfortably as though it was a kind of test.

'I don't understand why you didn't simply stay where you were,' said Antoine, 'in Place Saint-Bertrand, for the meal. Only the children accompany the effigy into the church.'

'I didn't know that and the butcher, Robert Petit, suggested that perhaps Barbara might be in the church, you know, waiting, not knowing, as I didn't know, that the procession didn't end there – or, I mean, it did, obviously, but not the whole town.'

Denis and Davide arrived, white-faced and wide-eyed, clearly aware of the tragedy. Antoine led them just inside the church door and pulled it almost closed so that no passer-by could see what had happened by chance. In reply to his questions, Denis and Davide told Antoine that they had been worried about Barbara for several days.

'I'm sure there was a decline in her health, her energy,' said one.

'Or perhaps it was just,' said the other, 'that she was no spring chicken.'

'No,' said the first, making Zoe frustrated that she could not yet decide which was Denis and which Davide. 'I think she was ill. Though she was often out, all day long, on her pins. I thought she was marvellous, but perhaps she was overdoing it? And she sometimes repeated herself, you know? But that's usual in age.'

This sympathetic but unhelpful comment was greeted by Antoine as if it were an oracular insight.

'You make a good point, but I believe we are all aware of what she was doing all the live-long day. Isn't that right?'

Denis and Davide made affirmative noises. Antoine turned to Zoe who was confused about what they all seemed to know but she didn't.

Am I being very stupid, somehow?

'And you, Madame Pascal, you say you arranged to meet her to walk the procession alongside one another. Were you good friends already?'

'I wouldn't say that. I knew her, of course, because she came into my shop a few times. But I only really spoke to her at any length this evening and . . .' Zoe pictured the moment. 'I thought she was lonely. That's why I offered to take her with me. She seemed to want to be at the meal, to be among people. Do you know what I mean?'

'What would you say, Denis?' asked the taller of the two guest-house owners, allowing Zoe to deduce that he must be Davide. They were both dressed alike, in black trousers and warm black puffer anoraks, but she would know Davide in future because he had a tightly styled beard and moustache, like a villain in a melodrama. 'I don't know about lonely. Did you think she was lonely?'

His companion – shorter, rounder, clean-shaven and wide-eyed – answered: 'Perhaps. Or she just liked to keep herself to herself? But it did seem to me that she was sickening.'

'Sickening how?' asked Antoine.

'I really couldn't say,' said Denis. 'We don't like to pry, do we, Davide?'

'Absolutely not,' said his partner, pursing his lips. 'That would be utterly wrong.'

Zoe was beginning to feel like a spare wheel. She asked Antoine if there was anything else she could help with, suggesting: 'If not, I'll leave you to it.'

'I'll need an official statement, but that can wait for the morning.'

Zoe thanked him for his consideration and went, with relief, back outside. The impassive and sinister effigy of Saint Bertrand was still there, on its platform, abandoned on the cobbles. She edged past it and walked slowly back down Rue des Templiers, round the curve, approaching the merry outdoor meal. It was in full swing, the sounds of crockery, glasses and high-spirited conversation carrying through the cold air. She hesitated in a deep doorway, not wanting to reveal herself.

It seems heartless for everyone to be celebrating while a woman lies dead on the church's cold stone floor. On the other hand, none of them knew her that well. She was just another unexceptional visitor, albeit an unusually elderly one to be travelling alone.

Zoe wondered if Barbara had a car.

And what has she been doing with her days? Without a vehicle, surely, she can't have been out hiking, day after day, in the countryside?

From where she stood, peeping round the stonework, it seemed to Zoe that the first courses had been devoured. Several tables were demanding refills to their carafes of red and white wine. Patrick from the Auberge Sainte-Catherine was moving at impressive speed, while an older waitress in a dazzling white apron circulated more slowly in his wake. Zoe assumed that the woman was a member of staff at Le Gourmand, whose prices she knew were considerably higher and whose service, therefore, was probably indulgent and slow.

Before anyone could notice her, Zoe decided to creep away home, weighed down by the sadness of an innocent life cut short.

At least, I assume an innocent life. Is it because I have been involved in other investigations with Maisie that I can't quite take it at face value?

Soon, though, she heard quick footsteps behind her and turned, with surprise, to greet the priest. He introduced himself for the first time by name.

'*Je m'appelle Julien Calmet.*'

'Should I refer to you as Father Julien?' she politely enquired.

'If you wish, Madame Pascal, but if you invite me to call you Zoe, Julien would be my preference.'

'Did you want something, Julien?'

'I was concerned. I noticed you – if you don't mind me saying so – cowering in that doorway, as if you hadn't recovered from what you saw.'

'It was a shock, but Denis Allard says that Barbara had been feeling under the weather and, it's true, when she came into my shop towards the end of the day, she did need to sit down and, thinking back, she appeared lethargic and vague, her balance a little off.'

'Was she breathless or sweating?' asked Julien.

'No, I don't think so. Why do you ask?'

'Just as a gauge of her physical state. Did she follow your conversation easily? She didn't appear disorientated?'

'I don't think so, perhaps a little, but it's difficult to say for sure. Just the fact of you asking those questions is making me doubt what otherwise seems a fairly innocent memory of our encounter. She didn't buy a book, so I suppose she just dropped in for company.'

'Or because she was weary and cold?'

'Perhaps. All she did was pet the dog, exchange a few words and then, because I took pity on her, I invited her to come with me and . . .' Zoe frowned, not sure what she had been about to say.

'And?' asked the priest with a surprising intensity in his gaze.

'And nothing, really.'

For a few seconds, Julien Calmet seemed to be weighing her up. She had an uncomfortable idea that he was calculating how many 'Hail Mary' prayers she would need to recite in order to achieve absolution for her unavowed sins. Then he smiled and gestured towards the restaurants.

'I must go back to the table. I think it is still a good idea for us to conceal what has happened, at least for the time being. Of course, once the ambulance arrives, it will no longer be possible. She will have to be carried down by hand on a stretcher.'

'How sad,' said Zoe. 'I mean, to have died so far from home, among strangers.'

'We are all among strangers,' said Father Julien. 'In the end, none of us knows our fellows as well as we like to think.'

He smiled again, creasing his gaunt features, and walked smartly away, disappearing round the corner towards the sounds of the *al fresco* meal.

Can he possibly think I have something to hide? What about him? Did I do the wrong thing when I left him alone at the door to fetch Antoine? We only have his word for it that he didn't enter the church.

She walked back up the lane, past the guest house, noticing that the lights were now on inside and assumed that either Denis or Davide or both had gone home. At the door of the church, she briefly spoke to Antoine who was waiting outside. He remarked: 'Not long now.'

She assumed he meant the arrival of the medical personnel.

'Has anything like this ever happened in Sainte-Catherine before – an unexpected death?'

'Why do you call it unexpected?' he demanded. 'Denis Allard is certain that she was unwell.'

'Oh, yes. That's true. All the same, people don't just collapse for no reason.'

'The reason might be because she was old.'

'Yes, I suppose. Goodnight, then.'

'One moment, if you wouldn't mind? You seem to have your own ideas. Would you care to share them?'

'I really don't.'

'Forgive me, but I can see them in your face.'

'What can you see?'

'That is what I ask myself,' he told her, a sharp expression on his face.

Zoe hesitated, wanting him to elaborate, but he didn't. Like with Father Julien Calmet, she began to feel that he was accusing her of something. It was extremely unnerving. She wanted to say: 'I barely knew her.' She resisted the temptation, not wanting to sound . . .

What, exactly? Defensive and guilty?

'I think I've shared everything I know, Antoine. Goodnight.'

She left him at the church doorway and crossed the empty Place Sainte-Catherine, beneath the almost-bare branches of the lime trees that caused the light of the orange street lamps to be broken up into splotches of brightness and shadow. On the welcome mat outside the door of her bookshop she found Russell, lying very flat. She thought at first that he was fast asleep, then she spotted that he had one cautious eye open, watching her approach.

'Hello, you,' she told him.

She leaned across to unlock the door with her new key on its shiny vulture fob and he jumped up to precede her inside, heading straight for his bowl under the counter, beneath the till. Finding it empty, he sat down and whimpered.

'All right,' she told him. 'One thing at a time.'

Russell stopped whining and waited. Zoe pondered his expression.

He looks like he's waiting for me to ask him a question.

She spoke to him aloud.

'Now, young Russell, here's the thing. You knew before I did, didn't you? You wanted me to go and see what had happened to Barbara in the church, but I didn't pay any attention. And, somehow, before all that, you got yourself shut in at the guest house. You went with her when she left, didn't you?'

Russell's expression didn't change. His immobility looked almost challenging, as if he considered the questions beneath him, the answers obvious.

'They aren't obvious,' argued Zoe, her voice a little echoey in the quiet bookshop. 'It all seems very mysterious.'

Nine

AN UNEXPECTED CONFRONTATION

Dawn broke the next day on another chilly morning. Zoë woke soon after, not feeling herself, having slept poorly, roused and haunted several times by the awful sight of the elderly woman's crumpled body on the chequerboard tiles of the creepy octagonal church.

Was it creepy, though? Or do I just think that because of the fact of death, illuminated by the bright bulbs of the chandelier, stark and final?

She sat up in bed, rearranging her pillows, unsurprised to see Russell asleep on top of her double duvet in the far corner, as if he knew he shouldn't be there, so was attempting to make his presence discreet.

And was her body crumpled? Perhaps she just sort of collapsed?

Like many French houses, the bookshop was equipped with electric convector heaters that came on according to a rhythm defined by thermostats and timers. She felt the one in her bedroom start working, taking the edge off the chill in the early-morning air. In addition, though, for downstairs, Zoë had decided to acquire a wood-burning stove. She thought it would completely transform the atmosphere in the bookshop, making it warm, dry and welcoming. She had asked Gato Merino to undertake the job. He had assured her that it was within his compass. She had accepted his price and today was the day.

Zoë got up, pushing her feet into her sloppy slippers and shuffling out onto the landing. Because she had been so busy, she still hadn't got around to removing the cardboard from the skylight, high in the rafters, and had come to suspect that it was there to prevent a street lamp from shining in. She found her dressing gown on the back of the bathroom door, put it on and went into the kitchen to make herself coffee. The pitter-patter of Russell's claws followed her.

'You know you have your own bed,' she told him, accusingly.

He looked up at her with an expression that seemed to mean: *It's too early for arguments.*

Zoe took her coffee downstairs, making sure that Russell followed her, and put her mug on the counter next to the till.

'That is your bed,' she said, pointing.

Russell gave it a suspicious look and went and scratched at the front door. Zoe turned the button on the new deadlock to open up. The light outside was lovely, the sky several different colours from orange through to blue. Almost all the leaves had come down from the lime trees, making a carpet of bronze across the cobbles, through which the terrier trotted away, on his own doggy errand.

Zoe thought, with a smile: *There goes Russell, rustling the leaves.*

Lights were on in most of her neighbours' houses. She liked the fact that the square was not lined entirely with shops, that it was a place where people lived. The windows were dark in the other retail premises: the estate agent with its flourishing holiday rental department; the man who sold and repaired electrical goods; the women's outfitters.

Zoe realised that she was standing with the door open, allowing the cold air in. She closed it and went back upstairs to dress, choosing jeans, a T shirt and a fleece-lined sweatshirt with the logo: 'I'd rather be reading'. True to its injunction, she finished the M. R. James story about Canon Alberic with a second and then a third coffee.

Gato Merino arrived just before eight o'clock with his son, Lali, in a very compact, diesel-engined VW van, packed to the gills with the equipment they would need.

'You did well to navigate the lanes,' she congratulated them.

'It was tight but we are practised,' said Merino senior.

She let them in and showed them what she wanted done, repeating it in part for her own benefit, to clarify her thoughts, because she still felt sluggish from her broken night, as well as on edge from all the caffeine – an unhappy combination. Gato interrupted.

'My dear Madame Pascal, all is well. We pierce the wall here for the chimney, which we will affix the to the outside, running up above the roofline in the courtyard, all according to the permission we have obtained from the town hall.'

It was, in fact, Zoe who had filled in the requisite forms and endured the pernickety visit from the self-important building inspector.

'And the stove itself?'

'In the van. It will be last to emerge. Everything is in hand. Before the day is out, you will be sitting beside it, drinking your hot chocolate and rereading your favourite book.'

Zoe smiled because that was exactly what she had imagined – not just for her customers, but also for herself. After hours, the bookshop would become her living room.

'In that case, Monsieur Merino, I will leave you to it. Will you need the front door key?' she asked, preparing to remove it from the vulture fob, leaving her with just the key to her van. 'It opens the courtyard door as well.'

'Please, call me Gato. No, we won't leave until we're done. Being Monday, you're closed?'

'Yes. You know where the kitchen is. Please, make yourself coffee or anything else. There are a few bits and pieces in the fridge.'

'We will have dinner in Le Gourmand,' said Merino junior, proudly. He was very fresh-faced, with a tilted smile. 'It's my birthday. I'm eighteen today.'

'Only if we make good progress, Lali,' said his father, attempting to appear severe. 'This work must be complete before Madame Pascal gets back.' He turned back to Zoe. 'How will you pass the time?'

'I'm going into Aix to look at some second-hand furniture. I want some comfortable chairs to occupy the space between the bookshelves and the back door, to group around the new stove. And I'll have lunch with my *notaire*, Caroline Robin.'

'*Ah, la belle Caroline*,' he said, nodding. 'Give her my best wishes.'

'I will, Gato.'

'How is her arm? Will you be going rock-climbing with her?'

'No,' said Zoe, surprised. 'Why would I do that?'

'I thought Caroline might enlist your help in her searches.' This meant nothing to Zoe but, before she could ask for an explanation, Gato told her: 'If we're to finish in the day, we must get all these lovely books shrouded.'

Zoe lent them a hand, spreading clear-plastic dust sheets over the nearby stacks and the till, fixing them carefully with masking tape. Then she slipped her frustratingly inactive mobile phone into the left-hand pocket of her camel-hair coat and departed, across the square and down past the church – from which she couldn't help but avert her eyes.

★

Inside the guest house, Davide Quillan was contemplating the closed door of Barbara Ercollani's room. The door hadn't

83

been locked or sealed with 'crime tape', but he had been asked not to disturb what could be found therein.

That's fair enough. That doesn't mean anything. Unless, of course, the silly old woman had actually found the Vulture.

He pursed his lips, reaching out a hand, hovering it close to the handle.

But, if she had, wouldn't she have made it known?

Davide withdrew his hand and went down the dark-stained stairs and the tiled corridor to the kitchen. Through the back window, he could see Denis busy outside in the small court-yard garden, tending the overhanging vine with the tiny, monogrammed secateurs Davide had bought him as a gift the previous Christmas. Davide approved. It was important to attend to such tasks, in order to 'keep up appearances'.

Davide Quillan was a driven man. He hated to come second. Throughout his school years, his demanding parents had instilled in him a respect only for first place, insisting: '*Everywhere else is nowhere.*'

As a counterweight, perhaps, they had also fostered in him a love of music and, on their family holidays each August, an affinity with the endlessly diverse landscape of the south of France: the giant rolling Rhône, its medium-sized tributaries, the rushing torrents out of the snowy mountains, the lush hills, the pleasant plains, the barren lunar landscapes above the tree line, even the overpopulated tourist destinations of the coast.

Davide had finally moved to Provence after taking early retirement from his job in banking – a middle-ranking man-ager without whom the business could not function, but notable only for the anonymity of his role. He had assumed that the guest house – that he'd bought with his retirement lump sum settlement, plus a contribution from his life part-ner, Denis Allard – would provide a lucrative hobby. It turned out to be the opposite, a draining money pit deepened by exasperating government regulation, with a demanding and penny-pinching clientèle.

It's proof of the old adage that if you want to make a million euros in the hospitality business, you should bring two million.

With an indulgent smile for Denis's attentive concentration on the outdoor vine, Davide sat down at the kitchen table, opened his violin case and applied rosin to the strings of his bow. Despite his grating financial worries, autumn was a period of the year that he enjoyed, travelling from village to village with the local folk band in their banged-up minibus, performing immemorial tunes to the sons and daughters of the parched but fertile soil.

And it gives me the opportunity – without Denis in my ear, telling me it's pointless – to search some new locations for the Vulture.

*

Zoe had never got to the bottom of why the previous bookshop owner at *La Librairie de Mes Rêves* had decided to sell. The entire transaction had been managed through third parties. She knew the woman's name, of course – Lucia Jacquet – from the multitude of documents that she had been obliged to sign, sometimes required to copy out whole paragraphs of 'assertions' to confirm that she had 'understood the foregoing'. Though, of course, she hadn't, despite her excellent French, because it was another language altogether – an archaic legalese.

One of the things she had understood, however, was that – as well as the bookshop itself – a garage at the bottom of the town and a vehicle were both included in the purchase price.

The enormous Peugeot SUV that she had hired on arrival a month earlier had been returned. Very fortunately, she hadn't had to drive it back to Marseille airport herself. Thierry – who divided his time between the exciting port city and helping Marcel on his wine farm outside Sainte-Catherine – had done that for her.

The garage belonging to the bookshop was at the foot of the slopes of Sainte-Catherine, to one side of the town hall, built into the hillside, opening onto the car park. It was one of four. Each had belonged, back in the mists of time, to one of the shops in the main square, placed there to provide storage facilities in a time when the estate agent had been a hardware emporium, the electrical goods place a greengrocer, the women's outfitter a horse butcher, and Zoe's bookshop – charmingly, she thought – Sainte-Catherine's tiny junior school. The other three had been sold off, but Zoe's garage had remained a part of her real estate purchase – plus the aged Renault van it contained, covered by a tarpaulin and an impressive network of cobwebs.

Zoe hadn't automatically trusted the roadworthiness of this surprise bonus. She had enquired around the town and discovered that the Total service station was equipped to ensure it was reliable. She was now the proud owner of an older French equivalent of the Merinos' compact VW.

She undid the combination padlock – that she had also set to 0511 – and opened the heavy wooden doors, thinking she ought to get the Merinos to repaint them before the weather turned. The space inside the garage was very tight. She sidled between the van and the wall and could only just open the door wide enough to squirm inside, slumping into the driver's seat. She pulled out onto the car park, then left the engine running while she shut – but didn't trouble to lock – the garage doors behind her.

She drove away with an odd sense that there was something she had forgotten to do.

Or perhaps some important object that I've left behind?

It wasn't until she was out between the sunflower fields, now harvested and barren, that she realised what it was.

Poor Barbara. For a little while, I forgot all about her.

Despite the shadow of the elderly woman's death, Zoe enjoyed the drive across country to Aix. The sky was bright, the roads – for the most part – clear of traffic, dipping and

rising with the folds of the hills. Creeping in through the sub-
urbs, she soon found the second-hand furniture place she
had been aiming for, a place called in French a *dépôt-vente*,
because people could 'deposit' their unwanted chattels there
to be sold on with a commission going to the 'vendor', like
an old-fashioned eBay.

The *dépôt-vente* was enormous and spread over two floors.
Zoe spent a delicious half hour browsing, finally deciding to
purchase a set of three matching club armchairs with leather
upholstery, like those she had once seen in Maisie's solicitor's
office in Chichester, comfortable but upright.

I don't want customers nodding off.

She paid with her debit card then gave the assistant her
keys so that he could put them in the back of her van.

'It's just outside, a Renault. They should just fit. You'll recognise it because it has the name of my bookshop on the
side, *La Librairie de Mes Rêves*.'

'We have a large book section, madame, at very good
prices. Would that be of interest?'

'I'll have a look,' she told him, despite the fact that it was
not her intention to begin selling used copies.

The books section was at the back of the second floor, a separate space divided off by a partial barrier of bookshelves in
random styles, presumably acquired in house clearances and
the like. She chose two volumes that she wanted to read herself
– modern detective stories by the brilliant medieval historian
Fred Vargas – then reminded herself that she ought to buy them
new.

After all, I can afford to.

The books were still in her hands when she heard a snap-
pish voice behind her.

'Madame Pascal, what are you doing here?'

She turned to see, with a pang of disappointment, a small
man with thin strands of grey-blond hair scraped across his
otherwise bald head. Dressed in a painter's blue smock, his

hands thrust into the front pockets – balled up in fists, she could tell – he regarded her with a malevolent expression on his pudgy face. On the floor alongside him were two large carrier bags of shopping in heavy-duty plastic from the Monoprix supermarket. From Patrick, the waiter, she had learned the second-hand bookseller's name.

She gave him a smile and said: 'Ah, Monsieur Etienne, how nice to see you. We never run into one another. I'm sure it's because we are both so busy, always on duty.'

'That may be your case and I suppose I ought to be pleased for you. What are you doing here?'

His tone was suspicious and frankly rude.

'I came to buy some things, including furniture, as it happens,' said Zoe patiently, 'to give people places to sit. I'm installing a stove in the hope of making the bookshop a sort of haven in the colder months, somewhere warm and welcoming.'

'I see,' he snapped. 'Have you considered my situation?'

'I beg your pardon?'

'Do you have no sympathy?'

'I don't follow. In what way?'

He indicated the two novels in her hands.

'It seems you wish to trespass on my territory.'

'Monsieur Etienne, I can't understand you.'

His top lip was quivering. Zoe feared he was about to start shouting at her in this public place, which would no doubt be very embarrassing for both of them. But he controlled himself, heaved up his two heavy bags of shopping from the floor, angrily shook his head and stomped heavily away.

Zoe wasn't sure what to do. For a few moments, she simply stood with an expression of bafflement on her face. Then she put the books back, taking care to find their rightful place, then tried to follow him downstairs – but had to wait while a man with two walking sticks climbed up. Then the man half-tripped and Zoe had to escort him to a chair so he could regain his poise. When she finally got downstairs, Monsieur Etienne was already outside, bustling away across the road.

She followed, out into the bright day but, before she could catch up, the light on the pelican crossing changed and a stream of surging traffic prevented her.

Ten

LA TABLE PROVENÇALE

Once Zoe's van was loaded, she asked the sales assistant if she could leave it where it was, explaining: 'In my experience, parking is very difficult in the centre of Aix and my appointment isn't far away.'

She deliberately gave him the impression that it was a rendezvous for business, rather than simply lunch with her friend.

'Of course, Madame Pascal.'

She set off on foot towards the centre of the historic city, with plenty of time to spare, spending nearly an hour in the Musée Granet, a palatial nineteenth-century building housing works by some of her favourite artists, including Degas, Bonnard, Giacometti and Cézanne. There was also an exceptionally interesting exhibition of sculptures of severed heads from the pre-Roman era, well before the birth of Christ.

Zoe found it all so fascinating that she made herself late and had to hurry through the busy streets because she feared that Caroline would only have time to snatch lunch. As it turned out, however, her friend was happy to tell her that she was able to take her time, having no appointments until late in the afternoon.

'I've made a reservation at a perfect little establishment by a charming fountain in a lovely square.'

La Table Provençale was everything Caroline promised. Because they were both warmly dressed – Zoe in her camel-hair coat and Caroline in an expensive ski jacket over her stylish slacks – they were able to sit at a table outside. In fact, sheltered from the wind and with autumn sun filtering through the wispy outer branches of an olive tree, they were almost too warm in their coats.

Zoe ordered two starters to come together – pâté with exquisitely vinegary cornichons and thin triangles of toast, plus a dish of green vegetables, parboiled then tossed in butter and pepper – while her friend chose a *steak tartare*, a mound of raw minced beef with a raw egg on top, dressed with tartare sauce. They shared a portion of double-cooked chips on the side.

Caroline's arm was much better and she no longer had to use the neoprene sling. There was, however, a moment when she winced, picking up the heavy wine bottle.

'Is it still giving you pain? You never did tell me how it happened.'

'Only when I do things at the wrong angle,' said Caroline, avoiding the implied question. 'Tell me about your business. Tell me about your neighbours.'

Zoe was interested that Caroline still wasn't prepared to share how she had come by her injury and it made her slightly suspicious. As she began her own answer, she also realised that she was avoiding, for the time being, the most dramatic news from Sainte-Catherine – the death of Barbara Ercollani.

'Things are going well. Better than I expected, in fact.' She gave some details of the most popular books and the pattern of purchases, generally coinciding with the opening hours of the street market. 'Oh, and I've adopted a stray dog, a Jack Russell.'

'*Mais tu es extraordinaire*,' exclaimed Caroline. 'It might have fleas or ticks or rabies.'

'I took Russell to the vet who gave him a perfect bill of health and all of the necessary vaccinations – which he hated – and he sulked for several days.'

'Which vet?'

'Recommended by Marcel Maurice.'

'Oh, that would be Firmin Séchan, with the bad teeth and the stoop. He must be a hundred years old.'

'I liked him,' said Zoe mildly. 'And his bill was very reasonable.'

'I imagine the dog sleeps on your bed?'

'He has his own bed, downstairs,' said Zoe, reluctant to admit that Caroline had guessed the embarrassing truth. She went on to describe her various interactions with her neighbours, concluding: 'By the way, what do you know about the priest, Julien Calmet?'

'I think it's a shame,' said Caroline.

'In what way?'

'That such a fine figure of a man with such an interesting face should cloister himself away from the world.'

'Good heavens, you're interested in him?'

'One cannot be interested in a priest, Zoe. This is not the Church of England. There are rules that may not be broken for such a man.' Caroline took a sip of her wine. 'Which is, perhaps, a part of his attraction.'

Both of them laughed.

'Oh, just now,' said Zoe, 'I had an odd encounter at the furniture place. I met, by coincidence, the little man who owns the second-hand bookshop in Sainte-Catherine. You know, Monsieur Etienne? He sells books out of his home and from tables in the square.' Zoe described the confrontation. 'Isn't that odd?'

'I expect he assumed that you were buying second-hand books to impinge upon his market. That's what he meant by "trespass".'

'Of course,' said Zoe, feeling foolish. 'That makes complete sense.' Then, because the meal was ending with coffee and tiny truffle chocolates, she realised that she had no choice but finally to tell Caroline the story that she had been so studiously avoiding, ending weakly with: 'It made an impression on me, though I don't know why. I barely knew her, poor thing.'

'Death is an uncomfortable topic,' said Caroline, 'and you were brought face to face with it out of the blue, without warning.'

'Denis and Davide took it in their stride.'

'Because they had seen that she was unwell and it was less of a surprise.'

'I don't believe that,' said Zoe. 'Yes, she seemed tired, but not sick. Then, Julien Calmet asked me some probing questions about her condition.'

'That would be because he was a doctor before he became a priest.' Caroline signalled for the bill. 'I will pay because I have a thriving legal practice in an important city whereas you are a country mouse in a dying industry, scrabbling to make ends meet.'

'That's very rude but also very kind of you. You must come and visit and I will buy you dinner at Le Gourmand.'

'Yes, please. That would be marvellous. The chef, Quentin Simone, is a genius.'

'I've not yet been. I'm friends with Patrick at the Auberge, so it seems disloyal.'

'Share the joy and your money,' said Caroline, decisively. 'And don't forget to drop in on the second-hand man and explain that he was mistaken. Do you know his ludicrous first name? It's "Napoléon".' They both laughed again, then her friend added, in a serious tone: 'In a small town, disagreements can fester.'

They got up and Zoe accompanied Caroline back to her office, feeling a slight chill from her final comment. To break the silence, she asked: 'Will the Sainte-Catherine market days continue right through the off-season?'

'On fewer days. I expect Maurice will have a calendar. Well, this is me.' Before they parted, Caroline told her: 'I'm so pleased things are going well. I hope winter doesn't last too long.'

'That sounds very *Game of Thrones*. In any case, it's still autumn – hot chocolate by the stove, comfortable chairs, happy customers.'

'Good, well, like I say, I'm glad. You deserve it.'

'You talk as if I am in need of reassurance and bucking up.'

'I have never thought so before,' said Caroline, thoughtfully. 'Today, though, it does seem to be the case.'

'No,' said Zoe, decisively. 'All is well, believe me.' She frowned, remembering something she had been meaning to ask. 'Is there any news about the mast? I suppose I feel cut off without my mobile phone and the landline won't be reinstalled for another week or two, it seems.'

'I have no idea. I imagine Marcel Maurice will know that, too. Or Thierry. The mast is on their land.'

'Are they the ones who damaged the cables?'

'That's what I've always assumed.'

'By accident or design?'

'How could it possibly be by design?'

Caroline's mobile began ringing. She told Zoe she had to take it and shuffled two steps away on the sunny pavement, but not so far that Zoe couldn't overhear the beginning of a heated exchange about Caroline's office rent. It gave her a flashback to the London life she had left behind, in which her schedule had been dictated by being 'always on', at the mercy of the insistent appeals of her own tyrannical mobile device.

'I'll leave you to it,' Zoe mouthed, blowing her friend a kiss.

She turned away.

I hope that's not as serious as it looks.

Eleven

DANGEROUS SMOKE

Exploring on foot, through the maze of ancient streets in the heart of historic Aix-en-Provence, Zoe lost her way until she came upon one of the principal avenues where the waters of a two-thousand-year-old, moss-covered Roman spring emerged at close to blood temperature. Beneath the same double alley of centennial lime trees, another fountain depicted the fifteenth-century Good King René, reputed to have introduced muscat grapes to the region, just before potatoes and peppers arrived from the New World. Further on, another fountain's enormous statues represented art, justice and agriculture.

Zoe was on the point of asking her way of a passer-by, then decided it would be better to let a little more time pass.

I don't want to get home before the Merinos have completed their work.

Because it was mid-afternoon, the air was still mild, the sun high in the sky, unobscured by clouds. She passed two different bookshops, briefly admired their window displays, but didn't go inside. She did enter the women's-wear sections in a department store, but didn't find anything she wanted to buy.

I'll never doll myself up every day like Caroline does, so there's no point.

By chance, she found herself back near the Musée Granet. Alongside was a magnificent, lopsided thirteenth-century church, dedicated to Saint John of Malta, a Benedictine missionary knight. She went inside and found that the choir were rehearsing a stately plain song. She sat down and enjoyed the delightful harmonies, created not by their voices – because they sang a single melodic line in unison – but by the echoes from the stone architecture.

The choir rehearsal complete, she went back outside and found another bookshop. As luck would have it, she located new copies of the two Fred Vargas novels she had coveted earlier and bought them, walking out into the late afternoon, wondering about sitting down with a cup of hot chocolate and making a start on one or the other of them.

No, you know what you're like. You'll keep telling yourself 'one more chapter' and end up chilled to the bone.

Soon, Zoe felt she had exhausted all that Aix had to offer the casual visitor. Also, she was impatient to see what the Merinos had accomplished. She wasn't entirely convinced that the work could be completed in a single day.

She successfully navigated her way back to the second-hand warehouse, pleased that she didn't have to ask a local. She looked with disquiet, however, at the squished suspension on her elderly Renault van.

Is this a good idea?

She went inside to ask about deliveries, receiving an enthusiastic answer until she told the assistant where she lived.

'Oh, dear, no. I'm afraid that's too far, Madame Pascal.'

'Never mind. I'm sure it will be all right.'

She checked the petrol gauge. It showed just below a quarter – enough to get her home and replenish from the local Total garage she liked to use.

Local is best.

She set off with her paperback books on the passenger seat, through the city streets, discovering something that she hadn't paid much attention to on the way in. Every couple of hundred metres, she had to slow to a crawl so as not to damage her undercarriage on the many speed bumps. On one of them, she felt an ominous scrape.

At last, she emerged onto the ring road, keeping a sharp eye out for the junction that would take her east towards Sainte-Catherine. She almost missed it on a tight slip road that doubled back on itself, looking directly into the sun.

Glad to be able to accelerate into the open country, all was well for a while. Then, discouragingly, she felt the engine intermittently missing a beat, as if trying to clear its throat. Then the accelerator developed a lag, a clearly perceptible delay between depressing the pedal and the drive she expected.

Zoe estimated that she was about three-quarters of the way home, but she still felt anxious. To the south, a field of stubble was being burnt, the smoke drifting lazily across the road because there was barely any wind to disperse it. It thickened as she approached into a dip, the car stuttering badly, like heavy fog. Then the carriageway took a leftward curve, into a deeper depression where the smoke had thickly pooled. Zoe could no longer properly see the road ahead.

Her eyes on the white line that divided her from oncoming traffic, she slowed and felt the engine hating it, losing power and spluttering. She pumped the accelerator and, suddenly, it caught, thrusting her forward, perilously close to the middle of the carriageway, just as a lorry came into view, its headlights unexpectedly emerging from the smoke.

Zoe wrenched the steering wheel to the right, bouncing her wheels in the gutter, right off the edge of the tarmac, fighting for control. Despite the faltering torque from her failing engine, she managed to climb to the top of a rise and coast to a halt in a semi lay-by, not really wide enough for her van, alongside some vines, already cut back for winter.

The engine died.

Heart pounding, Zoe opened the door and got out, finding she was a little unsteady on her feet. She moved to the rear of the van and put a reassuring hand on the roof, making her feel more grounded.

That was a drama. I'll have to remember the stubble burning, in case I come this way at the same time next year.

For the time being, there was no more traffic. The sun was very low and dazzling. With a feeling of 'hope over experience', she delved in the deep left-hand pocket of her camel-hair coat for her phone. Pulling it out, she saw – to her surprise and delight – that she had three good bars of signal.

The network problem must be limited to the stone streets of Sainte-Catherine. Who to call, however?

Just then, another vehicle came creeping up out of the smoke that still lay pooled in the depression, like dirty water. The driver was proceeding with extreme caution – which Zoe respected – crawling along unsettlingly close to the verge where she had inadequately pulled over. Then, she saw why. There was a little platoon of three cars, following one another closely, coming the other way, meaning there was scarcely room for all of them – three vehicles abreast – at this unexpected choke point.

The driver on her side slowed almost to a halt, grinding up the incline at walking pace. She was able to get a good look at him – and he at her. It was Napoléon Etienne.

Zoe waved and smiled. Monsieur Etienne stared, an expression like guilt on his pudgy features. She gestured, trying to explain, through mime, that she was sorry to be obstructing the highway, exaggeratedly mouthing the words: *Would you please stop?*

The oncoming traffic squeezed by and Monsieur Etienne, astonishingly, accelerated away, his eyes resolutely to the road ahead, leaving Zoe gaping at the side of the road. The situation seemed so absurd that she simply laughed, watching him disappear over another rise.

What an extraordinary little man. Caroline's right. I'll have to go and explain that I'm not going to try and steal his business.

The sound of multiple engines receded. Zoe turned her mind back to the question of who she might call. She had few useful stored numbers for any of the local businesses, but she did have the Total garage where her van had been serviced. Unfortunately, they had no tow truck available. She asked where she might find such a service and learned, with much sucking of teeth, that it would be very expensive if it had to come from 'the city', meaning Aix.

To Zoe's ear, the number quoted didn't seem unreasonable but – thrifty by nature – she was unwilling to waste money unnecessarily. She thanked the mechanic for his good advice, hung up and opened the maps app to find out precisely where she was, discovering that she was within walking distance of the Maurice farm. That decided her.

Marcel will have a tractor that might do the job as well as a dedicated vehicle. It's the end of the day. I might be lucky and find him free. But is this asking too much on such little acquaintance?

The internet provided a landline number. No mobile was listed. She dialled and stood listening to the sound of its double trill, vaguely watching the colours evolving in the beautiful sky, made still more lovely by the haze of slowly drifting smoke. No answer came. She lowered her phone from her ear, looking at the screen, willing it to respond. Finally, it stopped of its own accord.

Call failed.

She went back to the maps app, looking for the direction to the farm. Because the signal was so good, it told her clearly the direction in which to look. She could even see one of the buildings, now she knew where they might be, with a light on in an upstairs window. Pinching out the graphic, she estimated they were less than two kilometres away.

*

Marcel Maurice was out of doors, walking his vines, attentive to the wisdom of an old farming adage.

The best fertiliser is the farmer's boot.

And he was feeling sentimental.

I wish Thierry could hurry up and finish spreading his wild oats or whatever it is he needs to do in the big, exciting city. He needs to return to his roots, making the future something worth building.

In the distance, he saw a small platoon of cars on the road to Aix.

Perhaps it's our bedraggled old farmhouse. I've put every euro I've saved into the business. I can't expect Thierry to want to live like a peasant of a hundred years ago, with no central heating and no satellite dish and all the rest of it.

In losing his left arm in an avoidable farm accident, Marcel Maurice had endured bad luck. Because of this, perhaps, he knew good fortune when he saw it.

His choice of vine manager, for example, selected from a limited number of applicants, had turned out very well. Odile Charpentier was independent minded, well educated, in tune with his own ideas around biodynamic planting and harvesting, following the phases of the moon, and content with her isolated rural existence.

And a Vulturist, too.

He also felt blessed by the last few years' growing seasons, an encouraging balance of heat and cold, wet and dry, leading to excellent harvests, swollen with rain just before the grapes were brought in. This had allowed him to invest in new equipment, including mechanical assistance for weeding the fields and two new steel vats for fermentation. It had been a financial stretch but one which, he hoped, would pay off in the long run.

But, as someone once said, in the long run, we are all dead.

He drew a deep sighing breath, listening to the rhythmic scraping of his weeder, gazing at the multi-coloured sky.

If I could beat everyone to the Vulture, I know what I'd do with the money.

★

Zoe leaned into the cab of her Renault and put on the hazard lights, scolding herself that she hadn't thought to do so earlier. She crossed the road and navigated a ditch with one agile leap, glad she had chosen jeans, pulling aside the skirts of her long coat. She quickly walked five or six hundred metres north, slightly uphill. The alleyways between the rows of vines were not quite bare, with weeds trying to colonise the dirt, but the ground was well drained and not muddy.

At the top of the field, she found herself constrained by a tall hedge made up of poplar trees with thick undergrowth, a windbreak to protect the fruit from northerly winds. She followed the trees a little way to the east, then found a gap onto a track whose dirt was marked by the heavy tyres of tractors. She heard – before she saw – activity up ahead, the sound of a machine and a low voice, encouraging and warm, like a tender-hearted man might use when talking to a cat, trying to encourage it home for its tea.

As Zoe climbed the second field, she made out the shape of a man's head and shoulders above the cut-back plants.

I'm sure that's Marcel.

Close enough for his voice to become distinct, she recognised a few words.

'That's it, good girl. Keep going. You know what to do.'

Zoe supposed that the sound of the machine's electric motor was covering the sound of her footsteps. She was now so close that she hesitated to speak, so as not to make Marcel jump. She saw him wipe his face with a handkerchief and began: '*Je m'excuse . . .*'

He spun round, his usually merry face stained with tears.

'You startled me,' he said, accusingly.

'I'm so sorry. My car broke down and I thought I'd come up and ask for help. Is it Thierry?'

'Is what Thierry?' he asked, blowing his nose.

'You seem upset.'

'Yes, I suppose it is, in a way.'

'What's happened?'

'Nothing has happened. I'm a foolish sentimentalist. It's just he wants nothing to do with the vines. Or he's happy to help as a kind of hobby, but he doesn't understand them – that they can give meaning to a life, that they flow like nourishing blood.'

Good heavens. He feels this very deeply.

'And, of course, that's a sadness for you.'

'It is. I have no one else.' He sniffed and wiped his nose. 'Pay no attention. Tell me again, what are you doing here?'

She described her van breaking down, the engine losing power and then almost being smashed into by the oncoming truck in the smoke. She tried to make light of it, but couldn't help admitting: 'For a few moments, I was actually very scared.'

'He's a fool, that farmer. He's been told not to burn on still days. The smoke always collects in the dips.'

'I heard you speaking. Is Thierry here, somewhere?'

'No,' he told her with a sheepish shake of the head. 'I was talking to my robot.'

Twelve

A ROBOT AND A RESCUE

Zoe frowned, surprised by the idea of cutting-edge modern technology among the vines.

'Your robot?'

Marcel pointed down the row to where a chunky farm machine – like a large blue suitcase on rubber wheels – was creeping along, oscillating claws scrabbling at ground level, determinedly removing weeds.

'I know it's silly, but I like to watch it work sometimes and . . .'

He stopped and Zoe completed the thought.

'I know what you mean. I sympathise. You work, otherwise, alone. In London, I used to talk to my phone, planning my day, you know, asking it to remind me what I had to do and in what order I needed to accomplish all my chores. Of course, it did, because of the calendar and the other useful gizmos. But there was a downside, too. I think that was one of the reasons why I wanted to leave – because I felt life was in control of me, rather than the opposite, moulding me into too small a space. Does that make sense?'

'I've never wanted anything but this,' said Marcel, in his lovely accent.

'You've lived on the farm all your life?'

'I have.'

'Did you ever marry?' she asked, realising she had never wondered how Thierry came into the picture. 'If you don't mind me asking.'

'My sister married, but she and her husband died.'

'Oh. How awful.'

'It was a tourist ferry in the Greek islands. It sank, leaving me Thierry. He was only small, two years old, and one of the crew members saved him, keeping him afloat, awaiting rescue, treading water with him in his arms, then he got him into a lifeboat.'

The weeding robot was thirty metres away now, navigating the turn at the bottom of the row. Zoe supposed it was fitted with sensors and all kinds of clever computer intelligence, like a satnav.

'I've been thinking all along that Thierry was your son but I realise now that you always call him "my boy".'

'That's right, my nephew.' Marcel's tone changed. 'Anyway, is that your car?'

He pointed with his one good hand. Zoe turned to look. The hazard lights were intermittently visible in the distance, through the line of poplars.

'That's it.'

'What do you call her?' he asked with a smile in his voice.

'I don't call her anything.'

'My robot has a name, Rosalie the Robot. She's a Renault van, isn't she? You should call her Renée.'

'All right.' Zoe laughed. 'I will, in homage to Good King René who brought the muscat grapes.'

'Very good insider knowledge,' he told her. 'We'll make a local of you yet.'

'Thank you, Marcel,' said Zoe, extremely gratified. 'I hope so.'

They left the robot going about its business and walked up the field to the farmhouse, a poorly maintained stone-built building that, like the vines, seemed very big for one man to manage. Close by was a small, modern bungalow.

'That's my vineyard manager's house. By law, I have to provide accommodation, as well as a salary and benefits and all the rest of it.'

'Does he do a good job?'

'She,' he told her. 'Odile Charpentier. Yes, she's very good.'

Marcel showed Zoe a Toyota utility vehicle – that he called, inevitably, Toto – with an automatic gearbox and a spigot on the steering wheel to make it easier to control with just one hand. At the back of the Toyota was a motorised spool of steel cable. They both climbed in and Marcel drove a circuit of the vines, onto a farm track that came out further up the road, then found the place. He made a three-point turn and reversed up to Zoe's 'Renée'. Between the two of them, they located the tow point inside a small hatch in the front bumper and attached the steel cable.

'You'll need to get in, Zoe, and steer and be ready to use the brakes, so you don't roll forward and bang into the back of me when I have to slow down. Where are we going?'

'The Total garage. Do you use them?'

'I do. They're very good.'

'Well, they must have missed something because the engine coughed and spluttered and here I am stranded.'

The careful journey back to Sainte-Catherine only took a few minutes, but it felt much longer because it seemed precarious, with Zoe trying to keep herself a precise distance from Marcel's rear bumper. It was okay on the uphill drags, but downhill was more difficult when the cable became slack. Happily, they made it without mishap and they were able to leave the van in a corner of the forecourt. No mechanics were on duty, but the young woman who worked as a cashier told them she would leave a message for when they arrived in the morning. Then she warned Zoe that her van would have to join a queue: 'Of several days, perhaps. The mechanics are very busy.'

Zoe hid her feeling of frustration.

'Never mind. I can't thank you enough, Marcel. Can I buy you a drink?'

With a broad smile, he told her: 'That would be very kind.'

'Or perhaps a bite to eat? Will the restaurants be serving, yet? I only had two starters for lunch so I could do with something.'

'Le Gourmand won't open until seven, but we could get something simple at the Auberge.'

'Splendid.'

They walked up through the narrow lanes to the lovely square. Patrick was still on duty, as he always seemed to be, busy with a family with three teenage children. They ordered two delicious *croque-madame* toasted sandwiches and Marcel told her that Patrick worked all hours through the summer into autumn, up to the end of the tourist season, then he would disappear on holiday for six weeks, returning for Christmas and New Year.

'Who's in the kitchen?'

'Patrick's sister, Minette.'

'What's she like?'

'Very athletic with a sharp tongue.'

'Older or younger?'

'I've never wondered.' Marcel frowned. 'Maybe twins?'

That idea made Zoe think about family secrets and the complicated plot lines in mystery novels where twins were implicated in murderous crimes because of secrets from the dim and buried past. Then, because of all the drama, Zoe realised she had forgotten about the Merinos, busy with her new stove installation. She explained to Marcel and they carried their toasties away with them, wrapped in paper napkins to keep them warm.

The Merinos' van was still parked outside, with the door ajar. Zoe went in first, clanging the bell, asking: 'How did you get on, Gato?'

'Come, come,' called Monsieur Merino from the rear.

Zoe navigated through the stacks, noticing that the plastic dust sheets had all been removed, aware of an unaccustomed warmth, a dryness of the air. She found the two Merinos perched on her inherited kitchen chairs, the stove lit, set on a slab of local stone to protect the floorboards from ash and embers. Between them lay Russell, one of his ears folded back, making him look sad. Zoe bent down and straightened it.

'Please, sit. There is more,' Gato told her. 'Lali, turn off the lights.'

Merino junior got up and did so. The nook between the shelves – that Zoe was pleased to see would be just big enough to accommodate her worn but comfortable leather club armchairs – became magical, illuminated by the orange glow of the stove, through the fireproof glass.

'This is wonderful,' said Zoe. 'Where did you get the logs?'

'We brought them with us so that we could make sure all was well. It's just some odds and ends of *falabreguier*.' Zoe frowned and he spelt it for her, then said: 'That's the Provençal name for the tree it comes from.'

'This is delightful,' agreed Marcel. He and the Merinos shook hands. 'I must thank you again, Gato, for your help at harvest time.'

'It was our pleasure,' said Merino senior. 'Wasn't it, Lali?'

'It was,' said Merino junior. 'What's the point of living amongst the vines if you can't take part in the harvest?'

The young man insisted that Marcel take his chair. Zoe offered to share the two *croque-madame* snacks with her builders, but they reminded her that they had dinner awaiting them at Le Gourmand. She saw them out, then came back, marvelling once again at the change in atmosphere in the bookshop, conscious for the first time that there had been a kind of underlying worry tensing her shoulders, anxiety about the long winter months in this old and possibly damp stone building, especially because of the damage that might cause her precious stock.

She and Marcel ate, talking about the rhythm of farming life. She learned that the Maurice family had worked the land around Sainte-Catherine for at least nine generations, that Marcel had paperwork relating to the purchase of the farmhouse in the mid seventeen hundreds that specified an absurdly low price in 'argent sonnant et comptant', meaning 'silver money that rings and can be counted'.

They both had a glass of wine from Zoe's kitchen.

Luckily, she thought, *a Maurice vintage.*

Then Marcel got up and told her that he oughtn't to take up any more of her time.

'No, don't say that. You rescued me. I might have been stuck there all night – or I suppose I would have walked home and left Renée there, perhaps at the mercy of some inattentive truck driver, and found her smashed to smithereens in the morning.'

'All's well that ends well,' he told her and insisted he ought to go.

She showed him out into the square, worried that she had presumed too much on their frail acquaintance. Marcel strode away and she stayed where she was, trying to enjoy the scents of the evening, woodsmoke and autumn. A few neighbours were out and about, taking an evening walk and she realised she hadn't learned their names. Three medium-sized children were playing tag.

Zoe felt cold inside.

I'm still a stranger here. It all feels like it's happening behind glass.

She saw Antoine Grenelle in conversation with Napoléon Etienne. Then the policeman glanced up at her and came beetling across the cobbles in her direction.

And it looks like Renée the Van breaking down isn't the only disaster.

III

THE INVESTIGATION BEGINS

Thirteen

SUSPICION

Zoe stayed where she was, in her own doorway, looking across the cobbles of the square, as Brigadier Antoine Grenelle came purposefully to meet her. Because she had first noticed him over on the far side, it gave her time to think about how, sometimes, people's intentions are visible in their body language. In this case, she could already see that Antoine had something official to say to her that, she thought, she wouldn't enjoy.

'*Bonsoir, Madame Pascal,*' he said. 'I'm glad to have caught you. Shall we go inside?'

'You're inviting yourself into my home, Antoine?'

'Brigadier Grenelle, on this occasion, Madame Pascal.'

Antoine's usually vague eyes were bright and alert, reminding her of his incisive but – to her – inconclusive questions in the church.

'In that case, Brigadier, do I need to ask Caroline to be present?'

Zoe said it lightly, but the question just made Antoine look even more sombre.

'It would be your prerogative to summon a lawyer. For the time being there is no need.'

'I suppose I will have to take your word for that.'

'Can we step inside, please?'

'Go ahead.'

She gestured for him to precede her, but he hung back.

Does he think I'm going to bash him on the noggin?

'After you, madame,' he told her.

Zoe headed for the nook where the new stove was still burning, the only light the flames through the fire-proof glass. She sat down on one of the two hard chairs, but Antoine remained standing.

'Madame Pascal,' he began, 'certain elements of the investigation into the death of Madame Barbara Ercollani have led the police to the conclusion that the circumstances merit further elucidation, that it is possible that she did not die of natural causes.'

'I see,' said Zoe.

He gave her a penetrating look. 'You do not seem surprised.' Zoe didn't answer. Antoine asked, with an edge of impatience: 'Why do you not seem surprised, madame?'

'You told me I wouldn't need a lawyer present in this interview. Now, you ask me probing questions?'

'You are at liberty not to answer.'

Zoe sighed. There were good reasons why she had been able to keep her cool, to maintain her sangfroid, though she didn't really want to share them. She knew she would have to, though, in the end.

'I was surprised. I remain surprised,' she told him. 'But I wasn't frightened by what we saw. You see, I have experience of capital crimes.'

'You do?' asked Antoine, looking as though it would take him a moment or two to absorb this information. 'Might I ask—'

'When I was very much younger,' Zoe interrupted, 'I was a witness to several murder investigations.'

'How did that . . . It seems . . . How unusual,' said Antoine.

'When I say "witness", I don't mean that I saw the murders happen. I was a bystander to the events, but I got to know the investigating officers very well.'

'You were not a serving officer yourself?'

'No, I was not. And I was very young.'

'How young?'

'Sixteen.'

'And these murders all happened during one year of your young life?'

'Yes, remarkably, but it wasn't coincidence, exactly. There were connections between them. In the first, the police believed me to be in danger. But that was all very long ago. Can you tell me why you are sure that poor Barbara was killed?'

Zoe thought the circumstances suspicious because, of course, she had seen Barabara only an hour before, weary and confused, perhaps, but very much alive.

Antoine shook his head, evasively. 'I didn't say that anyone was sure. In any case, I cannot divulge . . .' He stopped, looking suspicious. 'I think you should explain how—'

Jumping in, Zoe tried to keep the exasperation from her voice.

'None of this is relevant, but I suppose it can do no harm to tell you. I was a foundling, left as a baby at a hospital, raised partly by the state and partly by inattentive foster parents. Out of that, the first murder investigation arose. I was incidental. But the person who saw through the complicated web of guilt and resentment was also a "civilian".'

'What was his relationship to you?'

'*Her* relationship,' Zoe corrected him. 'A friend, that's all – or, rather, someone who became a friend.'

In the back of her mind, she had an image of dear Maisie Cooper, now quite elderly.

I wonder if Maisie would be more frank than I am being. But I don't like him keeping me in the dark and expecting me to provide my answers blind.

'This friend was an active investigator?' he insisted.

'Maisie found herself drawn into the investigation for personal reason and, as I said, solved the mystery before the police did. But we're getting off track. You wanted to know why I didn't faint or exclaim in shock when you told me that Barbara didn't die a natural death. Now, you know. The idea is shocking, of course, but it's a road I've travelled down previously.'

'I'll need to know more about all this,' said Antoine, fussily.

'I'll need a good reason to tell you,' Zoe riposted. 'Do you have one?'

Antoine's tone became more official. 'An inspector from Aix has been tasked with preparing a dossier to submit to the examining magistrate.' The French phrase was *'juge d'instruction'*. 'You know what that means?'

'I do.'

'Only then will the next official steps be taken.'

'Do those steps involve questioning me as a potential assailant?'

'Why do you say "assailant"? Madame Ercollani might have been poisoned, for example.'

'Antoine . . .' Zoe began, then corrected herself. 'Brigadier Grenelle, I have no more knowledge of the death of poor Barbara than I have already shared with you. I used the word "assailant" but I might have said "murderer". That's what we're talking about, isn't it?'

'It is.'

Zoe decided, regardless of the fact that she was somehow under suspicion, to go upstairs and fetch them both a glass of wine from the kitchen.

'Please sit down, Antoine,' she told him. 'I'll fetch us a drink.'

Without a word, he did so, leaning forwards towards the flames, and Zoe ran upstairs. She found she had no red which she knew, from their first meeting, was Antoine's pre-ferred tipple, but there was still some of Marcel Maurice's excellent crisp white in the door of the fridge. She brought it down with two *ballons*, the bog-standard format of everyday wine glass. Placing all three things on the floor between her chair and the stove, she poured out two measures.

'*A votre santé*,' she told him, raising her glass, meaning 'good health'.

Antoine picked up his own and replied: '*A la vôtre*,' meaning 'to yours'. Then he added: 'And to the memory of Barbara Ercollani.'

They both drank, then Zoe wondered aloud: 'You did not know her well, but there is a connection between you. I'm right, aren't I?'

'It is for the officer to ask the questions,' murmured Antoine, looking at the flames. He sipped his wine. 'Especially where there is suspicion concerning the witness.'

'The witness being me,' said Zoe.

'I'm afraid so,' he told her. 'You were the last to speak to her, the last to see her, the one to discover the body. You had no reason to go to the church. The procession does not end there.'

'I didn't know that.'

'And the urgent desire of a murderer to return to the scene of their crime is well documented.'

Increasingly unnerved at being cast as a murderer, Zoe retorted: 'Well, I'm not worried.'

'Why is that?'

'Because I've done nothing wrong. I have nothing to be ashamed of or to regret.'

'All the same, I have recently come into possession of new evidence concerning your relationship to the deceased.'

'And what is that?'

'You were not on good terms. You were overheard in violent disagreement.'

'That is an outright lie,' Zoe blurted. 'Who told you that?' She remembered what she had seen in the square, just before Antoine came beetling over to find her. 'It was Napoléon Etienne, wasn't it? He's jealous of me and fears for his own business. No one likes or trusts him. You cannot possibly take his word against mine.'

Antoine slowly shook his head. 'I am obliged to inform you that you should not leave Sainte-Catherine.'

Zoe gulped and asked: 'What does that mean? Am I allowed to visit Aix, for example?'

'It would be better if you told me, were that your intention.'

'How about going to see Marcel Maurice on his vineyard?'

'Ah, I saw him leaving. Yes, that, too, especially if you were thinking of staying the night.'

'Why would I stay the night?' asked Zoe, then she came to the obvious conclusion. 'Because we might be embarking on some kind of intimate relationship? Well, that's not the case and I can assure you that I have no desire to sleep in any-one's bed but my own.' Zoe emptied her glass and, perhaps emboldened by the alcohol, added, in jest: 'At least, for the time being.'

Antoine looked up from the flames. His eyes were, for the first time since the oddly threatening conversation began, smiling.

'You would have no shortage of takers,' he told her, with a ghost of his former gallantry.

*

At just that moment, at the altar rail in the cold Templar church, kneeling on frigid flagstones, Julien Calmet was enduring a regular disappointment – yearning for a glimpse of the boundless charity of his chosen deity, but finding Him silently, dispiritingly, out of reach.

In early life, Julien's faith had been a matter of routine observance, abruptly transformed by a moment that still lived in his memory – a vivid perception of God's great-ness, one brilliant afternoon hiking through snow in the cold pre-Alps at the northern edge of the Verdon nature park, understanding for the first time that he should shift his vocation from medicine to religion, from care for his fellow humans' bodies to their souls.

His impotent prayers complete, Julien was able to stand without any involuntary gasps or creaks of his knees. His spare frame, lean and fit, was soon in motion, bending and stretching as he embarked on a secondary ritual of calisthenics that he employed as an antidote to the immobility of religious worship.

After his routine of physical exercise, Julien turned off the chandelier, allowing the church to darken, illuminated only by slant orange light from a street lamp outside that struggled to penetrate the stained glass of the ancient windows. A faint gleam caught the bronze plaque in the centre of the floor, calling to mind the place where Barbara Ercollani had lain, no longer prey to the vicissitudes of human existence and at one – he hoped – with her maker in death.

It is a mystery still, however. And perhaps the lives of my parishioners, here in Sainte-Catherine, will take a long time to recover.

He opened the heavy door, stepped outside and locked up. Then he hesitated, looking up the narrow lane towards the square and the bookshop.

Madame Pascal is a newcomer. There is much she does not yet know about this place and the people in it, including how the 'love of money' can lead to danger, as well as to sin.

★

Back at *La Librairie de Mes Rêves*, Antoine had gone, having said nothing else of any substance, leaving Zoe to reflect on an extraordinary day. She felt uncomfortably that she was under some kind of house arrest.

Definitely under suspicion. But why? It must be Etienne Napoléon's lie.

She opened the door of the stove, releasing a blast of superheated air into the room.

I'm not alone and friendless here in Sainte-Marie. Etienne is the exception, not the rule.

Underneath the firebox was a space for logs that the Merinos had, very kindly, left almost full of well-seasoned chunks of *falabreguier*, all of it twisted and full of knots, so unsuitable for furniture making or construction. The logs burned slowly because they came from the centre of the trees that had been sacrificed to provide her with warmth – the heartwood. She put two more on the fire, interested to discover how long they would last if she damped the stove down by closing all the vents.

Perhaps the embers will still be warm in the morning. That would be lovely – and very convenient for relighting.

She realised that there wasn't any kindling, so she put on her coat and went outside, locking up behind her. Because it had been windy, there were lots of twigs on the ground among the fallen leaves, snapped from the ends of the branches of the lime trees. Zoe picked up a good handful, thinking about tying them into a 'faggot', which was a good old Sussex word from her youth, meaning a bunch of thin pieces of wood bound tight together, for use in the absence of proper logs.

She put her handful of twigs on one of the granite bollards that ringed the square and took out her mobile phone, waking the screen with her code.

No bars. Out of range, again. It really is very frustrating and . . . isolating.

Zoe walked down through the quiet streets, past the church where the body had been found and the square where the Auberge was shut up and dark, while Le Gourmand was still serving indoors, the outside tables cleared and the chair cushions put away. In the car park at the bottom of the town, she remembered that she hadn't locked her garage.

But there's nothing in it.

Checking her mobile again, she found no improvement. She followed the suburban road a little way, just as far as the vet's house where she had taken Russell to be reluctantly given his jabs, then hesitated, looking down the road that led away across country, past the Maurice vineyard and on to Aix.

How far would I have to walk for a signal?

She thought about the tense experience of being towed all the way back to Sainte-Catherine by Marcel's Toyota pick-up.

Too far? I think so, yes.

Because it was pleasant being out at night with the knowledge that, back at the bookshop, she could find the stove burning and the whole house dry and warm, she decided to stroll through some of the quiet streets that she had never walked before, on the far side of the hill on which Sainte-Catherine was built. A few minutes later, she found herself standing at the foot of the 'stair' of clay roofs that she could see from the back bedroom.

On this side of the town, the houses formed a kind of wall, a solid terrace as if they had been built as a rampart against attack, without any street entrances between them. She had to walk on further, with the very fresh breeze on her cheeks, to find a narrow, cobbled lane, little more than a footpath.

She climbed past mostly shuttered windows, the only useful light coming from an old-fashioned orange street lamp on a bracket, at a turning a little way ahead. She heard faint voices of conversation and television sets, telling her that there were people inside these houses, living their everyday lives, perhaps joyful, perhaps anxious, perhaps full of sorrow.

Beyond the corner, well lit by the street lamp, she came to a house with a sign over the door that read *Livres d'Occasion*, meaning 'second-hand books'.

This is Monsieur Etienne's place.

or a minute or so, Zoe stood quietly, thinking about the
d and unkind way he had behaved, resolutely ignoring her
while she stood in danger of causing an accident at the side
of the highway.

Then his ridiculous lie.

She pictured the man with the two walking sticks who had
half tripped on the stairs of the second-hand shop in Aix
and prevented her from following Etienne. Then she pictured Monsieur Etienne's two heavy carrier bags of everyday
shopping and wondered what might have been in them.

A new thought crystallised.

*Renée the van was fine on the drive over. What could possi-
bly have gone wrong while it was parked on the forecourt of the*
dépôt-vente – *the furniture place?*

Monsieur Etienne's second-hand bookshop home gave no
answer. It was resolutely dark.

*If I could confront Napoléon Etienne right now and ask him
that same question, what might he say?*

She was on the point of banging on the door and demanding an answer when she found a different reason to hesitate.

*If I provoke him – and if I get carried away and challenge
him on lying about me to Antoine – he might become more
difficult still.*

Fourteen

WALKING OUT INTO DANGER

Days passed and, despite all of the dramatic events that had threatened to take over her life, Zoe began to experience a feeling of drift. No one came to question her a second time. She couldn't bring herself to confront either Antoine – to ask where the police investigation had got to – or Napoléon Etienne – to gauge his reaction and confirm or deny her unevidenced suspicions.

In part, too, her 'drift' was due to the changing season. Her flowering oleanders were apparently going into hibernation; her neighbours' plants were being cut back or shrouded in fleece in preparation for the frosts to come. Market days were reduced to Wednesdays, Saturdays and Sundays. The number of tourists declined in parallel.

And I feel people look at me differently – with more than a hint of suspicion in their eyes.

Fortunately, Sainte-Catherine was still a shopping destination for the constellation of lonely villages within twenty or thirty kilometres, meaning a fair number of local customers could still be relied upon. Furthermore, deliveries from larger towns such as Aix and Marseille were expensive – as Zoe had learned – meaning that internet purchases weren't always the most economical choice for the far-flung populations of the Verdon nature park.

One evening, after a very slow day, Zoe almost forgot that she was the owner of *La Librairie de Mes Rêves*, so happy was she sitting by her stove, reading one of her new Fred Vargas novels. The Merinos, father and son, had done her the favour of bringing the leather club armchairs up out of Renée the van, still awaiting investigation at the Total garage, and a big new load of logs, stacked in the rear courtyard.

She was interrupted by a knock at the door and a message from one of the mechanics, a handsome young man with 'Frank' on his name badge. Her van had finally reached the front of the service queue and, the following day, an investigation into what had gone wrong would commence, with a diagnosis and – hopefully – a prognosis, too.

She thanked him and, before he left, he seemed to weigh her up.

Is Frank wary of me, too?

From the threshold, she watched him go. The evening was already dark, the air crisp, scented with woodsmoke, the sky peppered with beautiful stars.

Time for some exercise.

Zoe put on an extra pair of socks and her new hiking boots, wonderfully lightweight in waterproof nylon, with excellent ankle support. Though she hated the look of it, she chose the warm-but-lightweight quilted gilet that she kept out of sight in a dark corner of her wardrobe, adding her own ski jacket – a much more economical version of the stylish one that Caroline wore – but warm and windproof, still. Slipping her mobile phone into her right-hand pocket, she went out into the chill evening. Russell followed, making darts left and right to verify his territory.

Zoe was so used to Sainte-Catherine – though she couldn't say she felt fully 'at home' – that things she had previously looked on as curious novelties now seemed completely ordinary. Among these were the odd, octagonal shape of the Templar church and the embossed designs of vines and grapes on the metal downpipes from the gutters. Likewise, she no longer asked herself how the two restaurants could possibly coexist, facing one another across the little square. It wasn't a question of each having a different clientèle, but of catering to different tastes and requirements at different moments in people's lives. The first clue had been the news that eighteen-year-old Lali Merino had been looking forward to enjoying a birthday meal in the very smart Le Gourmand – and that was a normal thing for a working-class lad to do on a special day.

Emerging alongside the town hall at the bottom of the town, she was glad to see the moon, looking very big because it was low to the horizon.

That will help me find my way.

Another, more insidious thought came into her mind.

And it will make it hard for anyone to sneak up on me.

Russell had disappeared, going about his own doggy business. On the far side of the car park was the *mobylette* she had noticed before, chained to a low rail beside the bench where she had first seen Antoine Grenelle. The lightweight motorbike was festooned with silver cobwebs, picked out by the moonlight. Beyond it, a path led west between the fields. She knew that it would bring her close to Marcel's vineyards, but that was not her destination. Her idea was simply to walk far enough to find a decent mobile phone signal, and no further.

It was very lovely walking alone beneath the star-strewn, inky black sky, with the moon like a dim silver searchlight showing her the undulations in the path. After a few minutes, she turned to look back at Sainte-Catherine and estimate how far she had gone.

Not far enough.

She left the sunflower field, ploughed over now, with burgeoning weeds or perhaps winter forage just discernible in the dark furrows. Entering the vines, she heard Marcel's robot hard at work on higher ground to the far side of the road, scratching the cold dirt to remove unwanted, opportunistic competition from the valuable crop. On her side, too, the land rose slightly as she approached the throughfare where she believed she would be able to make her call.

Arriving at the verge a little out of breath, she was momentarily dazzled by two cars driving along in a kind of procession, the second far too close.

That is the French way, however, the one behind up the chuff of the one in front.

As the noise of the two vehicles receded, she took out her phone, saw she had – as before – three bars of signal and made her call. Maisie answered on the third ring. Delighted to hear one another's voices, there followed a confusing sequence of overlapping greetings, then Zoe asked for her old friend's news.

'Nothing good, I'm afraid,' said Maisie, stoically. 'It seems I've broken a bone. My left wrist is in plaster.'

For a second, Zoe frowned, thinking about how that sort of injury seemed to be haunting her, with Caroline and then Marcel, too.

'How long do you have to keep it on?'

'Six weeks, they say, because I'm so old and frail.'

'Do you feel old and frail?'

Maisie laughed. 'No, I don't, but it is annoying to have one's independence taken away.'

For five minutes they talked about the charitable respite home in the Jacobean manor house of the Sussex village of Bunting that had, for a good few years now, in semi-retirement, been Maisie's professional responsibility. Zoe was pleased to hear that the residents – who were sometimes difficult to manage because they brought with them all kinds of traumas from their unhappy life experiences – seemed to be getting along well with one another.

'There are seven of them just at the moment,' said Maisie. 'In the New Year, I expect all of them to resume an independent existence.'

'They'll be with you right through the winter?' asked Zoe.

'Yes, I don't think we should oblige them to make their way unassisted in the dark months, do you?'

The question – almost poetically phrased – was rhetorical, so Zoe didn't answer. Instead, she told Maisie the story of Barbara Ercollani. She began with their first meetings, thinking her a pleasant but twittery old lady who just needed a book or two in order to while away the lonely evenings at *Chez Denis et Davide*. Then she described the close interest Barbara had taken in the topography of the Verdon nature park, buying guidebooks and detailed maps. She told Maisie about Barbara's surprisingly 'spicy' taste in fiction, then proceeded to the procession of the effigy of Saint Bertrand, the discovery in the church and the dreadful realisation that life had fled Barbara's crumpled body.

Maisie didn't interrupt. Then, when Zoe ran out of words, she asked seven or eight penetrating questions about the precise sequence of events, then went on to discuss what else Zoe knew of the characters and circumstances of the other residents of the town.

Zoe found the process draining but also rewarding, as it clarified her own thoughts. She was holding the phone horizontally in front of her mouth, using the speaker, so she could see the minutes adding up on the screen. Once they'd reached thirty, she asked Maisie if she ought to ring off because she was disturbing her friend's evening.

'No, not for that reason, but perhaps we should let all this settle. I'd like to know what the tipsy police officer is going to do next. And, you should probably make yourself ready to be interviewed officially, you know? If there is an investigating magistrate attached, then someone of more senior rank will be required to assemble evidence.'

'Yes,' said Zoe. 'That makes sense. But is there something in the back of your mind? Is that why you want to take a pause?'

'No, like I said, just in order to sit on it.'

Standing at the side of the road, with the vague hum of Marcel's robot beyond the tarmac between the vines, Zoe smiled at the extraordinary distance she had travelled in life from the moment when, decades before, abandoned and desperate, Maisie had come across her hiding in a chicken coop on a failing farm in the Sussex Downs, frightened and cowering from a murderer.

'All right,' she said. 'That sounds like a very good idea. Let's do that.'

They talked a little more about people they both knew – neighbours and friends, some still alive, others from an older generation and already dead – then bid one another goodbye with warm wishes for health and happiness.

'And prosperity,' added Maisie. 'I forgot to ask. Is the shop a going concern, do you think?'

'Had you asked me a week ago, I would have said yes. I'm becoming a little anxious about the quiet period, out of season.'

'Time will tell,' said Maisie. 'Keep in touch.'

With that, finally, they hung up.

Yes, time will tell – but that isn't actually a very reassuring idea.

No cars had gone past in all the time they had been talking but, just then, a rusty minibus went by, full of six or seven happy faces, clearly visible because the cabin light was on, meaning she could also see black cases for what looked like musical instruments propped between the passengers and the seats. She recognised the minibus as belonging to the local amateur orchestra that included some, but not all, of the band that had played for the *fête de Saint-Bertrand*. They called themselves *Les Vautours* – meaning 'the vultures' – and, of course, were all residents of Sainte-Catherine and of the villages round about.

Once the minibus had disappeared into the dip away to the left, to her surprise, Zoe heard gunshots and couldn't, at first, work out why. The irrational idea came into her mind that it might be an automated weapon, firing periodically to scare away crows.

But that makes no sense, not at night.

And the rhythm of the shots was random, coming in clumps, then pausing.

Oh, it must be hunters.

The sounds of shooting were coming from higher ground, on the far side of the road, distant enough that Zoe didn't feel in danger. She crossed over, interested to see if she might be able to pick out movement on the wooded hillside, and walked up between the vines, feeling happily connected to the landscape, drawn to this unusual night-time activity, wondering who the hunters might be.

Probably not Marcel, for obvious reasons.

She stopped, however, with a sudden intimation of danger, at the sound of a shuffling tread coming towards her, something like the uncertain gait of an elderly or infirm person obliged, painfully, to make haste. In the strong moonlight, she found it bizarre that she couldn't see them – or at least their torso – above the bare, woody stalks of last year's vines.

Or is it not actually a person?

Suddenly, there came an angry-sounding snort and she grasped the nature of the threat. The noises were coming from low to the ground, a wild animal disturbed by the hunters' guns, frightened and irritated, running down from the woods through the vines towards the road.

It must be a sanglier *– a wild boar.*

Gingerly, she turned to make her way back towards the road, trying and failing to make no sound, the dry and fallen leaves crunching beneath the soles of her hiking boots. She knew that the tusks of a wild boar were dangerous, even deadly, if the creature was a larger specimen and indignant at being disturbed. The snuffling and the heavy, pawing tread followed. She began to feel that it was she who was being hunted.

Does it understand it was being shot at and now it's simply making its escape? Or will it be frightened and desperate and lash out?

Despite her growing concern, she didn't want the animal to follow her and run out into the traffic, be startled by headlights and killed that way instead.

And a collision between a small car and a powerful sanglier *could easily be catastrophic for the vehicle's occupants, too.*

She continued down the alley between the vines, closer and closer to the road, aware that the wild boar was coming nearer, the sound of the animal's cloven hooves becoming more intimidating in the stillness of the night, its stertorous breathing no more than ten or twelve paces distant. In fear, Zoe turned to face the threat, now backing away. The heels of her lightweight walking boots reached the softness of the grassy verge.

At last.

Thankfully, the road was clear. Zoe spun round and ran across to the far side. To her dismay, she heard more rustling ahead of her.

Don't say there's another one on this side, too.

She felt pinned, caught between two enemies. She glanced left and right, but there was nothing and no one to protect her on the lonely road.

On the far verge, the wild boar appeared, its muscular shoulders and pinched face preceded by sharp, curving tusks. She wondered if the animal had good eyesight. She stood as still as she was able, anxious about the second creature that was rootling about behind her, equally close. Then, she felt her muscles tighten, involuntarily, as the nocturnal *sanglier* met her gaze.

Obviously, it has excellent night vision and it knows precisely where I am.

All at once, there was a commotion round her feet and a scuffling of tiny legs. A barrel-shaped body with close white fur brushed past her ankle and let off a volley of angry, fearless yapping.

It was Russell, of course, who must have followed her at a polite distance, down through the town and out across the sunflower fields and the vineyards.

Zoe had never seen the terrier so focused or energetic, determined to face down a wild animal more than ten times his size and – surely – twenty times his strength. The yapping continued, high-pitched and insistent. The wild boar was no longer interested in Zoe. All of its attention was focused on the source of the racket: a small dog with ideas above its station.

The boar pawed the ground, a horrible grating sound, like fingernails on a blackboard, edging closer, preparing to strike.

A sudden glare of headlights broke in, a vehicle cresting the brow of the dip in the road where the minibus had disappeared. For a second or two the vehicle itself would remain out of sight, but it would soon be upon them. There was a moment of stand-off, none of them knowing what to do. Russell became silent, but still unwilling to abandon his post as Zoe's defender, close to the white line in the centre of the road. The boar shook its bristly cheeks.

The vehicle crested the rise. Frightened by this overbright, human-made intrusion into the natural, moonlit world, the wild boar turned tail and ran. Emboldened by his victory, Russell jumped and danced in triumph.

With the onrushing vehicle almost upon them, Zoe strode forward, snatched him up and ran back to the verge, just as it surged past – a large white van being driven unnecessarily fast in the darkness of the unlit rural highway.

'Thank you, Russell. You're my hero, but also – what were you thinking?'

Tucked in her arms, surprisingly still and not struggling against being held, the terrier's only response was to quietly lick her cheek.

Fifteen

COLLECTING CLUES

Disappointingly, on the promised day, Renée the Renault van wasn't repaired or even investigated. There was some kind of autumn lurgy going round, meaning that both mechanics – Frank and his boss – were off, sniffling and sorry for themselves in their sick beds.

I feel a little trapped without a vehicle. On the other hand, I've not been anywhere – on a bus or taxi – in part because I don't want to have to tell Antoine my movements.

She saw the *brigadier* going past in the square and ran out to ask him, as discreetly as possible, if there was any news. His eyes shifty and unforthcoming, he didn't answer her directly. Instead, he reiterated his request – command, perhaps? – that she should 'keep him apprised of her movements'.

Frustrated, Zoe browsed a few of the tourist stalls selling novelties and local crafts, with an eye on the open door of her shop. She did her best to be friendly, but received little encouragement. She became more and more convinced that Babara Ercollani's death had sullied her reputation.

I remain a stranger to these people.

On her way back, she overheard Antoine chatting with the estate agent – a loud man with tightly curled grey hair and big teeth, called Ambroise Caille – and learned that both of them were hunters and had recently been out, after dark, looking for wild boar.

I'd really like to ask who else took part but I don't dare come across as too inquisitive – or defensive.

She wasn't certain why hunting felt important. She pictured the quiet of the countryside disturbed by human activity in the darkness, with barely any passers-by to observe what happened.

What else goes on in those lonely hills? Is it possible that Barbara Ercollani knew?

Then, because they hadn't noticed her presence, she overheard them discussing her, with Ambroise asking: 'Is she on the trail already? She has an intelligent look in her eye and far too innocent a smile.'

'That's what my sister thinks,' replied Antoine, 'that she is searching in secret.'

Unhappy at being the subject of this incomprehensible gossip, Zoe walked on.

As a response to the declining autumn trade, the market traders were in the habit of beginning to pack up much earlier. And, in another change to the rhythm of activities in the town, the Auberge Sainte-Catherine had closed its doors and shutters, stacked up its tables and chairs and hidden them beneath tattered grey tarpaulins. One day Patrick was there, vigorous and smiling, making her coffee and serving her a pastry in the morning or a *croque-monsieur* as a snatched lunch, the next he was gone.

It was another slow day in the shop. Those who did cross the threshold of *The Bookshop of My Dreams*, however, declared themselves delighted to find the charming nook where she invited them to sit and begin to enjoy the copies that she hoped they would buy.

This, though, created a new problem. If Zoe wasn't careful, these 'reading' editions would soon become too well-thumbed to be sold to anyone else. She toyed with the idea of installing a bookcase of volumes set aside specifically for people to browse, perhaps even allowing them to turn down the corners of pages or break the spines to make them easier to read – and as a way of distinguishing them from her 'new' stock.

But I absolutely can't do that. It would appear to put me in direct competition with Monsieur Etienne.

That wasn't really true but, since their confrontation, she had felt an earnest need to avoid any future unpleasantness.

Even if I'm not selling this 'reading' stock, it might seem as if I were.

Zoe checked the time and decided to pop back out and buy one or two groceries before the square emptied of stalls, even though she had customers. She spoke briefly to them – a pleasant family of English tourists, a mother and father and a three-year-old boy, sitting by the stove.

'I'll be no more than ten minutes. Stay where you are and enjoy the warmth.'

'Thank you,' said the mother, an intelligent, friendly-looking woman with short auburn hair. 'That would be lovely.'

Zoe bought olives, fresh bread and four bottles, two red and two white, from Marcel Maurice, then ran into Antoinette Grenelle, Antoine's sister, at Robert Petit's butcher's stall. She had barely spoken to the haberdasher since becoming aware of the odd feud between her and her brother. To make conversation and try and dissolve the invisible barrier between them, she asked Antoinette if she knew where Patrick had gone 'for his well-earned holidays' and when he might reopen the Auberge. It turned out she did.

'He's in Italy, on their Riviera, in a village nobody goes to because not many people know that it's there, down a very steep road to a sheltered cove, like in a story.'

'Does he have family there?'

'Perhaps. Why?'

'Because then he would be Italian and there seem to be a lot of Italian connections around here. Barbara, who died. Lucia, whose bookshop I bought. I know her second name was Jacquet, which is solidly French, but I've always assumed her Christian name must derive from a different heritage. And now Patrick.'

'That is normal.'

'How so?'

'The border isn't so far away and, in history, frontiers were more flexible than they are today.'

Zoe left a pause, then asked: 'You have decided not to be my enemy, then?'

'I told you. You cannot be friends with both my brother and with me.' For a second time, Antoinette gave her a wink and Maisie wondered what it was that she was not picking up on. The haberdasher's words seemed simultaneously serious and bantering. Then Antoinette added: 'But anyway, you cannot be friends with my brother while under suspicion, under investigation. Isn't that so?'

'Who says I am under investigation?'

Antoinette waved a hand, dismissively. 'It is well known. People are wary of you.'

Zoe's heart sank.

That's exactly what I feared.

'Please tell me, why did you and your brother fall out?'

'We did not fall out. We find ourselves on different sides, that's all.'

With a dismissive shake of her head, Antoinette bustled away.

I wish I understood what that means.

Zoe paid for the rotisserie chicken that was now her regular order, then found herself face to face with Denis Allard and, instinctively, recoiled – not because she had taken against the smaller and rounder of the two guest-house owners, but because he was clearly unwell. His eyes were red and running, as was – revoltingly – his nose. Encumbered by his market shopping, he was clumsily trying to use a large blue-and-white-checked handkerchief to stem the flow.

133

'Oh dear, Madame Pascal,' he spluttered. 'Don't come too close. I'm sure it's not serious but, all the same . . .'

'Please, call me Zoe. Have you had it long?'

'Almost a week.'

'Then I expect you're not infectious any longer.'

'Poor Mrs Ercollani died and left it for me – that's what I think.'

He desperately wants everyone to believe Barbara was ill. Why?

'Is Davide suffering, too?'

'No.' Denis sniffed. 'Davide is never ill. And I've people coming and not enough room for them all.'

'Is Barbara's room still out of commission?'

'What do we do with her things? That's what I'd like to know. It gives me the shivers, thinking about it, having to collect up her bits and pieces, packing her suitcases.'

'You mean everything is just as she left it?' asked Zoe.

'Worse,' he said mournfully, once again wiping his nose. 'The police turned it all upside down.'

'No one has been in touch since?'

'She must have been all alone in the world.' He paused to give a good wet blow, before continuing: 'You knew her, didn't you? I don't suppose you might . . .'

He left an implied question hanging. Zoe wasn't sure what it was.

'Let me just say, for clarity, that I didn't know her well. What is it you want help with?'

'Packing her things up and, perhaps, storing them?'

That's a surprise. I'd like to be helpful but is this something I ought to do?

'I understand you feeling uncomfortable,' she told him. 'Does Davide feel the same way?'

'No, he's nowhere near as squeamish as I am, but he's not here this week.'

'Is he on holiday?'

'A holiday from me, perhaps,' said Denis with a self-deprecating smile. 'He plays the violin, you know. Perhaps you don't, though? There's a local chamber band and he is one of the leading lights. At this time of year, they go from village to village. It's a tradition.'

'Folk music or classical?'

'Old local tunes, like at the *fête de Saint-Bertrand*.' Denis sneezed and Zoe took a precautionary step back. He went on. 'Only the better musicians. And, of course there's the Vulture. Anyway, I stay home to mind the guest house.'

Zoe didn't know what he meant by that or by 'vulture'. From the way he said, it, she wondered if she should think of it with a capital 'V'.

Perhaps a performance venue? The Verdon nature park is famous for its birds of prey so it wouldn't be surprising to find that there's a concert hall named after one.

'To be clear, you'd like me to come and tidy away Barbara's things. Do you have permission from the police?'

'I suppose I should have asked that shambling Inspector Sicarie, over from Aix-en-Provence, but he gives me the heebie-jeebies.'

'Did Inspector Sicarie find anything of interest?' she asked, not wanting to look like she was prying, but intrigued all the same.

'I don't know. He wouldn't tell me. Will you help? Please say you will. I would be so grateful. I shudder each time I go past her door. And you were her friend. The inspector was very interested when I told him that.'

Oh, dear, Denis. I wish you hadn't, but it might help to have a look at her bits and pieces and understand more about her. I'm worried her death will somehow come back to bite me. Denis seems to be telling people that I knew her well. If there is to be an investigation, I would rather be on the inside than the outside.

Zoe came to a decision.

'All right. I'll come as soon as I've closed up.'

She returned to the bookshop. The English tourist father – who had thick hair tied back in a ponytail and tattoos peeking out from beneath his clothes – was reading to his little boy from a large-format illustrated book about trucks and diggers. Because the text was in French, the man was having to improvise – and was doing so delightfully. The mother, clearly having a break from parenting duties, was entirely absorbed in a contemporary English novel, a murder mystery by the celebrated author and screenwriter Anthony Horowitz.

It was getting past teatime. Despite her decision to do Denis a favour and tidy the belongings of the late Barbara Ercollani, Zoe didn't like to send them on their way.

They seem so happy and . . . What's the word? Yes, rested.

She had an intuition that the couple's holiday with a small child was proving exhausting. She decided to pop out for five minutes and have a look at the room Barbara had inhabited, then go back once she knew the lie of the land. She put this to the mother who immediately insisted that they couldn't presume any longer on her hospitality.

'We've been here for almost an hour already,' said the mother. 'But I'd like both of these books, please.'

She showed Zoe the novel – that she was well into, at least fifty pages – and an illustrated book of pictorial riddles, based on the landscape of the Verdon nature park called *Au Pays des Vautours*, meaning *In the Land of Vultures*. It was one of Zoe's most consistent sellers and she hadn't got to the bottom of why so many people wanted it. It reminded her of Denis's unexplained remark that she had heard as: '*And, of course, there's the Vulture.*' She decided she ought to have a closer look at another copy.

I'll do it later this evening.

The father added: 'And these two.' He showed her a field guide to local trees, native and imported, as well as the child's picture book. 'And perhaps we might come back when we are next in Sainte-Catherine?'

'You are staying locally?'

'We're nomads in our Mazda Bongo. It was a treat to be able to relax by your stove.'

'Of course. Please do.'

Zoe rang up the sales and they went out into the square, the little boy running ahead, kicking the crisp leaves. Zoe stood at the door, watching the parents hanging back, comparing images from the tree guide and the riddle book, looking very focused and interested.

I wonder what that's about.

Zoe shut the door and made everything tidy – which only took five minutes because of the slowness of trade – put on her ski jacket and followed them out, carefully locking up behind her. As she hurried past the few remaining stallholders, packing away their things into the toy-town-style vehicles that were the only ones capable of climbing up through the narrow streets, she thought about buying a coffee machine.

I don't want to step on anyone's toes but, all the time the Auberge is shut, it would be fair enough for me to provide hot drinks. And it would help make my bookshop a destination.

She arrived at the guest house, tucked into the cul-de-sac on the hairpin bend of the cobbled street, and knocked on the door. From beyond it, she heard dragging feet, then Denis opened up, looking blurry and confused.

'I am here, as promised,' she told him.

'Yes, yes,' he replied vaguely.

'You do look poorly.'

'I've not been sleeping. I dropped off. Do you know where you're going – first floor, door on the right?'

She gave him a smile and climbed the stairs, made of very dark wood with prominent knots and twists in the grain. The treads were all slightly misshapen – or, rather, they had more natural shapes than plain sawn timber. Zoe wondered if the guest house was even older then her bookshop.

Or perhaps the same age. That would make sense for the heart of the village.

On the landing, she hesitated. The door was firmly closed, as if something shameful was concealed inside. She turned the handle – an old-fashioned iron one, a sort of hollow knot of strands of metal, sharp in her fingers – and stepped inside.

Denis had spoken the truth. The room was a mess. A large old-fashioned wardrobe had been partly emptied on the bed, a quantity of Barbara's clothes tossed down, still on their hangers. The ones remaining on the rail were hanging askew. Some of the pockets had been turned out, the linings visible like Russell's sad, turned-back ear. Three suitcases could be seen, a small one on the writing table beneath the window, a large one on a low piece of furniture designed for that purpose, and a medium-sized one in the middle of the floor. The lids were all propped open, revealing disordered contents.

Because the room was fairly large, it also accommodated a small chest of drawers. Clearly, the contents of Barbara's three suitcases had been difficult to stuff into this modest piece of furniture, made of lovely golden pine, because the drawers were overflowing.

Or perhaps that's because the police disturbed everything and didn't bother to fold her clothes up and put them back nicely.

Either side of the bed were two small nightstands, little cupboards that didn't match one another, although both were made of similar dark-stained wood. The books Barbara had bought from Zoe we're on top of the left-hand cabinet. She picked up the top one and found the spine broken, with many of the pages turned down, not just the corners but large triangles that seemed to point to items within the text.

Odd.

Another book was the one that the English mother had chosen, that her French distributor had recommended as likely to provide consistent sales, the illustrated book entitled

In the Land of Vultures, held open with the compass Zoe had seen in Barbara's hand in the square at night. It made Zoe suddenly suspicious of the English 'van nomads'.

Is this a coincidence or is there something more to it? How many people – locals and visitors combined – did poor Barbara have reason to fear?

Zoe realised that, from a kind of accumulation of details – above all the police investigation for which she seemed inexplicably to be a target – she had reached a firm conclusion.

There can be no doubt. The weight of evidence says poor Barbara was murdered.

Sixteen

THREE UNSETTLING ENCOUNTERS

Zoe left Barabara Ercollani's abandoned bedroom and found Denis in his kitchen, with his head under a towel over a bowl of steaming mentholated water. Once she'd got his attention, he told her: 'I'm trying to clear my tubes.'

'Denis, I've thought about it and I can't tidy Barbara's room today. I have to ask Antoine and make sure it's not the wrong thing to do, but I promise I'll come back tomorrow if he says "yes". Is that all right?'

'I'd be so grateful,' he told her.

'Fingers crossed, then.'

She returned to the bookshop and put a couple more logs in the stove, then fetched her vacuum cleaner from the tall cupboard in the kitchen to gather up the ash that had spilt on its slab of stone. That done, she sat down and watched the flames for a while, daydreaming about starting a book club or a reading group.

What about a writing group, as well? Maybe I should go into partnership with Denis and Davide and set up creative holidays.

She went to search the shelves where the local guide books were located and found that the copy of the illustrated book that she had sold to the young English family had been her last.

That's a shame.

Wishing she had brought Barbara's copy home with her, she went upstairs to the kitchen and made herself a delicious chicken sandwich with a good length of baguette, adding thin slices of salty black olives as a garnish, plus a few shavings of strongly flavoured red onion from the bottom of the fridge, using mustard mayonnaise instead of butter. She ate her lip-smacking dinner in front of the stove with her second Fred Vargas novel in her spare hand, a story about wolves inhabiting a Provençal landscape and a murderer who used their frightening presence as a smokescreen for his crimes. It was called *L'homme à l'envers*, meaning something like 'the upside-down man' or 'the backwards man', which she didn't think worked in English.

Having finished her sandwich, she heard Russell scraping at the door and let him in, discovering his paws were muddy from digging. She rubbed them clean with the old towel she kept under the counter, then dragged his bed in front of the stove for him to lie in. Studiously, he ignored it, curling himself up on the floorboards alongside.

Zoe returned to her novel, but became distracted by the idea of buying a reading lamp or two that could be positioned between the armchairs, so as not to have to use the many little LED ceiling lights when the shop was closed. Then she refocused and pressed on to the denouement of *The Upside-Down Man*, finding herself stiff from immobility when, finally, she got up to go to bed. From the bathroom, brushing her teeth, she heard Russell's surreptitious pitter-patter on the stairs and decided not to send him back down.

What harm can it do? It's not as though I'm likely to be sharing my bed with anyone else.

That idea gave her a chill and she had to make an effort of will not to let herself once more doubt the wisdom of her decision to begin a new life in a remote southern-French hill town.

The absence of a phone signal isn't helping. Neither is poor Barbara's death – perhaps murder?

She told herself not to make assumptions.

Underneath it all, though, I believe I can be happy here, even without yet having lots and lots of friends. I just need to give it time.

*

The next day, Sunday, reasserted Zoe's sense of drift. A few people came in to browse but she made very few sales. After lunch, just as she was wondering whether to close up early, water the oleanders and go for a hike through the chilly fields, three men entered, speaking rapidly in German. They wore walking boots and weatherproof clothing, with ruck-sacks on their backs with detailed local maps in clear plastic pockets for ease of use, should it rain. Their baffling conversation was intense and focused as they searched the stacks, eventually ending up in the part of the bookshop where she displayed tourist information and local history and so on.

Having not found what they wanted, they approached her counter, still speaking intently to one another. She wondered if they might be brothers because they had a strong resemblance – or perhaps that was just a coincidence of their friendship. Though German wasn't a language that Zoe was fluent in, she did recognise the word '*Raubvogel*', meaning bird of prey, because they used it several times. Also, each had an embroidered patch sewn onto the left breast of their weatherproof jackets, an image of a vulture and the word '*Geier*', which Zoe assumed must be the German word for it.

There was a pause with none of them certain, it seemed, what to say. She smiled and asked them in French if she could help them. The tallest of the three asked, haltingly: '*Parlez Anglais?*'

'Yes, of course.'

'Picture book,' he said, enunciating carefully, 'with . . .' He frowned and tapped his embroidered patch. 'With "*Geier*", like this.'

'Vulture,' Zoe told him. 'No, I'm sorry. I sold my last copy yesterday.'

There was a pause while he took this in then translated for his two companions. They all had the slightly unkempt look of men who live solitary lives, their hair not particularly clean and very much unstyled.

'You know the picture book?' the tall one asked.

'I've sold plenty of copies but I've never read it.' She saw that she had spoken too fast, so she gestured to herself, shaking her head, and repeated: 'I have never read it.'

He nodded and translated for his companions: '*Sie hat es nicht gelesen.*'

One of the others replied: '*Sie kann uns nicht helfen.*'

This was not beyond Zoe's rudimentary German, meaning: 'She can't help us.'

'I will have a new delivery on Tuesday, in two days,' she told them. 'More books, in two days. You understand?'

'Ah, good. Two days. I come. But my friends go home.'

There followed a much more rapid conversation in German whose detail she couldn't follow but she understood that the leader was trying to convince his friends to stay on with him. More and more, Zoe wished she had paid attention to the picture book. She would have liked to know why it seemed so deeply to motivate people of very different backgrounds.

'I see you Tuesday, good,' the leader told her. 'For "*Geier*" book.'

'Vulture,' she reminded him.

'Yes, I learn. Spell please?' He took a card from his pocket for her to write on. It was inscribed: *Oskar Weiss, Der Wiesbadener Geocaching Club*.

'Geocaching,' said Zoe. 'That's looking for hidden things in the landscape, isn't it, following clues?' She made a broad gesture. 'And you are Oskar Weiss, from Wiesbaden?'

'*Ja, das stimmt,*' he told her. 'That's right.'

She wrote on the reverse of the card and showed it to him, repeating the word aloud: 'Vulture.'

He did the same, left her the card, then added, very formally: 'Thank you, madame.'

The three geocachers left, deep in conversation. Zoe was surprised to discover that the time was only two o'clock.

Just for once, I'm going to shut early. I need more physical exercise. I'm becoming a blob.

She turned off the strings of overhead LEDs, leaving just the desk lamp on her island counter and the pleasant glow from the stove towards the rear of the shop. She had just sat down in one of the leather club armchairs to change into her hiking boots when she heard the clang of the bell on its loop of steel.

'*J'arrive*,' she called, meaning: 'I'm coming'.

She laced up her second boot, behind and in front of her ankle, and hurried to her counter, finding a very unprepossessing man in a shabby overcoat, worn over a sagging cardigan and an unironed off-white shirt. He had come in without being invited – it was a shop, after all – and the German visitor's card was in his hand. He was frowning, as if it had surprised him somehow.

Or perhaps he's just interested that there are words in two languages, some printed and one handwritten, none of them French.

'I was about to close up on this quiet Sunday but,' she offered, 'if there's something particular you want, I'll do my best to help.'

Her visitor put down the card. His eyes were dark and suspicious, his brows wiry and long. The expression on his face wasn't friendly.

'What I want,' he told her, 'is you.'

*

By this time, Oskar Weiss and his two companions were already in their hire car, heading south towards Marseille. Oskar was driving because he was the leader – of the geocaching club, of the holiday organisation, of the friendship group. Sometimes he wondered why the others followed him so readily.

Because they have nothing else in their lives?

Oskar was glad he would soon be alone. He knew himself to be very close to finding the '*Geier*', the Vulture.

That is a word I know in English. Why did I forget it?

The reasons were simple – the excitement of the chase, the disconcerting presence of the attractive bookshop owner.

Once the others go home, I will return to Sainte-Catherine. There is no reason for me to share the prize.

He thought about what the woman might know, remembering his friend's remark.

'*Sie kann uns nicht helfen.*'

He pursed his lips, navigating a tight roundabout.

Maybe that was a lie. Or she can help us – help me – but she doesn't know it yet.

*

A little later, once the policeman had gone, Zoe wished that she had told off 'the inspector from Aix' – the same officer who had so unimpressed Caroline – for his cryptic remark.

'*What I want,*' he had told her, '*is you.*'

It had caused a surge of adrenaline to course through her, so much did his words remind her of the sort of thing a serial killer might say in a thriller.

His visit was intimidating and they didn't leave the island counter. He had brought with him the statement Zoe had made for Antoine and he took her through it, line by line, asking her detailed questions about the sequence of events, ending up with a final enquiry about something that had remained lodged in Zoe's subconscious, too.

'You do not believe Madame Ercollani was ill?'

'I didn't, but I'm no longer sure.' This answer seemed to satisfy him and he nodded and turned to go. Zoe rebuked him: 'You realise you haven't bothered to tell me your name?'

'Sicarie,' he told her, then spelled it, letter by letter.

'Yes, I knew that. Denis Allard told me. Perhaps I ought to mention that he has asked me to help tidy Madame Ercollani's things. Is there any reason, from the point of view of the police, why I shouldn't?'

He gave her a distrustful look, half turned in the act of leaving.

'Why would you do that?'

'As a favour to him. He's unwell and the fact of her clothes remaining all strewn about the room upsets him.'

'What does that have to do with you, though, who claim not to have known Madame Ercollani well? Are you not a stranger to Sainte-Catherine?'

Zoe was aware that she wanted to do it in part because she felt lonely and needed friends, but she said: 'It's a neighbourly thing to do. Davide Quillan, his partner in the business, is away. I like to help people.'

'It seems an imposition.' He contemplated her, still half turned, his eyes shadowed by his wiry, dark brows. His skin was dark, too, and she assumed he was of Mediterranean heritage, short and stocky. 'Do you frequently allow yourself to be drawn into other people's lives?'

'You appear to be judging me on very short acquaintance.'

'It was a question, not an accusation.'

Zoe knew she had become defensive, but couldn't stop herself.

'Well,' she asked, 'am I allowed to help?'

'By all means, go and be neighbourly. The police have no objection.'

With that, he left. Zoe ran upstairs to fetch her ski jacket then hurried downstairs, wanting to see where he went next. By the time she had gone outside and locked the front door, however, he was out of sight beyond the final market traders, dismantling their stalls.

Zoe crossed the square and descended Rue des Templiers to the guest house. To her surprise, she met Davide Quillan at the front door. He looked weary from his musical tour, with a violin case in one hand and another longer, thinner bag in the other. Zoe explained why she was there and he told her there was no need.

'I'll deal with it,' he told her, firmly. 'The last date on our tour was cancelled because of a problem with the hall and I am returned.'

'Are you sure? Denis was very keen that I—'

He interrupted with a sigh. 'It's too much of an imposition. I don't know why he's got so het up about it. When I'm away with the Vultures, he lets things get on top of him.'

Zoe remembered seeing the name on the side of the minibus that had passed her in the night.

'Why are you called "The Vultures"? I keep hearing about birds of prey one way and another.'

'The Verdon nature park is famous for them, especially in the area around the gorges, with the torrents out of the mountains and the celebrated rock-climbing places.'

'I need to read up some more on the history and geography of the area. I have an excellent guide book but I haven't got around to—'

'Yes, you ought to make that effort,' he told her with, she felt, a note of criticism.

'Even if I can't help, I wonder, could I pop up? There's a book I wanted to borrow, one that I sold to Madame Ercollani and I've been meaning to look at.' Davide gave her an inquisitive look and Zoe, for reasons that escaped her, decided to lie and not mention *In the Land of Vultures* by name. 'It's a romantic novel that she enjoyed very much, though I don't think it will be to my taste.'

'Go ahead,' he told her, with an air of not being able to think of a reason to refuse. 'Mind my suitcase in the hall.'

She went inside, catching a glimpse of Denis at the end of the ground-floor corridor, bent over his bowl of mentholated hot water, part-concealed by a towel. Davide's suitcase was at the foot of the stairs and open, with a small pile of clothes to one side, presumably ready for laundering.

So, this is his second trip up from the car park.

Zoe went upstairs and opened the first door on the right. She was struck by an intuition that the room looked different.

Is it tidier? Not exactly, but the things seem more piled up, less strewn about.

She went to the pile of books on the bedside table, expecting to find the large-format *In the Land of Vultures*. The compass that had held it open was there, but not the book. She bent down to look under the bed then picked up and put down several piles of clothes.

It's gone.

Davide appeared in the doorway.

'Can you not find it?' he asked.

'No, I mean, yes,' said Zoe quickly, picking up the 'spicy' novel, *Infinite Desire*, and showing it to him. 'Here it is. I really don't think it's for me, but it's useful in my business to know the sorts of things that people are buying.'

Zoe smiled. Davide didn't reply straight away. He had a hand on the door frame as if for balance.

Or to prevent me from leaving.

'I saw Inspector Sicarie in the square. Did he question you again?' he asked.

'For the first time, actually.'

His eyes narrowed as he waited for her to divulge further details. Zoe chose not to speak, holding his gaze. Eventually, he sighed and told her: 'I've had a very busy week. Would you mind very much . . . ?'

'Of course, I'm sorry to be disturbing you. Let me get out of your way.' Zoe couldn't do so immediately because he hadn't moved. That fact made her realise for the first time that Davide was a strongly built man, at least six inches – fifteen centimetres – taller than she. 'Will you excuse me?'

'What did Denis tell you?'

'In what regard?'

'About the Vulture.'

Again, it was obvious that he said it with a capital 'V'.

'Nothing – not even your band's name.'

Davide sighed again. 'Never mind.'

He stepped aside and Zoe left, out of the room onto the landing, brushing past him uncomfortably close, then down the stairs and outside into the bright afternoon, glad to have escaped from the oppressive atmosphere in the guest house.

Do I mean 'escape'? Isn't that foolishly melodramatic?

She walked away, down the hill towards Place Saint-Bertrand, putting the spicy novel in one of her large patch pockets.

No, I don't think it is. Davide wished me ill. Was it because he thought I was prying?

At the sight of the shut-up Auberge Sainte-Catherine, she stopped.

And, if he'd already been in with his suitcase before going back down to the car park for his musical instruments, then he easily had time to speak to Denis about me and go and hide Barbara's copy of In the Land of Vultures.

Seventeen

LUXURY – AT LAST

Having left Davide Quillan to his post-tour laundry and Denis Allard to his mentholated steam, Zoe was standing outside the shut-up Auberge Sainte-Catherine, thinking about the visit of the inspector of police.

I wish Julien Calmet had examined Barbara's body more closely. I would like to know what the police are doing. Have they decided there's nothing to investigate, that it's just a sad story of a fairly old woman's heart giving out on a cold evening when she'd been overdoing things? If so, I fear they are wrong. Barbara was here in Sainte-Marie for too long; her behaviour was too mysterious.

Vaguely, Zoe's eyes took in the windowsills of Le Gourmand, lit with little electric lamps in the shape of candle flames.

I'm sure Barbara looked done in, weary not ill. And perhaps confused?

Zoe's eyes became unfocused, all her attention on the sequence of thoughts inside her head.

I wonder how much I ought to be worried for my own sake. Inspector Sicarie was non-committal, but he took me through my statement with a keen eye for details. He wasn't obviously trying to trip me up, but it wasn't far from it.

With a start of surprise, she realised that she was blankly staring at the waitress she had seen working with Patrick on the evening of the procession of the effigy of Saint

Bertrand – the evening of Barbara's death. The waitress was in the doorway of the restaurant, gazing at her, a questioning expression in her eyes. She looked severe with a resemblance to the spooky central character in *The Woman in Black* that Zoe had seen with Maisie at the Fortune Theatre in London.

'Good afternoon. My name is Pascal, Zoe Pascal. We've not been introduced. I've taken over the bookshop.'

'I know. Would you like to come in? The lunchtime service runs late on Sundays.'

Zoe was about to refuse. Her intention – inspired by an austere idea that it would be good for her – had been to go for a hike and get her blood pumping. But, now that she was faced with the choice, she felt much more inclined to revel in the prospect of a splendid meal, eaten in blissful solitude, without interruption from either the clanging doorbell of the bookshop or the distressing repercussions of Barbara Ercollani's unexplained death.

'I would be delighted. Thank you.'

The waitress stepped aside so that Zoe could precede her indoors. Le Gourmand was low-ceilinged with dark-stained beams only just above head height. There were three couples having a late lunch, all of them strangers to Zoe. In the centre of the room was a fireplace, open both sides, under a substantial chimney.

Zoe took off her ski jacket and was shown to a table by one of the front windows through which – past its imitation candle – she saw Inspector Sicarie go by in conversation with Antoine. The waitress returned with a bottle of filtered water. Zoe was about to place an order for a small carafe of house wine, when she was informed that there were 'pairings' – in other words particular wines, served at the chef's discretion, with each dish.

'So, I should order the food first?'

'Yes, that's right.'

Zoe had already scanned the menu, so she did what she often did, hoping it wouldn't give offence.

'I'd like two starters, please, the medley of autumn vegetables with smoked salmon and pickled courgettes, and the parmesan *panna cotta* with herb salad and preserved tomatoes.'

'The wine recommended with those choices would be the Maurice Marbrières.'

'What's that like?'

'A noble white, very crisp and dry, made from Cinsault grapes that enjoy the harsh ground of the *marbrière*, where marble was once extracted.'

'And it's from Marcel Maurice?'

'Yes, that's right.'

'Splendid. That sounds perfect.'

The waitress glided away – very much like 'the woman in black' – to communicate her order to the chef, leaving Zoe to contemplate a tall glass containing six or seven hand-made breadsticks flavoured with rosemary and crystals of salt. Her hand strayed to them, then she told herself to wait, turning her attention to the flames in the fireplace, busy consuming a pile of twisted prunings from old vines, known as '*souches*', very sought after for barbecues and the like because the wood was very hard and burnt for a long time.

A feeling of peace came over her and she realised that this would be the first time she had properly treated herself. Every day since her arrival in Sainte-Catherine, with the removal men following her down through France, she had maintained a steely focus on her project: to make a success of her new life. And, because of the precarity of the idea of making a living from a bookshop in a relatively isolated Provençal hill town – as Caroline Robin never hesitated to remind her – she had made a point of shopping economically, religiously turning off unnecessary lights, and generally behaving as if . . .

Well, as if I'm on my uppers, when I'm actually not.

Zoe gave in and nibbled the end of one of the breadsticks, finding it delicious. Luckily, before she overdid it, the waitress brought out her two starters and Zoe attacked them with gusto, finding each flavour more freshly satisfying than the last. The pickled courgettes were tangy without having lost the lovely earthy savour of the vegetables themselves. The salmon tasted of fish as well as the smokehouse. The medley of salad leaves and herbs included some delightful edible flowers. The autumn vegetables were crisp, even though they had been parboiled then braised with butter and salt and pepper. Between mouthfuls, she had to remind herself to sip her superb dry white wine, its complex flavours excited and enlivened by the food.

Zoe emptied her two small starter plates in what seemed to her an indecently brief lapse of time. She put her knife and fork together and sat back, delighted with her choices. The waitress asked if she would like to see the menu for a dessert and she said yes and ordered a second glass of wine, but was told – once again – that the correct vintage would be brought once she had selected her next course.

Zoe contemplated her choices: caramelised hazelnuts with poached peach and apricot, plus broken muscovado biscuits; a chocolate mousse with praline 'leaves', whatever that might mean; a grapefruit supreme with coffee-flavoured cream. In the end, with an apologetic smile, she chose the plate of seasonal cheeses.

'The recommendation is for another Maurice wine, made principally from the Carignan grape, also adapted to poor soils.'

'Is the land hereabouts not good for vines?'

'That depends on the *viticulteur*,' said the waitress. 'Marcel is one of the best.'

She slipped away again and didn't return for some time because two of the other three tables wanted their bills. Zoe allowed her mind to wander, less anxious now because her body had been warmed by the wine and the excellent food. She felt her breathing slow, as if she had finally accepted the rhythm of a sleepy Sunday afternoon. Her eyes became heavy and it was a shock when the waitress was back at her elbow with a dark slate on which three sperate cheeses sat, each in perfect condition to be eaten today or, at the very latest, tomorrow.

'This is a Banon,' the waitress told her, pointing, 'named after a small village in the mountains, from which it comes. It's fairly soft with a natural crust and must always be matured wrapped in chestnut leaves, which is unique to this region.' She indicated another. 'This is a Cabrioulet, much stronger-flavoured, made from goat's milk and allowed to mature. This last is a Brousse, goat's milk once more, but only two days old. The Brousse can only be made from goat's milk from a particular local breed, the Rove.' The waitress smiled. 'It's my favourite.'

'That all sounds marvellous.'

The waitress indicated the glass of wine she had also brought.

'Some find this wine a little overpowering, but it pairs well with all three cheeses.'

'Thank you.'

Zoe tried each in turn, using the neutral black crackers served alongside, finding each one more delicious than the last. Because she had already devoured her two starters, she managed to take her time, thinking about how food and drink were a kind of ritual pleasure in France – not always but quite often – rather than just a response to the obligation to refuel, like putting petrol in a car.

Thinking of fuel, she was again struck by the sinister suspicion about what Napoléon Etienne might have done that she had pushed to the back of her mind, awaiting the news from the Total garage.

I must remember to go down and ask the mechanics tomorrow morning.

The third couple got up and paid, meaning the restaurant was now empty, apart from her. The fire had burnt down and the waitress didn't show any sign of wanting to stoke it up. Zoe wondered if perhaps that was it for the day, that the restaurant would soon close and not reopen in the evening.

She finished her cheeses, making sure she had a tiny sip of the excellent red wine to complete the 'ritual'. Then the waitress was at her elbow, wondering if she needed 'coffee to finish'.

'No, thank you.' Zoe frowned, feeling a little tipsy. 'I don't remember if I introduced myself—'

The waitress didn't let her finish.

'You are Madame Pascal and you have reopened the bookshop. Everyone is very pleased.'

'Oh, good. Thank you. I'm afraid I don't know your name.'

'Simouno Simone.' Seeing Zoe frown, she spelled it and explained: 'Simouno is the Provençal version of Simone, a name my parents liked very much. My husband, in the kitchen, is Quentin Simone, because he was a fifth child, and I have ended up Simouno Simone.'

'I see,' said Zoe, sharing her smile. 'How interesting. Well, it's a lovely name.'

'Will there be anything more?'

Zoe realised that the time had definitely come for her to go. From outside in the street, she heard a church bell begin to chime.

'Is that an afternoon service?'

'Vespers,' said Simouno Simone. 'Will you be attending?'

'Yes,' said Zoe, on a whim. 'I think perhaps I will.'

'Then I will see you there,' said Simouno, patiently.

'Yes, of course. Please bring me my bill.'

The waitress already had it to hand. Zoe paid with her bank card, experiencing a small internal shudder of shock at just how far she had gone, financially speaking, in extravagantly treating herself. She stood up and pushed her arms into the sleeves of her ski jacket and went out into the street.

Sainte-Catherine was a picture, the biscuit-coloured houses and red-clay roofs profiled against the fading light of an autumn afternoon, the sky painted with mauve and orange, as well as the traditional gorgeous blue of southern France.

A family went past, looking like two grandparents and three grandchildren, dressed smartly for church. Zoe fell in behind them, climbing the cobbled street to the threshold of the octagonal house of worship. Father Julien Calmet was at the door, greeting his parishioners with warmth, each one by name. When he recognised Zoe, his eyes revealed surprise and . . .

What is that expression? I think I've caught him on the hop by being here. Does that mean that he suspects me of wrongdoing, too? Or has he got guilty secrets of his own?

Eighteen

An Unexpected Social Call

The ritual of an excellent late Sunday lunch at Le Gourmand had made Zoe feel better about herself – and about the slow start she had made, integrating into Sainte-Catherine. She entered the church, her eyes going automatically to the place on the stone-flagged floor where Barbara Ercollani's crumpled body had lain.

Abruptly, her sense of well-being vanished.

Oh dear, I wish I hadn't come. This feels like a mistake.

Then, to her surprise, the church ritual did her good too. The language of religion was comforting, with its heightened patterns of speech and sonorous cadences. The vespers service was short, only half an hour. The image of Barbara Ercollani's broken body was cleansed from her mind by the sequence of devotional words: a psalm, announced as 'number twenty-nine', giving thanks for God's strength in combat with ill-defined enemies and unspecified disasters; a prayer that appealed for God's assistance in the troubles of life; another that was an acknowledgement of His permanence; a hymn about joy and light; then a second psalm, number thirty-one, about the relief and happiness that flow from repentance and absolution.

Zoe enjoyed the fact that everyone seemed able to join in, even the smaller children, carried along by the tide of words. Pretty much everyone she knew was there: Marcel with his nephew Thierry; Antoine and Antoinette, on opposite sides of the congregation; Robert Petit, the butcher, with three children and a vivacious-looking wife; Denis Allard, looking a little better, and Davide Quillan who Zoe thought nodded off briefly in the second psalm; Gato and Lali Merino with a dark-haired, robust woman who looked inadequately dressed for the season in a floral-print dress and a thin cardigan; Napoléon Etienne who seemed ill at ease and unable to meet Zoe's eye; the elderly vet, Firmin Séchan, who had given Russell his jabs and talked about how much he had liked her predecessor, Lucia Jacquet; Simouno Simone, who had effected a quick change from her plain black waitressing outfit into a very chic two-piece suit. As far as Zoé could see, her husband, Quentin Simone, wasn't present.

Father Julien Calmet was an impressive preacher, lending depth and conviction to every phrase. He recited by heart a passage about the congregation's faith being tested by all kinds of challenges, to which the assembled townspeople replied, as one: 'You are the Way, the Truth and the Life.' There was no sermon as such and this response was followed by a brief closing statement in which Julien, his gaunt features very still and determined above the pristine white of his ceremonial garb, sent them back out into the world with the assurance that God would always be with them: 'His grace is infinite, His forgiveness also, for centuries and centuries.'

And that was that. The church cleared quickly, without Father Julien moving to the door to shake everyone's hands, as Zoe had expected. Happy in her own head and not wanting to get drawn in to any conversations, Zoe stayed where she was, on a wooden chair with a rush seat, allowing the others to disperse. Old Firmin Séchan, however, came to ask about Russell.

'He's a lovable scamp, I'd wager,' he told her.

'Yes, but very intelligent, too.'

'You can't beat a terrier. Don't forget his booster jabs. Good evening to you.'

Zoe stood up to follow him out, the last to leave. Aware of another presence close behind, she turned to see Julien Calmet, on the verge of speech.

'Good evening,' she said. 'That was a beautifully delivered service.'

'Thank you. I observed you following but not fully joining in. Did it seem very foreign?'

'Yes and no.'

'Are you a believer?' he asked her lightly. 'Either Catholic or Protestant?'

'No, not as such, but I admire the way the church brings people together to contemplate things greater than themselves.'

'That's very well put.' He left a short pause, during which Firmin Séchan slowly exited the Templar church, leaving them alone. He surprised her by saying: 'I have no more duties on this chilly Sunday. Would you enjoy a glass of port?'

Zoe smiled and laughed.

'No, I wouldn't, too sweet, but that's very kind. Can I, instead, offer you a glass of Maurice wine by my new stove? You would be the very first.'

'You haven't yet made many firm friends?' he asked, surprising her for a second time.

'Why would you say that?'

'Forgive me. That was presumptuous.' He gestured to his ecclesiastical regalia. 'It is a habit of this role.'

'I am self-sufficient and do not need to be saved,' she told him, deliberately echoing the language of the church service, but still smiling so he knew that she wasn't being facetious. 'I appreciate you asking.'

'Then I would be delighted to see your new stove. It will take me a few minutes to disrobe.'

'You know where to find me.'

Zoe exited the church with a puzzled frown on her face, remembering Caroline's cryptic remarks about Julien Calmet: '*I think it's a shame that such a fine figure of a man with* such an interesting face should cloister himself away from the world.'

Zoe had replied: *'Good heavens, you're interested in him?'*

Caroline's response had been more interesting still: *'One cannot be interested in a priest, Zoe. This is not the Church of England. There are rules that may not be broken for such a man. Which is, perhaps, a part of his attraction.'*

★

The burglar – now, of course, a murderer, too – was very close. Frustrated by the memory of pointlessly rifling and vandalising Caroline Robin's office – because the locks of the bookshop had been changed too soon – they were strolling through the square, among the dispersing congregation, without the need for a disguise. Their presence wasn't especially remarkable.

Where is Madame Pascal? I didn't miss her, did I?

As the inhabitants of Sainte-Catherine returned to their homes, the murderer found a place of concealment, in the alleyway between the butcher and the estate agent, in shadow, behind two tall rubbish bins. The position provided a view of both the door of the church and of the bookshop.

Ah, there she is.

★

Russell was once again waiting for Zoe, looking droopy and sad on the doormat, as if he resented her absence but expected nothing better. She let him in and he perked up and went straight to his bowl of dry kibble.

Although Zoe had been out for more than two hours, the stove was still slowly burning, damped right down, turning the logs to charcoal. She opened the door and the flames surged up, making her lean back from the blast of hot air. She placed two more carefully on top of the embers and left the door open because the glass was black with soot, making it less joyful to sit beside if it was closed.

She put her ski jacket on the coat stand and went upstairs to the kitchen for the bottle of white wine from the door of the fridge. It was about two-thirds full. Happily, there was another alongside should they need it.

When she got back downstairs, she saw her own reflection in the front window, the one that gave on to the square.

I hope he's not coming because he feels sorry for me and is taking pity, out of a sense of duty.

For a moment or two, she thought about getting changed out of the clothes she had chosen for her aborted hike, then decided against it.

I would feel foolish if he noticed – which he inevitably would. He's a noticing sort of person.

Abruptly, her reflection in the window glass was replaced by the gaunt features of Julien Calmet approaching beneath the gentle street lamps. She waved and went to open the door, finding him already on the mat, his hand extended, about to let himself in. The impression of presumption was so clear that he apologised.

'I'm so sorry. I was behaving as if I had the right to enter, as if I was visiting a bookshop, rather than your home.'

'Never mind. In the daytime, people are supposed to just come in unannounced.'

She stepped aside and he immediately enthused about what he called 'the rejuvenation'. He admired the improved lighting, the spotless floorboards, the dust-free shelves. When he saw the reading nook by the stove, he became positively effusive.

'This is a wonderful *cantou*,' he told her, using a Provençal word that she knew could be translated as something like 'cosy corner'. 'You've been very clever, making the deepest, darkest, least propitious area of the shop a destination. But how will you ever get people to leave?'

'I suppose, generally speaking, I don't want them to, until closing time, that is.'

'This would be the most wonderful spot for my Bible classes.' He corrected himself. 'No, not classes. We discuss scripture but not in a didactic way – in order to give form and shape to our lives.'

'How interesting.' Zoe wondered if that was something she might want in her shop and if there could be a significant market for devotional books alongside the other self-help and wellness volumes that were an important part of her turnover. 'Are you seriously asking if that might be possible?'

'Oh, the idea just popped into my head,' he told her. 'I shouldn't be asking you to think about work when this was supposed to be a social call. You are doing me a favour.'

'In what way?'

'Like many people, I find Sunday evenings difficult.'

'For most, that's because their brief leisure is over and they have to refocus on work, whereas for you—'

'True,' he interrupted. 'Sunday is a working day. Perhaps because of that, my duties done, I experience a sense of emptiness.'

'That makes complete sense,' said Zoe, although surprised at the admission. 'Did you ever feel that before you were ordained, when you were a doctor?'

'Caroline told you that about me?'

'She did.'

'Yes. As I said, many people detest Sunday evenings.'

'Why did you change direction in life?'

'Not so much a change, as a resumption. Early in life, I trained for the priesthood, then switched to medicine. After a fairly successful career, I had a *crise nerveuse*, what the Anglo-Saxons call a "nervous breakdown".' He spoke the English words carefully with a reasonable accent. 'I was driven, you see, only satisfied when striving, unable to switch off. The breakdown was purely physical, if you follow me, but it had psychological sequels.' He stopped. 'Am I being boring?'

'Not at all.'

'Or perhaps you are simply kind.' He explained himself further. 'After the *crise*, I no longer felt the same sense of purpose. Somehow, I couldn't shake the idea that, if I couldn't be a kind of medical superman, what was the point of anything?'

'And that led you back to the church?'

'To God,' he told her. 'The church is just a way of framing our perception of the infinite.'

'To repeat your earlier compliment, that's very cleverly put. I'm not being a very good host, am I? Can I serve you a glass of white wine?'

Julien Calmet laughed and it sounded very natural and unforced. 'I thought you'd never ask.'

Zoe was finding Julien surprisingly easy to talk to. The unexpectedly intimate revelations with which their conversation had begun didn't then make it difficult to discuss more mundane matters, such as her acquisition of a stray dog, the breakdown of Renée the Renault van, her delightful lunch at Le Gourmand, the hunters in the hills. In turn, he gave her more insight into how he knew Caroline – from professional circles in Aix where he had practised medicine – and a little of the history of *La Librairie de Mes Rêves*.

'Lucia Jacquet was an unhappy woman, one of those unprepared for widowhood.'

'Oh, I didn't know she was bereaved.'

'The business was her husband's and, when he died, she struggled on, but she didn't really know what she was doing. He had never shared his expertise. I don't think she liked books.'

'That won't do. People who like books like people who like books. It's central to why customers come to me or any other bookshop like mine, rather than just buying what the supermarket stocks – or the internet.'

'Your offer to buy the business came as a blessing, she told me. She was on tenterhooks until it was all signed and sealed.'

'Where is she now?'

'She moved back to her people. I believe she is happy there. She wrote twice and I replied, then she didn't write again.'

Zoe frowned and asked: 'There isn't some kind of mystery about her, is there?'

'In what way?' he asked, looking interested.

'There's nothing more to her departure than not making a success of the bookshop? How did she become widowed?'

'Her husband was a hunter. He went out alone – which is unwise – and was gored by a wild boar, severing the femoral artery in his right thigh. He would have bled out in just a few minutes. He was not found for several days. No one knew where to look.'

'Poor man,' said Zoe, not sharing the details of her own close shave with a *sanglier*. 'Poor Lucia.'

'Indeed, but was there some other element of mystery you were hinting at?'

'It's very vague, just something about the fact that Barbara Ercollani was Italian or of Italian descent or married to an Italian and so, I supposed, was Lucia Jacquet. Where are "her people" as you described them?'

'Saint-Raphaël, closer to the Italian border. I don't understand, though. Lucia was long gone before Barbara arrived with her unlikely purple tracksuit and her ferreting about in the landscape.'

'Do you know why Barbara was in Sainte-Catherine?'

'Well, yes. Don't you?'

'No, I have no idea, and Inspector Sicarie and Antoine Grenelle both seem to think I had something to do with her death, which is completely inexplicable to me – and to you, I hope.'

'They might as well say that I had some guilt in the matter. We found her together.'

'It's all profoundly unsettling and I think my neighbours look at me with suspicion, too.' Zoe realised that her voice had become thin and tense and she covered her discomfort by serving them both some more wine. 'So, anyway, is it something you are able to share?'

'To share?'

'Why Barbara was here. It wasn't a private matter divulged in the secrecy of confession or anything like that?' asked Zoe, attempting to introduce some humour into what she felt had become an awkward moment.

'No, nothing like that.'

'So, why was she here?'

'For the Silver Vulture,' said Father Julien Calmet.

IV

STEPS FORWARD AND STEPS BACK

Nineteen

The Truth about the Vulture

'Oh, really,' said Zoe. 'This is absolutely exasperating.' Then she laughed and told him: 'Please enlighten me so I can finally get to the bottom of this mystery.'

'I beg your pardon?' said Julien, his ascetic features creased into a frown.

'Everywhere I turn there are people talking about birds of prey – looking for them, wanting books about them. Now you're talking about a silver one? What am I not grasping?'

'She was a Vulturist,' said Julien, as if that was all the explanation necessary.

Zoe laughed again and told him: 'That doesn't help.'

'Are you not aware . . .' Julien hesitated. His eyes became vague, calculating something in his head. 'It was ten years ago, almost to the day. Or it will be at the end of the month, the eve of All Hallows.'

'What was ten years ago?'

'That the Vulture was hidden.'

'It sounds like you keep saying that word with a capital letter. Am I right?'

'Yes. The Vulture. It was in all the papers and on the radio and television. And, of course, the book came out at the same time. It was quite the story, catching people's imaginations. Ever since, people have been looking for it.'

The various fragments of information began to come together in Zoe's mind.

'Oh, it's like *Masquerade*.'

'What's that?'

'*Masquerade* was a lovely book, published in the late Seventies in the UK, a sort of treasure hunt.'

'What was the treasure?'

'A golden hare, buried somewhere that could be discovered by solving the cryptic clues in the poems and paintings.'

'And it was solved and the treasure discovered?'

'Yes, absolutely, just three years later, I think it was, but that created another scandal because the person who dug it up – in a clay box, to shield it from metal detectors, as I remember it – apparently guessed the location because the author of the book had let it slip to a mutual acquaintance and . . .' Zoe stopped and frowned. 'I can't remember how it played out, but you see what I mean? And your thing, the Vulture, is the same? It's related to the puzzle book, *In the Land of Vultures*?'

'Precisely. Barbara Ercollani was a Vulturist. She thought she was on the trail, that she had penetrated the mystery.'

'There's a difference of opinion about her. Denis Allard says, with absolute conviction, that she was sickening for something, a cold or flu or even worse. I'm not sure. For myself, I drift between "definitely ill" and "possibly just old and tired". Denis's partner, Davide Quillan, seemed at first to agree with me but, now, I don't know. As a doctor, do you have an opinion?'

'An ex-doctor. I never examined her. I didn't speak to her in the last week of her life.'

Somehow, that answer sounded evasive, though it made complete sense.

'Was she a member of your congregation?'

'Not in the first few weeks but later on she became assiduous.'

Zoe decided to share the information that most deeply gnawed at her.

'You know that I've been questioned several times by the police, that I am somehow under suspicion?'

Zoe noticed a gleam of interest in his eye and had a fleeting idea that he was pleased.

But that's ridiculous. Why would he be pleased?

'I know Inspector Sicarie,' he told her. 'Like Caroline, we used to move in the same circles in Aix. I believe he is a capable officer, despite appearances. Caroline, too, is a Vulturist,' he told her, lightly.

'No!' Zoe exclaimed.

'It's how she hurt her arm. She was scrambling in some rocks alongside the Rigolet, believing herself on the trail of a key clue, and slipped with her hand in a crack and wrenched it, straining the ligaments.'

'And you know this because she came to you for help?'

'Yes, Sainte-Catherine was closer than the hospital in Aix. I told her she needed an X-ray and, happily, the damage was to the soft tissues, not to the bone.'

Zoe pursed her lips, wondering what else she should ask. She felt that she was, figuratively, close behind her prey.

And what is my prey, precisely? Some nugget of information that I might one day need in order to exonerate myself? I think it is. I need to solve this mystery for myself, not just for Barbara.

'Do you know if she found it?'

'Caroline?'

'No, Barbara.'

'Ah, you are wondering if she might have located the treasure and, therefore, been killed for it?'

'I am, though it sounds ridiculous when you say it out loud.'

He became serious, very much 'Father Julien Calmet' once more.

'Do you know why the scripture says that "the love of money is the root of all evil"? I mean, why it says "the love of money", rather than just "money"?'

'I suppose because when people acquire wealth, they discover it's never enough and they always want more?'

'Yes, that's right. The puzzle book, as you called it, *In the Land of Vultures*, seems to me to be an evil thing, exciting its public with avarice. If I knew who its author was, I would recommend that they bring the hunt to an end – perhaps at the end of the month, on the tenth anniversary.'

'You sound very serious.'

'I am.' He sipped his white wine, then apologised. 'I'm sorry. I am being excessively judgemental. I have upset you. It is a book you sell, of course, and I have made you feel you are doing something sinful.'

'Oh, it would take a good deal more than that to persuade me that I am bound for eternal damnation.'

Julien smiled and told her: 'I am not allowed to joke about such things, but I take your point.' He paused, then added with a wink: 'Confirmed heathen, that you are.'

They both laughed and Zoe made another deduction.

'Antoinette and Antoine Grenelle are on different sides of the search, aren't they, refusing to share ideas and clues. That's what they fell out about.'

'I believe so.'

'But is the Vulture so very valuable? I mean, is it worth a life-changing amount of money?'

'That would depend on how much money one had to begin with. Your purchase of this lovely bookshop – that you have improved so much, let me repeat – was a life-changing boon for Lucia.'

'The Vulture is made of silver. Is it very heavy? Does it contain a lot of precious metal?'

'Yes. More to the point, though, there is a fund. The author of the book has drawn no royalties from the sales. All the monies are accumulating in an interest-bearing account. The longer the challenge remains unsolved, the more valuable it becomes – not just for the prestige and the vulture-shaped trinket, but also for the profits from the book's decade of success.'

'And that is a substantial sum?'

'I have always supposed so. You are much better placed to estimate than I am.'

'To go back to your idea of the book being "evil", have there been fiercer disputes than Antoinette Grenelle pretending to refuse to speak to her brother? Oh, and I suppose I ought to tell you, she mentioned the feud to me with a wink, as if she thought I ought to know that it was foolish or not entirely serious.'

'I am not aware of any, but the Vulturists keep their cards very close to their chests. No one wants to be seen approaching what they think might be the key clue or hiding place, for fear of others following and taking advantage of their ideas.'

'So, people search in secret?'

'That's right.'

'At night?'

'Often, I believe.'

'Lucia Jacquet's husband might have been a Vulturist, using hunting as a cover.'

'That thought hadn't crossed my mind.'

'And others?'

'Perhaps.'

Zoe thought about the other 'confirmed hunters' among those she had met.

Antoine and the estate agent, Ambroise Caille . . . Am I forgetting someone?

She asked: 'If Barbara had a firm idea of where she wanted to look, might she have tried to blur her tracks by repeated forays into random parts of the countryside?'

'That's very perceptive. Doing so would be trying to *noyer le poisson*,' said Julien, using a French expression that meant, literally, 'to drown the fish' – concealing the truth by smothering it with a myriad of unimportant additional facts.

'Do you know how she got about?'

'You never saw her?'

'I'm mostly cloistered in my shop, you know.'

'She buzzed around on a *mobylette*. It's still chained to a railing at the edge of the car park.' He hesitated, then asked: 'You are not a Vulturist yourself?'

'I've not even read it and I have no idea how the puzzles work.'

'Do you have copy we can peruse now?'

'I'm awaiting new stock from the distributors on Tuesday.' Zoe changed tack. 'I think Barbara was on the verge of something, at the same time as being lonely and needing company. That's why I invited her to come with me to the Saint Bertrand procession. I even got Patrick to set a place for her, even though the restaurant was all booked up.'

All the light had faded from the sky. The rear windows onto the small courtyard of the bookshop were dark, the alpine plants in the stone planter no longer visible, nor was the charming bas-relief of a child reading. They hadn't turned on the lights. The only illumination came from the logs burning down in the stove, like during her conversation with Marcel, after he had towed her van back to town. The creases in Julien's severe face were deeply shadowed.

'I have overstayed my welcome,' he told her.

She realised that he had said that because she had allowed a silence to grow too long.

'No, you haven't. Let's talk about pleasanter things.'

Zoe gave him her impressions of their neighbours, happy to learn some details of their home lives and who had what children and who was related to whom. When she came to Napoléon Etienne, the second-hand book salesman, Julien laughed.

'He's a silly, self-important little man, the Lord bless him. I'm sure you know what I mean by "*déterminisme nominatif*"?'

'Nominative determinism, the idea that our personalities are shaped by our names, or we take jobs that correspond, like someone called Baker making a living by selling cakes.'

'Exactly. Poor Napoléon has taken his given name to heart. He believes himself an emperor, much more important than, in fact, he is. He's very certain in his ideas, even when they are not shared.'

'Such as?'

'Silly things, like insisting the street lamps don't go off until two in the morning or the correct day for the rubbish lorry to come.'

'But he's genuinely a book lover?'

'He was behind the *village du livre* signs, getting the *mairie* to invest as a way of promoting tourism to Sainte-Catherine.'

'Could he be the author of *In the Land of Vultures*?'

Julien pondered, then replied: 'I suppose he could, but where would he have found the money to make the silver object – or to get the object made? And, once the book became a success, I can't see him allowing all that income to slip through his fingers. That doesn't seem in character.'

'But he might consider there are other ways of profiting from the book, by publishing another one, for example, or the way the monies are invested might not be as transparent as you suggest?'

'There are other people I might suspect ahead of him.'

'For example?'

'Marcel Maurice is very learned. Did you know? Though his life is his vines, he was an honours student in human geography and went on to write a thesis on the topography and geology of the Verdon nature park.'

'I see.' Zoe didn't know what to make of this new information. It seemed odd that it hadn't come up. 'Coming back to Napoléon Etienne, I've not warmed to him,' said Zoe. Then she told the story of him driving past her when she had broken down on the road. 'I'm sure he saw me and chose not to stop and help out of spite.'

'Not the Good Samaritan.'

'No, indeed. Plus, he lied about me having an argument with poor Barbara. Does that seem in character for him?'

'I'm afraid it does. It's not the first time he's been known to spread unsubstantiated rumours.'

Zoe felt a chilly draught from under the front door. It coincided with a repeat of the horrible sense that she was not among friends, here in Sainte-Catherine. She made a determined effort to banish the negative thoughts, offering to make Julien something to eat.

'I don't have much but I could whisk together a fricassee of chicken and rice with vegetables from the freezer.'

'That's very kind, but I do not eat in the evenings. It disagrees with me.'

'How un-French,' said Zoe with a smile.

'Alas, yes,' he said. 'But I would be delighted to buy you lunch one day. Perhaps when Patrick returns and the Auberge reopens? My priestly stipend doesn't run to the prices at Le Gourmand.'

'Actually, I ate there today and it was fairly reasonable, given how good . . .' Zoe stopped, thinking to herself that the only reason the bill had not seemed completely excessive was because she could afford the extravagance. 'But, yes, the Auberge would be lovely, too. Will Patrick be back soon?'

'He will reopen for Christmas and New Year.'

'Then we don't have long to wait,' said Zoe.

Julien was perched on the front edge of the leather cushions in the low club armchair and looked like he was about to leave, but wanted to share another fragment of information before doing so.

She asked: 'Was there something else you wanted to say?'

'Just that you should be wary of Inspector Sicarie. He is a very determined character. He will not easily let go of an idea, once it is firmly implanted.'

Zoe glanced at Russell, lying contented on the floorboards in front of the open door of the stove.

'Like a dog with a bone,' she remarked, 'as we say in English.'

'Yes, precisely. Or a dog with a rat.'

'I would be the rat, in this analogy?' asked Zoe, lightly.

'I hope not. But, to extend the image, Sicarie, if he were a hunting dog, would be a very unkempt and coarse one.' With this harsh description, Julien stood up, towering over her. 'I will leave you. I have an early service at six o'clock. I must wake well before dawn.'

'You will enjoy your breakfast,' said Zoe, thinking about the fact that he wouldn't have eaten any dinner.

'I will not break my fast until after lauds,' he told her, using the Latin name for the service.

No wonder you are so gaunt.

'Thank you for being my first proper social call,' she told him. 'I have very much enjoyed our chat.'

'As have I.'

He left her without shaking her hand or kissing her on each cheek in the typical style. She followed him to the door and watched him cross the square. Russell came to sit by her foot, looking up at her as if to say: '*Shut the door, won't you? It's chilly out.*'

Zoe did so, turning the button to lock it, then went and closed the door of the stove so it wouldn't burn up too fast or spill hot embers on the stone slab or even the ancient floorboards. She put her keys on the shelf beneath the counter, thinking she ought to put a hook there so she didn't lose them, then tidied away the empty bottle and glasses – she hadn't needed to uncork the second – and took them upstairs. She pondered getting ready for bed then coming back down to read, but found she didn't want a book, that she would be quite happy just watching the flames through the sooty glass.

Father Julien Calmet is a very interesting man. I can absolutely see what Caroline meant.

She thought about the Vulture treasure and the 'love of money'.

He's right about that, too.

The German tourists – the geocachers – came into her mind.

Their leader, Oskar Weiss, will be back on Tuesday for a copy of the book. I suppose it must have been translated into German, because he doesn't speak French. Perhaps he thinks the original will have additional clues. I wonder if he'll ask me to help him understand it.

The logs settled in the firebox and Zoe contemplated adding more.

Or I could go to bed?

She did just that, leaving Russell where he was, enjoying the fading warmth. At some point in the night, she was roused by his claws on the stairs and the slight bounce in the mattress as he jumped up to ensconce himself on the far corner. Later, too hot under the covers, she threw a layer off, smothering Russell who yapped in complaint and ran away to scrape at the front door until the sound became too annoying and she felt she had no choice but to go down and let him out.

'Do not bark, however,' she told him severely.

He ran off on his little legs, through the crisp leaves, and Zoe realised that there had been a change of air. The wind had come round, all the way to the south, out of Africa, and the night was mild. She contemplated the dark doors and windows of her neighbours.

Perhaps I've made a breakthrough, having Julien round. I should organise a gathering. I'll invite all the other residents of the square and everyone else I've met, even Napoléon Etienne. It'll be a chance to get them all across the threshold and stop them thinking that I'm a peculiar stranger from across the seas who climbs through windows and doesn't fit in.

She went back to bed, already planning.

And I can find out more about this 'Silver Vulture'. Yes, this is a good idea. It will be hard work, but a lovely step forward.

As things turned out, she couldn't have been more wrong.

Twenty

THE PAST ZOE CAN'T ESCAPE

The next day, Zoe's mood plummeted.

Despite the repeated decision she kept taking to try and be more positive, to make the most of things, to assume she was integrating, even if she wasn't, Zoe woke up sluggish and weary, as if, all night long, she had been swimming against a rip tide or treading water, just to keep herself from drowning.

There were several reasons. Partly, it was because Monday was the day she had selected not to open the shop and, therefore, she felt at a loose end, purposeless and back in the uncomfortable feeling of 'drift'. There was also the nagging unpleasantness of being suspected of something unspoken, like the hero of Franz Kafka's *The Trial*, who complained that he was being arrested without having done anything wrong.

And the poor man is never told what it is he's accused of.

Most important, though, and most insidious, was something she had been obliged to learn to live with, which came in waves; an oppressive anxiety and gloom out of the distant echoes of childhood, the trauma of repeated abandonment that she had, if truth were told, wrestled with all her life long. However warm and secure her present, the broken-and-mended parts of her psyche were still capable, decades later, of dragging her back to the years in which she had been alone and friendless, unloved, uncared for and, ultimately, thrown out by her foster family to fend for herself.

She had told Antoine the bare bones of being a tiny infant foundling at St Richards Hospital in Chichester. The truth was, her childhood in care and at the mercy of inattentive or downright unkind foster parents only came to an end on her sixteenth birthday when she had been abandoned a second time at a dismal rural bus stop, with no money and a small suitcase of meagre childish possessions.

I felt sorry for Barbara because her loneliness mirrored my own.

Zoe felt another pang, remembering what Maurice had said about having no one to whom he could pass on his vines – or pass on his love for them.

If I dropped down dead, would anyone in Sainte-Catherine miss me? Would they let the bookshop go to rack and ruin?

Zoe had never been to therapy but she had read many books about the legacy of childhood pain. She had always felt equipped to deal with it.

Until now?

She took a steadying breath.

Have I underestimated the time and energy it will take to begin a new life? I'm not a child or a teenager. That makes a difference.

A kind of slideshow of her new acquaintances flickered through her mind.

Suspicious acquaintances, too.

Zoe lay very still, concentrating on the rhythm of her breathing and focusing her mind on leaving the shadows of the past behind, trying to persuade herself to live in the present.

In the end, there is only now.

It didn't immediately work. Self-knowledge was all very well, but the unexpected coldness of her neighbours had made her feel a failure, amongst their successful lives.

You can't compare how people appear to the outside world with the messy, gloopy, nebulous worry and shame inside and—

Zoe brought her spiralling internal monologue to an abrupt halt, berating herself.

Stop festering and pull yourself together.

She still thought her 'bookshop party' idea from the middle of the night was a good one. She dressed, drank a large glass of water in the kitchen then went downstairs, opening up her laptop on the counter. She set about crafting an invitation, one that she could deliver by hand to her neighbours.

That is, the neighbours who I hope will become my long-term friends.

It didn't take long, formatting it with two invitations to the page so that the A4 paper from the printer could be cut in two to save ink.

And the invitation will appear less ostentatious.

On a previous lonely day, Zoe had used some free art software to design a logo for the bookshop, basing it on a pencil sketch she had made of the premises. Pleased with her efforts, she incorporated it into the invitation. Despite the fact that, for the time being, no one would be able to reach her, she added her mobile phone number, hoping people would save it to their own devices in order to be in touch with her more easily in the future, once the cables to the mast had been repaired.

That is, if this party does manage to make me some proper new friends.

Because she had woken early, all this moping and then organising was complete by nine o'clock. Before printing, she strolled down through the town to the service station, with Russell trotting beside her. She left him outside, determinedly sniffing along the perimeter of the forecourt, and entered through an automatic glass sliding door. The young woman – whose name was Cécilie and whom she had got used to seeing staffing the payment cubicle – greeted her in an off-hand manner that, counterintuitively, she found reassuring.

If Cécilie doesn't feel the need to make an effort, that means I'm a regular, a local.

Like most modern French service stations, the Total garage had a sophisticated shop attached, selling a range of pre-packaged food stuffs, as well as workwear, boots and hats and gloves, plus phone accessories and some other everyday electricals. There were two tall vending machines capable of providing coffee, hot chocolate and tea in a dazzling range of options. Waiting for the mechanic to come through to speak to her, Zoe selected her habitual *café allongé* and drank it standing at an island outside the entrance to the toilets.

Before she had finished, Frank arrived, pulling some blue nitrile gloves from his hands, reminding her of a junior surgeon in a television drama because of his dark hair, high forehead, chestnut-brown eyes and wide generous mouth. He looked about sixteen, but Zoe was aware that her impression of young people's ages had shifted since she had become what people referred to as a 'mature woman'. She decided he was probably twenty-four or twenty-five.

'I'm sorry about all the delays,' he told her. 'We'll get to it shortly.'

She described the problem with Renée's engine for a second time, losing power intermittently and then, ultimately, having to pull over, the road not wide enough to properly get out of the throughfare. He told her that he knew the place.

'Did you or your colleagues not discover a fault when you did the service? What was that? Four weeks ago?'

'Absolutely not,' he told her, and she thought she might have wounded his professional pride. 'I took care of her myself and she was in perfect working order. But these things happen.' He shrugged. 'I hope you don't think—'

'I don't know what to think,' Zoe told him, apologetically. 'But it was very worrying. I nearly caused a serious accident. I assume you took her out on a test drive?'

'Of course.'

'A good distance?'

'I took the country roads towards the gorges. It's a good test because it's up and down and windy, then there's a roundabout where it's easy to make a U-turn and come back. She was impeccable,' he concluded, abbreviating the last word to '*impec*'.

Zoe decided to take the plunge.

'I had a thought. Please don't think I'm trying to tell you your job. I just wondered if somebody might have sabotaged my van by putting something in the petrol tank. Does that sound plausible?'

The young man had his back to her because he was ordering his own cup of coffee from the vending machine, a tiny espresso in a little plastic goblet. He turned and told her: 'From your description, the very same thing had already crossed my mind. When I was at the Lycée in Aix-en-Provence, I knew someone who fell out with his best friend and put sugar in the petrol tank of his *mobylette*.'

Zoe nodded, imagining the ubiquitous lightweight mopeds beloved of French teenagers.

And that was how Barbara Ercollani got about and her moby-lette is still chained up in the car park.

'There's no lock on my petrol cap. This could have been the same thing?' she asked.

He shook his head.

'The thing's a myth. Sugar doesn't dissolve in petrol and, if it stays in granules, obviously it would get caught by the filters. Anyway, I'll start by draining the tank. If it's a fuel problem, I'll find out.'

'Could it have been dangerous? Might the engine have blown up?'

'From sugar? No,' he said with a chuckle. 'But, to be fair, you're right. Pulling over where you did might well have caused an accident involving not just you but other cars as well. So, there's no "could" about it.'

Zoe felt that the conversation had taken a melodramatic tone. It did, however, tie in with her own idea that Napoléon Etienne had been the culprit.

'If not sugar, what else?' she asked.

'I've not heard of any other substances causing the problem you described, but I'll ask Raymond.'

Zoe assumed that 'Raymond' must be the senior mechanic on the premises.

'Thank you very much. Should I come back later or—'

She had been, pointlessly, about to say: *Will you call me?* But he interrupted.

'Come back at twelve. Okay, I'd better get on. I have a *contrôle* to do first.'

Zoe knew that a '*contrôle*' was the French equivalent of the MOT test.

'Would you tell me your second name so I know who to ask for?'

'Frank Séchan.'

'Oh, like the vet?' Zoe asked, remembering that Julien Calmet had, in fact, mentioned the relationship.

'My grandfather.'

The mention of the elderly large-animal vet gave Zoe the distinct impression that there was something she had forgotten. Before she could work out what it was, she became distracted because Frank, rather than simply disappearing through the staff-only door into the section of the building devoted to maintenance and repairs, went and leaned across the counter of the payment cubicle, put a clean hand either side of the young woman's face and kissed her long and languorously. Cécilie responded in kind, making Zoe feel uncomfortably like a voyeur.

She turned away and heard – but couldn't make out – their low voices, presumably exchanging vows of love or lust. After a rapturous pause, Frank exited the public area to get on with his work.

Zoe had wandered away from them into a far corner of the shop. She noticed, among the electrical appliances, two coffee machines, one a bog-standard filter device and the other a space-age alternative that required small aluminium pods. Under the display counter were boxed versions. Zoe chose the filter coffee machine and took it to the counter. She was about to pay when, taking out her purse, she noticed the dateline on the display on the till and an appointment that she had forgotten came rushing back into her mind.

'Oh, I'm late. Will you excuse me?'

Cécilie asked: 'Shall I put this back?'

'No, keep it for me, please.'

Outside, Zoe found Russell still sniffing around the roots of the weeds that grew just beyond the edge of the tarmac forecourt. She called him and he looked up with an inquisitive air but seemed disinclined to leave off from his urgent task of finding who else and what else had been this way before him. Impatiently, Zoe hurried over, picked him up and carried him away, the dog impotently writhing as she made her way across the ring road and down a side street into the neighbourhood of suburban villas, mostly single storey, where the elderly vet had a consulting room in a converted garage.

Russell's little doggy brain began to work out where it was that they were going and decided he wanted none of it. He struggled more fiercely in her arms. Zoe tightened her hold on his back legs, squeezing them between the inside of her elbow and her waist. After a few more convulsions, with whimpering reluctance, he seemed to accept his fate.

Apart from the professional sign on the door of the garage, the little ticky-tacky *pavillon* – as such bungalows were called in French – looked little different from its neighbours. It was the sort of house that could be purchased from a catalogue, amongst a range of four or five styles, built using the same methods and the same materials, not designed to stand out.

Firmin Séchan, however, had made a difference with at least two dozen plant containers, some of them big enough to hold trees. The front yard, either side of the path, was a riot of fruiting olives, thriving oleander, vigorous purple-flowering bougainvillea and bright red geraniums.

Zoe wove through the planters and knocked on the door of the converted garage. Hearing no response, she went in and found the waiting room empty, but voices were audible from the consulting room beyond. She sat down on an uncomfortable foam-filled chair, letting Russell explore, and picked up a puzzle magazine from the low table. She leafed through the pages – a sequence of crosswords, sudoku, maths games and so on – finding that every single one had been completed. At first, she thought this might be because the magazine had been there for a long time but, looking more closely, she saw that it was only a week old.

The door to the consulting room opened and the man who ran the estate agent on the square came out.

Tightly curled grey hair, big teeth – that's Ambroise Caille. Antoine's friend, a hunter.

Ambroise was carrying a cat basket inside which, behind a wire grille, a tiny kitten cowered. Russell was immediately interested, climbing up at the man's leg, an expression of polite enquiry on his charming, pointed face.

'I'm sorry,' said Zoe. 'Get down, Russell.'

'That's all right,' the estate agent told her. 'I like dogs.'

He didn't wait, however, to see if Russell's interest might become more insistent. In any case, Zoe picked him up so he couldn't escape when Ambroise opened the door to leave. Firmin called her from the consulting room and she went through, apologising that she was late for the booster jabs that were required to follow on from Russell's initial inoculations.

'All is well. Ambroise was early, in any case.'

Firmin Séchan administered the injections with a distracted air and a slight tremor in his bony hands, as if his mind was on other things, which Zoe thought was reasonable given he must have done this precise same thing many thousands of times. Once the process was complete and Russell had made the complaints that he seemed to think suitable, she lifted him down off the table and told Firmin: 'I'm having a get-together in the bookshop tomorrow, Tuesday, towards the end of the day's trading, at six. I wonder if you might be able to come? I'm inviting more or less all the friends and neighbours I can think of. It would be a pleasure to see you there.'

'How kind, how very kind. I tried to encourage Lucia to do just such a thing. But don't you think Wednesday might be better?'

'Because it's a market day? Of course, you're right.'

'Did you say six o'clock?'

'Does that not seem to you the right time?'

'I might choose four, giving the traders time to dismantle their stalls, but before they've all gone.'

'That makes sense.'

Zoe paid Firmin's very modest bill, shook his hand and left, opening the outer door onto the pleasantly mild autumn day. Russell shot past her and galloped away between the pots and other planters, clearly determined to put as much distance as he could, as quickly as possible, between himself and the shameful events of the vet's consulting room.

Zoe wandered away much more slowly, enjoying the sun on her face, taking off her gilet and folding it over her arm. She returned to the petrol station to buy the filter coffee machine, delighted with the idea that it would make the bookshop more welcoming and homely. As she carried it up through the streets, she felt another brief pang of guilt on the way past the restaurants, not liking the idea that she might be accused of stealing Patrick's trade.

Back at the bookshop, she unlocked the front door and went inside, leaving it open because the smell of woodsmoke from the previous day was very strong. She tossed her keys on the shelf under the counter, put the boxed coffee machine on top and stood for a moment, thinking about where she might install it. She realised a coffee table would be a good idea, between the three leather armchairs and the stove, plus a side table alongside the back door.

Do I want to schlep over to Aix again to buy them? I suppose I might, if Frank gives Renée a clean bill of health.

That, of course, led her mind her back to Napoléon Etienne and his extraordinary behaviour when she broke down at the side of the road, leading to the suspicions that she couldn't shake.

I suppose I'll know for sure at midday.

Convinced by Firmin's argument that Wednesday would be a better day for her 'gathering', Zoe amended the details on her laptop then printed a sheaf of pages. As she cut them all in half, separating the two invitations on each A4 sheet, shuffling the papers brought her mind back to the puzzle magazine in the vet's waiting room.

Puzzles seem to be a thing in Sainte-Catherine. I wonder if Firmin knows who sat there and filled in all those answers. I should have asked him. Whoever it was has to be someone who loves cryptic games and is, therefore, bound to be another local person on the trail of the Vulture.

Twenty-One

A Change of Mood

Zoe delivered her invitations to every house and shop in the square, unsettled by the fact that she had to repeatedly explain herself.

'Just a gathering, to thank everyone for their kindness in welcoming me to the village.'

By the fifth time she said it, she didn't believe it herself, but the warmer weather meant she felt much happier than she had on waking up, out without a coat, wearing just a clean white T-shirt and jeans.

Once she had completed her circuit of the square, Zoe made her way into Rue des Templiers and then the less-frequented side streets, delivering invitations to the two restaurants and even to the house of Napoléon Etienne, taking care to rattle the letterbox so that he couldn't think that she was sneaking up on him or doing something nefarious. She even hung around for a minute or so, wondering if he might open up so that she would be able to speak to him.

It's just possible that he was simply too frightened to stop because of the oncoming traffic and the poor visibility.

No answer came to her ostentatious delivery.

No, there must be more to it. He bad-mouthed me to Antoine.

Having invited everyone that she knew in the town proper, she decided to put an invitation through the letterbox of the vet who seemed to her an entirely benign presence in Sainte-Catherine. She found him pottering about out of doors, picking microscopic weeds from the dirt in his planters.

'It isn't that they are noxious,' he told her. 'It's that they steal the nourishment intended for the plants that I value. A weed is not a bad plant, *per se*, but simply something growing in the wrong place.'

Zoe came closer and, before she knew what she was doing, asked him: 'Am I an invasive plant, growing in the wrong place?'

His deeply lined face expressed uncertainty.

'Good heavens, why would you ask that? You are the most marvellous addition to our community.'

'Good,' she told him quietly, unconvinced.

'You astonish me, Madame Pascal. The bookshop, itself, makes a difference to the culture of our town. But had you opened a new clothing store or a bike shop or a delicatessen, I'm sure your neighbours would have been just as pleased at your friendly, optimistic presence.'

Zoe could not at first reply. She was so moved by his kind words that her own seemed to catch in her throat.

This is different from the automatic, routine gallantry of men of my own age. Firmin isn't couching his compliments in a froth of flirtation. I think I have to take him at his word.

'It's so kind of you to say that. I've been having doubts.'

'Desist from doubt,' he told her, robustly. 'Take it from an old man. Life is for living – and where might one live better than this glorious landscape, by turns rugged or lush, grassy or wooded, parched in the summer but running with torrent streams in autumn, winter and spring?'

'Is that a quotation, poetry perhaps?'

'No, just my own idea.'

'Well, it's exactly what I thought when first I saw Sainte-Catherine.'

'When was that?' he asked her, perching on the edge of an enormous clay planter in which a three-metre olive tree was flourishing. As he leaned against its trunk, a little shower of dry leaves fell onto his sparse grey hair and his bony shoulders, concealed beneath a plaid shirt and a threadbare cardigan. 'Recent or ancient?'

'Ancient. My half-sister – who is eighteen years older than I am – brought me to the theatre festival in Avignon. It was a huge adventure.'

'How marvellous. What was the reason for your visit?'

Zoe hesitated. The trip had, extraordinarily, involved another mystery, involving Zoe but solved by Maisie, so she didn't want to say more, wary of word getting around and exciting further suspicions in Inspector Sicarie.

'It's a long story. Perhaps I'll tell you about it another time. Afterwards, we went on a driving tour through Provence. By chance, therefore, I saw Sainte-Catherine when I was at a very impressionable age and never forgot it. More recently, working under constant pressure in London theatre, I suppose I started to become oppressed by the traffic and the roadworks and the buses and the taxis and the ambulances and the sirens. I was brought up in the countryside, you see.'

'That makes complete sense. First impressions matter – the place where one becomes aware of oneself as an individual, separate from parents and family.'

'I've never said this out loud before but I do wonder if, ultimately, I'm not sort of reverting to type, a kind of throwback in my own life.'

Although Firmin was listening attentively, he didn't answer straight away. Zoe worried that she had become boring, droning on to a relative stranger about her own heartfelt psychological discoveries. It did not appear so, however.

'I think that is the most interesting thing anyone has said to me in several years.'

'You do?'

'At my age, nothing is a surprise. Everything makes you think of similar events from your own past. Often, I am unable to place them on the timeline of my own personal history. Did they happen in my twenties or my thirties or my forties? I won't go on listing my other decades,' he told her with a smile. 'It would take too long. But what you've said, your generous sharing of your own private emotions . . . I really am very touched that you should display, on so brief an acquaintance, such confidence and trust.'

He pushed his right hand deep into the pocket of his gardening trousers and drew out an unsavoury red-and-white-checked handkerchief with which he dabbed his eyes.

'Oh, I'm sorry. Have I upset you?'

'Not at all. These are happy tears.'

'I don't know what to say.'

He smiled and adjusted his seat on the hard rim of the planter.

'Tell me more about your life. Old age is lonely, you know.'

'All right.'

Zoe described the renovations at the bookshop. He asked if she had replanted in the courtyard and she told him it wasn't a success.

He gave her an amused smile, telling her: 'Oh, that is a shame.'

She asked about his favourite authors, discovering they both admired Fred Vargas. The conversation became less intense. She gave him his invitation and he complimented her on her 'charming logo'.

'You recognise it as the shop?'

'I do, I do. I sketch myself. Where else are you going?'

'It's such a beautiful day, I thought I might trek through the fields, along the main road and up to the vineyard farmhouse. I would like Marcel to come, and Thierry if he's at home.'

'Then I must delay you no longer.'

He offered his hand and she realised it was to help him up off the big clay tub. He gave her a sober handshake and she left, the road through the suburb bringing her out on the edge of the vines, not far from the place where Russell had come to her rescue, confronting the wild boar. In a break in traffic, she crossed over and headed uphill, listening out for Marcel's weeding machine that she imagined must be somewhere near, pursuing its Sisyphean objective.

No sooner does Rosalie the Robot pass by, pulling the weeds out of the fertile soil, than they will begin growing back. It's probably best that its poor mechanical brain doesn't know that.

Feeling hot, with the remaining invitations stuffed into her hip pocket, she wondered what time it was. Because, for her, today wasn't a working day, she hadn't put on a watch. From the position of the sun in the bright blue sky, she guessed it might be one o'clock. Her growling tummy reinforced this idea. She wondered if Marcel might be prevailed upon to give her something to eat.

Climbing between the bare vines, Zoe quietly hummed to herself – the same musical theatre number she had sung in the cab of the SUV on the way from the airport on the day of her arrival – then stopped as she began to feel pleasantly puffed. She tried to remember who it was who said something along the lines of horses sweating, men perspiring and women 'glowing'. She seemed to remember reading it in a clever Terry Pratchett fantasy novel.

But it must be older than that? I am definitely – and at the very least – perspiring.

At the edge of the wine-farm buildings, not far from the one occupied by Marcel's manager, Zoe took a quick breather. Close by was a galvanised tap on a vertical stand-pipe. She let it run for half a minute, then cooled herself down by splashing the cold water on her face and neck. Unfortunately, she was clumsy, leaving her white T-shirt clinging and semi-transparent. Just then, Marcel emerged from the manager's grace-and-favour accommodation, accompanied by a small woman who wore a dirty blue boiler suit, smudged with oil stains. Both Marcel and the woman looked confused.

'Hello,' said Zoe. 'Am I interrupting?'

Marcel introduced her as the new bookshop owner to which the manager replied, inevitably: 'Oh, yes. Madame Pascal.'

'Call me Zoe, please. And you are?'

'Odile Charpentier.'

'That's a lovely name.' She remembered Julien's remarks about Napoléon Etienne and nominative determinism. 'Did you feel a pressure from it to become a carpenter?'

'In what way?' asked Odile.

'Odile has been up all night,' said Marcel. 'You'll have to explain—'

'Oh, yes,' interrupted Odile. She gave a weak smile. 'I should have been called "Delavigne" or something like that.'

'Anyway,' said Zoe, who had her arms folded because of the clinging T-shirt, 'I wanted to invite you to the bookshop at the end of market trading on Wednesday, at about four o'clock. I sort of feel the need to formally introduce myself to everyone all at once, otherwise I'm just interminably telling people who I am, only for them to reply: "Yes, we know." Do you see?'

'I'll be there,' said Marcel.

'I'll come if I can,' said Odile.

'Why were you up all night?'

'Our harvest isn't yet complete and our press jammed. I had to take it apart and rebuild it.'

Zoe waved a fly out of her eyes, unfolding her arms. 'How very clever of you.'

Odile smiled then asked: 'Why are you wet?'

'I was beginning to wonder, myself,' said Marcel, chuckling.

'I was hot,' said Zoe, gesturing to the tap, 'and I . . .'

She stopped. They all looked at one another and, after a pause, laughed.

'Why not, though, on a hot day?' asked Odile, rhetorically.

'No complaint from me,' said Marcel.

'Well,' added Zoe, 'that was all I came to say.' She gave them each an invitation. 'See you Wednesday.'

She turned away and strode back down the field, making an effort not to turn round and check whether they were watching her or even, perhaps, talking about her. When she reached the road, she did permit herself to glance back up the slope but the angle of the terrain meant she could only see the roofs of the buildings.

She returned home through the ploughed-up sunflower field, by chance meeting Russell at the edge of the car park in front of the town hall. There was something lying on the ground that he seemed very interested in. She approached and discovered that it was the corpse of a rat, just beginning to swell because of some hidden putrefaction going on beneath its dirty brown fur. Zoe found the sight disgusting but didn't feel she had the right to criticise Russell for his specialised canine interests.

'*Tu viens?*' she asked him and his expressive face gave her a look that seemed to say: '*All right, yes, I'm coming.*'

They walked up through the town together, Russell trotting ahead, then running back, then trotting ahead once more. The warm day was beginning to cool and Zoe was still hungry. Although there was no outdoor market stall, in Robert Petit's butcher's shop she was able to buy two handmade stuffed peppers, not even asking what they contained, knowing by experience that his speciality products were always delicious.

Back at the bookshop, she ate her stuffed peppers from a tray on her knees, in front of the unlit stove, identifying minced pork, garlic, shallots, leeks, sweetcorn, pine nuts and lots of salt and pepper. She thought about whether it might be a good idea to convert the second bedroom into a kind of living room, perhaps with a pull-out sofa or a sofa bed, but definitely with a dining table.

Isn't it slovenly to be always eating on my lap?

Having finished her lunch, she noticed the book that she had picked up in Barbara's bedroom in the guest house in order to give herself a kind of pretext for being there, observed by Davide Quillan. It was on the seat of the adjacent armchair. She reached over for it and read the blurb on the back. It described a steamy erotic adventure in trite, uninspiring terms. Once again, it seemed a strange choice for her elderly acquaintance.

Zoe put the tray on the floor and told Russell that it wasn't for him to lick her plate. Then she opened the book and began to read.

The text itself was just as clunky and guileless as the blurb on the back. Weirdly, though, Barbara seemed to have paid it close attention. As Zoe had noticed, every so often, a corner of a page was turned down, sometimes a small triangle and sometimes a larger one. Despite herself, she read on, becoming absorbed by the will-they-won't-they drama.

Obviously, they will.

They did, several times.

Then, perhaps because she had been thinking about puzzles so much, Zoe began to wonder if there might be more to it. She began trying to identify the precise words indicated by the turned-down corners.

Is it possible that they comprise a cryptic message?

Just then, she was interrupted by the rattle of her letterbox and something being pushed through and allowed to fall on her doormat. She went to find out what it was – a small sheet of printer paper, folded over. She opened it up and recognised it as one of her invitations. Scrawled across it in thick black pen was an angry message in capital letters.

NON – RENTREZ CHEZ VOUS!

Zoe opened the door and looked outside, just catching sight of Napoléon Etienne as he hurried away, his shoulders hunched, his fists balled up in the front pocket of his navy-blue painter's smock.

She was shocked. Not only did the message refuse her invitation, but it also told her to 'GO HOME!'

Is there nothing I can do to defuse his irrational enmity?

She frowned.

Why do I assume it's irrational, based in his jealousy and loneliness? What if he's looking for a scapegoat for his own actions? What if he's the murderer?

With a need, once more, to be active, and to try and forget Etienne's one-sided hatred, Zoe shut the door, fetched pen and paper and made a note of all the words that the turned-down corners seemed to indicate in Barbara's erotic novel. They didn't obviously form a sentence or any kind of meaningful message. Zoe looked more closely, wondering if Barbara had been more accurate still, pointing out particular letters.

It was hard to be absolutely sure which ones were indicated because it wasn't the most accurate method and Zoe had unfolded and refolded a few of them while reading. She began to wish that Barbara had instead annotated the book with a pen or pencil, even though, as a book lover, that was not something she would normally recommend. She persevered, however, and decided the corners were supposed to point to individual letters. She noted them down, ending up with a sequence with a few alternatives that didn't seem to form a word – at least, not one she knew.

M, I or A, C, O, C or R, D or O, U or R, L or A, I, E or T, R or A.

The novel was written in French, but that, of course, didn't mean that the word or message that Barbara had spelt out with her peculiar method also had to be French.

It might be Italian, for example. Or, it's possible that it's an anagram. There are enough letters to make several short words.

Zoe wrote the most likely letters down in a sort of jumble to see if any patterns jumped out at her.

Nothing immediately occurs. What I really need is a copy of In the Land of Vultures. *That would at least give me a context for what all this might mean if, as seems likely, the hunt for the hidden treasure is linked to Barbara's death.*

She leafed through the pages of the novel once more, to double-check those letters where she felt she had a choice. Looking very carefully and making sure that she wasn't deforming the folds, she came to the conclusion that the most likely sequence was as follows:

M, A, C, O, C, O, R, L, I, T, A.

Intrigued, Zoe went and found a dictionary in the reference section of her bookshop. It wasn't a very sophisticated volume, being intended for tourists or secondary school children, developing their knowledge of the French language. She was not surprised that the word wasn't listed. She opened her laptop on the shop counter and connected to the internet, typing the sequence of letters into the search box of her browser.

Unusually, the search function didn't return any positive results at all. It did offer her several ideas for alternate spellings:

mario colita
macrolide
marco carta
macrolite

None of them seemed very meaningful, but she went a step further and studied each of these terms in turn, without further inspiration. Then, looking again, she changed her mind about a couple of the letters.

M, I, C, O, C, O, R, L, I, T, R.

That returned a suggestion of 'microliter' which didn't seem to get her anywhere.

I think perhaps I'll leave this alone. When the distributor comes tomorrow with more copies of the puzzle book, I'll think about it again. Perhaps I'll even show it to my German friend, Oskar Weiss, and see if it provides him with any inspiration. As a Vulturist himself, he's bound to be interested.

Zoe smiled, imagining an unlikely conflab between the unkempt German puzzler and Barbara Ercollani, bent over their maps and their puzzle books, warily sharing ideas and clues. Then she had an entirely new thought.

Or is it I who should be wary of him?

Zoe felt the cold shadow of loneliness once again invading her mood. It was easy to forget that Inspector Sicarie had promised to return and question her again.

What if Oskar Weiss is connected in some way to Barbara's death? Maybe, if I could find good reasons to suspect him, that would help to clear my own name.

The brief flare of optimism provided by that idea soon dissolved.

But if Oskar is connected to Barbara's death, shouldn't I be worried about him turning up at my shop tomorrow? He's a Vulturist, that's certain. Was he in Sainte-Catherine on the evening of the Feast of Saint Bertrand? Possibly.

She gulped.

Am I, in fact, merrily looking forward to the arrival of a murderer?

Twenty-Two

OPPORTUNITY AND MOTIVE

Having eaten her lunch, Zoe began to fret about the fact there was no message from the garage, then Frank Séchan knocked on her door with news that there would be a further delay because he had been called out with the tow truck to remove a broken-down car from one of the narrow country roads where its presence was, as he put it, 'a danger to road users'. Zoe found that frustrating because she had decided she would, after all, like to make another trek into Aix to choose a coffee table and side table for the stove corner.

The idea that I shouldn't leave Sainte-Marie is ridiculous. And I'd be back in couple of hours.

'I do apologise,' said Frank.

'It can't be helped,' Zoe told him.

'A lovely day for a hike?' he suggested.

'I've already done that,' she told him, a little grumpily.

'Till tomorrow, then.'

Zoe fetched her second Vargas novel and perched herself on the square top of the granite bollard just outside her door to read in the fading sun – or, rather, to give an impression of reading. Inside her mind, she was thinking about the key period of time between when Barbara had left her and when she and Julien found her body, shooing away the children before they could know why.

Has anyone explained what happened to the team of boys and girls? There must have been gossip.

Zoe had a good memory and she remembered very clearly noticing the time when Barbara had come into the shop for her final visit, looking weary or ill . . . and definitely lonely.

Ten past six.

She had browsed and then they had chatted. Once Barbara had gone, looking pleased with her invitation to the *al fresco* dinner, Zoe had made herself busy, tidying, cashing up and sending emails. That had taken her until maybe ten to seven when she'd got ready to go out, opening the front door and seeing the inhabitants of Sainte-Catherine, her neighbours from the square, in their finery, all making their way down through the cobbled streets towards the *mairie* for the start of the procession.

Worrying that she had led Barbara astray, telling her there was no need to dress up, she had followed them under the trees, past the impressive door of the church and down Rue des Templiers to the little cul-de-sac where the guest house was located. Then, she had knocked and waited.

Getting no reply, she had knocked again and waited for a minute or two before the heavy tread of Denis Allard frightened her, pounding up the hill because he had forgotten something.

Was it a piccolo? If he were an instrument, he really ought to be a French horn.

Zoe smiled to herself, her mind wandering as she attributed different musical instruments to a few more of the people she knew.

Firmin Séchan, the vet, would be a cello, warm and sympathetic. His grandson Frank would be a snare drum, busy and percussive. Caroline would be something formal and lovely and a little distant – perhaps a violin.

She frowned.

No, Davide Quillan plays the violin in the local band. And something else, as well? He had a second case . . .

Zoe became very still, struck by a sudden inspiration.

Or maybe Davide's second case wasn't for another musical instrument. Maybe it was for a metal detector. It would be the right shape and size, I think.

Zoe wondered about what this might mean.

Didn't Julien tell me that the Vulture is protected from metal detection by a clay casket?

She frowned again, trying to relive her conversation with the unusual priest.

No, that was me talking about the golden hare from the Masquerade book. He didn't say anything of the kind. Does that mean the Vulture isn't protected from metal detectorists and their tools? If so, it can't be out there buried somewhere because it might be found by accident – even by someone who doesn't know what they're looking for – like an archaeologist from the museum in Aix, the one who found the severed heads.

Zoe had a flashback to the marvellous exhibition that had almost made her late for lunch with Caroline.

Or was Marcel digging for it when he severed the cables to the mast?

She realised that she was getting off topic.

So, Barbara came in just after six and left at maybe twenty or twenty five past. I cashed up and all the rest of it, then was outside the guest-house door at seven. Denis came pounding up for his piccolo or whatever it was and it turned out that the guest-house door had been unlocked all the time. He gave me permission to run up and check her room and, of course, she wasn't there – but Russell was in the hallway, presumably having followed her home in the hope of illicit treats.

Zoe shifted position on her granite perch, still enjoying the warmth of the autumn sun, though it was slipping quickly down the sky.

When she left the bookshop, Russell followed her out into the square. I remember that clearly. There's only about half an hour unaccounted for. She must have shut him in at the guest house when she went back out, presumably to the church to meet me,

203

thinking that was where the procession began because I didn't explain myself clearly enough.

Zoe hesitated before framing the next thought.

And someone met her there or followed her there and killed her?

She thought about Inspector Sicarie and his investigation, wishing she knew the cause of death. She remembered his close questioning of her movements.

He must have been doing the same thing I am now, but obviously with much more practice and authority. Has he asked everyone else who knew her the same things?

Zoe realised that she had made an assumption about what Barbara had done that might not correspond to reality.

Maybe Barbara went directly to the church from the bookshop. She was still in her sagging purple tracksuit, after all. Maybe Russell snuck into the guest house when Denis and Davide came out, slipping in without them noticing. In any case, Barbara could have been killed any time from two minutes after she left my shop.

She shut her book, weary of holding it up in pretence. She saw the estate agent, Ambroise Caille, locking up his premises, talking to a man in a smart suit, presumably in order to take the prospective buyer out and show him properties for sale.

It's so frustrating. If I had the authority to ask my own questions, I bet I could work out the key moment in time. And it would be easy to discover who had opportunity because most of the village would have been down in the car park in preparation for the procession, giving one another alibis.

She went indoors, leaving the Vargas novel on the counter and turning on her computer, with the idea of typing out everything she thought she knew in order to send it by post to Maisie. It took about twenty minutes and, once it was printed, she thought she had done it well. Folding it over twice to fit inside a business envelope, she discovered she had no stamps, rarely having a use for them.

She took her letter to the Hyper U supermarket where, she knew, stamps were available from each till. The letterbox was outside the *mairie* in a corner of the car park. She slipped it into the slot and noticed the tow truck parked at the edge of the harvested sunflower field with a battered Mercedes sports car attached behind.

She walked along the ring road to the garage and asked Cécilie, the cashier, if Frank was back, discovering that he was and had finished his examination of Renée the Renault.

'Can I speak to him?'

Cécilie called him through, using an intercom, referring to him as '*chéri*'. While waiting, Zoe wondered about a coffee but decided it was too late in the day. Frank came busily through, rubbing his hands on a paper towel.

'You were right, Madame Pascal, about the cause, even though I can't tell you for sure who did it.'

'Sugar in the tank?'

'No,' he reminded her with a chuckle. 'That's a myth, remember. It was water.'

'Water? How can you tell?'

'I have experience looking at fuel and it's easy to see when it's not right. Petrol contains ten per cent ethanol which is very hygroscopic – it absorbs water easily. In modern cars, this shouldn't be a big problem.'

'But surely it would prevent combustion and the engine would lose power, like mine did?'

'That's what I'm getting at. If your Renault was a new one, the oxygen sensors and on-board computers would automatically try and compensate for the more dilute mixture and the engine would run fine without injuring itself. In an older car . . .' He stopped, shaking his head and pursing his lips.

'How much water?' she asked.

'That depends how much fuel was in the tank, but a couple of two-litre bottles of Evian on top of ten or fifteen litres of fuel would cause a problem, for sure.'

Zoe tried to picture Napoléon Etienne's shopping bags. They had seemed heavy. She remembered him struggling to make his dramatic exit because of it. Each two-litre bottle of water would weigh precisely two kilograms, about the same as a big bag of potatoes.

I have to confront him.

'But Renée is good to go, now?'

'She is,' said Frank, with another chuckle. 'I filled her up.'

'Don't mention it to anyone, will you?' she asked him. 'For the time being.'

'Okay,' he said, with a hint of uncertainty. 'But Cécilie knows.'

'No one else?' suggested Zoe.

'I'll tell her to keep it to herself. Shall I bring her round?'

'Yes, please.'

Frank disappeared through a staff-only door, leaving Zoe with a picture in memory of Napoléon Etienne bustling away across the road with the light on the pelican crossing changing, the traffic surging past, preventing her from following.

If that memory is reliable, his bags were suddenly very much lighter and he was moving more quickly.

Cécilie presented her bill and she paid, including the cost of a full tank of petrol. She went outside and met Frank at the side of the road. He got out, leaving the engine running, confirmed that Renée was fit for a journey into Aix and she took his place behind the wheel.

Antoine can go whistle. I'll be back before anyone knows it.

The roads were clear and she made good time. At the *dépôt-vente*, she found a coffee table and a side table that she thought would do for the stove corner and drove back again to Sainte-Catherine without incident. She carried each one up through the town, one at a time, then put the car away in her garage, carved into the base of the hillside, and padlocked the weather-worn door. Then, for the third time in twenty minutes, she trudged wearily home.

Enough steps and enough climbing for one day.

She was, though, pleased with all she had got done – the thinking and the talking and the useful chores.

But I'm no closer to knowing what happened in that crucial half hour on the Feast of Saint Bertrand.

Zoe thought about hiking out to make a mobile phone call to Maisie to warn her about the letter she had sent – or even a social catch-up with one or other of the friends she had left behind in the UK – but her legs and feet were sore and she couldn't face it. She finished her second Fred Vargas novel soon after another pot-luck dinner eaten on her knees, when Russell came scratching at the closed door. She let him in and had to rub down his little paws because he had been digging once more. That made her think about detectorists and their metal detectors and she wondered if there might be a crossover between that community and the hunters.

It would be useful to know who belongs to each group. Are there any women who hunt, for example? What about Odile Charpentier, not really being up all night fixing the wine press, but out in the hills, doing something suspicious?

Her mind went back to the crucial time.

But how would that connect to a body in the church on the night of the feast?

The unwelcome idea bubbled up that, if everyone else in the village was accounted for in the crucial period, getting ready for the procession, then only she was unaccompanied, without alibi, in the spreadsheet of timings that she imagined Inspector Sicarie had drawn up.

No, he's not the spreadsheet type. I bet he's got an untidy notebook full of bits and pieces of paper, random scraps of knowledge.

She sighed.

But Julien Calmet warned me that his brain is razor sharp.

★

Zoe didn't know it, but the murderer of Barbara Ercollani was, at that moment, in Place Sainte-Catherine, standing beneath an almost-bare lime tree, in an area of shadow between the pools of light thrown by two old-fashioned street lamps, shaped like lanterns and fixed to the façades of the buildings. The murderer wasn't exactly hiding – because there was no reason for them not to be there – but they had no desire to advertise their presence.

From their partial hiding place, they were looking at the door of the bookshop, thinking once more about the infuriating fact that they had gone to the trouble of breaking into Caroline Robin's office in order to steal the keys to the deserted building, then found they were too late. The sale had gone through and the new owner had taken up residence.

That hadn't entirely deterred them. After a long day's travel and the hustle and bustle of moving in, the murderer had expected the woman to sleep soundly in her new home. The following night, using the stolen keys, they had attempted to gain access.

But she had taken the precaution of shooting a bolt at the foot of the door.

In that moment of frustrated opportunity, it had crossed the murderer's mind that the door might be forced, but they had swiftly disregarded the thought.

No, this place is far too public.

In any case, trying the lock had caused a disturbance of the doorbell on its curved strap of steel.

And, now, I've been standing here too long.

The murderer strolled away across the cobbles, heading for Rue des Templiers.

Never mind. Another opportunity will soon present itself, I'm sure.

★

Zoe went to bed later than she meant to, having 'wasted', as she reproached herself, a couple of hours down an internet rabbit hole made up of discussion groups and French Wikipedia entries about the Vulture and the puzzle book. She discovered that the publishers were assiduous in getting reproductions of the pages from *In the Land of Vultures* taken down, which made sense.

They need people to buy it, not just browse scans online.

Once she was under the covers, her restless mind refused to settle and she tossed and turned, aware of two o'clock and then three o'clock creeping past between fitful slumber.

Twenty-Three

'So, You Knew Barbara?'

When 'tomorrow' – Tuesday – finally came, it turned into Zoe's most difficult day yet in Sainte-Catherine. Once again, she had to fight a wave of psychological gloom. Plus, the warmer weather brought on a day of downpours, great thundering torrents falling vertically out of an iron-grey sky.

The market didn't operate, of course, because the regular trading days were now limited to Wednesdays and the weekends, and her mood sank deeper and deeper as she sat alone, wondering where her next customer might come from.

She had set up the coffee machine on the new side table, next to the stove, to improve the atmosphere. And she had drunk too much of it herself. It all reminded her of a W. H. Auden poem she admired in which he bemoaned those miserable days when nothing came easily. The trouble was, Zoe wasn't sure that there was anything else that she could do. There was no way of forcing customers to queue at her door.

You know this, she told herself. *It's the nature of the retail trade. You make your investment in money and energy and time and hope, then you wait for people to come.*

Zoe tried to focus her mind on ways she might boost her footfall.

The Bible discussion group is a possibility, as is the idea I could partner with the guest house for writing retreats. And a reading group for local people, even if that just means selling half a dozen copies of a paperback novel each month.

Finally, around lunchtime, the English family – intelligent-looking mother, ponytailed father and bright young child – pushed open the door with an air of escaping from Noah's flood, standing on the generous doormat and shaking their good-quality wet-weather clothing. Zoe helped them hang it all up on the old-fashioned coat stand and told them: 'There's coffee available in the stove corner.'

They told her how grateful they were, how they had not expected the change in the weather and – caught out on a hike in the worst of the downpour – more or less everything they owned was either wet or dirty.

'We were delaying getting laundry washed and dried at the supermarket until we had a good big load,' said the mother. 'We left it too late and now it won't be ready for a couple of hours.'

Although the weather wasn't really cold enough, Zoe lit the stove and moved the coat stand with its burden of damp coats and hats alongside. The mother sat in one of the leather armchairs with the three-year-old on her lap, encouraging him to watch the flames and imagine that they were lithe, dancing people with amusing things to say to one another. Meanwhile, the father complimented Zoe on her alpine rockery in the little rear courtyard: 'Though it looks a little undernourished.'

'Are you a gardener?' she asked him, thinking that would fit with his tattoos and outdoorsy air.

'I used to work at Kew, in the glasshouses, but we've taken time out.'

'You mean from work, both of you?'

'Yes.'

'Have you been travelling for long?'

'Since the spring.'

'Does it become wearing, ever, when it's hot or wet or cold?'

'Now and then,' he told her with a smile, 'but not as much as work.'

Zoe turned away and tended to her stove. The kindling was already burning well. She shaped a pyramid of larger logs so they would quickly catch. In the back of her mind, she was trying not to compare her choices to theirs, but failed.

I've tied myself to this place when I could have been a carefree itinerant traveller with almost no bills to pay.

Once she was satisfied that the logs were properly burning, she stood up and offered them coffee again: 'From my new machine.' They both accepted and she went upstairs for mugs from the kitchen. She put the mother's coffee in her hand and went to find the father in the stacks. He was on his haunches looking at a row of field guides to the flora and fauna – the plants and animals – of southern France. He stood up with a groan and a creak of his knees, thanking her for the coffee, cupping the mug between two hands, like someone whose extremities easily felt the cold.

'What was it that persuaded you to leave everything behind?'

'We wanted tomorrow to be different from yesterday,' he said simply, but with an edge. Zoe didn't want to probe but he went on of his own accord: 'We both lost parents far too young. They were hard workers, never giving themselves a moment's freedom. We didn't want to follow their example, to repeat their mistakes, for that to happen to us.'

Zoe reflected that she seemed to be becoming a magnet for unexpectedly deep confessions – Julien Calmet, Firmin Séchan and now this stranger.

'Why the Verdon nature park? Did I ask you that the other day?' She caught a look of wariness in his eyes, then remembered that she knew. The man had bought her last copy of *In the Land of Vultures*. 'Oh, you're a Vulturist,' she told him. 'That's why you're looking at my books on local nature.'

'Kind of,' he told her, adopting an air of inconsequence that she couldn't quite believe in. 'It's fun to try and puzzle out, but others take it much more seriously than we do.'

'You say "we". Both you and your wife are interested?'

'Like other people do crosswords – nothing more than that.'

Zoe didn't believe him, but she smiled and agreed. The bookshop was becoming stuffy so she went and opened the back door a crack onto the little courtyard and the child asked if he could go outside. The mother told him he would have to wait for the rain to stop. It was still falling vertically. She picked the child up and showed him the bird's-eye-view map of Sainte-Catherine in its slender oak frame on the wall, pointing out the square and the bookshop in the centre. The child wasn't very interested. The mother took out her mobile phone and made it play a children's video, giving Zoe an apologetic glance.

'It's *Shaun the Sheep*. I hope you don't mind. We're not disturbing anyone, are we?'

'No, I've no other customers, as you can see.'

'How much for the coffees?'

'Oh,' said Zoe, thrown by the fact she hadn't thought about it. 'It's free.'

'Don't say that. You should ask at least for a token amount.'

'All right then. Two euros each, like the vending machines in the garage.' The mother got up and found some change in the pocket of her coat. 'Thank you,' said Zoe. 'How long have you been looking for the Silver Vulture?'

'A few weeks, on and off. We have the English translation and we wondered if the clues might be different in the French one. That was why we bought it the other day. But it's exactly the same.'

'Do you have it with you?'

'No.'

'Can I ask where you've been looking? Or is that a professional secret among Vulturists?'

'We've been all over,' said the woman, airily. Zoe wondered if she was being evasive. Then, indicating her three-year-old son, she said: 'It's a good way of entertaining Benjy, you know, a reason for scrambling about among the rocks and hiking through the woods.'

The mention of the little boy's name prompted Zoe to introduce herself. She discovered that the parents were Clare and Toby, names she had an idea she had heard before, not long after arriving.

'Stay as long as you like,' Zoe told them.

The husband emerged from the shelves with a book on native and non-native trees. He paid for it with an English debit card from a bank Zoe hadn't heard of but the transaction went through all right and she learned that their surname was 'Day'.

'In the puzzle book, what exactly are the clues?' she asked. 'I sold you my last copy before I had a chance to read it myself.'

'People have different ideas,' said Toby. 'Some think the trees and hills and mountains in the landscape paintings can be identified and there are buried clues in each location. They study the images with people, wondering if they refer to actual human beings alive today.' He laughed. 'But that would be too simple, wouldn't it?'

'You don't agree?'

'If there were people out there who knew, it would have been found by now.'

'I've been told the answer doesn't require digging. Is Sainte-Catherine definitely at the heart of the mystery?'

'Yes.'

'Why do people think that?'

'They know it.'

'Because?' insisted Zoe.

'I wish I could show you,' said Toby.

Clare took over: 'In one of the early paintings, there's a tree that grows in a woven circle with flowers sort of spread out around it, as if they were sparks.'

'Oh,' sad Zoe, catching her drift. 'You mean it looks like a Catherine wheel.'

'That's right,' said Clare, looking impressed. 'Do you know the story?'

'I have a vague memory. Can you tell me the details?'

'It was Catherine of Alexandria, an early Christian who was sentenced to death on what was called a "breaking wheel". Suddenly, a burst of fire from heaven split the wheel asunder. Instead, she was executed by beheading but the dramatic image of the burning wheel persisted.'

'What are the paintings like? Are they very detailed like old botanical illustrations? I mean, are the trees identifiable as opposed to being just sort of generic?'

'They can absolutely be identified,' said Toby. 'Whoever painted them has a gift for draughtsmanship and an understanding of the features that distinguish one species from another.'

'And are they common trees?'

'People talk about chestnuts and beeches and oaks but often get them mixed up and can't go much further. There are lots in the book that are widespread but whose names people probably don't know. For example, would you be able to identify a hackberry?'

'Absolutely not.'

'I think hackberries are important.'

'In the book?'

'In the solution,' he told her. 'They're on half the pages.'

'And where do people mostly search?' asked Zoe. 'Somebody mentioned the Verdon Gorge?'

'That was an obvious place to start because it's associated with the vultures who roost there. Some rock climbers from a local club made a big thing a couple of years ago of examining inaccessible ledges that could only be reached with ropes and belays, attached to pitons hammered into the cliffs.'

'What did they find?'

'Nothing, obviously. How would a painter and riddle maker have managed to access those remote ledges?' asked Toby, reasonably. 'And the climbers were wrong to make a huge show-off thing of it. They ought to have done it in secret. They were fined afterwards for installing their gear in a protected landscape.'

'Plus,' said Clare, 'the book launch promised that anyone is capable of retrieving the treasure.'

'Even an elderly lady,' mused Zoe, lost in her own thoughts.

'You mean Barbara,' said Toby.

'I do,' said Zoe, surprised. 'Did you know her?'

'You know the road to Aix?' he asked. 'There's a deep dip and a stream that runs under the tarmac through a culvert.'

'Yes, I know the place,' said Zoe, remembering the smoke from the stubble burning that had made driving through so dangerous. 'But I didn't know about the culvert. But what does that have to do with Sainte-Catherine?'

'It's the main road. In another of the paintings, there are lots of fountains and most people think that's a reference to Aix-en-Provence which is known as—'

'Yes, the city of fountains. So, the road from there to the "Catherine wheel" town and . . .' Zoe faltered. 'Sorry, I shouldn't have interrupted. So, you knew Barbara. Please, go on. You were talking about the culvert?'

'It was more the fact that this obviously elderly lady was there, poised precariously on the bank, trying to bend down and peer into the darkness of the wet tunnel under the road.'

'Was the culvert running?'

'Yes, at least two feet deep. It's fed by springs and melt-water from the mountains all year round.'

'Why did you stop?'

Clare said: 'We weren't thinking about the Vulture at that point. Was it three weeks ago? We were just worried about a grey-haired woman who seemed stuck or lost.'

'I thought perhaps she might be "wandering", you know,' said Toby.

'It happens,' said Clare, 'because of Alzheimer's, for example.'

'And you stopped to help. That was very kind.'

Toby laughed. 'I soon regretted it. She was vague but still persuaded me that there was "something precious" down there, and could I wade in and look for it. She was very evasive when I asked her questions. Kind of desperate, too. Do you know what I mean?'

Zoe thought about her own interactions with Barabara. 'Yes, there was an undercurrent of desperation. Oh, did she speak English?'

'With an American accent. Apparently, she lived in the States for a time with one of her husbands.'

'Then what happened?'

'I wasn't keen but, in the end, I gave in,' said Toby, with a shiver. 'And, blimey, it was cold.'

Twenty-Four

THE BOOK AT LAST

The story that Toby told was actually very straightforward. He narrated taking off his boots and his hiking socks and the thin cotton socks he wore beneath – to prevent blisters – putting them aside on a dry corner of the terrain. He rolled up his trouser legs and climbed down into the running water. He reiterated exactly how cold it was, rushing down out of the mountains to flow through the culvert beneath the tarmac road.

'Does it flood the road in spring?' she wondered aloud.

'I don't know. Why do you ask?'

'Because it might be important in relation to the Vulture clues.'

'I hadn't thought of that,' said Clare.

Then she made a joke about the fact that, had Toby bought the hiking trousers with zips at the knee so they could be turned into long shorts – which he had been coveting on the internet – it would have been the perfect moment to employ them. Zoe assumed this was conjugal banter and didn't join in.

'It was dark, of course,' Toby resumed, 'in the tunnel under the road – and hard to see.'

'But you have no shortage of kit, Toby,' said Clare, in the same amused tone.

'Yes, all right. I am prepared like a Boy Scout,' he joshed back at her.

There followed a digression during which Zoe learned all about the many clever gadgets that the little English family had acquired for camping and for their itinerant lifestyle. The list included an elasticated torch that Toby strapped around his forehead so that wherever he angled his gaze, he could see whatever there was to see. Then he went on.

'Wading in, I touched a hand against the damp wall, built of bricks and mortar probably a hundred and fifty years ago, an impressive bit of construction. I turned my head from side to side and, I have to admit, it felt creepy.'

'Like in a ghost story?' asked Zoe.

'No, a thriller, like I was suddenly going to see the gaping mouth of a—'

'Shush,' said Clare, indicating the little boy. 'Not in front of Benjy.'

'He's all right,' said Toby. 'Anyway, the bricks were slimy and the mortar in between was all blackened by mould. I didn't go too far because I was concerned that the air in the tunnel might not be good.'

'In what sense?'

'Bad, noxious.'

'Is that something you have experience of? Oh, maybe from caving?'

'Yes, I love a bit of speleology,' he said with a grin.

'Are there any significant cave systems in the Verdon nature park?'

'Not vast, but some.'

'Could the Vulture be secreted underground?'

'Again, there's the issue that it's supposed to be readily accessible, once its's found.' He described how disappointed Barbara was that he could find nothing of interest. 'The thing is, when I told her that there was nothing there, obviously I asked her what I was supposed to be looking for, if she thought there might be a carved message in the brickwork or possibly a niche inside which a clue was hidden. "What sort of clue?" she asked me. I replied: "Well, to the treasure from the book, *In the Land of Vultures*." She went very quiet.'

'Did she know that you were Vulturists, too?'

'Well, she did then. She seemed pleased and also, at the same time, not pleased.'

'What does that mean?'

'I wondered if she was sort of doing a double bluff, wanting people to think the culvert was important when it wasn't.'

'She already knew you were searching and was trying to lead you astray?'

'Maybe. Anyway, can you guess what I did next?' asked Toby.

'I'm going to assume that you waited for a gap in the traffic and crossed the road to have a look in the other end.'

'Yes, but there was no point because it was absolutely choked with a metal grille that had collected sticks and leaves, all sorts. Barbara wanted me to come back to the other end and creep right inside. I wasn't rude but I told her I couldn't just take that risk on the strength of her inquisitiveness. I needed a reason. That was when she told me about the hackberry.'

'Yes, you mentioned them,' said Zoe. 'Are they rare?'

'Not at all. There're loads in Paris and they've been in Provence for five hundred years.'

Zoe guessed that might tie in with the European discovery of the Americas in 1492 and asked: 'From the New World?'

'Yes. Anyway, Barbara became more open and sharing again all of a sudden. She showed me a detail in one of the paintings reproduced in the book that was the spitting image of an actual, real-life hackberry tree, looming over a culvert. I wish I had it with me to show you. *Celtis occidentalis*. There are eight of them in the book, all drawn and painted with real skill, even down to the distinctive super-rough bark. In each landscape, there's an interesting feature nearby.'

'For example?'

'Well, the culvert or a special shape of rock or a couple of peaks on the horizon with the tree in between. Do you see?'

'I'm trying to visualise. Some more copies will arrive later and I'll make sure to find time.'

Clare chimed in: 'Barbara told us that she had been trying to decipher the symbolism or the imagery – I can't remember which word she used – but had come to a grinding halt.'

'I didn't believe her,' said Toby. 'I thought she was sus.'

'In what way?' asked Zoe.

'Knew more than she let on – much more.'

Zoe asked, tentatively: 'You don't seem to mind sharing your ideas. You're not worried about word getting out about where you're looking and someone finding the Vulture before you. Why is that?'

For the first time in a while, Clare spoke in a more serious tone. 'The truth is, we hadn't ever taken it seriously – and this was a few weeks ago, remember, before she died.'

'Yes,' said Zoe quietly. 'Of course it was.'

'And we didn't know about the enormity of the prize. We had no idea the book had sold so well. You know it amounts to several hundred thousand euros?'

'No,' said Zoe. 'I didn't. That could represent a powerful motive.'

'There's a website run by the publisher where you can see the numbers going up, like the jackpot in a lottery.'

'Crikey, let's look.'

She moved towards her laptop but, just then, they were interrupted by some customers, a party of wet but jolly Dutch tourists who told Zoe proudly that they were happy to read guide books in French or in English if she had nothing in their native tongue. From their conversation, Zoe discovered that they were simple tourists and not Vulturists – which, given everything, came as a relief.

No sooner had the Dutch party left than another group of blond northern Europeans came in, browsing the shelves and telling one another – she hoped – what a charming shop it was, perhaps in Norwegian though she couldn't be sure. She offered assistance in French and in English and it turned out that they were looking for picture books for their two small children, perfect little blond creatures, dressed in unisex hiking gear but in tiny sizes.

Zoe enjoyed showing them her stock. They bought an illustrated French alphabet and three different picture books for which the parents said: 'We will invent Norwegian words.'

The transaction complete, they fell into easy conversation, in reasonable English, with Clare and Toby and their little boy, who left off watching his video in order to join the Norwegian infant book club, with every appearance of understanding everything that was said in the Nordic language, which everyone found charming.

The bell clanged again and some more damp tourists came in, exclaiming in delight at the smell of fresh coffee. It became obvious that they knew the Norwegian family and Zoe discovered that there was a tour company, based in Aix-en-Provence, that, in the off-season when the vehicles weren't busy otherwise, brought people by minibus into the villages of the Verdon nature park, showing them the sights and letting them out in a few chosen locations to enjoy the landscape and the lovely villages and hill towns.

Zoe was delighted with this news. She determined to find out who ran the company and get in touch with them directly, with a view to learning the schedule and perhaps developing some kind of preferential relationship. While these thoughts were running through her head, she replenished the filter coffee machine and fetched more mugs from upstairs, glad that they all matched from a set of twelve that she had bought at the Royal Festival Hall in London, decorated with a very characteristic 1950s design from the era of the Festival of Britain.

Soon, the muggy autumn afternoon in *The Bookshop of My Dreams* turned into a full-on caffeine party. Luckily, Zoe had plenty of oat milk and even a pot of single cream that she had bought for making dauphinoise potatoes but hadn't got around to using. Charging only two euros a cup – as well as selling more than two dozen books – the afternoon turned into a financial success. One of the Norwegians asked her: 'Why is there no café in Sainte-Catherine?'

'There is a café,' she explained, 'but they work so hard all summer that they have a few weeks off in the autumn.'

'You should become a café yourself,' he told her. 'A book-shop café.'

'If I did,' said Zoe, her commercial instincts aroused, 'what else do you think I should serve?'

'Oh,' he said, 'tea, herbal tea, maybe cakes? Easy things.'

'Is there any particular reason why you're travelling around the region?' she asked.

'We came in summer. We liked very much, but too hot for walking so we come back in the autumn. We do not organise and worry it was late, you know, for good weather. A few days ago, "bitter cold", like you English say. Then perfect. Now wet.'

The tourist had a lovely manner and Zoe laughed. A small dark man in a shiny black suit came into the shop, a peaked cap in his hand. He spoke to the assembled tourists in French, telling them that he would be waiting in the car park at the foot of the town and that, to remain on schedule, they ought to leave within the next fifteen minutes. Identifying him as the driver, Zoe asked him: 'Where are you going next?'

'We will drive the Verdon Gorge and, I hope, we will see the vultures wheeling. It'll be a good day for it if the rain stops with the warm air creating thermals on which they like to glide.'

Zoe instantly took to the little man. He seemed to have a genuine enthusiasm for the park and for his job of showing it off to tourists.

'Have you been doing this for long?' she enquired.

'No, this is my first year.'

'How did you come to love the park so much? It's obvious that you do.'

The man looked around the shop and lowered his voice, not wanting to be overheard. He needn't have bothered because the conversation was jolly and general.

'I'm not a Vulturist,' he told her. 'I took the job because I love the region. I explore it and I'm paid for it. Don't laugh at me.'

'I absolutely wouldn't dare,' said Zoe.

Soon, the driver and the tourists all drifted away. The English family followed. Zoe checked her watch. It was almost teatime, the hour at which she expected the distributor to arrive with her order of books.

In the gap between their departure and this appointment, she checked her stock and reordered the books that she had sold. Then she did an internet search, trying to find the company that brought the tourists round, whose name the driver had given her. The website was well maintained and stylish and the prices charged seemed reasonable, which gave her pleasure because most tourist activities, in her experience, were fiercely expensive, gouging a captive market.

She made a second search, quickly finding the publisher website for *In the Land of Vultures* – and the dramatic ticker screen that showed the value of the prize fund.

Impressive. Worth killing for? Certainly.

The bell clanged once more but no one came in. Zoe went to open up, finding a delivery woman sent by the book distribution company pushing an awkward hand trailer with thick rubber wheels, reminding her of the cleaning women from the beginning of her Sainte-Catherine adventure. She made space on the counter to stack three cardboard boxes, checking through their contents against the delivery note. Everything was in order.

She drew out a copy of *In the Land of Vultures*, itching to look inside. The delivery woman asked for a signature and wondered aloud: 'Are you trying to solve the puzzle?'

'No, but I'd like to know more about it.'

'What if it's a hoax?' The woman had a pugnacious air, reinforced by her uniform of a brown shirt and shorts, making her resemble a bad-tempered Cub Scout. 'What if it's not out there at all? They'd never have to pay the prize fund but people would still keep buying the book, getting more and more desperate, not knowing they're being . . .' she paused, looking for a suitable expression, then said: *'menées par le nez'*, meaning 'led by the nose', like farm animals pulled from barn to field and back using the iron rings threaded through their nostrils.

'But surely that's not possible?' Zoe protested. 'It would be the most enormous scandal and a criminal offence, a fraud. Surely the publishing company couldn't risk that?'

'What if the publishing company didn't know? What proof is there?'

'I was on their website just now and there seems to be a lot of very convincing documentation.'

'You can't trust what you read on the internet,' argued the woman. 'Everyone knows that.'

Zoe wasn't finding her visitor *'sympathique'* so she didn't pursue the conversation any further. She held the door open for her to leave and watched the trundling of the rubber-wheeled trolley, bouncing across the cobbled square. In the far corner, she noticed Russell, sniffing a drainpipe.

Left alone, Zoe went to sit by the stove – whose fire had burnt right down – in order to leaf through the puzzle book. It was true, what Toby had said. The images were beautiful and rendered with exceptional precision in pen and ink and watercolour, reminding her of botanical sketches of exotic plants that she had seen in antiquarian books compiled by eighteenth- and nineteenth-century explorers and naturalists. There were eight landscapes that alternated with eight double-page spreads with people. The spreads with people, too, were rendered in exquisite detail.

It must be possible to identify the hills and the mountains. People ought to be able to stand in the same positions that the artist stood. But I can't be the only person to have thought of that.

Turning the pages, Zoe noticed that the edges of the images overlapped in the sense that some of the tiny details from the borders on each sheet of glossy paper were repeated. Zoe felt a thrill of insight, imagining cutting the pages out and lining them up on the floor, turning the book into a large frieze.

I couldn't . . .

Looking more closely, she saw more evidence that she was on the right track, but with a further refinement. Items on the upper and lower edges of the pages – birds in flight, animals in the fields – were also repeated, meaning the pages formed not just a frieze, but maybe a map, connected top and bottom, as well as side to side.

For a delicious few seconds, Zoe allowed herself to imagine the sacrilege of taking this brand-new copy of the book apart, aligning all the pages, and seeing the answer to the riddle, revealed by her flash of inspiration.

Someone else must have seen that, too. I bet my German friend, Oskar Weiss, has done exactly that and has the book's pages taped together and pinned up on the wall of his study or his man cave.

Visualising that, Zoe realised something else.

The printing is – obviously – double sided. The 'people' images are all separate compositions and don't fit together, but the 'landscape' double pages . . .

She frowned, imagining a possible sequence of events.

Anyone who wanted to make a complete 'map' of the puzzle, visible all at once, fitting the eight landscapes together, would then need a second copy.

Zoe wished that Toby and Clare – and their delightful little boy Benjy – were still there so she could ask them what they thought. Then the doorbell clanged and she stood up, expecting to greet Oskar with his untidy, greasy hair and formal, broken English.

'Madame Pascal,' said Inspector Sicarie, 'I wonder if you might have time to answer some more questions?'

Twenty-Five

INTERROGATION

Although the inspector had framed his request as a question, Zoe didn't think that she had the right to refuse. Hoping the interview wouldn't last very long, she didn't invite him to sit down but stood at her counter, as she had done before.

'This may take some time,' he told her. 'Perhaps you would be more comfortable in your own accommodation, upstairs.'

'I would prefer not to close the shop. It's important, in retail, to respect the advertised hours of opening.'

'Our conversation will not be one that you would wish overheard,' he told her, his voice low and – she thought – threatening.

'Are you trying to intimidate me?' she asked, lightly. 'I have experience of police procedure.'

'I know. I have been briefed by Brigadier Grenelle and by the British police. The wheels of justice turn slowly but, in the end, they inevitably reach their intended goal.'

'Perhaps you should go on.'

'Some might consider it ancient history, the dramas of your teenage years, but it is an interesting insight into your character.' His eyes flicked up to meet hers for a second, then he promptly changed the subject. 'I wonder if you would tell me how it is that you came to choose this lonely place.'

'By lonely place, I suppose you mean Sainte-Catherine? Did we not cover this the other day and, if you don't mind, before answering your questions about my dim and distant past, I think I would be within my rights to know why you have been researching me so thoroughly.'

'I believe you know.'

'I can assure you that I don't.'

'Then let me explain. First, there is the fact of your relationship with the deceased. Second, your presence at the discovery of her body. Third, your lack of surprise at that event. Fourth, your desire to associate yourself with the brigadier's investigation. Fifth, your repeated insistence on visiting her accommodation in the guest house. Sixth, Monsieur Napoléon's evidence of your dispute with the deceased.'

'Which never happened,' she insisted.

'Seventh, your manner.'

'My manner?'

'In the context of these dramatic events, you seem to me too calm, too easy.'

'You would prefer me to be hysterical and fall on the floor, to rend my garments?'

No sooner were the words out of her mouth than Zoe regretted them. Although she had intended them to be facetious, she felt uncomfortably that they had sounded suggestive. Fortunately, the inspector didn't seem to notice.

'It is not a question of what I would prefer,' he told her. 'It is a question of what would seem more natural.'

'You're suggesting that I'm an "unnatural woman".'

'Am I?'

'It seems to me that you are.' Zoe heard herself doubling down, her tone increasingly combative. 'Would you like to get to the point?'

'You were sixteen years old when you were associated, for the first time, with a capital crime. Your behaviour was not above suspicion. It is a matter of official record that your motivations and actions were suspected, although ultimately exonerated. Soon after, however, you were a witness to the

229

circumstances surrounding several other murders. This seems extraordinary to me.'

'I'm not sure that I should concern myself with whether or not you find the circumstances of so long ago "extraordinary". Do you have anything else to say about your current investigation, other than your meaningless pretexts for importuning me?'

'I suppose, at some point, all those years ago, an investigating officer must have told you that the innocent have nothing to fear, that the role of the police is to uncover the truth – and the truth can only harm the guilty?'

'Whether or not they did doesn't enlighten me with regard to your presence in my home.'

'In your shop,' he quibbled.

'Which is also my home,' she insisted.

All the time this conversation had been taking place, Zoe had been standing very still, her hands gripping the edge of the counter. She realised this gesture betrayed her tension and folded her arms, then regretted doing so as she knew it must look defensive. He, meanwhile, had been standing at an angle to her, his round shoulders in his shabby coat swaying slightly as he shifted his weight from foot to foot. Only now and then did his eyes meet hers. His attitude made her think that he was listening for some clue in her tone of voice, some subtle frailty or nervousness that would indicate how he ought to progress his interrogation – for that was what it was, she saw clearly. She was a 'person of interest' in the investigation into Barbara Ercollani's death.

'What do you say to my seven reasons?'

'Non-reasons, I would call them.'

But they aren't "non-reasons", not really. Enumerating them like that, I can see how they might seem to add up to something.

'Why were you so keen to look through the deceased woman's belongings?' he demanded.

'That is not an accurate description of the circumstances. I believe I told you that Denis Allard, being unwell and upset by the mess Barbara had left behind, asked me to help out.'

'Davide Quillan suggests that it was the other way around, that you put yourself forward not once but twice.'

Zoe didn't know what to say.

Does that mean that Davide is deliberately trying to implicate me? And, if so, can it be in order to divert suspicion away from himself?

'I believe I've already answered this point,' she told him.

'Did you remove anything from her room?'

'Antoine told me that the police had finished their investigation,' she prevaricated, 'and left the place in a complete state.'

'That isn't an answer to my question.'

'If you know, why are you asking?'

'Because it is interesting for an investigating officer to hear for himself how honest a witness or a suspect is prepared to be.'

'Which am I?'

He used the phrase she had just imagined.

'You are a "person of interest".'

'To whom?'

'To the investigating magistrate who has tasked me with the collection and organisation of facts. Do you refuse to tell me what you took?'

'A book,' said Zoe. 'Barbara suggested I might want to read it.'

'Could I see it?'

'Now?'

Zoe would have liked to refuse, but her eyes had automatically gone straight to it, lying innocently on her second-hand coffee table. She fetched the novel with its racy cover and many turned-down pages, wondering what the inspector would make of it, feeling very awkward at the idea that he would think her a devotee of erotic fiction, despite the fact that she was very open-minded herself.

The problem isn't the fact of the 'spicy' story, it's what goes through other people's minds.

The inspector contemplated *Infinite Desire*, hesitating over the image on the cover – a cartoonish, chesty young woman with absurdly large eyes, and two different, shadowy male figures in the background, clearly competing for her affection. Beneath the title and the author's name, Erica Noll, the two men's faces were each caught in the two circles of the infinity symbol, like a figure eight on its side. He stroked a finger across the image and she saw his gaze sharpen.

Has he seen something I missed?

He opened it, taking in the fact of the many folded corners, doing as Zoe had done and placing his finger repeatedly on the text as if deciding which sentence or word or letter was indicated. After what seemed a long pause, he raised his eyes and looked at her.

'What kind of message do you think this is?'

'Who's to say it is a message?'

Sicarie sighed. 'Why pretend not to understand? This vandalism is not normal behaviour for a lover of books.' He put the paperback into a large sagging pocket in his overcoat. 'You are an intelligent woman, though you seem determined not to face facts in your current dilemma. You will have searched for meaning, concealed within these pages. I know that. I can see it in your face, in your stillness, the wariness in your eyes. Why do you think yourself cleverer than I?'

'I don't think anything of the sort,' she snapped. 'Were you not here, I wouldn't be thinking about you at all.'

At this, Zoe was surprised to see him smile – not to her but to himself, his eyes down once more on the ancient floorboards. She wondered what he was thinking and if she was in the process of making an enemy.

'That was like a line in a play,' he told her. 'Would you like to give me a reason why Etienne Napoléon might invent a noisy argument between you and the deceased?'

'Because he resents me as an incomer and fears that I will steal his trade. He's been unpleasant to me from the day of my arrival.' The inspector made no comment. 'Is that all?' she demanded.

Very quietly, still without meeting her gaze, he explained: 'I gave you seven reasons earlier why I consider you an enigmatic presence, one that, from my point of view, needs to be understood. There is an eighth.'

'Is that so?'

'It is.'

He went to leave and she found herself calling after him. 'Are you not going to tell me?'

He hesitated at the door and seemed to be waiting for the clanging of the bell to cease before replying.

'You will find out in time.'

Twenty-Six

ILLUMINATION

Inspector Sicarie left her, closing the door quietly behind himself. Zoe simply stood, wondering what she ought to do next. The bookshop seemed unnaturally quiet. There was a slightly burnt fragrance in the air from the hot plate beneath the filter coffee jug that she had allowed to become empty but neglected to turn off.

I need to get on top of things. I need to find out for myself what's going on.

As these words formed in her imagination, she felt the need to go out and search, visit the church, knock on people's doors, drive out and examine the culvert. But none of these unfocused occupations was really necessary. With the clues from the erotic novel leaving her baffled – and the inspector having taken it away with him – she decided she ought to be studying *In the Land of Vultures*.

She sat down in one of her club armchairs and opened the book at the imprint page, where details of the date of publication and so on were listed, including a copyright line that said: © *Fondation Vautours*. That she found interesting because no one had yet mentioned that there was a charitable foundation attached to the whole extravaganza. Zoe determined to research that just as soon as she had a moment.

Charities in the UK have to publish their accounts so it's probably the same in France, isn't it?

She leafed through the book, getting a sense of the whole. There were only sixteen double pages, making thirty-two pages in all. They alternated between eight double-page landscapes and eight closer-up double-page depictions of people at work: tending to goats and sheep in the fields; cutting up a carcass in a butcher's shop; someone snipping a length of fabric from a roll; bottling up in a wine cellar; serving customers in a greengrocer's premises; preparing the symbolic bread and wine for communion mass; happy people eating and drinking at café tables; little children hard at work in a classroom.

Zoe flipped through these eight human-centred images twice, thinking that there was definitely a message in them that she ought to recognise, but she couldn't summon it from her subconscious.

Is it about the order, ending up with the infants writing in their little exercise books?

All the pictures had an olde-worlde look, as if they depicted scenes from the previous century.

Maybe from just after World War II?

But there was no sense of deprivation or poverty.

Whoever drew and painted these scenes did so in celebration of a bygone way of life.

In addition, each 'human-centric' image included words that could be read. For example, the barrels in the cellar picture had the names of grapes clearly visible on their ends. The seamstress, with her roll of fabric, stood before shelves on which were inscribed the French words for velvet, satin, silk, wool and a couple of others that were illegible because partly obscured. In the butcher's shop, several cuts of meat were named and she realised that behind the man's head were the words *Boucherie Chevaline*, meaning 'horse butcher'.

Zoe flicked through, sort of assembling a sense of all these words in a jumble in her imagination, but they didn't coalesce with meaning or lead her to another deduction.

She turned her attention to the eight landscapes. Each one was very lovely, composed with a subtle appreciation of form and light, depicting different times of day and, she realised, different seasons of the year. The trees in the first image were draped with snow and leafless. Then, as the eight landscapes pages progressed, spring burgeoned, then summer, then autumn, ending once more in winter. Other details – such as the running of rivers or the presence of flowers in the meadows – reinforced this sense of eight chronological snapshots from the calendar of a single year.

Thinking about the running of rivers, she found the image that had sent Barabara in search of the culvert under the main road.

Is it because I know the place – and spent time close by when Renée broke down – that it seems so accurate? Am I sort of pasting my own memories over the top of this reproduction?

It was the third image.

Given there are eight landscape pictures to the year, dividing fifty-two, that makes six and a half weeks for each one. So, the third double-page panorama depicts somewhere between thirteen and nineteen and a half weeks into the year.

The hackberry tree – as she had learned it was called – was plainly visible, in early leaf.

The first landscape image is the end of winter, then there are two for spring, two for summer and two for autumn, then the eighth and final one is the beginning of winter once more.

Turning the pages, she tried to find common features, paying close attention to the distant mountains. The sky was, by turns, iron grey or clear blue or broken by fluffy white clouds or bruised with purple storms. In two of the paintings, dark jagged peaks were silhouetted against an inky-blue, starry firmament. All eight landscapes included a vulture, always flying, gliding on outstretched wings or diving after prey, with eyes that seemed to shine, even in the ones depicted at night.

Zoe tried to put herself into the paintings, to see what it was that the vultures were looking at but, of course, that made no sense. They were looking out of the page at her. She went back to the third one, depicting late spring, and touched the glossy paper with the road and culvert in the foreground, noticing that the vulture in this one was profiled against the partly cloudy sky in a kind of arrow shape, its wings slightly folded back.

Plunging, almost as if indicating a direction.

She got up for a sheet of A4 from the printer and laid its straight edge along a line from the tip of the vulture's tail feathers, through its one visible eye, finding that the prolongation of the line went through the trunk of the hackberry, into the opening under the road.

Well, that explains why Barbara was so interested in that location.

Zoe contemplated her loose sheet of paper.

But why did she fold down all the corners in the novel? Was it because she was making a note of something she had seen that she feared she might forget?

She turned the pages to a landscape that showed the confluence of the canal and the river, the Rigolet, thinking about the day of her arrival in Sainte-Catherine and the children she had seen playing there. The canal was shaded, she remembered, with parasol pines, but there were other trees growing close by, perhaps including another hackberry?

There were no words in the landscapes and Zoe felt a bit lost because she was much more a 'literature person' than an 'art person'. She turned back to the images of twentieth-century people going about their business several generations ago. Because they were all interiors, there were no vultures on the wing but, in each painting, one of the carrion birds appeared in other guises: as an inanimate ornament in two of them; in paintings-within-the-paintings in two others; as a child's toy in the classroom; a live one outside the window of the horse butcher's looking hungrily in.

Zoe slid her sheet of A4 paper across each double page, lining up the tail and the eye of these vultures, too. Every line led her to a fragment of text. For example, in the name of the shop, behind the butcher's head: *Boucherie Chevaline*. Because the two words were on top of one another, the line indicated two letters, a 'c' and an 'r'.

Zoe fetched a pen and wrote them down, then went through all the other 'people' images, ending up with eleven letters that, once again, she wrote in a jumble, like the ones she had thought to identify in the text of Barbara's raunchy novel, *Infinite Desire*. Luckily, she still had her notes to compare with, even though Inspector Sicarie had taken it.

If both books contain anagrams or codes, they must be connected.

With a growing feeling of excitement, Zoe realised that she now had the means to refine her two lists. Comparing the first jumble with the new one from *In the Land of Vultures*, she decided that there were eleven or maybe twelve letters that she could be certain about because they were on both.

She stood up at her counter and woke her laptop, hesitating over how to search. Then she thought of trying an online anagram solver, typing in the whole string: O U L C O C I E R M I H L.

The longest possible answer was 'heroicomic' which only had ten letters and was a word Zoe had never heard before.

That seems to be a dead end.

She tried again with a French anagram solver. The longest answer was an eleven-letter word, MICOCOULIER. Not knowing what it meant but thinking it looked plausibly scientific, Zoe copied and pasted it into a new search and found a French-language Wikipedia page that gave her a detailed and vivid explanation.

A *micocoulier* was a tree, from the genus *Celtis*, capable of tolerating both extremely cold winters and prolonged hot summers. It had a deeply-grooved cork-like bark, edible autumn berries and a useful timber often employed in the manufacture of whip handles, walking canes and other useful but decorative items.

I think I can see where this is going.

With a sense that she wouldn't be surprised by the answer, Zoe pasted the word *micocoulier* into a translation engine. Sure enough, the instantaneous reply confirmed her suspicion.

Hackberry.

She went back to the French Wikipedia page, discovering that the hackberry also provided timber for spindles, wood sculptures and even musical instruments. Because it often grew with three smaller branches sprouting from a larger one, it lent itself to the manufacture of wooden hay forks in the shape of tridents.

Her mind swimming with all this taxonomical and practical information, Zoe returned to her club armchair, in front of the stove, opening the door to find just a few red embers glowing in the bed of ash. Zoe remembered Gato Merino telling her that he and his son, Lali, had brought some 'odds and ends of *falabreguier*'. She went back to her laptop and searched for that word, too, relying on her memory of Gato spelling it out for her.

Sure enough, *falabreguier* was the common, non-scientific Provençal name for the *micocoulier*, or hackberry.

Once again, Zoe subsided into one of her leather armchairs.

This is progress. I now know much more than I did before, thanks to finally getting the chance to browse a copy of In the Land of Vultures. *The trouble is, I'm not particularly clever at this sort of thing and I have no idea what any of these cryptic clues might mean.*

239

She wearily shook her head as another problem bubbled up out of the swamp of her troubled imagination.

And if I can't crack the puzzle, I'll have no way of escaping Inspector Sicarie's suspicion that I'm a murderer.

Twenty-Seven

Darkness Falls

Closing time at *The Bookshop of My Dreams* – half past six.

Zoe tidied up, put a couple of logs on the stove in case it got cold later and donned her ski jacket and hiking boots, ready to go outside. Before leaving, she went back for the puzzle book and her mobile, then exited, carefully locking the front door.

That's a mystery I haven't thought about since I arrived. I never found out from Caroline if somebody stole my keys from her office. Why on earth would they have done that? Could it possibly be connected to the Vulture?

She tried to imagine Barbara Ercollani breaking into the notary's office and turning the place upside down.

That doesn't seem likely. But I was woken up in the night by somebody or something on one of the first nights. Could it have been the thief trying my door, finding it bolted?

Zoe crossed the square – lit by street lamps though the sun wouldn't fully set until seven o'clock – in a contemplative mood, but not certain what to focus her mind upon. She stopped in front of the octagonal church, listening to the vague sounds of her neighbours inside their homes, busy with their individual lives.

Then the locksmith changed the mechanisms, front and back, making the stolen keys redundant. But whoever took them wasn't to know that.

She continued downhill, past the restaurants, and arrived at the well, putting her hands on the parapet wall that surrounded it, looking down, trying to make out the water far below.

I suppose, because it's a dryish autumn after a hot summer, it's quite deep down.

She thought about another M. R. James story in which a treasure of some kind – she couldn't remember exactly what, perhaps a bag of coins – was concealed in the wall of a well. At the climax of the story, as the protagonist awkwardly manoeuvred himself in the slimy obscurity of the tight shaft and reached into the damp niche, there was a wonderfully creepy description of a strange wet arm being laid almost tenderly across his neck and shoulders in the moist darkness.

What a hiding place this would be. There are even metal hoops on the wall to climb down.

Zoe shuddered, smiling to herself.

No need to give myself the heebie-jeebies.

Instead of taking her usual route down to the car park and the town hall, she followed the facing lane that traversed the slope between biscuit-coloured stone houses. It led her out of Sainte-Catherine on the north side, where a country lane wove into the fields, little used with grass growing along the centre. After two hundred metres, she was stopped by a five-bar metal gate with a printed sign that told her that the rising fields beyond belonged to the Maurice farm and that no dogs were permitted due to the presence of sheep. She looked around to make sure that Russell hadn't sneakily followed her on his naughty little legs. He was nowhere to be seen.

The lock on the gate was a simple mechanism, a sprung bar that could be pulled back to release a catch. She shut it carefully behind her and followed a dirt pathway worn in the grass at the edge of the field because, due to the recent heavy rain, the rest of the terrain was sopping wet.

The moon had risen before the fall of night. The field climbed ahead of her and she followed the path, becoming pleasantly puffed. Near the top of the slope, she found a small digger, known as a bobcat, used for minor earth moving. It was parked beside an intersection with another lane that led away to the west, again protected by a metal gate, she thought towards Marcel's farmhouse.

Zoe pressed on towards the summit of the green hill, heading for a tall, dark silhouette, like a spear of slender darkness against the fading light of the sky. The closer she came, the more certain she was of what she would find.

The mobile phone mast.

Close to the summit, the path was blocked by a fallen tree, one that she recognised.

Cork-like bark and branches that sprout like tridents – a hackberry.

When still alive, the *micocoulier* tree must have been twenty metres tall with a spread in its canopy at least as wide. She made her way around it, towards a root ball that looked as though it had pulled itself whole out of the ground, together with a heap of dirt and stones. Next to it, looking very out of place on the rural hillside, were some functional municipal barriers in heavy orange plastic, protecting a damp hole in the ground where, she had to assume, the damage to the cables connecting to the cellular network of the mast must be located. She looked at the sky.

I need to do this quickly. Otherwise, all the light will be gone.

She opened the puzzle book and angled the pages towards the west, making sure not to cast them into shadow from the last orange rays of the setting sun. She compared the skyline in several of the painted images before settling on the fifth one because it included a lonely tree on a grassy summit, just like the one she was standing on. The jagged teeth of the mountains away to the north matched the painting precisely. The only substantial difference was the lack of a decorative flock of white sheep.

The images in this book are snapshots. It doesn't mean everything has to be exactly as depicted every hour of every day.

Zoe turned on the spot, looking in all directions across the gorgeous countryside that was disappearing into deeper and darker shadows. She wondered if there was a pathway she could follow towards the thick forest beyond the Maurice farm.

Presumably through the gate where that bobcat is parked. That would probably take me straight to the place where Lucia's husband was gored by a wild boar and killed, poor man.

Zoe became very still.

I wonder if that was investigated by the police. How hard might it be to give the impression of such an injury when, in fact, the wound was caused by a knife – for example a hunter's knife?

Zoe had never met the man nor seen a photograph of him, but she visualised a stocky local in a khaki jacket with many pockets, wet brown hair sticking to his forehead, lying among fallen leaves, a dark pool of sticky blood soaking through them into the soil.

If that was a method I was going to use, I wouldn't employ my hunter's knife. I would try and get hold of a wild-boar tusk and use that as my weapon, like the murderer in the Fred Vargas novel, The Upside-Down Man, *who pretended to be a wolf.*

She turned her mind back to the solid evidence, close at hand.

Now I think I know how the mobile phone connection was broken. This massive hackberry tree must have fallen in strong winds. Up here on the top of the hill, the soil is probably thin.

She looked at landscape five in the puzzle book again, but it was becoming less distinct in the advancing dusk.

If this tree is one of the key objects depicted in the eight landscape images, what will it mean for the hunt for the Vulture if it's no longer there? Soon, Gato Merino is going to come up here with a chainsaw to cut it up into logs.

She contemplated the mast itself, a narrow, unnatural shape in the rural environment.

Or maybe it wasn't the strong winds off the peaks. Maybe the phone company brought a bigger piece of machinery than that bobcat and pulled the tree over in order to make room for their mast. They weren't to know it was crucial to a literary puzzle.

She retraced her steps downhill. Because it was getting hard to see, she stumbled twice, the second time reaching out for a fence post to help her balance, catching the heel of her thumb on a strand of barbed wire.

'Ouch,' she said aloud and sucked the wound and spat, wary of infection.

She carried on more carefully to the five-bar gate, released the catch, pushed through and approached Sainte-Catherine from the north, entering through the narrow gap in the houses that would bring her past Napoléon Etienne's home.

The shutters were closed on his three-storey building, but slivers of light were visible through cracks in and around the shutters on both the ground and first floors. Illuminated by a street lamp, attached to a building a few doors away, Zoe could read the sign advertising the premises as a second-hand bookshop, engraved in bronze, the deep-cut letters painted with black enamel. The font used was one that she knew the Emperor Napoléon's memorials in Paris, such as the Arc de Triomphe, also employed.

I bet that's not an accident. But I don't care if he thinks of himself as an emperor. I'm not going to let him tell lies about me and I'm definitely not going to let him mess about with my van again. I need to put him on the spot.

There was no knocker so she rapped on the door with her knuckles, left a pause of two or three seconds, then repeated the gesture. The door was heavy and close-fitting and she heard no sound from within until it opened a crack and she saw the little man's suspicious face – or rather a sliver of his suspicious face, between the edge of the timbers and the frame.

'I'm busy. You can't come in.'

'I didn't ask to come in,' said Zoe. 'I just came to tell you that I know what you did.'

The expression of guilt in his eyes was inescapable.

'I don't know what you mean,' he said, impulsively.

'Yes, you do,' she told him. 'I haven't yet mentioned it to the police, but I might.'

'You're in enough trouble as it is,' he hissed.

'No, I'm not,' she retorted.

'Do you think people don't know?'

He tried to shut the door, but Zoe had taken the precaution of putting the toe of her hiking boot in the gap.

'You realise you might have caused a serious accident. I've spoken to the assistant at the second-hand furniture shop. He has closed-circuit television cameras inside and out. I could easily get hold of the tapes and pass them on to Inspector Sicarie. What do you say to that?'

'I don't believe you,' he told her, but there was apprehension and calculation in his eyes.

'I don't like people lying about me, especially to the police.'

'I told them what I thought I heard.'

'You were mistaken. I think we need to have a bit of a chat,' said Zoe, feeling a need to press home her advantage.

If indeed I do have an advantage.

'Why?'

'Let me in and we'll get to the bottom of this.' Though she felt no respect or affection for the little man, she forced herself to smile. 'There's no need for us to be enemies.'

'Except you are forcing your way into my home,' he retorted, truculently. 'How would you feel?'

Zoe sighed and told him: 'I'm not the one who—' She stopped, having glimpsed a large poster on the wall behind him. 'Is that from the launch of *In the Land of Vultures*?'

'It's none of your business. You're not welcome here, either in my home or in Sainte-Catherine.'

'I don't think that's up to you,' said Zoe.

'You're just a tourist. You won't last.'

'I assure you I'm not a tourist. Sainte-Catherine is now my home and, if that's a problem for you, you'll have to get used to it.' Zoe could hear herself and felt self-conscious, jousting in a public street. 'As I said, I was in Aix to pick up a couple of bits of furniture. I didn't ask for the video tapes, but I will if I consider you not to have learned your lesson. Do you understand?'

The same look of doubtful calculation came into his eyes. She could still only see a sliver of his face and that was only because her strong rubber toe was stopping him from closing the door. She thought he was trying to remember if it was true – that there were security cameras outside the *dépôt-vente*. Then he surprised her by saying: 'I have something for you.'

In a quick movement, he snatched up something out of sight and prodded her with it in the stomach – an umbrella. She stepped back, instinctively, and he forced the door closed, leaving Zoe alone in the quiet street.

She laughed.

That was an unexpected interlude. I surprise myself.

She walked away, feeling that she had won the encounter on points.

He doesn't know I made up the story about the security cameras. That shook him. At least, it ought to have done, but what if he's a cold-blooded murderer himself?

The lane took her through the narrow houses to the central square, Place Sainte-Catherine, where she put the puzzle book through her own large letter box. Then she walked down the cobbled streets to where the haberdasher, Antoinette Grenelle, had her premises. The front window was open, revealing an Aladdin's cave of buttons, ribbons, braid, zips, bolts of cloth and so on, plus a large cutting table with a brass rule set in the edge. Antoinette was busy with a bucket and mop, washing the floor of terracotta tiles. She caught sight of Zoe looking in and told her: 'Have a seat. I'll be out shortly.'

Beside the front door was the weathered kitchen chair on which Zoe had first come across the *mercière*, smoking a dark-brown cheroot. Zoe didn't sit down because a bird had pooped on it. She contemplated the sky, now almost completely dark, thinking about the position of the stars in the heavens and whether that might be important in the two paintings from *In the Land of Vultures* that represented night-time scenes.

Antoinette came outside, leaving the front door open 'for the drying draught'. From a pocket of her apron, she took out a loose cheroot and lit it with a cheap BIC lighter.

'When we first met,' Zoe told her, 'I believed you when you suggested there was a feud between you and your brother. I was actually worried about what I might have let myself in for, moving to Sainte-Catherine. I began to visualise all kinds of simmering resentments. Then Barbara Ercollani made a passing remark about "factions" that I found unnerving.'

'It was just my little joke. I thought you would have known, being a bookseller.'

'No one's heard of the Vulture in England. I mean, some people might have, but not I.'

'I reckoned that you'd have been aware and knew to take it in jest.'

'On the other hand,' said Zoe, pointedly, 'Barbara Ercollani was a Vulturist and she's dead, so maybe the whole thing shouldn't be taken in jest? And Julien Calmet thinks it's evil, that it's evidence that the love of money always leads to sin and danger.'

'Father Julien is a troubled man,' said Antoinette, drawing contemplatively on her cheroot. 'He won't last.'

'How do you mean? Here, in Sainte-Catherine?' Zoe asked, reminded of Napoléon Etienne's unkind judgement on her.

'No, I mean as a priest. He doesn't believe deeply enough for the sacrifice.'

'How can you be so sure? What sacrifice, exactly?'

'He's a man, a proper man, not a eunuch,' said Antoinette. 'Ask your friend Caroline.'

'Were they in a relationship?'

'They were and, as I heard it, all through his theological training, just up until he was ordained and put a stop to it. She's not renounced, however.'

'Why do you say that?'

'She's in Sainte-Catherine more often than is necessary.'

'Necessary in what way?'

'For someone with occasional conveyancing to do for Ambroise Caille, the estate agent.'

Zoe thought about what Julien had told her about the way Caroline injured her arm.

'Did you know she's a Vulturist, too?'

'Of course I did.'

Zoe changed tack. 'I was up by the mast earlier his evening, just before dusk. Are you aware of what's happened there?'

'A tree came down.'

'Yes. Is that what ruptured the underground cables?'

'Apparently.'

Antoinette looked like she was holding something back. Zoe decided to share what she had worked out.

'That fallen tree is one of those pictured in the puzzle book. Did you know that?'

'I did.' Antoinette dropped her cheroot and crushed the butt under her masculine, lace-up shoe. 'Lower your voice.'

'All right,' said Zoe, more quietly. 'I was just thinking, what if the tree fell because someone was digging up there, thinking it might be where the Vulture was buried, maybe

249

even using the bobcat I saw parked lower down the hill, and that's what undermined the tree as well as damaging the cables.'

'That's a big "what if",' said Antoinette. 'Who were you thinking of?'

'I suppose it's Marcel Maurice's bobcat?' Zoe asked.

'And he certainly wouldn't be able to dig by hand, having only one of them,' said Antoinette, brutally. Then she sighed. 'It looks like you're good at this. It's a shame you didn't come sooner. We might have made a team for finding the treasure, you and I.'

'Except, the treasure is much more valuable for having been in the ground for so long.'

'Not necessarily in the ground,' said Antoinette, gnomically.

'Where else, though?'

'Barbara was often in church. Did you know that?'

'I think someone mentioned it.'

Zoe actually had a vivid memory of Julien commenting that her attendance had become '*assiduous*'. Zoe didn't say so out loud, but she wondered if that meant that Barbara had discovered something – possibly based on the deciphering of what must have been a major clue about the *micocoulier* trees – and whatever it was pointed to the church and that meant that she wanted to attend every service she could.

And, of course, that was where her body was found.

Zoe came back to herself to find Antoinette weighing her up.

'You're keeping back,' said the haberdasher. 'I'm sorry to see that. I might have helped you.'

'Helped me how?'

'I could tell the inspector that we were together at the crucial time, give you an alibi.'

'How do you know the crucial time?'

'My brother told me.'

'Why would you do that?'

250

'Like I said, we could be a team to find the Vulture. I've an idea you've seen something others haven't, perhaps from coming to it fresh.'

'You shouldn't speak so lightly of lying to the police.'

'Who's to say it would be lying? Who's to say I didn't see you creeping into the guest house and coming back out.'

'How do you know about that?'

'People talk.'

'Including your brother, again?'

'Yes. You've grasped that we've not really fallen out. That's just for a joke.'

'Did you see me, though? Weren't you down at the *mairie* with the band as everyone was gathering and tuning up?'

'If you don't know yourself, how would the inspector be able to contradict me?'

'True,' said Zoe, feeling she was out of her depth with all the wheels-within-wheels of Antoinette's ideas. And the haberdasher's gaze was mesmeric and unblinking, yet still with a ghost of the 'wink' Zoe had seen at their first encounter, as if what Antoinette meant was never quite what she said. 'What else do you know?'

'That your friend Caroline was here on the evening in question but she didn't join the procession.'

'Do you know why not?'

'Because she had a fierce argument with her ex-boyfriend. In my doorway, would you believe? I'd turned off my lights ready to go down and they thought I was out, I suppose.'

Zoe tried to imagine Caroline and Julien in a 'fierce' argument and found it might suit her friend's lively personality but not the more reserved priest.

'Where does that leave us?'

'Ready for dinner,' said Antoinette, decisively. 'Come back and talk to me some more, when you've had a chance to think things through.'

'All right,' said Zoe. She still had a few invitations in the back pocket of her jeans. 'Or you could come to my party?'

'Perhaps I will.'

Antoinette went inside, shutting the door behind her, then reached through the open window to close the external shutters. Zoe walked away, deep in thought, past the well and Place Saint-Bertrand and the guest house in its brief cul-de-sac, up to the heavy doors of the church. She turned the handle, finding them locked.

I suppose it isn't left open for fear of robbery or vandalism. That could be why Barbara became an assiduous churchgoer, as her only opportunities to examine the place and understand it as a repository of clues. Then it was probably left open ready for the arrival of the effigy. In fact, it was. I remember. Julien didn't have to unlock it. But I wish I'd paid more attention to the statuary and so on when I was there for evensong the other day.

Behind her, she heard the doors of Le Gourmand opening and went back down the cobbled street to find Simouno Simone, the waitress and proprietor, wife of the chef, Quentin Simone, watering the stylish steel boxes out of which the thick trunks of her vines grew. Zoe greeted her with a smile and asked if she would soon be opening up.

'This time of year, we just do Wednesday into the weekend. But the supermarket will still be open if you hurry.'

'Never mind, I've got some bits and pieces in the fridge. But I wanted to ask you a question.'

'Yes,' said Simouno, her drawn face politely attentive. 'What would that be about?'

'Are you a Vulturist as well?'

Twenty-Eight

EIGHT HACKBERRIES

Simouno Simone didn't seem unnerved by Zoe's question – *'Are you a Vulturist as well?'* – though Zoe had surprised herself by asking it.

This isn't systematic in any way. I'm just blundering around, challenging whoever I run into.

'Yes, I am,' Simouno told her, smiling.

There was a short pause.

'If you don't have time to speak now, I'll leave you in peace,' Zoe told her.

'Have you caught the bug too?'

'I've been reading the book and I was just comparing one of the locations, the fallen tree by the mast.'

Simouno looked confused, so Zoe explained.

'Oh, I've not been up there for ages,' said the restaurateur, then she added a phrase that Zoe didn't immediately understand because it was an English word pronounced in French: *'Sur le quad.'*

'You mean a four-wheeled motorbike?'

'I do.'

'How dashing and exciting.'

'Would you like to try? We could make a circuit. You can ride behind.'

Simouno was beaming, like a teenager inviting a new friend to a sleepover.

I can't refuse. This is the sort of thing that friends do together, on the spur of the moment. What's the alternative? 'No, I have to go home and wash my hair.' And it'll be an opportunity to find out more from someone who knows the landscape intimately.

'All right, let's do it.'

'Excellent. I'll meet you down at the garages.'

'No, I'll wait. But won't your husband want to come with you?'

'Quentin's not interested. In any case, he's in his kitchen, trying new recipes.'

'Not a Vulturist?' Zoe asked, feeling like a scratched record.

'No, he thinks we're all silly.'

Simouno disappeared indoors, leaving Zoe with a feeling of excited anticipation.

Exploring the landscape after dark on a quad bike – that's not what I expected when I was hoping to become more integrated into the everyday life of Sainte-Catherine.

While Simouno was getting changed, the evening was becoming chillier, though nowhere near as cold as the previous few days, before the rain began to fall. Zoe hoped they weren't caught out in another shower, though it would be a good test for her Decathlon ski jacket.

Simouno emerged from the front door of the restaurant dressed in similar clothes to Zoe – practical hiking boots, jeans, and a warm and waterproof coat.

'Let's go.'

As they walked down through the quiet streets, Zoe asked why Quentin thought that the Vulturists were silly.

'I think I told you that he's a fifth child?'

'How does that influence things?'

'First-borns bask in their parents' attention, then they get pushed aside by the new baby and become sort of mini-adults, diligent and desperate to excel. They score higher on IQ tests and fear failure. With the second child, parents are less attentive, so they become people pleasers, in order to get attention. Then another turns up, all cute and lovely and fawned over, but not for long, as the sequence continues. By the fifth, it's all just routine. "Oh, hey, there's another kid." Fourth and fifth children have to find their own thing, inside themselves, that gives their lives meaning.'

'And that's your Quentin? He found cooking?'

'Precisely. Merciful heavens, did he find cooking.' Simouno laughed. 'I'm glad for him though.'

'Local?'

'Born and bred. Loves to forage in the countryside. Knows every nook and cranny.'

Interesting . . .

'But why does that make him think the Vulturists, like you, are silly?'

'That late-child self-sufficiency also means they think only their chosen path is the right one.' Simouno sighed. 'He doesn't understand how people can get so involved in the mystery. And he's Asperger's so he's ultra-focused.'

Or, maybe, thought Zoe, *that means he likes puzzles and pattern-seeking and he's the author of the book and he pretends to despise it in order to cover that up. Born locally and as a forager for natural ingredients for his kitchen, he would be well placed.*

They had reached the car park. Simouno unlocked the fourth garage along.

'Did you buy this from the . . .' Zoe paused, trying to remember who had originally owned which one. 'Did it belong to the horse butcher, back in the mists of time?'

Simouno stopped and said: 'Ah, so you are properly on the trail.'

'I suppose I have been thinking about it. The old-fashioned horse butcher is in the book. It has to be a clue of some sort.'

'That's what we think.'

'We?'

'Me, Antoine, Antoinette, Davide, Denis but not so much, Marcel and Thierry and Odile when she's not too busy, Robert, Ambroise. And Caroline though she plays her cards very close to her chest.'

'And poor Barbara,' said Zoe, wondering what Simouno's reaction would be.

'Was she? I hadn't heard.'

Simouno pressed four buttons on an alarm pad, unlocked a pair of close-fitting timber doors with metal frames and swung them open. An automatic light came on, revealing industrial racking stacked high with dry goods in packets, boxes and tins, plus unused pots and pans and kitchen equipment. In the middle stood the quad bike, looking very out of place. Simouno wheeled it outside and carefully locked up again.

'Do you worry about thefts?' Zoe asked.

'Never happened yet, touch wood.' Simouno swung her leg over the generous padded seat and fired the engine. 'All aboard.'

Zoe got on behind. 'Helmets?'

'We'll mostly be off road.'

'What do I hold on to?'

'There's a frame at the back of the seat or you can put your arms round me.'

Simouno revved the throttle on the handlebars and pulled away, meaning Zoe was only just in time grasping the cold metal behind her. They circumnavigated the town then Simouno asked Zoe to get off and open the five-bar gate so they could climb up to the mobile phone mast, bouncing and lurching on the uneven ground, twice making Zoe's teeth bang together. They arrived at the place, stopping alongside the fallen hackberry tree. Simouno spoke over the idling engine.

'Do you know how this happened?'

'I don't.'

'We could ask Marcel?'

'All right, let's go that way. Run down and open the other gate.'

Zoe jumped off and went to open the one where the bobcat was parked. Simouno drove through and Zoe shut it behind them, jumping back on. The field track followed a curve of the hill then dipped down towards the Maurice farmhouse, a couple of kilometres further on. Simouno stopped in the courtyard and Marcel came outside, wearing an apron over his clothes, clearly – Zoe thought with a pang of sympathy – in the process of cooking a sad, solitary dinner. Then Thierry emerged, looking delighted to see them both. Marcel invited them to stay.

'I can stretch my risotto to four, though it won't be anything like Quentin's creations.'

'No, thanks,' said Zoe. 'Simouno is showing me the places she's identified from *In the Land of Vultures*.'

'Have you seen the size of the prize fund?' asked Thierry.

'Actually, yes,' said Zoe.

'That's a surprise,' said Marcel. 'Have you become obsessed?'

'No,' said Zoe, not wanting to reveal that she was most motivated by exonerating herself of Barabar's murder. 'But you have to admit it's interesting.'

'It is,' said Thierry.

'But it brings strangers out here traipsing through our vines,' complained Marcel.

Zoe asked: 'We were wondering what happened to the tree by the mast. How did it come down? All you Vulturists seem to agree it's pictured in the book, so the fact that it's fallen means that the mystery has been disrupted, maybe even destroyed?'

'That's right, but I just found it like that one morning,' said Marcel.

'Recently?'

'A few weeks ago.'

'Meaning it happened overnight?'

'Hard to say. I don't go that way every day.'

'Might it have been the telecoms engineers,' Zoe suggested, 'making room for their mast because they wanted the very highest point of the hill?'

'I suppose it could have been.'

'Or, if it was someone local, who would have the equipment necessary?'

'Frank Séchan,' said Thierry, 'from the garage, with his tow truck? And he's a Vulturist so he might think it a good idea to—'

'That doesn't make sense,' said Simouno, interrupting, and Zoe felt this was a good indicator of the enthused style of conversation between people focused on finding the silver treasure. 'Frank would know,' continued Simouno, 'that people would still be able to find the location from the landscape picture in the book, but there wouldn't be a *falabreguier* there any more.'

'Or you could have done it,' said Zoe to Marcel, 'using the motorised cable on your Toyota.'

'Why would I do that?' asked Marcel.

Zoe smiled and told him: 'For the same reason – because you are a secret Vulturist and you wanted to conceal the clue.'

'Except that wouldn't get in the way for people who already know that location,' insisted Simouno.

'But what does the location mean?' asked Zoe. They all looked at her, expecting her to answer her own question. She told them: 'I have no idea. I really was asking.'

'No one's got to the bottom of that,' said Simouno. 'Davide's been up there with his metal detector.'

Zoe felt a self-satisfised glow that this confirmed her own suspicion.

'But with no results?' she asked.

'Had he found anything, we would have heard.'

'But he wouldn't have let on,' said Zoe, 'unless he'd found the big prize. If he'd discovered just an, er, an intermediate clue, he'd have kept it to himself.'

'But there's not supposed to be any digging involved,' said Thierry.

'Tell me more about that?'

'At the launch ten years ago,' said Marcel, 'it was something the publisher made clear up front, that it was an intellectual puzzle, not a physical adventure. That's why things like the climbers in the Verdon Gorge were never going to be the answer.'

'Speaking of climbing,' Zoe asked, 'do any of you know what Caroline was doing or where she was when she hurt her arm?'

'She wouldn't tell us,' said Marcel. 'Have you found out?'

'Julien Calmet told me it happened when she was, I want to say "vulturing", on the rocks along the Rigolet. She came to him because they know one another from back in the day when he was a doctor. He told her to go to hospital for an X-ray where they gave her that sling that she hated.'

All three looked very interested but not one knew – or was prepared to share – why Caroline had been searching on the river. Standing in the wine-farm courtyard, the four of them discussed other locations in the book, taking turns to describe them for Zoe who was less *au fait* with the geography than the locals. Gradually, she began to picture them.

'So, there's another one above this wine farm, towards the thicker woods where the hunters have been shooting and then there's another location down by the road, next to the culvert. What about south of the main road?'

'I can show you,' said Simouno. She described a couple more locations. 'Can you stand some more bouncing across country?'

'I absolutely can.'

They bid goodbye to Marcel and Thierry Maurice, climbed back onto the quad bike and drove down through the vines. Zoe shouted above the engine for Simouno to stop at the culvert and she had a good look round. The thickening darkness meant there was nothing much to see – despite the dim headlight – that she hadn't already imagined from Toby's detailed description.

They crossed the road and drove on along the edge of the ploughed sunflower field, jolted more and more by the uneven ground. She was pleased when they stopped, beneath the looming shadows of the parasol pine trees, with the night air scented by the water in the canal and the Rigolet, all other sounds covered by the rushing of the weir.

'When did the river last overtop the lip?' Zoe asked.

'Just in the last twenty-four hours, I expect,' said Simouno, 'with the heavy rain.'

'Would that have been enough?'

'Not if it was only local rainfall, but it also fell on the mountains and has run down in tributaries to join us here.'

'Does the Rigolet ever flood?'

'Not massively.'

'Or dry up completely?'

'Ah, you're imagining something concealed in the riverbed.'

'I wasn't but, now you say it, the treasure could be under a slab of stone, you know, so the publisher wasn't lying, the slab just has to be lifted up, not dug up, but it can only happen when the Rigolet stops running and reveals it.'

'I don't think so.'

'Why not? It would be a good way to make sure that the mystery lasted a good long time, until there's a severe enough drought.'

'I don't believe that's ever happened or is likely to because, as well as rain, there's snowpack on the mountains that gradually melts through the summer, maintaining the flow.'

'Fair enough. But this is definitely a location pictured in the book,' said Zoe, thinking about the day of her arrival. 'Where is the hackberry?'

'On the far bank,' said Simouno, 'but there's no crossing place for the quad, not without going back to town.'

'That's a shame.'

'You could walk across the lip of the weir. It's shallow.'

'But I can't see. It's too dark.'

'I was joking.'

'Yes, of course. Where are the other locations?'

'To the south and the east of Sainte-Catherine. Do you want me to drive the long way round and show you?'

'I'm not sure there's any point. There's no light left in the sky and, to be truthful, I'm not sure my teeth can take any more clacking together.'

'Fair enough. I'll go more carefully.'

Simouno was as good as her word, driving more slowly. The towpath along the canal was a better track in any case. Zoe's mind cleared and the germ of an idea began growing in the fertile soil of her imagination – something to do with the arrangement of landscape views around Sainte-Catherine, each one centred on a Provençal *falabreguier*.

In modern French, it would have an accent on the first 'e' – falabréguier – *but a tiny language detail like that can't possibly be crucial, can it?*

They arrived back at the garages on the car park. Simouno put the quad bike away, locked up and reset that alarm, then they walked up through the town.

'Will you be able to come to my little reception tomorrow?' Zoe asked. 'It won't interrupt your working day?'

'I expect Quentin will be busy with prep for the evening service, but I'll be there. It's very nice of you.'

'Good. Thank you for that adventure.'

'Any wiser? Any nearer cracking the case?' Simouno asked with a smile.

'I feel I don't know the landscape well enough to interpret what any of it means,' Zoe told her.

But that was no longer the truth. She thought she did have an idea and it related to the detailed local maps she had sold Barbara and seen beside her bed in the guest house.

They bid one another goodbye and Zoe wandered up through the cobbled streets, past the front door of the church, dark and locked up for the night. Turning into the square, she was struck by the complete quiet.

Sainte-Catherine is like a stronghold or a fortress, built on a rocky prominence with the houses themselves forming its walls, a bastion against invaders. Inside, people live secret lives – or, if not secret, just private, like Quentin Simone in his kitchen, beavering away, creating new recipes, or Julien Calmet, praying and drafting his sermons, or Napoléon Etienne plotting revenge.

She grimaced at the memory of her confrontation with the second-hand bookseller. She didn't feel she entirely had the upper hand, but she hoped she had given him pause.

Russell was on her doormat, waiting for her. She unlocked and they both went inside. Zoe turned on the lights. Russell headed straight for the stove and looked disconcerted to find that it had gone out, glancing up at her with an enquiring expression in his deep-brown eyes.

'It isn't cold,' she told him, aloud. 'In fact, it feels stuffy.'

She opened the back door onto the courtyard. Her alpine plants looked sad in the stone planter with, on its side, the stone carving of a child reading.

I suppose they don't get enough sun. Maybe I should have replaced the soil. It was soaked through with . . .

She made a face, remembering the acrid odour of cats that she had been in a hurry to dispel. A new idea came into her mind.

Is that carving a memento of when my bookshop used to be the village school?

Leaving the back door open, she headed for the book-shelves, looking for a local map, finding one designed for hikers with fine detail and a generous scale. She opened it out on the coffee table, perched on the front edge of one of the leather armchairs, and frowned as she tried to identify the places where Simouno had shown her the locations depicted in the puzzle book. They had visited four in person and, after a minute or two, Zoe thought she knew how they corresponded to the contour lines and other technical features on the map.

It's a shame it was so dark. I would have liked to see the others and make sure there's a hackberry tree in each place. I bet there is.

Zoe traced a finger across the map, linking the four locations she knew about. They formed a curve from north-east of Sainte-Catherine by the mobile phone mast – which wasn't marked, of course, being brand new – to south-west and the confluence of river and canal.

Or maybe not a curve.

That was the idea that had come into her mind as Simouno drove more carefully along the canal towpath.

Not a curve because there are eight places depicted in total and, if you connect these four with straight lines, they look much more like they are half of an octagon than points on a circle.

Zoe pictured the octagonal Templar church.

That can't be a coincidence, can it?

Almost against her will, she visualised once more Barabra Ercollani's slack limbs, collapsed and folded unnaturally on the cold flagstones.

An octagon inside an octagon. But what does that mean?

That thought led her to Barbara's unexpected taste for 'spicy' fiction and the novel she had used as a coded reference to the *micocoulier* tree in Erica Noll's *Infinite Desire*.

What's the connection, there?

She no longer had the book to look at because Inspector Sicarie had taken it, but she remembered the cover very clearly.

The infinity symbol, a bit like a figure eight on its side.

Plus, she remembered that the heroine of the novel – the one whose passion alternated between the two lurking men, framed by the two circles of the infinity symbol – was called Octavia.

Eight, again.

V

LIFE AND DEATH

Twenty-Nine
WHERE IS OSKAR WEISS?

Zoe got up soon after seven the next morning with an urgent desire to inspect the octagonal Templar church. Being a Wednesday, there would be an early mass at eight o'clock, lasting about half an hour, giving her plenty of time to attend before she opened the bookshop at nine-thirty to coincide with the arrival of visitors to the market. As she washed and brushed her teeth and dressed, she could hear the traders assembling their stalls outside.

A kind of rogues' gallery went through her mind – all her neighbours and friends. She was trying to decide if anyone that she had met could possibly be the author of *In the Land of Vultures*. Obviously, it would have to be someone who knew the region well. But, as it happened, Sainte-Catherine seemed to have a very strong centre of gravity. Most of the people born there didn't move away. Even those who had occupations in other places – bigger cities, such as Caroline in Aix and Thierry in Marseille – could be relied upon to visit.

She paused in her brushing to consider the case of the elderly vet, Firmin Séchan. It crossed her mind that he might be the person who had completed all the puzzles in the magazine on the table in his waiting room. That would make him a prime candidate for the role of author. Plus, he was old enough to have imagined the 'people' scenes with their dated clothes and so on from the last century – because he would have seen them with his own eyes.

How hard might it be to discover if he has any skill as an artist? Someone must know – unless he practises in secret, possibly in order not to be outed?

Pulling on her jeans, Zoe wondered about another possible candidate, someone who came into her mind because of the very vivid way that Simouno had described his unusually focused cast of mind – Quentin Simone.

No, that doesn't make sense. He already has his 'thing'. He wouldn't be the sort of person to flip about between fine cuisine and a frivolous treasure hunt.

She considered the two young people she had met at the garage: Frank and Cécilie.

Not strong candidates at all – much too involved in 'love's young dream'.

Brushing her hair, she pondered the known Vulturists: Denis and Davide, Simouno herself, Marcel and Thierry and Odile, Caroline, Antoine and Antoinette. She decided they were all out of the picture.

If any of them was the author, they wouldn't be working so hard to find the treasure.

For a second, her gestures became still.

Or is one of them working super-hard as a bluff?

She resumed the regular, grooming stroke.

The exception is, perhaps, Marcel Maurice. He's different. He does just enough to appear interested, but he's not obsessed. If he were the author, he wouldn't be giving himself away through lack of interest but, at the same time, he's not putting himself out to find it. Oh, and the fallen tree is on his land. And the ruptured cable. That's a big deal for anyone new to the region who needs a good phone signal because they want to use a maps app to navigate and triangulate and assemble clues.

She put down her hairbrush, wiped round the sink with some toilet paper, tossing it into the bowl, and brought to mind the people she didn't know so well, including Ambroise Caille, the estate agent, and Robert Petit, the butcher.

I was on a roll yesterday. It's a shame I didn't start sooner. I could have confronted more of them, putting them under unexpected pressure.

She smiled at herself in the mirror.

'What came over you?' she asked herself, aloud.

Her face became more serious, answering the rhetorical question with a sober warning, inside her head.

It was the visit of the police inspector. That was what did it. I was forced into action because I became worried for myself, with who knows what suspicions hanging over me.

She left the bathroom and fetched a two-litre bottle of mineral water and a bag of coffee grounds from the fridge, taking them downstairs to set up the filter machine. Soon, the delicious fragrance began to permeate the open-plan, low-ceilinged ground floor. She noticed a triangle of white paper poking beneath the door. She went and picked it up off the mat. It was another one of Oskar Weiss's oversized calling cards.

She took it to the counter and turned it over. On the reverse was a brief message, written in a very square hand.

I come too late. I see you tomorrow.

She poured some kibble into Russell's bowl.

I wonder, has he just dropped that off or was it there last night? I don't think I would necessarily have seen it when I got home. Firstly, it was dark and, secondly, Russell would've been sitting on top of it, scrambling to get indoors ahead of me, a blur of white himself.

Because she had time still before having to cross the square to church, she booted up her laptop computer in order to research the novel *Infinite Desire*, and its author, Erica Noll. The first references were all to online shops where it seemed quite prominent in its category, variously referred to as 'spicy', 'torrid' or 'erotic'. It had published just six months before. She clicked through to see what else the author had written and if, perhaps, there might be a photograph. There was and, as was often the case, it looked nothing like the author, having been taken at least fifteen or even twenty years before.

Zoe knew this to be so for one simple and obvious reason. The face in the frame, the author of *Infinite Desire* was none other than Barbara Ercollani herself. Baffled, she racked her brain for a reason why Barbara should have bought her own book.

Was it vanity, then? Did she buy it so that I would order another copy and make it more prominent on display?

Beside her on the counter was the piece of paper on which she had written out the two jumbles of letters that made up '*micocoulier*', one heap from the turned-down corners in the novel, the other from the arrow-like gaze of the vultures. Almost without thinking, she doodled the author's name, Erica Noll, writing the letters in a random sequence as if trying to conceal their meaning.

LONARELCI

The answer stared back at her.

Erica Noll is simply an anagram of Barbara's surname, Ercollani. That's two anagrams associated with her: the turned-down corners and her pseudonym. No wonder she was well on the trail of the Vulture.

Time was now short. Because she was going to church, Zoe put on her long camel-hair coat rather than her economy ski jacket. She went outside, with Russell snuffling around her heels, clearly surprised to be out and about with the sun barely risen.

Zoe crossed the square, heading for the church, saying good morning to the stallholders as she dodged between them. The octagonal building was still dark and the door locked with five people waiting outside.

I know where Julien lives. I'll go down to meet him.

She didn't have to walk far. Their paths – hers downhill and his up from the little modern suburb – coincided by the well. He was bare-headed but warmly dressed in a dark over-coat. It was hard to tell if it was black or very dark blue.

'Good morning. Can I speak to you please?'

By the light of the street lamps, she recognised that Julien had a serious, closed-off expression on his face, as if he was already contemplating the mysteries of the spiritual mass over which he was about to preside. In his eyes, she thought she caught a sense that he was frustrated or even annoyed to be drawn out of this special state of mind. Then, after a pause, he told her, politely: 'We had better stay where we are for a moment, for privacy.'

Recapturing some of the momentum of the previous day, Zoe asked: 'You remember I asked, did Barbara confide in you at all?'

'I told you we spoke several times,' said Julien.

'But did she ask for advice? Was she suffering from some kind of crisis? The more I think about her, the more I won-der.'

'She was old and not in the best of health.'

Before answering, Zoe let his words sit.

What is he trying to tell me, without saying it out loud?

'Were her health issues solely to do with age?'

'I believe they were,' said Julien.

'In the sense that they were problems that we associate with ageing. For example, she was worried about . . .' Zoe stopped then changed tack. 'I think I said to you the other day that I don't want you to divulge secrets from the confes-sional or anything like that.'

'She never made confession. Our conversations were informal.' He stopped for a second. 'I think perhaps you've guessed what it was that was in her mind.'

Zoe's gaze met his and she was struck once more by the startling austerity of his gaunt features.

'She felt that her memory was failing,' she said.

'And with it,' Julien replied, sombrely, 'her sense of self.'

In ponderous silence, they walked on to the door of the church. Julien took a large iron key from the pocket of his overcoat, and inserted it into the lock. The mechanism turned easily, but the sound was surprisingly loud, echoing in the pre-dawn street. He turned the iron handle releasing the door catch and pushed the heavy timbers inwards. Inevitably, the action gave Zoe a flashback to the moment when she had done the same thing and got her first glimpse of Barbara Ercollani lying dead on the flagstones in her awful purple tracksuit. Julien stood back to allow her to enter but she insisted he should go first. She didn't want to stand in the darkness, groping for the light switch, feeling the ghost of the tragedy on the back of her neck. Then she let the other five congregants precede her, too.

Once the chandelier was illuminated, she followed them, taking a seat in the back row of folding chairs while he disappeared behind the altar, where there was presumably a robing room. The light from the many bulbs was unnecessarily stark, she thought.

Not exactly conducive to an atmosphere of prayer and contemplation.

The chairs were laid out in eight or nine rows, completely filling the nave at the centre of the eight-sided building. The place where Barbara had lain was therefore partly inaccessible.

On the night of the procession for the entry of the effigy of Saint Bertrand, the space had been cleared, the chairs all stacked away somewhere. This is how the church is normally laid out, like for vespers the other day. Is that why Barbara snuck in here when she ought to have been meeting me, because she knew there was access to something that normally was hidden?

There was no sign, as yet, of Julien re-emerging. Three more worshippers arrived. Zoe got up and went to find the place where the dead woman had been discovered, in the very centre of the building, beneath the summit of the domed roof, in the midst of the rows of folding chairs. She sidled into position, nudging aside the ones in front.

That's very interesting.

There was a plaque set within the flagstones of the floor, made of bronze and well-worn with the passing of many generations of feet. The engraved image it depicted was still visible, however, partly thanks to the brilliance of the chandelier. It was a figure of a woman wearing what Zoe would probably refer to as an *abaya*, draped over her head, as female figures from the early Christian church in the Middle East were often depicted. She was holding a book and was accompanied by a child.

If you didn't know that this church is dedicated to Saint Catherine, you could easily wonder if that was Mary and Jesus, but I don't think the mother of God is associated with learning. I should find out if Saint Catherine is. It's idiotic only to know about the firework.

She also made a mental note to investigate on which day the Feast of Saint Catherine might fall. Then, feeling foolish because the other congregants were watching her, she bent down and felt at the edges of the bronze plaque with her fingernails.

If the octagon of hackberry trees in the landscape is supposed to bring Vulturists to the octagonal church, you can imagine people thinking that this plaque might be a hatch or a cover for a secret compartment in the floor. That sounds like something out of a movie, but it makes sense.

The square of bronze was solidly cemented in place and gave an appearance of not having moved for many, many years. Zoe stood up and returned the chairs to their original positions, obscuring the plaque. A bizarre idea came into her mind.

Did someone come across Barbara inspecting the inlaid slab of bronze – someone who knows about the Vulture and wants it

273

for themselves — and decide to despatch her there and then? Who though? It really is very frustrating not to know the precise cause of death.

Julien reappeared, clothed in white satin investments, carrying a tray with three silver receptacles for the symbolic bread and wine: a jug with a narrow neck, a chalice that she supposed was currently empty, and a silver plate on which lay two dozen wafers. He placed all of this in a niche beside the altar then bent his head in prayer.

An immense stillness descended. Zoe surprised herself with a feeling of peace and serenity.

Julien has a powerful personality. It's communicating itself to me right now. And, each moment in our conversations has been coloured by his ideas: his strength of feeling about sin and 'the love of money', his deep sympathy for poor Barbara, his kindness and his attentiveness to the children in the procession, his closeness to Lucia Jacquet. Whenever I'm with him, I've felt sort of enveloped in whatever aura he projected.

An elderly couple entered, people Zoe had never spoken to but had seen in the market. She smiled at them, not wanting to break the silence. They sat down close to the rear of the church.

What have I learned? That Barbara was concerned that her memory was failing. It seems to me that she must have bought her most recent book, Infinite Desire *— her own work although written under a pseudonym — as a way of reminding herself of who she was.*

Another grey-haired couple arrived.

But that still doesn't answer the question of why she turned down the corners of the pages, spelling out the French name of the hackberry tree. Was it because she was worried that she would forget that essential clue? And did she come to the church on the Feast of Saint Bertrand to follow up some new revelation, inspired by rereading In the Land of Vultures?

Half a dozen more congregants entered, people she might normally speak to, but the atmosphere of silence persisted and seemed to be shared by all the worshippers. There were now twenty people present, most of them elderly, not one of them among Zoe's list of 'persons of interest'.

Julien turned to face them and the early mass began. Like the vespers on the previous Sunday evening, the service was brief, lasting just twenty-five minutes, delivered in Latin, which Zoe thought must be a feature of this particular mid-week eucharist. The longest element was the blessing of the bread and wine, and the shuffling steps of the congregation to the altar rail in order to partake in the mystery of transubstantiation. After the blessing and valediction at the end of the service, Zoe had a sense that she shouldn't wait behind and try to speak to Julien again.

Is this a new mood I've detected in him? Have I become an awkward presence, prying into things that he thinks shouldn't concern me?

She went outside and found that the sun was up, but behind a bank of cloud in the east, so the day was still very gloomy.

And what about his 'fierce' argument with Caroline on the night of Barbara's death?

She followed Rue des Templiers up into the square to find Russell sitting pertly on the cobbles beside the rotisserie that Robert Petit was just plugging into a trailing cable and setting in motion. Twelve pasty white birds began rotating in the glazed cabinet as the cooking elements glowed red. Zoe ordered one for herself and went back to the bookshop with Russell following, but the terrier kept glancing back at the butcher's stall with an air of disappointment, then up at Zoe.

'*You know he gave me nothing?*' he seemed to say.

Once indoors, at first Zoe didn't want to take off her coat. She had become cold and stiff in the church. She tossed her keys on the dark shelf under the counter then told herself that the way to get warm was to be busy. She knelt down in front of the stove to organise a little wigwam of kindling with a firelighter that smelt of petrol. She struck a match and the dry timber very quickly began to burn up, the individual sticks toppling over into the bed of ashes, creating a set of embers on which she could lay some thicker logs.

It's a good job I've got plenty out in the courtyard to keep the place warm and friendly for this afternoon's party.

Still a little chilled, her fingers feeling bony and stiff and bloodless, she poured herself a mug of coffee and wrapped her hands around it. Through the front window and the glazed portion of the door she could see the sky was lightening, with a kind of second dawn breaking well above the horizon through a gap in the clouds. Despite this harbinger of the day, Zoe felt another kind of cloud descending.

I'm still trapped, not supposed to leave town. And I'm not busy enough in the shop and that makes me feel passive, waiting for customers who may or may not come. I think it'll be all right in the holiday seasons, but I'll need something else to occupy my mind in the long winter months. Surely the hunt for the Vulture and the murderer will be over and done with by then, though?

With her coffee in her left hand, she made a circuit of the shelves, pulling the books forward with her right so that they all aligned with the front edges because that was how she liked them to look. The bell clanged and she peered through a gap to see Oskar Weiss standing irresolute on the mat, his unwashed hair sticking sparsely to the white dome of his scalp. She went to meet him.

'Good morning,' she said carefully, clearly, in English. 'How are you, Mr Weiss?'

'Yes, good morning. The book? You have it?'

'I do.'

'I buy,' he told her.

'Perhaps you'll be disappointed? I don't think it's any different in the various language editions.'

'Ah, but my copy is no good.'

'Why is that?'

'Excuse, please. I cannot say.'

'It's because you've cut it up and stuck it on the wall, isn't it – perhaps more than one.'

Oskar Weiss looked utterly astonished. '*Wie können Sie das wissen?*'

Zoe felt smug that she understood this and felt she was on a roll.

'You want to know how I know. I didn't know. I guessed, you understand?'

'How guess?'

'I was looking at the book myself and I imagined it cut up and pasted on a wall, you know, or glued or sellotaped, to make a single large image, aligning the landscape pages. Is that what you did? Do you understand "aligning"?'

'*Ausrichten, ja,*' he said. 'Line right.'

'I thought so.' Zoe grinned broadly. 'Did it help?'

'*Jawohl,*' said Oskar, shiftily.

Zoe hesitated, wondering if what she was doing was wise but excited to know if her suppositions were correct.

'Let me tell you how I think it works,' she said. 'When you cut up the book, the landscapes didn't line up as a grid, they overlap to make a perimeter with a gap in the middle.'

'Yes,' he agreed warily. 'They make empty shape.'

'And, if you connect the trees in that perimeter together, you know, drawing lines from one to another, it makes an octagon. Is it the same word in German?'

'*Ja, Oktagon.* Or *Achteck* which is *Acht* for eight and *Eck* for side.'

'Okay, so the octagon in the landscape must refer to the octagon of the church in Sainte-Catherine.'

'*Nein,*' he told her, shaking his head.

277

'But surely—' she began.

'*Nein, nein,*' he told her interrupting. 'The church is not the middle.'

He put a hand over his mouth and she thought she heard him cursing under his breath.

That's very interesting. I'm glad I rattled on. He didn't mean to tell me that.

Thirty

THE CAUSE OF DEATH

'I buy book,' Oskar Weiss told her, firmly. 'And thank you.'

'You don't want to talk about the Vulture any more?' Zoe asked, intrigued by his behaviour.

'I buy and I go.'

He could no longer meet her gaze. She fetched a copy of *In the Land of Vultures* from the shelves and placed it beside the till. He looked at it hungrily, proffering his debit card. In order to have a further opportunity to question him, she put a party invitation inside the book and processed the transaction. He picked up his prize, leaving the shop without another word. Zoe followed him outside, watching him bustle away through the market stalls, like a shoplifter fearful of being followed. For a second time, Zoe wondered if she had done the right thing by being alone with him.

Or is he afflicted with a different kind of guilt?

She saw the dark uniform and peaked cap of the tour driver leading a group of tourists through the stalls towards her. He approached, shook her hand and belatedly introduced himself.

'You are Madame Pascal of course. My name is Bernard Dupin. The morning is gloomy and chilly. I will come in and sit with you and drink your coffee, if that's all right, and make your shop the meeting point for when we must leave?'

'That's very kind of you,' said Zoe, warmly. 'The coffee, Bernard, for you will be free.'

'We must all work hard to make the wheels of commerce turn,' he told her with a nod.

'Come in.' She invited him to sit by the stove and prepared his drink. 'You are earlier than the other day?'

'It's the approach of the half-term. More people. I will be back this afternoon as well, for a second half-day tour.'

'Marvellous,' said Zoe.

For the next hour, she was kept busy serving coffee and selling her most popular books – those associated with local history, local hiking, the natural world and so on. It struck her that there must be more novels out there that were set in the region, other than the sinister Fred Vargas thriller.

If I can track them down, it would be a good idea to offer a selection of them and display them prominently.

Though she had plenty of coffee – a packet open in her fridge and two unopened in her cupboard – she saw that she would soon run out of milk, cream, and caffeinated and herbal tea. Luckily, the stall in the market that sold specialist infusions of local herbs was there, so she was able to briefly skip out and buy three different packets to offer to those people who didn't want coffee – all beautifully packaged, making her think she ought to charge more for them than just two euros. The driver went to the supermarket on his own initiative and returned with a bag of three sickly-sweet apple *beignets* – doughnuts.

The shop grew busier as the moment for the coach party's departure approached, with Bernard Dupin in his peaked cap rounding all the visitors up and leading them away through the town. In the quiet that ensued, Zoe realised that she ought to prepare more comprehensively both for the second coach party of tourists and for the reception that she had planned for the end of the day.

She propped the door ajar with the old coat stand and went out into the market with a large bag for life in the crook of her elbow. At one of the baker's stalls, she bought several hand-tied packets of artisan biscuits, both sweet and savoury, and a dozen each of croissants, *pains au chocolat* and *pains aux raisins.*

They can go in the freezer if no one wants them.

She took all that home and then went back out to the olive stall where a variety of the savoury delicacies were offered in large steel bowls, mixed with chilli or bell peppers or garlic or Provençal herbs. The man was all set up to package them in little plastic tubs that Zoe didn't really approve of because they added to landfill waste.

But I can use those pots for serving at the party, later on.

She bought two tubs each of four different kinds of olives and was delighted to discover that the man also sold cocktail sticks with which to serve them. Her next stop was with the *crémier* – the milkman and cheesemonger – where she bought eight different local cheeses that people could eat with the savoury biscuits.

Back at the shop, she took all that upstairs to the kitchen then came back down for the mugs that she would need to wash up and dry. She spoke briefly to Marcel Maurice at his stall close to her front door, asking him to give her a shout if he saw anybody entering the shop.

'Because I'll be busy upstairs for ten minutes.'

'Put your faith in me,' he told her with his habitual gallantry.

'How is the harvest? Have the changes in the weather, the cold and the rain, made things difficult?'

'All is well. These things are sent to try us and Thierry has been a great help, taking time off work.'

'That's interesting. Do you think he's changing his mind about living in the country?'

Marcel couldn't answer because Simouno Simone arrived with a very particular order for specific vintages that, Zoe knew, she would offer as 'paired wines' with her husband Quentin's exquisite culinary creations. As it turned out, Zoe was able to complete her washing up and tidy away her shopping without interruption.

The minibus tourists are a bonus. As Marcel said, all will be well. I've lots of ideas for making this place work. I just need time.

Needing time, of course, was just another way of saying: 'I need money.' That idea led her, entirely naturally, back to the prize fund for whoever had the wit or blind luck to locate the hidden Vulture.

Standing at her counter, with the front door still open because the day was mild and the wind, if there was any, from a different direction, she tried to think again through all of the people that she had met, but in a more systematic way. On the one hand, she was trying to anticipate who might be there at teatime to enjoy her hospitality; on the other, she was again pondering the question of who might be driven to desperate acts by what Julien had more than once called 'the love of money'.

On a sheet of A4 printer paper she made an exhaustive list of potential and confirmed Vulturists: '*Thierry and Marcel Maurice; Antoine and Antoinette Grenelle; Caroline Robin; Patrick Lagrasse and perhaps his unseen sister; Robert Petit (and wife); Denis Allard and Davide Quillan; Julien Calmet; Gato and Lali Merino, perhaps; Napoléon Etienne; Firmin Séchan; Simouno and maybe Quentin Simone; Ambroise Caille; Odile Charpentier; Frank Séchan and Cécilie Something at the garage; the Day family, Clare and Toby, with their sweet little boy, Benjy; Oskar Weiss.*'

She came to a halt.

Is that everyone? The most likely must be the monstrous and paranoid Monsieur Etienne.

She drew faint lines through the names that she considered too far-fetched for proper consideration as murderers – such as Frank and Cécilie – then regretted it.

I ought to be more suspicious. I bet Maisie was always suspicious, never trusting what people said to her, questioning their honesty and motives. People probably called her 'judgemental', or they would have done, but that wasn't really a word people used back in the Seventies. Am I too weak and gullible?

She remembered how she had faced down Inspector Sicarie.

I didn't let myself be brow-beaten, there.

She frowned, a little hopelessly.

Maybe that was the wrong thing to do. Perhaps I ought to have been – to use another old-fashioned expression – more 'biddable'.

She sighed and moved on to another idea that had just bubbled up out of her subconscious.

Clare and Toby Day are interesting. I was, for a bit, jealous of their freedom and their itinerant van life. In reality, it wouldn't suit me. I like proper kitchens and bathrooms and a big warm bed.

She thought back over their extended conversation.

They were definitely in no hurry to leave. My bookshop was a kind of safe harbour for them on a miserable wet day, when anything else would have been hard work, trolling around outdoors in the damp or trapped in their Mazda Bongo.

Zoe smiled.

'Bongo' is a funny name for a model of van. I bet it's pretty old.

She looked it up on the internet and was surprised to discover that Bongos were first manufactured in 1966 and were still rolling off the production lines today.

Okay, so their van's not an ancient wreck, but there was friction between them, albeit covered up by banter, about shopping, as if they have to budget carefully. Perhaps they've got a plan of how much to spend each month while they're on the road, in order to keep the adventure going as long as possible, and they've exceeded it and their travels will have to be cut short.

Zoe tried to imagine doing something similar in her late twenties or early thirties.

I was far too busy making my way in musical theatre.

She smiled to herself, thinking about the fact that barely anyone in Sainte-Catherine had any idea that she had appeared on West End stages, that she had been paid to sing and dance and act, that she had been what the casting agents called 'a triple threat', before she went into management herself.

That seems so very long ago.

Shaking off her nostalgic digression, Zoe tugged a new sheet of paper out of the printer and wrote down: '*Clare, Toby & Benjy Day.*' After a pause, she added: '*Broke?*' Then she embarked on a new list of the people she genuinely considered might be involved in Barbara Ercollani's death, however remotely, with brief notes for potential motives. She arrived at Partrick Lagrasse from the Auberge Sainte-Catherine, at first discounting him because he was away.

But the Auberge was open on the night Barbara was killed. Would he have been too busy preparing for the dinner? Maybe not. His sister would have been doing that 'backstage' as it were. He could easily have slipped away for five minutes and . . .

Once again, she came up against the problem that she didn't know precisely how Barbara had died.

How was she killed?

She went and stood in the doorway, looking out at the market traders. It was a slowish day. The stallholders outnumbered, in total, their customers. But, as she had told the inspector, that was the nature of retail.

You have to be always available as advertised.

Antoine suddenly came strutting across. 'You went to Aix without telling me.'

'How do you know? No, never mind. I'm sorry. It was a spur-of-the-moment thing, there and back.' She took advantage of his presence to ask: 'What was the cause of death?'

'That's a very sensitive question,' said Antoine.

He strolled away to Marcel's stall for a glass of white wine. Zoe wondered if he was on duty. It was hard to tell because he always seemed to be wearing the same colour of shirt. On this occasion, though, it had no insignia so she decided not.

He came back, a small tulip-shaped glass held daintily by the stem so as not to make it warm.

'Will you answer my "sensitive question"?' she enquired with a smile. 'Aren't we friends?'

'Of course we are friends.'

'Come inside. There's no one else about. Perhaps I will join you in a drink.'

She gestured to the interior and went to fetch a glass of wine herself, promising Marcel that she would come back and settle up later. She took a spare one, too, that she thought to ply Antoine with, should he prove – as she expected – thirsty. Back at the bookshop, she found him sitting in front of the smouldering stove, gazing at the sooty glass as if searching for flames.

'Is that for me?' he asked.

She smiled and gave him the second glass. He put his empty one on the floor by his feet.

'I was wondering,' she began, 'if you could help me with something else, even if you're not allowed to tell me about the cause of death. It's this. Inspector Sicarie told me that he had eight reasons to be interested in me as a witness or a suspect. He went through the first seven and I can't remember each one but, the thing is, he didn't tell me the last. I don't know, but it sounded like it was the most damning. Do you know what I mean?'

Antoine was still gazing at the sooty, glazed door of the stove. Zoe wondered how much he had been drinking. In the end, the silence she left seemed to get through to him and he roused himself and told her: 'That would perhaps be a detail of the forensic investigation.'

'If I had sneezed, for example, there might be evidence of that on her clothing? Or is that just silly? I don't know how it works.'

'That's not a bad example,' said Antoine. 'It wouldn't be important in a case like this because she is known to have

285

come into your shop and spoken to you not long before she was found dead.' His voice became stronger as the phrases he was using became more formal. 'Indeed, she had become well recognised in the town and there are several independent witnesses who confirm that she walked away from your door looking either weary, or unwell, or positively unsteady – but very much alive.'

That gave Zoe pause.

'Weary', 'unwell', 'positively unsteady' – which was it?

'And I didn't sneeze on her, anyway,' said Zoe, aloud. 'I've been in the best of health ever since I've been here.'

'Sainte-Catherine is a very healthy place,' said Antoine.

'Unless it isn't,' quibbled Zoe, meaningfully.

'No,' he replied. 'Unless it isn't.'

'Anyway, if it's not that, DNA from a sneeze or something like it, what is the eighth clue or the eighth piece of incriminating evidence?'

'It's hard for me to say without answering your other question.'

'You mean about cause of death?'

'I do.' Antoine sighed deeply, leaned forward in the chair – so his nose was over his toes – then launched himself upright. 'Thank you for your hospitality. Those oleanders you put either side of your door are very beautiful. They were not there before. They were your idea?'

He stopped, looking as if nothing that he had said was of any importance.

'What?'

'They are very particular plants.'

'I don't know what you're getting at,' Zoe protested. 'There's no one else here, Antoine. Can't you speak more plainly?'

'There are such things as professional pride and professional responsibility. Give it some thought.' He indicated her laptop computer, open on the counter. 'Look them up. They

286

may be very beautiful but perhaps they have other attributes as well.'

He went to leave but got involved in sort of side-to-side shuffle because two local people who Zoe recognised from vespers on Sunday were just then coming in to browse the new fiction section. Antoine weaved past them and slipped away, and she was unable to follow because she was immediately involved in looking up unknown names and titles, because neither customer could remember those details from the book review programme that they had watched on television the previous evening.

Finally, following clues from the partial synopses that they did remember, Zoe located the two books online and also, fortunately, on her shelves, part of the previous day's delivery. The two customers paid and left, then Zoe used her favourite search engine to look up 'oleander'.

The first three pages of references – maybe more, she didn't go any further – were all concerned with where to buy them, how to plant them and how to care for them.

That can't be what Antoine meant. He was trying to put me on the trail of the cause of death.

She didn't like the idea, but he was clearly suggesting something more sinister.

Could it be poison?

She added that word to the search box and pressed enter, making an unsettling – perhaps even terrifying – discovery.

Oleander poisoning will occur where the victim eats the flowers or chews the leaves or stems of either Nerium oleander or Cascabela thevetia. Active poisons include digitoxigenin, oleandrin, oleondroside and others. Symptoms include but are not limited to: irregular or slowed heartbeat, hypotension, muscular weakness, headaches, blurred vision, diarrhoea, loss of appetite, nausea, stomach pain, confusion, depression, disorientation and death.

Thirty-One

The Wrong Mood for a Party

The revelation that Inspector Sicarie's eighth reason for suspecting her was the innocent – but apparently poisonous – shrubs growing either side of her front door seemed, to Zoe, to be completely unfair.

I put them in entirely by chance, because Elise Guillaume had some on her stall that first day and because I'd seen one outside Denis and Davide's guest house. I didn't even know that every part of them was . . .

She frowned.

If I'm to be suspected for cultivating murderous shrubs, what about the guest-house owners and what about Elise herself?

Zoe remembered her chat with Julien in which he had told her about all the complex familial connections in Sainte-Catherine, including, she now recalled, the fact that Cécilie at the Total garage was Elise Guillaume's daughter.

But I can't see either – or both of them together – as murderers. It's much more likely to be Davide Quillan.

She remembered Denis Allard at his kitchen table with a bowl of mentholated hot water. What had he said?

'I'm trying to clear my tubes.'

Zoe shuddered as a different image came into her mind.

Denis is supposedly convinced that Barbara was ill – or he wants everyone to believe she was ill. Is that because he made her do something similar, sit with her face under a towel, breathing in steam that was laced with oleander rather than healing menthol?

Zoe went back to her laptop, intending to research whether such a thing might be possible – death by inhalation of oleander vapour – but stopped with her fingers suspended over the keyboard.

No, I mustn't. Inspector Sicarie might seize my computer and use its search history against me, including my investigation of 'oleander poison'. And I won't be able to tell him that I only looked into it because of Antoine's hints because that would get Antoine into trouble.

After this moment of indecision, Zoe remembered seeing flourishing oleanders outside Firmin Séchan's home and consulting room.

Firmin is someone who would have the means to extract a tincture or whatever it would need to be, what with his scientific background as a vet. And he would have the local knowledge, acquired over many years, to interpret the puzzle book and find the key location.

The tab in her browser was still open so she glanced at the list of symptoms once more, thinking that they correlated – some of them, at least – with what she had seen in Barbara.

Is that why the police investigation is taking so long? Are they trying to isolate evidence of digitoxigenin or oleandrin or oleandroside poisoning in Barbara's corpse? Is that even possible?

She sighed.

I'm such an ignoramus. Every question I ask myself makes me feel less equipped to solve my own mystery – even though I need to do so for my own protection.

Aware that she was in entirely the wrong mood for a party, Zoe forced herself to begin getting things ready, reviving the stove because it might get chilly later on but opening the back door onto the courtyard so the place didn't become stuffy. She hesitated over her suffering alpines in the outdoor planter, thinking she ought to ask Elise Guillaume – if she turned up – why they weren't doing well.

On one of her trips up and down the stairs, as the afternoon was becoming gloomier with the sun behind thick grey clouds, she turned on the landing light only to hear its bulb pop. She had no spare so she fetched a kitchen chair, climbed up upon it and removed the square of cardboard from the skylight at last. As she had guessed, she could see a street lamp attached to the eaves of the adjacent budding.

That will be annoying in the evening, but I can't have people tripping over themselves if they need to come upstairs for the toilet.

Zoe paused in her labours.

Oh dear, I don't think I really want people traipsing through my private quarters. I wish I had a downstairs bathroom.

She checked her watch, finding the time was almost four. She went outside and discovered Marcel and Thierry Maurice and Elise Guillaume chatting. On the other side of the square, Robert Petit was just pulling his rotisserie indoors to the butcher's shop, bouncing it across the cobbles on its casters. Napoléon Etienne was on his way home with a stack of second-hand paperbacks in a rubber-wheeled handcart.

'Why don't you come in?' she asked Maurice and the others. 'I hope that's why you're here?'

'It is. Thanks.'

They all went inside and Zoe's mood lifted with the easy, friendly conversation. Robert followed them with a clang of the bell and Zoe propped the door open with the coat stand to stop the noise repeating for no reason. She asked Thierry to begin serving drinks while she put her laptop and cash tray away in her safe, then had a shiver of worry that she might have allowed any one of them to see and memorise her four-digit code.

Don't be so foolish. These people are not your enemies.

She stood up and made an effort to smile.

Someone is, however. I'm more and more sure of it.

To her surprise, Oskar Weiss arrived next, in halting English conversation with Firmin Séchan who looked very frail and bony by comparison with the much younger, stockier German. They were followed by Odile Charpentier who quickly drank two glasses of wine, then became involved in a detailed debate about soils and weather with Marcel. Thierry joined Oskar and the elderly vet, impressing Zoe by being able to converse with the tourist in his own language.

Of course, Thierry would have to be multilingual in his job at the car hire desk at the airport.

The van nomads, the Days – Clare, Toby and Benjy – were next to arrive, noticeably cleaner in their freshly laundered clothes. The little boy wanted to know: 'Where are the other children?' His mother explained that the Norwegian family might come or they might not – then they did, telling Zoe that they had enjoyed their minibus tour so much that they had hired a car to do the same visits all over again: 'But with more time and independence.' This gave Zoe a real boost, the idea that she was definitely on the way to making her shop a proper destination in the off-season.

Frank Séchan turned up, telling her: 'I can only pop in. I've taken my break to coincide.' She asked if Cécilie might come too with, in the back of her mind, her slight but festering suspicion about Cécilie's mother, Elise, related to oleanders as a source of poison. The answer was negative for both of them. Apparently, they had a hairdressing appointment alongside one another at the *coiffeuse* lower down the town, near Antoinette Grenelle's *mercerie*.

Despite the absence of the Guillaumes, there was no shortage of guests. Ambroise Caille and his wife and children came in, demonstrating to Zoe that they were well liked from the reception they obtained. Zoe spent five minutes showing the kids her selection of 'junior fiction' and Ambroise insisted on buying them a book each to read in the armchairs by the stove – two copies of the first Harry Potter novel, so they each had their own. Zoe told him he could pay for them on another day. Then he spoiled it, for Zoe, by encouraging his kids to compete to see who could finish first.

Just then, she noticed Oskar Weiss had gone out into the courtyard and was bending to inspect her alpine plants. She supposed he was finding the loud buzz of competing conversations in a language he didn't speak a strain and went to explain that the plants had only gone in recently and weren't perhaps in a suitable location. He gazed at her with a bemused expression on his wide face, so she repeated herself in simpler English and he nodded, ponderously, and went back into the bookshop proper, but not without a glance over his shoulder that, if asked, she would have described as 'yearning'.

While she had been with the Caille children and with Oskar, more guests had arrived, including Gato and Lali Merino who were telling Marcel about the installation of the stove and hearing his plans for the renovation of his farmhouse – a topic that Thierry seemed to find extremely interesting. Antoine and Antoinette Grenelle came in together and made a beeline for Zoe, Antoinette telling her brother: 'This one may make a fine Vulturist. She has the eye.'

Zoe demurred, insisting: 'Don't worry. I'm not about to become an obsessive Vulture hunter.'

By some accident of the rhythm of general conversation, her words seemed to land in the midst of a coincidental pause, like a heavy stone falling into the middle of a deep pond. She glanced round.

Someone – perhaps more than one person – is paying more attention to me than they should.

She drew Antoine aside and whispered: 'I have no idea how anyone would go about extracting poison from an oleander plant.'

'Not even from the case of poisoning you were involved with when you were a girl?'

He was referring to a murder that had taken place decades earlier alongside a country fair, solved by her half-sister Maisie Cooper.

'No, that had nothing to do with me. I was barely involved.'

'But the connection is there in the police records,' he told her with a sad and, she thought, sympathetic shake of the head.

Zoe would have liked to question him further as a glass of Marcel's excellent wine seemed to have given her a surge of impetuous energy. But she was distracted by the arrival of Caroline with Simouno Simone on her arm. They came straight to her and Zoe learned that the two women had grown up together. They reminisced about their shared childhood, then went further back in time.

'I'm talking,' Caroline told Zoe, 'about the period when our mothers and fathers were ineffectually educated in this very building, back when it was the village school.'

Zoe dearly wanted to know more about the history of *La Librairie de Mes Rêves* but, between the heads of her guests, she noticed Napoléon Etienne, the second-hand bookseller, lurking outside. She excused herself to go and speak to him.

'There is no need for us to be enemies. I understand from Julien Calmet that you were instrumental in the designation of Sainte-Catherine as a *"village du livre"*. It seems to me that we should work together to make the most your initiative.'

She held his gaze. His determination to resent her seemed to be wavering. Then, unfortunately, Russell came scampering over, pinned back his ears and barked, as if he was trying to face down another *sanglier*. Monsieur Etienne jumped back, scolding: 'Get away from me, you awful mutt.'

'Stop it, Russell,' snapped Zoe. She bent to snatch him up, angry and wriggling in her arms. 'Pay no attention, please. He's overexcited by all the people.'

It was too late. The moment of possible détente had passed and the second-hand bookseller was bustling away with his habitual angry gait, his shoulders hunched and his fists balled up in the front pocket of his painter's smock.

Zoe put Russell down and he ran away with an angry bark. She went back inside, glad to see that – among others whose names she wasn't certain of – Denis Allard and Davide Quillan had arrived and were each pronging olives with cocktail sticks while Simouno talked at them about going into partnership.

'We could organise together and share the marketing costs – your delightful accommodation and our exquisite cuisine.'

'More costs,' said Davide, unconvinced.

'I think it's a wonderful idea,' said Denis. 'For the off-season, especially.'

Zoe was pleased to see that her neighbours were thinking the same way she was – apart from Napoléon Etienne – co-operation rather than competition. She was about to join in when Julien Calmet appeared at her elbow to suggest: 'I can open some more bottles of wine, if you have any. The bar you've organised on the counter is running dry.'

'Thank you. That would be very kind. They're upstairs in the fridge.'

He made his way to the foot of the stairs and Zoe had a sudden qualm.

Is everything a slovenly mess up there? I hope not.

Zoe made a circuit of the room, disconcerted to find four or five people reading books from the shelves. Two were paperbacks and they were straining their spines.

Oh, well. I mustn't introduce any bad feeling.

She came across Oskar Weiss once more who was studying the bird's-eye view of Sainte-Catherine in its thin wooden frame on the wall. She approached and saw that, shielded by his substantial body, he was comparing the drawing with sketches in his own notebook. When he became aware of her presence, he reddened and hid his papers inside his water-proof coat.

'This is a good picture,' he told her, unconvincingly. 'It is interesting, the Sainte-Catherine history.'

'And in its connection to the Vulture – the *Geier*?' she asked lightly.

'Yes,' he told her with an angry shake of the head. 'You know this.'

Julien had returned with three more bottles of white wine and two of red that Thierry was helping him to uncork. Marcel, his uncle, approached, wondering: 'When's the speech?'

'Oh, dear. Do I have to make a speech?'

Caroline joined them, offering: 'I'll introduce you, Zoe. An event like this needs some kind of punctuation.'

'If I have to.'

In a loud voice, Caroline called the room to order and several people chinked their glasses together to ask for quiet. It took a little while for the people concealed in the book stacks to emerge and crowd round, then Caroline said: 'A town is made up of buildings and shops, yes. More importantly, it is comprised of the people who live there. We, in Sainte-Catherine – and, though I live and work in Aix, I count myself still a daughter of this place – are very fortunate to have welcomed my good friend as a new neighbour and a commercial dynamo who no doubt will contribute for many years to the prosperity of our home. I give you, Zoe Pascal.'

There were a few cheers and lots of applause, though muffled because people all had glasses in their hands. Zoe shook her head, smiling.

'Well, I didn't intend to make a speech and I've nothing prepared. This party is almost as much of a surprise to me as it no doubt was to all of you, but I wanted to give a general thanks for your kind welcome.'

She paused because, just then, Inspector Sicarie had appeared in her doorway.

What does he want?

She pulled herself together and continued.

'First of all, I must second Caroline's kind words and say that they are reciprocated.'

She paused again because she could see Bernard Dupin over Inspector Sicarie's shoulder with another gaggle of tourists, all of them clearly expecting entrance to the shop.

'Secondly, some of you know this already but it bears repeating. I first saw Sainte-Catherine when I was just a teenager. The sight of it remained with me all those years. I feel, today, that I was always meant to be here. I dearly hope, in time, that you will all agree with me.' She smiled broadly and was gratified by a chorus of approval. 'Let's toast the future of the town itself.' She raised her glass. '*A l'avenir de Sainte-Catherine.*'

Everyone repeated her words and drank. Then Marcel added: 'And your good health, Zoe.'

A second toast was drunk. Zoe thanked everyone once more and the speechifying moment came to an end. Within a couple of minutes, a third of the attendees had drifted away – some, like Frank, on their way back to work – making room for the new arrivals. Inspector Sicarie shambled in and engaged Caroline in hushed conversation by the foot of the stairs. Robert Petit's wife very kindly ran across the square to fetch a tray of additional glasses because there was no time to wash up.

With the second cohort of tourists, Zoe was kept very busy discussing novels and guidebooks and maps, helping them search the stacks. Then she had to get her laptop and payment equipment out of the safe and boot it all up in order – with great satisfaction – to take their money. She noticed Clare Day kindly going round tidying, gathering up books that had been left lying around and piling them neatly on the coffee table for reshelving. Toby and Benjy were outside in the courtyard, looking at the alpines, then it came on to rain again so they rushed inside, shutting the door behind them.

People kept going up and down the stairs to use the bathroom. The pots of olives were soon all emptied and the sweet and savoury biscuits all devoured. Even the wine began to run out, so people slipped away, most of them taking the trouble to come and thank her and wish her good luck, until there were only Marcel, Caroline and the English family left. Zoe wondered if the party had helped her to avoid another interrogation by Inspector Sicarie and wished – despite her misgivings – that she had been able to speak to him and challenge his intentions before he left.

Perhaps it's the wine I've drunk, but I'd like to know precisely what he intends to do. If he arrests me tomorrow, I will at least have gone out with a bang.

Toby told her: 'Those plants you've put in, I think they've not got enough dirt. You ought to dig it out and replenish whatever's there.'

'I will,' she told him. Then she realised she simply had to sit down, slumping onto one of the two hard chairs. 'But not today. I'm bushed.'

He perched on the other chair, looking as though he wanted to confess something.

'You know, this is sort of our dream,' he told her.

'I thought you were happy on the road?'

'Yes, for the time being. But this is the sort of thing we'd love to find, you know, once we've done enough drifting.'

'That's funny,' said Zoe. 'I've been thinking of drifting as a bad thing.'

Caroline came to say goodbye. 'Lovely party. Don't get up.'

'Thank you for making the effort and coming all the way from Aix.'

'It was lovely to have a proper chat with Simouno. We were best friends at school.'

Marcel went with her and Zoe wondered if there was the possibility of some kind of romance between them. Then she regretted not finding a moment to ask Caroline about the argument Antoinette had told her about, the one that had taken place just before Barbara died or was killed, between Caroline and the doctor-turned-priest, Julien Calmet.

I ought to have thanked him for his help. I wonder when he left.

Clare and Benjy Day came downstairs and Clare told her that they had taken all the dirty glasses and empty bottles up to the kitchen. Zoe looked round. The bookshop was fairly tidy, all things considered.

'Can I give you something more substantial to eat?' she offered.

After a brief protest, they agreed, but only if allowed to help wash up and clean. Zoe accepted with alacrity and she and Clare post-mortemed the event as they went, with Toby and Benjy siting on the floor by the stove, drawing and colouring on a stack of Zoe's printer paper. The washing-up complete, they all ate on the floor. The sun went down just before seven, as they were finishing their odd meal of scraps from the party and leftovers from Zoe's fridge.

'You must be very pleased with how that went,' said Clare. 'I'm a little jealous.'

'I told her,' Toby told his wife. 'This is exactly the sort of business we would love to be able to afford.'

'But we don't have the capital to invest in buying either the building or the goodwill,' explained Clare.

'In this case, there was no goodwill because it had been shut for so long, but yes,' said Zoe, 'that's always the barrier.'

'And if you have to borrow,' Clare continued, 'you end up spending all your profit on servicing the interest payments.'

'You become asset rich but time and money poor,' said Toby with an air of repeating himself.

'You don't come from money, either of you? You don't have a "bank of mum and dad" to support you, of course. You told me, your parents are dead.'

'No,' said Toby, abruptly. 'We don't.'

Clare gave Benjy her phone to watch another *Shaun the Sheep* video and Zoe felt she had overstepped. After a few moments, though, conversation became easier and the three grown-ups talked on about the difficult search for freedom, what Clare called: 'A life in which self-determination and obligation are in balance.' Zoe began to understand that she and Toby were only just getting by on their nomadic adventure and felt, in her comparative luxury and security, that she had been extremely self-indulgent with all her mental complaints.

Though I didn't tell anyone else. They were just in my head.

The 'after-party' broke up around eight because Benjy became tired and bored and fractious, all at once. They left and Zoe stood on the threshold to watch them go, the little boy between his parents, holding their hands and swinging and kicking at the fallen leaves, less crisply satisfying now because of all the rain. Russell came nosing round the edge of the square as if keeping a low profile or making sure there were no more strangers that he disapproved of, invading his patch, before deigning to return.

'Come in, you silly dog,' she told him.

He stopped and looked up at her, a quizzical expression on his face. He seemed to ask: '*What was all that about? Why did you stop me giving him a piece of my mind?*'

'I know,' said Zoe. 'He's a horrible little man.'

She stepped aside but Russell wandered away.

Oh dear, he's in a huff. But Napoléon Etienne was the only black mark on an otherwise perfect evening.

Zoe shut and locked the door, turning the button to slide the bolt home into the keep. Then she paused, her hand on the cold metal.

That isn't true, though. There was also Oskar Weiss poking nosily around. I like him less and less. And there was the unexpected visit from Inspector Sicarie.

Physically tired and mentally drained, she went and sat in one of her leather club armchairs, leaning forward to open the stove door to encourage more flame.

I'm weary of mysteries. I wish someone would come along and tell me who did what, when, and to whom – and we could all be done with it.

Thirty-Two

'No One Can Get In'

Zoe didn't trouble with the lock on the courtyard door because, of course, it was inaccessible.

Unless someone decides to climb over the clay roofs of the adjoining houses.

She wasn't sure where she had put her keys. She groped in the dark shelf under the counter where she often left them, but they weren't there. She found she was too tired to search for them or even to put her computer and other paraphernalia back in the safe.

It doesn't matter. No one can get in.

In the stack of books on the coffee table – which Clare had tidied for reshelving – two paperbacks had indeed been damaged by straining their spines. Zoe decided she would leave them there, but with stickers on their front covers: *Reading copies – not for sale.*

She made a circuit of the shop and found two wine glasses that they had missed and took them upstairs to wash up. The bookshop and first-floor apartment felt very empty in comparison with the noise and bustle of the party, but the event seemed to have left a kind of echo.

I no longer feel so alone with my books and my thoughts.

And Russell hadn't returned.

He'll probably come back in the middle of the night from some nocturnal adventure and scrape or yap to be let in.

She wondered what to do with the rest of her evening.

Perhaps put some more order in my thoughts?

She sat back down in front of the stove. In the back of her mind was something someone had said to her about Inspector Sicarie.

'*If he were a hunting dog, he would be a very unkempt and coarse one.*'

Zoe couldn't remember who.

It was probably Julien, though, wasn't it? It sounds like his tone of voice and he would definitely have mixed feelings about him because . . .

Zoe's ideas came to an indecisive halt.

Why would he have a downer on the inspector? I have an idea I know, but I can't quiet crystallise the reason.

She picked up the copy of *In the Land of Vultures*, turning the pages, allowing her mind to drift, hoping to discover some new insight into the clues in the lovely landscapes with their cleverly chosen locations.

Eight hackberries making the shape of an octagon, like the Templar church. Are there enough hackberries out there, randomly, that it was always going to be possible to find eight to describe an octagon, or did someone plant them, maybe as much as twenty years ago or more, in order to set up the pattern so that they could become a clue for In the Land of Vultures?

Zoe decided it could easily be the former, that there were so many *micocouliers* across Provence – Toby had told her that they had first become widespread five hundred years before – that the author of the puzzle book would have had their pick.

Another memory came into her mind – of Barbara's copy going missing from beside her bed. She was sure that it was Davide who had taken it, in between her own two visits to the dead woman's guest-house bedroom.

Davide is definitely a Vulturist, but could he possibly be a murderer? I don't think he was close to solving the mystery. When I saw him that day, he'd come back from his musical tour exhausted. I bet he was out late after each concert, searching with his metal detector. I wonder, though, if there were clues or notes Barbara made in her copy of the puzzle book – even turned-down corners, like in Infinite Desire?

Zoe revisited her intuition about why Barbara had vandalised the novel, putting together her own sense of the woman and the hints from Julien's conversation.

She was losing her memory, either from age or something awful like dementia, and was leaving herself clues. She bought a copy of her own novel to remind herself of who she was, and she created her own key to the landscape element in the puzzle book.

Her satisfaction lasted only a few moments.

I'm not sure that gets me anywhere.

Zoe thought about the fact that Barbara had been found in the church, perhaps inspecting the bronze plaque of Saint Catherine featuring a book and a child.

The church is usually locked but was open just then because of the procession for the Feast of Saint Bertrand. She took advantage to go in alone and inspect the plaque.

Zoe made a sound of frustration.

Surely the inspector has a clear idea of who had the opportunity to find her there? That ought to be routine police work, correlating statements and alibis.

She saw a slideshow of the key moments, like a flick-book in her memory.

As far as I can see, there was no one available. Everyone was with everyone else, many of them down in the car park by the mairie. *Anyone who came back up would have been seen by Patrick or Simouno because they were busy in Place Saint-Bertrand setting up the dinner. If somebody stayed behind – Robert Petit or Ambroise Caille, for example, at their premises in the main square – I would have seen them.*

She looked round for the dog, then remembered that he was out ratting or rabbiting.

Russell – if he could speak – might be able to tell me.

*

Zoe's adopted stray dog was nosing along a quiet lane on the north side of the hill town, below the stair of clay roofs that she could see from her rear bedroom window. His lively canine brain was entirely focused on the pursuit of a rat that, he knew, lived in the dank dark beneath a broken drain cover. He looked up, though, when he heard a car door open and smelt the distinctive sweet odour of a pastry.

There was a human close by, sitting in the open doorway of the vehicle, tearing the pastry into pieces. The human held his gaze and extended a hand.

Russell approached, trusting and unwary, and took the proffered shred of *croissant*, swallowing it whole, almost as a pelican gulps down fish. Then he looked up to enquire: '*Is there more?*'

The human put the remaining pieces on the floor in the footwell. After only a brief pause, Russell's brain told him: '*You may as well get in. That's what seems to be required.*'

Once he was in the car, however, the door was closed and – after all the croissant shreds had been eaten and he was able to apply himself to his new circumstances – Russell realised that he was trapped.

★

Frowning, Zoe pondered Barbara's behaviour in the first weeks of her stay in Sainte-Catherine, a time she only knew of from hearsay. She visualised the elderly woman buzzing about the countryside on her *mobylette*, back when the weather was warm and dry. Then she considered the fact that the lightweight moped had gone unused for a spell.

I don't think that was just because of the cold and rain.

She put the copy of *In the Land of Vultures* down – well thumbed by both her and by some of her party guests – and leaned back in the leather armchair.

Barbara stopped buzzing the countryside because she had learned all she needed to from exploring.

She asked herself why Toby and Clare had come across her down at the culvert.

Because, as Toby sort of guessed, it was a kind of bluff, suggesting the underground tunnel was important to divert attention from her true goal, which was . . .

Zoe found herself, in her mind's eye, back inside the church, with the slack body, like an abandoned puppet on the flagstones.

I feel I have everything I need in order to understand, but the answer won't come clear.

She tried to recapture the triangular conversation with the Days about what they wanted from life – the revelation that their nomadic existence wasn't actually an end point, just a gruelling compromise.

They're not like vultures, happy to be wheeling and swooping, effortlessly, on life's thermals. They'd rather find somewhere to safely land. I wonder how far they would go to achieve that goal?

She stood up to look more closely at the drawing of Sainte-Catherine in its slender oak frame by the back door. It really was a lovely thing in the 'draughtsman' style, though the paper had wrinkled with age beneath the glass.

Did Oskar take such an interest in it simply because he's very focused on that kind of thing, or is there an additional clue, perhaps the fact that there is a kind of resemblance to the style of drawing in the puzzle book? But that might be a coincidence.

Looking at it close up, she realised, for the first time, that the picture was signed. She had never noticed before because the signature was in the top-left corner, rather than bottom right, as was more usual. And it was disguised by seeming a part of the pictorial detail – almost certainly the Maurice wine-farm buildings and the woods beyond.

Zoe fetched her phone and used its torch to look more closely, angling it to reduce glare. Faded with age and confused with other spidery lines, she found the signature impossible to make out.

What does it matter, anyway?

She touched the thin glass, positioning her forefinger on the drawing of the octagonal church.

It's funny. It ought to be in the centre of the town, because Sainte-Catherine itself has a kind of eight-sided form, with the outer houses forming a bastion. I think it's called enchâtellement, *making a castle out of the people's homes. But Place Sainte-Catherine is lopsided when the church ought to be like the bull's-eye in a target.*

Thinking about the church made her reflect on the character of the town's priest.

I can imagine Julien solving the puzzle. I can't remember if I ever asked him if he'd read In the Land of Vultures. *I know he disapproves of it, of course. If he had worked out the location of the treasure, would he keep it to himself – I mean, not declare it and cash it in – out of contempt for the whole process? No, he'd be much more likely to want to bring the adventure to an end and stop it from exciting people's avarice and greed.*

The thought of these archaic, deadly sins made Zoe feel nervous. She turned the steel button on the lock on the back door and looked round the shop.

Maybe I should leave the lights on tonight?

She felt foolish, like a child afraid of the dark.

I wish Russell was back.

She flicked the switch, anticipating that the space should be plunged into darkness, as usual, but it wasn't thanks to the street lamp that shone through the skylight over the landing at the top of the stairs.

I'm glad I removed that square of carboard.

Glancing again at the drawing of Sainte-Catherine and the nearby hills and fields, Zoe found herself embroidering a wholly new scenario in her overstimulated imagination, one involving the hunter apparently killed by a wild boar.

What if Lucia Jacquet's husband was the author of In the Land of Vultures? *Could he have been killed by someone who tortured him for the location of the treasure?*

She considered again her idea of 'death by wild boar's tusk'.

Then, his murderer wouldn't necessarily announce what they knew because, with every day that passes, the fund grows and grows. But how would they decide when the time was ripe to claim their prize? Before someone else solves the puzzle and steals it out from under them, I suppose – Barbara Ercollani, for example.

Zoe sighed.

This is awful.

She went upstairs, oppressed by the same feeling that she was no longer alone, that the presence of all her party guests had somehow spoilt her solitary occupation of *The Bookshop of My Dreams.*

It doesn't feel mine any longer. It feels like I'm just passing through and the ghosts of all the previous residents are clustered around me, out of sight, but definitely there, watching and waiting.

Thirty-Three

Inside and Outside

It was absolutely true that Zoe was not alone in *La Librairie de Mes Rêves*. But it wasn't the lurking ghosts of the previous residents – Lucia Jacquet and her dead husband or Caroline's and Simouno's parents, practising their letters with soft pencils in cheap exercise books.

Someone had taken advantage of the comings and goings, up and down the stairs to the kitchen and the bathroom, to conceal themselves in the built-in hanging niche beside the chimney flue in the front room.

Uncomfortable in that confined and dusty space, surrounded by dresses and blouses and coats, nervous of being discovered, they were waiting impatiently for time to pass, in order to be certain that Zoe was asleep before they emerged.

*

Having enticed the Jack Russell into the car with a pastry purloined from the party, the burglar-turned-murderer was now in Place Sainte-Catherine, standing – as before – in a pool of shadow. In their pocket were the keys to the bookshop that they had stolen from the shelf beneath the counter.

They rubbed a thumb and forefinger across the smooth metal of the vulture fob, waiting for the street lamps to go out at two o'clock before making their move. In their other hand, discreetly, by their side, they held a *matraque*, a heavy truncheon, the traditional weapon of the French police.

★

Zoe had slept but now she was on the edge of wakefulness once more, lying as still as stone beneath her duvet, one leg of her White Company pyjamas rucked up to her knee. Through half-opened eyes she could see the glow of the orange street lamp on the landing because she had left the door open for some air.

The thing that she thought had half-woken her was a sharp and intrusive memory of the moment when Barbara had come into the bookshop for a final time. The elderly woman had wandered over to the bird's-eye view of Sainte-Catherine on the wall, then tried the door to the courtyard – which had happened to be locked.

Like both Oskar Weiss and Toby Day at the party, earlier, though both attempted to disguise their interest, one way or another.

With the clarity that sometimes comes from an in-between state of consciousness, Zoe abruptly remembered Antoinette telling her about the row she had overheard between Caroline and . . .

Who was it?

That was precisely the question. Antoinette hadn't named him.

'. . . *she had a fierce argument with her ex-boyfriend. In my doorway, would you . . .*'

And, although Zoe had jumped to the conclusion that the 'ex-boyfriend' was Julien Calmet, it might have been someone else.

Inspector Sicarie, for example.

Zoe remembered seeing him in hushed conversation with Caroline by the foot of the stairs.

309

Their liaison must have ended badly. That's why every time she's mentioned him, there's been a harsh undertone, right back to when she referred to him as 'the inspector from Aix' who investigated the burglary at her office. And it's come up several times that all three – Caroline, Julien and Sicarie – used to inhabit the same professional and social circles in the city.

Zoe felt herself becoming more fully awake but resisted the temptation to move because her subconscious had moved on to a memory of the elderly vet, Firmin Séchan, telling her: *'Life is for living – and where might one live better than this glorious landscape, by turns rugged or lush, grassy or wooded, parched in the summer but running with torrent streams in autumn, winter and spring?'*

At the time, she had almost thought it might be a quotation, perhaps even poetry. Of course, back then, she hadn't studied *In the Land of Vultures*. If she had, it would surely have brought the lovely landscapes to mind.

And didn't Firmin go on to tell me: 'I sketch myself'?

Certain she was right, that Firmin was the author of the puzzle book, Zoe became fully awake, her eyes wide, though she still hadn't moved.

He's the correct age to have created the distinctive mid-twentieth-century scenes of people going about their daily lives.

She remembered describing to him the renovations at the bookshop. In reply, the vet had immediately asked her if she had replanted in the courtyard and – now she thought about it – he had seemed amused when she had told him that the alpines weren't a success.

The obvious conclusion is that the Vulture is concealed in the planter in my courtyard. That's the answer to the conundrum about the fact that the church is not at the centre of the village in the drawing, the eight-sided bastion. Place Sainte-Catherine is off-centre, so my bookshop is the bull's-eye. And the alpines are doing badly because, as Toby said, there's not enough dirt, meaning there must be a board or something just beneath the surface, hiding the Vulture.

Remaining as still as a recumbent statue, Zoe tried to piece together how the events must have played out.

Firmin Séchan was good friends with Lucia Jacquet and her husband, after whose death he tried to help Lucia with ideas for keeping the business alive. He could easily have found a reason to . . .

She frowned.

No, that's not it.

She reassessed.

I have to remember that I'm thinking about at least ten years ago, when Monsieur Jacquet was still alive. He might even have been in league with Firmin and made it possible to hide the Vulture in the planter, thinking the whole puzzle-book idea was a brilliant commercial wheeze, just as I keep looking for opportunities to boost my trade.

Two images came into her mind: the bronze plaque of Saint Catherine with a child and a book set into the flagstones of the church; the stone carving on the side of the planter.

I bet, if I looked closely, I would see that it's the same child. That's how the church is supposed to lead people to the bookshop. That's what Barbara was working out in her befuddled way, but she never had a chance to examine my stone carving up close because the courtyard door was locked and, then, she died.

Zoe remembered Firmin conversing in halting English with Oskar.

Perhaps Firmin knew about Masquerade, *the English puzzle book, and took inspiration from it.*

She wondered what time it was, remembering what Julien had said about Napoléon Etienne always wanting to have his own way in the organisation of the life of Sainte-Catherine: '*Like insisting the street lamps don't go off until two in the morning or the correct day for the rubbish lorry to come.*'

She glanced towards the landing, able to see – because she had left her bedroom door ajar – that there was a strong orange glow from the street lamp, through the skylight she had uncovered. Then, for no reason that she could fathom, a shadow was suddenly cast, blocking out the light, then moving on.

Oh no.

Then she heard something like the soft tread of a rubber-soled boot.

If Russell were here, he'd be off the bed and barking fit to raise the dead.

Zoe knew that the stairs of the bookshop were very solidly built. It was possible to descend them in silence – but only if one knew where to tread. On a couple of the steps, putting one's weight on the right-hand side would bring forth a creak.

She flinched, hearing precisely that.

There it is, once and then twice.

Unsure what to do, but with an icy finger of fear stroking a sharp fingernail down her spine, Zoe sat up, careful not to make a sound. She drew the duvet off her legs and swung her feet to the ground, gently rising from the mattress. Then she stood and listened.

That's the sound of someone turning the steel button on one of the locks, maybe the one to the square but maybe also the one to the courtyard.

Feeling almost naked and definitely unprotected in her pyjamas, Zoe moved gingerly across the bedroom. She heard the door to the courtyard swing inwards, then almost silently – but not quite silently – close.

Whoever it is must now be outside. I should be able to get downstairs without being seen and maybe slip out into the square. Then I can fetch help, perhaps rouse Antoine from his house in the side streets.

She slipped out onto the landing, turning sideways so as not to have to move her bedroom door and perhaps make the hinges squeak. Descending the stairs, she clung to the left-hand side to avoid any unwanted creaks. At the foot, in the same place she had seen Caroline and Inspector Sicarie in their hushed conversation, she peered round an ancient timber post.

Yes, someone's outside in the courtyard.

Through the glazed back door, she could see them carefully removing the egg-shaped stones of her rockery, gently placing them on the ground, discarding her failing alpine plants.

Who is it, though?

She couldn't tell. Not only was her view obstructed by the door frame, the courtyard was in shadow. Her curiosity got the better of her and, instead of making for the front door and the exit, she crouched and edged forward towards her island counter. At the same time, the street lamp over the landing went out, plunging the bookshop into blackness.

That must be two o'clock on the dot.

Zoe's heart was beating very loudly, she thought. On her knees on the floorboards, she had even less chance of identifying who it was in the courtyard in the gloom. Then she heard another sound.

Oh, no, what's that?

It was a new danger, signalled by the characteristic scratching of someone using an unaccustomed key in an unaccustomed lock, in darkness at the front of the building.

That's why I couldn't find the vulture fob. Someone stole it.

Her attention was jerked back to the courtyard where there was a sudden white illumination, a darting beam that, frustratingly, didn't reveal whoever was there, preparing to dig beneath her rockery and remove the Vulture from its decade-long hiding place.

That's a head-torch, which means—

Zoe had no time to complete the thought because the front door had just opened, infinitely slowly to avoid jangling the bell. Despite the absence of street lamps, peering round the edge of the counter she recognised the dark silhouette – a shambling, round-shouldered form in a long overcoat, solid black against the slightly lighter night.

Inspector Sicarie. I never liked him.

Zoe was torn. She didn't want Toby Day to get away with invading her privacy in order to steal the Vulture out from under her nose. If Inspector Sicarie had stolen her keys, then – surely? – he was also the murderer of Barabara Ercollani and, what's more, the person who trashed Caroline's office.

Is Toby just as good a suspect? Maybe he's the murderer and Sicarie is just after the money. He must have been on the trail of the treasure before I moved in, but he worked out all the clues just a little too late. Then I changed the locks and, since then, he's been biding his time, trying to distract me with his accusations, in case I found it for myself. He was there on the night of Barbara's death, arguing with Caroline. I bet the whole oleander thing is just a smokescreen and—

Zoe had no time for further conjecture because Sicarie was moving past her hiding place and definitely would have seen her, had his attention not been entirely fixated on the darting white beam beyond the glass of the courtyard door. The headlamp flickered across the glass as Toby moved the last large stone out of the planter. A glimmer was refracted, revealing to Zoe that Sicarie had a weapon in his hand, a *matraque* – an evil-looking black truncheon.

Toby stood up and Zoe was momentarily confused because, upright, his dark silhouette seemed too large, too heavy. He bent down again and she clearly saw his fingers groping into the tired soil beneath her fresh compost, attempting to find the edge of something, a board, in fact, that he raised, the torchlight revealing a shower of dusty dirt falling from it. He put the board aside and a reflection from the door glass revealed his pale face and unbecoming dark hair.

314

Oh, it's Oskar. Of course, I watched Toby leave.

The German tourist's eyes widened and Zoe grasped that he had seen Sicarie through the glass. The inspector surged forward, grabbing the door handle and heaving. The door swung inwards then was tugged back because Oskar was heaving in the other direction.

Sicarie hissed two harsh words Zoe couldn't make out, then gave another mighty tug. The door lurched open and Oskar fell into the room, staggering two clumsy steps then tripping over the coffee table and landing with a thump. Sicarie raised his truncheon above his head in order to strike and Zoe rushed at him, knocking his arm away, but she also fell, her momentum carrying her into the side table and the coffee machine that crashed to the floor with a tinkle of broken glass.

She rolled onto her back in time to see Sicarie coming at her, swearing comprehensively in Provençal vocabulary that Zoe didn't understand but whose meaning was obvious. The heavy truncheon was raised and, ineffectually, she put up her hands to ward off what would inevitably be a crushing – perhaps fatal – blow, screwing up her eyes, wishing she had slipped away when she had the chance.

But I never had the chance. He was already out there, waiting.

The blow never fell. When she opened her eyes, it was to see Oskar grappling with the much smaller police officer, squeezing him in a bear hug. They pirouetted together as if locked in some kind of bizarre dance, the head-torch sending beams of bright-white light around the room, making their combat look as if it was lit by a strobe. Then one of them trod on one or other of the 'reading copy' paperback books and it skidded on the beeswax polished floorboards and they both slipped and fell.

Sicarie hit the floor first with a sudden exhalation. As he lay winded, Oskar got to his feet then sort of 'bombed' him, like a child jumping into a swimming pool, landing with his heavy backside on the inspector's solar plexus.

Zoe thought she heard the snap of one or two ribs as Sicarie moaned and gasped. Then, with admirable economy of movement, Oskar got to his feet, found a roll of Sellotape on the counter by the light of his head-torch, turned Sicarie over and wound it round and round his wrists behind his back.

'*Vielen Dank, gnädige Frau,*' he said to her when this task was complete.

'Never mind "thank you". What were you thinking, Oskar, sneaking about my home in the middle of the night?'

'I am sorry. You know what I thinking, please?' he told her, looking contrite, his accent very strong. '*Der Geier* – the Vulture.'

'Never mind,' she retorted, breathlessly. 'I suppose, in a way, it's lucky you did.'

EPILOGUE

The answer to Zoe's unasked question about the feast day of Catherine of Alexandria was the twenty-fifth of November, by which time Inspector Sicarie – whose first name turned out to be Thibaud – had been convicted of the murder of Barbara Ercollani on the basis of incontrovertible forensic evidence that he had apparently attempted to conceal. He was therefore also convicted of 'attempting to pervert the course of justice'.

The murder had been accomplished by lethal injection beneath Barbara's hairline, making the puncture wound hard, but not impossible, to find. At one point, Zoe was told what the poison was, but the scientific name refused to stay with her. In court, Sicarie refused to describe the precise circumstances of how he had managed to keep Barbara still while he administered the fatal fluid, but Zoe supposed it hadn't been difficult.

Poor Barbara was tired and old and ill. How cruel.

Zoe had received a letter in reply from Maisie that predicted many aspects of how the mystery had, in fact, played out, even though Maisie hadn't been in full possession of the facts. Maisie had, for example, advised Zoe to drop 'the Italian connection' as 'pure coincidence' – and so it had proved. Because her landline had finally been installed and the mast reconnected to the cellular network, she and her elderly half-sister had been able to chat several times on the phone.

The fact that the Silver Vulture had finally been located after ten years of searching was kept quiet until after the end of Sicarie's trial. Oskar Weiss came back for the *fête de Sainte-Catherine*, in order to be interviewed by the local press, radio and TV stations who had got into the habit of referring to it as 'the French bookshop murder', forgetting that the capital crime had actually taken place in the church. Firmin Séchan, as the author of *In the Land of Vultures*, was also suddenly in great demand.

Oskar, obviously, was delighted with his winnings, the prize fund of more than two hundred thousand euros. In an access of generosity and in recognition for Zoe's part in the drama, late at night in the bookshop, he insisted that she should keep the Silver Vulture itself.

'On the wall you must put,' he told her. 'People come and see.'

'I couldn't,' she told him.

'Why not?' he asked, looking hurt.

Zoe enlisted Thierry's help in trying to translate and explain that it was 'too rich a gift', but Oskar was adamant.

'For you it must be. I invade your home. I am sorry. This is fair. I do not discuss more.'

'I don't think he's going to change his mind,' Thierry warned her.

'Thank you, Oskar,' she finally told him, accepting his lavish gift. 'You are very kind.'

'I come back again,' he told her, 'and you forgive me. In the next summer. We will be friends?'

'Yes, Oskar,' she told him, a little exasperated. 'We will be friends.'

Firmin, too, was delighted with this arrangement. Two days later he came back with his grandson, Frank, carrying a secure display case for his silver creation. It had a heavy wood-and-steel frame and the Vulture itself was protected by 'bank grade' toughened glass. They bolted it to the wall, next to the bird's-eye view of Sainte-Catherine – which turned out also, of course, to be Firmin's work, a gift for his friend Lucia Jacquet.

Zoe reminded him of their conversation, perched on the olive-tree planter outside his *pavillon*.

'You asked me if I'd replanted in the courtyard and, when I told you the alpines weren't doing well, you said: "Oh, that is a shame." You must have been worried I might find the Vulture by accident.'

'I was,' said Firmin, laughing.

She asked him about Lucia Jacquet's husband and her fleeting suspicion about how he might have died.

'Is it certain he was gored by a wild boar?'

'Oh, yes. The animal was identified and euthanised.'

On a beautiful late-autumn day, the sun surprisingly warm, the Day family came to visit. Benjy went to stroke Russell, who was lounging in front of the stove. Zoe told them how, to her surprise, early the next morning after the drama and arrest, Napoléon Etienne had come to complain about her dog: 'He is shut in a car below my outer window, barking and barking.'

Zoe had enlisted Antoine's help in freeing Russell, popping the lock with an unfolded wire coat hanger, like in the movies, none the worse for his ordeal.

With great sadness, the Days wanted Zoe to know that they would soon have to give up on their nomadic existence, giving Zoe an idea.

'What if you came back sometime and stayed here for a week?'

'Why would we do that?' Clare asked.

'I told you,' insisted Toby, 'we're out of money and time.'

'I mean here, in *The Bookshop of My Dreams*. Look, in the new year, I'd love to take a trip back to England, just as a visit. While I'm away, you two could look after things.'

'Are you sure?' asked Toby. 'You don't really know us and, as you admitted to me just now, for a while at least you thought it was me digging up your courtyard planter.'

'That was just the stress of it all. What do you say?' They looked at one another and Zoe saw that they were going to agree. 'Excellent,' she told them, decisively. 'That's settled. We'll be in touch with one another in the spring.'

The Days left and Zoe tidied up, then there was a knock at the door. She went to answer, wondering if it might be Bernard Dupin with another mob of tourists in his minibus. Instead, she found Caroline Robin and Julien Calmet standing shoulder to shoulder in the sunshine on her doormat.

'What's happening? Is it bad news.'

'Of course not,' said Caroline, impatiently.

'Why would you think that?' asked Julien.

'I feel I've yet to be properly accepted in Sainte-Catherine,' said Zoe honestly, her voice tight and sad. 'At more or less every turn, I've done or said the wrong thing.'

'Nonsense,' said Caroline.

'It is we, the *sainte-catherinois*,' said Julien, using the complicated French adjective for the inhabitants of the hill town, 'who have neglected our duty as hosts.'

He stepped aside and Caroline did the same, revealing that the centre of the square had been laid out with trestle tables, converted from the market stalls for an impromptu feast. Lined up on either side was almost everyone she had met since her arrival on a scorching hot afternoon a couple of months before – Marcel and Thierry and Odile, Antoine and Antoinette, Elise and Cécilie, Frank and Firmin, Gato and his robust wife with their son Lali, Denis and Davide, Simouno as ever without her mysterious husband Quentin, Ambroise the estate agent and Robert the butcher with their wives and children.

'What's happening?' pleaded Zoe. 'I don't understand.'

'It's the Feast of Saint Catherine today,' said Caroline. 'But we decided to make it the Feast of Zoe, too.'

'This is too much—' she began.

'No, it's not,' insisted Julien. 'In thanks for you solving "the French bookshop murder" and bringing to light the Silver Vulture at last, it is actually nowhere near enough. Come.'

They each took her arm and drew her forward, into a crowd of smiling faces, every one of them a neighbour.

But now, at last, Zoe thought, *my friends.*

The End

ACKNOWLEDGEMENTS

Thanks to Luigi Bonomi whose idea it was that I should write cosy crime, and to the team at LBA; to my magnificent editor Audrey Linton, plus all her colleagues at Hodder & Stoughton; to the booksellers, festival co-ordinators, podcasters and all the others whose dedication and enthusiasm are so essential to a flourishing book industry; to all the generous writers who have supported this playwright's unexpected transition to novel writing.

And, of course, to the person from whom I learnt to write books – the best and only Kate Mosse.

**Love Greg Mosse?
Don't miss the Maisie Cooper Mystery series . . .**

**. . . where crimes and murder
are around every corner.**

RAISING READERS
Books Build Bright Futures

Dear Reader,

We'd love your attention for one more page to tell you about the crisis in children's reading, and what we can all do.

Studies have shown that reading for fun is the **single biggest predictor of a child's future success** – more than family circumstance, parents' educational background or income. It improves academic results, mental health, wealth, communication skills, and ambition.

The number of children reading for fun is in rapid decline. Young people have a lot of competition for their time, and a worryingly high number do not have a single book at home.

Our business works extensively with schools, libraries and literacy charities, but here are some ways we can all raise more readers:

- Reading to children for just 10 minutes a day makes a difference
- Don't give up if children aren't regular readers – there will be books for them!
- Visit bookshops and libraries to get recommendations
- Encourage them to listen to audiobooks
- Support school libraries
- Give books as gifts

Thank you for reading: there's a lot more information about how to encourage children to read on our website. www.JoinRaisingReaders.com